Beautiful Strangers

by

Ellen Dean

Bloomington, IN Milton Keynes, UK

AuthorHouse™
1663 Liberty Drive, Suite 200
Bloomington, IN 47403
www.authorhouse.com
Phone: 1-800-839-8640

AuthorHouse™ UK Ltd.
500 Avebury Boulevard
Central Milton Keynes, MK9 2BE
www.authorhouse.co.uk
Phone: 08001974150

This book is a work of fiction. People, places, events, and situations are the product of the authors imagination. Any resemblance to actual persons, living or dead, or historical events, is purely coincidental.

First published by AuthorHouse 8/18/2006

ISBN: 1-4259-5446-4 (sc)

Printed in the United States of America
Bloomington, Indiana

This book is printed on acid-free paper.

Chapter 1

Beth was excited. The adrenaline pumped through her body making her glad to be alive. Although she'd hardly slept she didn't care. It was the first time she had felt this good in over a year and today was her first official day at St. Gregory's.

After forcing down a cup of tea, her substitute for breakfast, she felt able to take on the world. Checking her appearance in the hall mirror she was stunned at her reflection. A mystical stranger stared back. Long sleek brunette hair elegantly swept up into a stylish knot, enhancing her sparkling brown eyes and fine chiselled features. Her pristine white coat glowed in the lamplight. Fashion conscious to the end, under the white coat she wore a cream cheesecloth top over a long denim skirt, and neat designer shoes on her feet. Light makeup and diamond studs in her ears completed her ensemble. She believed it was important to look good for the patients.

Pinning her name badge in the left lapel, checking she had four pens in her breast pocket, one red, one blue, one black, one green, checking again her stethoscope was safely tucked in her right hand pocket along with other necessary bits and pieces, she was ready. Well, almost ready. Her hair wasn't quite right. Pulling it loose she started again twisting it into a knot then securing it at the back of her head with a comb. Right, that's better, now I'm ready. She switched off the lamp, pushed some money into her skirt pocket along with her keys and left the apartment shutting the door firmly behind her.

During the short walk to the hospital Miss Elizabeth McConnell, Surgeon, was bid a cheery 'good morning' by several members of staff, and loud wolf whistles sounded from a nearby building site. She blushed, but turned and gave the builders a wave of acknowledgment. It all added to her buoyancy.

As she walked she reflected on the events of the past year, events that had brought her here today when to all intents and purposes she would have still been in Edinburgh.

Sadly, it was all down to her father's untimely fatal heart attack the previous year. Unsurprisingly, Isobel, her grief stricken mother, had completely gone to pieces, as had her younger sister, Catherine, who totally shunned the support of Giles, her husband, and sank into depression. All turned to Beth needing her comfort and strength of character which made her feel duty bound to put her surgical career on hold and return home to support them and run the family estate. Property, stock, tenants and such, could not look after themselves.

Beth believed the Universe has a way of providing, and eventually their overwhelming grief started to level out, helped by Catherine's news. She was expecting a baby, the first grandchild. Isobel had done a complete turn around with the news, persuaded them to move back into the family home, and was busy helping Catherine redecorate the East Wing and plan the nursery.

By a lucky co-incidence Beth found Angus, an experienced and honest estate manager, keen to move his family to the Durham Dales, and more than able to take over the reins of the estate. Her intuition told her he was the right man for the job, plus his lovely wife Shona got on like a house on fire with Isobel, and their two adorable children would help cheer the place up.

Then the position of General Surgeon with Mr. Dickinson's Team in Newcastle had fallen into her lap, as had the perfect two bedroomed apartment an estate agent friend found for her. Not only was it close to the hospital, but also to the newly built Hogan's Health and Leisure Club. To Beth's finely tuned mind, this was all meant to be. Synchronicity that's what it was.

She intended to join Hogan's, having a vague idea of getting herself back into shape. She didn't need too. Her slim five foot four figure was perfectly proportioned, most women would die for a body like hers. As can be the way with natural beauty, she was unaware of the fact that most people regarded her as drop dead gorgeous, but sometimes a bit more confidence in that department wouldn't have gone amiss.

Not only beautiful on the outside, she was beautiful inside too. Naturally caring and sympathetic, her wicked sense of humour bubbled up when least expected. Many regarded her as docile and pliable, which she was for most of the time until someone might try to push her into a corner where she didn't want to be. Then her determined character and strong will kicked in big time, but it usually took a lot to get this reaction.

The only clouds on her horizon, if you could call them clouds, were the pesky visions. Pushing through the hospital doors she crossed her fingers in the hope they would leave her alone.

Waving to the girls on Reception she opened her office door to the smell of freshly ground coffee permeating the air. Janet, her assigned secretary with over thirty years of St.

Gregory's history behind her, was already busy at her desk and looked up over her old fashioned spectacles to bid her good morning.

Looking around the room she was delighted to see the vase of fresh daffodils Janet had brought in especially for her. Beth knew they were going to get along. It is good to be here she thought taking the mug of steaming coffee Janet handed to her.

Beth settled in easily. She enjoyed working alongside David Dickinson. He was a big, caring man with a shock of black hair and a moustache to match and was famous for his selection of outrageous dickey-bow ties. An approachable man, who was graced with the natural ability of putting worried patients at ease, he welcomed her into the fold as though she'd been part of his team forever. Beth quickly discovered that most of his time was spent between the hospital and delivering seminars. He seldom seemed to go home.

Within days Beth met Stuart, a senior houseman, pleasant and easygoing. They had lots of patients in common so frequently met for lunch in the hospital dining hall to discuss patient progress. This was a perfect excuse for Stuart, who fancied Beth like mad, but he was very aware of the difference in their professional status. Because she was relaxed and approachable he eventually worked his way round to asking her out to dinner. They were seen in one of the smart city restaurants and immediately the hospital grapevine swung into action and had them married with children.

Beth had had her fair share of boyfriends, but never felt truly comfortable with any of them. She refused to acknowledge why that was, always shying away from analysing her feelings. Could Stuart be the one? After a couple of dinner dates she realized Stuart was not going to be the exception. But he was good company, so Beth kept the relationship going aiming to keep it purely platonic. Stuart had other ideas, naturally he wanted to take things further. Beth made every excuse imaginable to stall things in the sex department.

Every hospital has its characters. St. Gregory's was no exception. Most of the staff were genuine and helpful, yet Beth was saddened to find a couple of Ward Sisters who were openly hostile to her. Even in this day and age they bitterly resented having to deal with a female surgeon. Was it plain old jealousy rearing its ugly head? Beth wondered, especially after the extremely difficult Sister Armstrong completely forgot her manners. Beth, dripping with tact and diplomacy, rose above the silly situation earning her brownie points from the entire ward. Nursing staff, cleaners and patients gave her a round of silent applause. She might have won the battle, but she knew she hadn't won the war.

She didn't care. She took it all in her stride, including the cranky Ward Sister who insisted her staff turn all the wheels on the beds to face the same direction. Crazy woman thought Beth, as if that's going to make any difference to the well being of the patients. Hardly surprising her nickname was The Sergeant Major. She ruled with an uncompromising rod of iron.

Then there was the Nursing Officer who expected student nurses to stand to attention and remove their cardigans whenever she appeared on the ward. Discipline being her keyword. Our Teaching Hospital is supposed to nurture and produce first class nurses, not terrify the poor things to death in the process, thought Beth after witnessing a first year reduced to tears.

One night after being called in to attend an emergency, Beth was delighted to discover the Night Sister who had summoned her was her old friend Val Taylor. They first met at the beginning of Beth's medical career when Val appointed herself as one of Beth's guardian angels. Naturally, they had a lot of catching up to do, so after their patient was settled, Val sent the student nurse currently undertaking a stint on night duty, to make them all some tea.

She arrived back at the nurse's station, carefully balancing her heavy tray just as Val looked up and boomed, 'Good evening, Daphne!'

The student paled, turned too quickly and completely overbalanced. A glorious cacophony of shattering china filled the air as cups, saucers, and chocolate biscuits all crashed to the floor, smashing into a thousand pieces. On silent feet the dreaded Nursing Officer had followed the student from the kitchen. Now, standing right behind her wearing a voluminous dark cloak showing just a slash of scarlet lining, the Nursing Officer the poor girl feared most in the world towered over her.

My God, thought Beth, the woman looks like Countess Dracula. No wonder the kid dropped the tray.

Sleeping patients were unceremoniously awakened and later Beth thanked her lucky stars that no one had had a heart attack, especially the one she had just attended.

Feeling sorry for the student, Beth bent to help her pick up the broken China, and surprisingly Countess Dracula melted and bent to help pick up too, something unheard of. Nursing Officers were regarded as Gods and tended to act that way.

Val despatched the embarrassed student for fresh tea, whispering out the corner of her mouth to take her time, giving her a chance to pull herself together, then she too helped to pick up the debris.

Returning with a freshly laden tray, the pretty young student tried to apologize. Daphne laughed and made a joke out of it. Being kind-hearted was way out of character.

Now what's she up to? Val pondered. She knew Daphne well enough to know she always had an ulterior motive. Daphne doesn't get on her hands and knees for nothing.

With the broken china cleared up and the ward settled, Val made the formal introductions. Beth and Daphne had not met before. Val watched Daphne look at Beth a little too appraisingly. After Daphne continued on her rounds, and the student was sent to tidy the linen cupboard, a long job that would keep her busy for ages if she took the given opportunity to skive, Val and Beth finally sat down to catch up.

Family news exhausted, hospital gossip was their inevitable topic. Beth, sipping tea, said, 'Daphne seems nice. Has she been here long?'

'Long enough! She came here after splitting up with her partner. Couldn't stand working in the same hospital as her!'

'Her? Did you say her?'

'Yes. I did.'

'Go on...tell me more.' She bit into a chocolate digestive.

'I don't know how you manage to stay so slim, you do like your chocolate. I don't know, look at me, if I so much as look at chocolate I put another pound on.' Val placed her hands on her large hips. 'Anyway, back to Daphne. Well...rumour has it...that she got herself involved in some kind of woman's circle - if you get my drift! Her other half was *not* amused and gave her her marching orders just like that!' Val clicked her fingers.

'Mmmm...fascinating. Anyway, must go, got to get some sleep. I'm on duty in the morning. Tell you what Val, I'll stay in the doctor's restroom tonight then I'll be on hand in case you need me again for Mr. Green. Oh! It is lovely to see you again.' As she stood up Beth checked her pockets for her stethoscope, then hugged Val taking comfort from her ample frame. She was delighted to find her old friend working here.

She looked on her as a mother figure even more so now her bleached blonde hair had been allowed to turn into natural steel grey.

Val fussed her, 'Yes, yes and you dear. Now off you go. Go and get settled in, I'll try not to disturb you.' Val's tone changed, 'By the way, did you notice how Daphne kept touching your hands while we were picking up the china?' She narrowed her eyes giving a knowing look.

Beth shook her head, laughing. 'What? No! Don't be silly! You're imagining things. Honestly Val. You never change! You've been on nights too long!'

'Oh and Beth…the visions…are you still having them?'

'Oh no, don't ask. I try not to dwell on them, and then hopefully I'll be left in peace.'

'You haven't got a handle on them yet then? It's a gift you know. I always knew you were special…wish I had them.'

'You're welcome to them. Now shut up and don't mention them again.' She waltzed off along the corridor, anxious to get her head down so that she could think about Daphne and her girlfriend.

Beth was more than a bit curious about Daphne's particular lifestyle. She tried to visualize what her partner would look like, wondering what kind of woman she might be, until sleep overtook her.

Chapter 2

Southampton Marina shimmered in the early morning sunshine. Hyacinth stuck the last stamp onto the final envelope, satisfied she had finished the invitations to their annual fund-raiser. Scooping them carelessly into an oversized Chanel shoulder bag for posting when she went ashore, she picked up a small purple velvet pouch from the table and held it reverently in her hands.

You'll make me a fortune you little beauties she thought as she clutched the pouch to her breast before carefully fastening it into the inner zip pocket of the bag.

She stood up, brushing herself down in case any unwanted bits of fluff were sticking to her black pinstripe Versace suit. They wouldn't have dared. She was almost ready to leave, a stickler for appearance she ran her perfectly manicured nails through her mane of blonde hair, blended into three shades by her hairdresser to create a soft tawny hue. When she was satisfied it was perfect enough to be seen in public she applied her lipstick, a strong vibrant red, one of life's little essentials.

After methodically checking everything was secured on board The Amethyst, her half million pound cabin cruiser, she collected her belongings, locked the main cabin door and oozing confidence walked along the gang plank heading for her Mercedes jingling the keys as she went. This morning, despite the dreaded forthcoming boring charity bash, Hyacinth was happy, or as happy as it was possible for her to be. Last night she and Penny, her closest friend, spent a wonderful evening celebrating the Spring Equinox together. It was a pity Penny had to leave so early this morning, Hyacinth smiled to herself, remembering. She was a restless spirit, always seeking excitement and she knew just how to get it. A true pleasure seeker, she didn't care who she hurt in her pursuit of it.

Three hours later she placed the purple pouch safely into her deposit box at her London bank. The concierge standing guard by her car deferentially tipped his cap as he bent to open the driver's door for her. She rewarded him with a smile and casually pushed a twenty pound note into his hand before sliding into the leather seat. Lighting a cigarette before putting on the designer sunglasses she was never without she headed out of London. There was one stop she had to make on the way home.

Chapter 3

Stuart started working alongside Beth. She should have been pleased, instead she was irritated to death. His strong personality and rugged good looks meant he was well sought after by most of the female staff, and half of the male. Right now Beth wished one of them would take him off her hands. She started sniping at him, hating herself for being mean, but unable to stop.

The Dickinson's annual charity bash was due to take place in early May. Beth and Stuart were invited as a couple. He was ecstatic; she wasn't amused at all, but couldn't say so as this invitation was highly prized. People kept saying how David's wife, Hyacinth, chose her guest list with great care and that only a handful of staff had received invitations this year. Perhaps she should offer hers to the highest bidder and give the money to their damned charity.

Beth really didn't want to go, willing a good excuse to present itself. She moaned about the invitation to Val when they next met over a midnight cup of coffee. If she had expected sympathy she didn't get it, instead Val told her they would enjoy the 'do'. She had been a guest herself the previous year and launched into a euphoric description of the house.

'It's a classy place the Dickinson's have. Not like your family estate Beth, you understand, but it is a big house all the same, out Jesmond way with beautiful gardens…ultra posh it is. Wait till you see the swimming pool, indoor of course, straight out of Homes and Gardens with changing rooms big enough to spend your summer holidays in. From what I can remember of last year nearly all the youngsters ended up skinny-dipping at midnight, come to think of it, it wasn't just the youngsters! I didn't bother though. Not wanting to be centre-stage!' Val roared with laughter at her own joke, rocking backwards and forwards in danger of overbalancing and falling off her swivel chair. Then the tone of her voice changed, ringing her hands together she became serious, 'Listen…' she bent forward, looked up and down the ward to see if anyone could hear, making sure no-one was lurking in close proximity, she patted Beth's knee as she said, 'Hyacinth can be one to watch out for mind.'

'Oh! What do you mean?' Beth automatically copied Val looking left and right. 'One to watch out for, Val? Why? What does she do? Apart from being married to David, that is.'

'Don't you know?' She looked around again not wanting to be overheard. 'Oh you are slipping up. Well, she's a gynaecologist. Gave up a brilliant career when she married. Had two children before you could sneeze, hired a nanny and returned to work before a decent amount of time had elapsed. Not full time though just part-time, for appearances sake. They say she can wrap him around her little finger. She looks more like a film star than a Doctor, dresses like a film star too. Must cost him a fortune. Probably buys her knickers at Harrods.' Val rocked back in her chair again. 'Anyway, she travels to Carlisle a couple of days most weeks, she has a clinic come hostel over there.' Val paused weighing up her words, 'A bit of a card that one.'

'A bit of a card, Val?'

'She has lots of friends.'

'So?'

'Female friends. About half a dozen of them.' Val paused expecting a reaction, when none came she continued. 'I think she takes them to her place in Scotland…at least that's what the hospital grapevine says. Don't know what they get up to there. Funny how David never goes though.'

'Well, what's wrong with that?' Beth was becoming impatient and bored by Val's gossip. 'Everyone needs friends and from what I can see David's hardly ever at home. I expect she's the type to be on lots of committees.'

'Yes, I know he's away from home a lot, probably 'cos of her carryings on and I know there's nothing wrong with having friends. I expect she misses her kids. They're at boarding school…or maybe they've moved on to university now, time flies doesn't it? Anyway, enough of this silly chatter, just you be careful though, that's all I'm saying. She's a bit different is our Hyacinth…Committees, eh?' Val chuckled, 'Well I guess that's one way of putting it. Now will I go and get the Tarot cards out of my bag and give you a reading, or not?'

Beth shook her head, 'Not tonight thanks Val I'm too tired. I've been on my legs all day. Another time, okay?'

Chapter 4

Beth woke early on the morning of the charity bash. Blue sky and sunshine promised a warm spring day. Guests were invited to arrive from two pm. Beth still didn't want to go. Her hoped for emergency didn't happen. She dressed listlessly, not caring what she wore, but knowing she should look at least half way presentable. She rejected everything in her wardrobe as unsuitable, and then started again. Finally she settled on a simple white linen dress, tan leather flat sandals for easy walking on grass, she couldn't really wear heels they would sink into the ground, fastened her hair back into a ponytail and slicked on some lipstick. That'll do, they can take me or leave me. Better take a jacket she thought, as she sprayed on Chanel No 5. Without intending to, she looked gorgeous.

Hyacinth was in a black mood. She wasn't looking forward to the fund-raiser; she'd become utterly bored with the whole thing. She only put on a pleasant face to keep David sweet, life was much easier that way. Poor David, he was like an old toy she was still rather fond of, except she couldn't pop him into a box and store him away in the back of a cupboard. They'd been married for what seemed like forever, the novelty had worn off long ago, but he was from an old respectable family and allowed her to do pretty much what she wanted. Freedom and old money carried a lot of clout with Hyacinth. She really should stop being such a miserable bitch with him, after all he unwittingly provided her with a marvellous smoke screen. Despite being a big man, where Hyacinth was concerned he wasn't strong and didn't object, as he should have done, when she packed both their son and daughter off to boarding school at the earliest opportunity. Only once had he been on the receiving end of her ferocious temper and he never wanted to go there again. Sex was no longer an option and hadn't been since the birth of their daughter, their second child. But he had his work, that was really his family now, and his precious secretary, Tara, was very accommodating. Unknown to him Hyacinth had made sure of that. They were old school friends and of course she'd had her long before David.

Hyacinth had been raised in South Africa and her close family still lived there. Hers had been a cosseted upbringing as would befit the child of rich parents. Years at one of the best English boarding schools meant she hadn't seen much of her family while she was growing up, but she had formed a loyal following among the girls. Nearly every one wanted to be her special friend and by her sixteenth birthday she'd lost count of her teenage conquests. She flirted outrageously with her teachers, staying in their good books she had a knack of getting her own way. None succumbed to her charms, although one or two came perilously close. The tutors at her Swiss finishing school loved her and the pretty French mistress fell into her arms within six weeks of the start of the first term. During her gap year she toured the world before going to university to study medicine. Of course she excelled and her professors expected great things of her. However, to their dismay she married David shortly after meeting him. She loved life's luxuries, was a natural sailor, enjoyed immense popularity, and travelled abroad whenever the whim took her, often sailing The Amethyst to warmer climes. For all of this she was still restless. The skeleton she kept in her cupboard reared its ugly head now and again, but she was always able to control it, with the help of her girls.

At least the girls would be here, and they were *all* coming today. She might manage a quickie with Serena, their newest and youngest recruit. She felt a terrific connection with Serena, who reminded her of herself twenty years ago, long tousled blonde hair, firm young tits, and plenty of attitude.

And today she had to welcome David's new female surgeon. She was dreading it. In her minds eye she could see some already dried up old swat going by the name of Elizabeth McConnell who would probably simper around her for the entire afternoon being a bloody nuisance.

She cast a practiced eye over the lawn layout noting everything was in place. She needed to check there were sufficient fluffy lilac towels dotted around the swimming pool and give her caterer a word of thanks before she went upstairs to get ready. Why the hell did she put herself through this? It would be so much easier to simply write a cheque and give it straight to the bloody charity.

Back in her bedroom her mood was no sweeter. Her fortieth birthday was looming. She refused to acknowledge it, flatly and icily rejecting David's feeble offer of a celebration. As far as she was concerned there was nothing to celebrate.

She stripped off. Standing naked in front of the full-length mirror she examined herself critically from all angles. She knew she had a stunning body. No sign of cellulite thankfully, and no real stretch marks from the birth of her children. Her blue eyes flashed back at her, she didn't feel forty, finally satisfied she didn't look it, she studied her natural blonde pubic hair, letting the fingers of both hands slip into the curls; she could turn herself on in an instant. And she had time. Her left hand moved to fondle her breast, squeezing the nipple as the fingers of her other hand probed a little deeper into her warm, slick opening.

Stuart, sensing Beth was not happy when he called to collect her, was wise enough not to comment except to say how delicious she looked. They drove to Jesmond in silence.

Arriving at the Dickinson's house both were surprised to see many people they recognized from the media. A television presenter, a well known agony aunt and a local racehorse trainer were laughing together under one of the stripy blue and white sunshades. Because the Dickinson's were well connected in many circles there was a well heeled and diverse mix of guests in attendance. Most were willing, and able, to dig deep into their pockets to support the Dickinson's chosen charity. Beth had already been tapped for a substantial donation.

The party was in full swing, spread out across their beautifully manicured gardens. Fearing the wrath of Hyacinth, the team of gardeners had done themselves proud. As Beth and Stuart walked across the lawns to join the other guests, Beth was captivated by the scene in front of her, a Bedouin tent billowed in the breeze instantly taking her back to childhood dreams of starry Arabian nights.

Hyacinth, discussing something trivial with her caterer, turned to check who was arriving and stopped mid-sentence. Removing her sunglasses, instead shading her eyes with her hands, she watched the expression on the young woman's face, feeling a familiar stirring in her psyche. Smiling to herself, Hyacinth asked the caterer if she had seen this beautiful stranger before. The caterer shook her head. Maybe, thought Hyacinth, the party was going to be fun after all. She immediately started to imagine ways of drawing this beauty to her. She would have to be subtle, probably quite cunning, but she could format her plan when she found out a little more about her. The idea of introducing this woman to her personal lifestyle sent uncontrollable shivers up and down her spine.

Beth had no idea she was the subject of Hyacinth's intense scrutiny. Coming out of her reverie she held Stuart's hand as they walked towards the marquee. Inside a sprung dance floor had been laid and a local band played as energetic youngsters danced to the live music.

David Dickinson greeted them warmly and thanked them for coming, apologizing for his wife's absence. He waved his hand towards the crowd explaining she was in there somewhere dealing with something, probably the catering, but he would introduce her later. After talking shop for a little while and ensuring they had drinks he went off to greet more guests.

Over two hundred and fifty people chattering like mynah birds and swigging champagne surrounded them. Almost instantly a uniformed waitress pressed another champagne flute into Beth's hand. Sipping the fizzy liquid she glanced around noticing most of the women had dressed in a similar fashion to her. So she'd got it right without trying. The men wore casual slacks and polo shirts. Beth thought she had never seen so many designer labels at one meet, or such a glamorous crowd of women.

Empty champagne glasses were immediately re-filled by the sharp eyed, unobtrusive waitresses who hovered in the background beside the long purpose built bar. In another section of the marquee comfortable chairs were thoughtfully arranged around tables enabling guests to sit and relax in the shade.

Val was right about the food. 'Davinia's Catering' had prepared a sumptuous buffet, artistically presented along one complete side of the marquee under shaded windows dressed with long purple drapes. Beth had two immediate thoughts. It seemed a crime to spoil such a vision by eating it, and purple - what a peculiar choice of colour.

Caterer Davinia, the daughter of Lord and Lady Macfarline, had enjoyed a privileged upbringing. After the birth of her daughter it had taken all her powers of persuasion to convince her father that she did not want to return to University. He eventually agreed, on condition that she stayed at home to raise the child herself, wrongly assuming his condition would change her mind. When Felicity eventually started attending primary school Davinia was offered a part-time position by one of her father's friends who owned an exclusive jewellery shop in Newcastle. Although she had no need to work she had a tremendous love of jewellery and felt she had been offered the perfect opportunity to broaden her knowledge of precious stones. She had accepted the offer before her father could interfere and soon she became regarded as one of the north's leading authorities on diamonds. She had loved her job and enjoyed being in a position of trust and authority until recently jumping ship. Laughingly blaming her actions on a mid-life crisis, she set about establishing a superb five star catering service, using daddy's money and contacts of course.

Today, Davinia was standing at the head of the banquet table guarding the food like an anxious parent, proudly proclaiming to anyone listening that food had always been her first love.

Davinia wasn't what you would call an attractive woman, although kindness radiated from every inch of her rotund body. She had grown so round because of her passion for food and the fact that she personally tasted *everything* she cooked. She was barely five-foot tall, with tight curly hair and twinkling grey eyes. A veritable roly-poly.

Beth thought Davinia's food looked worthy of inclusion in the glossiest food magazine. Plates of fresh salmon, mushroom vol-au-vents, canapés, quiches and coronation chicken graced the white linen tables. Cucumber sandwiches rubbed shoulders with rich chocolate fudge cake and individual lemon cheesecakes sat alongside dishes of strawberries soaked in champagne surrounded by jugs of fresh cream. Mouth-watering.

As Beth stood with Stuart admiring the display, Davinia turned and introduced herself. Then without batting an eyelid she introduced her partner, a woman.

Wow, what a statement to make Beth thought as she shook hands with ginger haired Julie, a rock climbing, sailing fanatic. Stuart's smile became fixed, he said nothing. Beth suppressed an urge to kick him on the ankle to jerk him out of his silent posture.

Julie and Davinia were the same age, but Julie was tall in comparison to Davinia. At five foot seven she was slim and looked extremely fit. It was evident how much they loved each other; they had no qualms about being known as a 'couple'. Beth was fascinated, wondering what on earth they would get up to.

Julie latched on to Beth and Stuart, who had managed only the limpest handshake with her, telling them how she helped Davinia with her catering business. She didn't look the type who would see eye to eye with a cooker, and Beth reckoned she wouldn't have a clue how to make anybody's soufflé rise. Perhaps she went along with Davinia to keep a watchful eye on her. She came across as the possessive type. Stuart wandered away bored with Julie banging on about the virtues of real quality catering and the joys of organic carrots.

Loosing the drift of Julie's conversation, Beth became uneasy, on edge. She sensed eyes boring into her as the hairs on the back of her neck stood on end. As though compelled, she turned to meet Hyacinth's gaze.

Chapter 5

Giving herself up to the sheer pleasure of successfully gaining Beth's attention, Hyacinth's smile was genuine for the first time that day. For a millisecond Beth imagined Hyacinth was encouraging her gaze, not turning away as she looked directly back at her. Beth did not know she was looking into the eyes of the mistress of the chase.

She still knew very little about Hyacinth except what Val had told her. She had a crazy thought, while their eyes locked, that Hyacinth was enjoying holding the eye contact. The look between them was intense. She felt as though Hyacinth was putting her into a trance. It must have been that second glass of champagne; she knew she'd drunk it too quickly, giving her silly thoughts and hiccups. After what seemed an eternity, she forced herself to tear her eyes away, successfully breaking the contact. She was disturbed, feeling as if Hyacinth had been peering deep into her soul. Val's words rang in her ears - be careful of Hyacinth.

Delighted with the effect she was having on her quarry, Hyacinth moved towards Beth, gliding effortlessly through the melee of guests. Easily re-establishing eye contact again, although Beth tried hard to resist, Hyacinth would not allow it. Then standing so close, their body heat mingling as their arms touched, Hyacinth introduced herself and completely threw Beth by talking about the food. The last thing Beth expected was a conversation about food. Telling herself not to be so stupid she struggled with the small talk.

She didn't know what she'd expected her to say and she hadn't needed the introduction, she'd just known this was Hyacinth. Beth was flattered by her attention.

She thought Hyacinth was beautiful with her model looks, slender five foot five figure, and her thick mane of blonde hair. Her voice spoke only to Beth, and even though other people surrounded them, Hyacinth made her feel as if they were the only two people in the world. Was this what Val meant? But what exactly was 'this'?

Hyacinth was buzzing. She was immensely attracted to Beth. She knew some others who would be too.

Throwing her usual caution to the wind she lost no time in telling Beth how much she enjoyed hill walking and in the next breath suggested they go for a day's walking together in the Lake District.

'To blow the hospital cobwebs away, darling, there's nothing to compare with the sun on your back and a bit of Lakeland solitude.' Hyacinth lifted a fresh glass of champagne from the tray of a passing waiter. Taking Beth's hand she pressed the ice-cold glass into it, holding on. 'And I could have you all to myself, couldn't I?'

Beth hiccupped, 'Sorry! What did you say?' she laughed nervously, 'Really, this champagne is very strong. I think I must be hearing things. I thought you said something about having me all to yourself.'

'Mmmm...did you?' Hyacinth raised her eyebrows quizzically, sensually sucking a juicy strawberry. Taking Beth's elbow she moved even closer, 'Come with me, darling. Let me introduce you to some of the other guests and some of my special friends. It's so good that you've joined the surgical team, David speaks highly of you and how tough a time you had after your father died. It takes guts to do what you did.'

Beth was smitten by Hyacinth's charm.

'Now, darling, these are three of my special friends.' Hyacinth stopped beside a group of attractive, ultra-smart women, 'Alison, Clarice, Serena, I'd like to introduce Beth McConnell, whom I hope we will all get to know *much* better.'

All three women greeted Beth warmly. She was intrigued by their identical diamond pendants. Beth loved diamonds, indeed she was wearing her favourite diamond earrings today. These women had great taste in gems, but how weird they'd all chosen to wear the same necklace.

'Look over there, darling. That's Felicity, Davinia's daughter.' Hyacinth pointed to another glamorous young blonde who turned and waved to them. Again taking Beth's elbow she led her further round the gardens, pointing out more guests to her, introducing her to others. Beth felt like a filly in the parade ring. She knew she would never remember so many different faces, never mind their names, but it wasn't important, as she didn't envisage meeting any of them again. After completing a full circuit of the gardens, Hyacinth suggested a date to go hill walking. Beth surprised herself by agreeing to go.

Once she had confirmed their arrangements, Hyacinth forced herself to leave Beth. She must go and mingle with the other guests before David noticed how much time she'd spent with the newest member of his team. Before moving away, she leaned into Beth, feeling the warmth of her body, squeezing her arm. It was only a light touch, yet Beth was overwhelmed by the force of energy that surged through her accompanied by a vision of Hyacinth wearing a purple cloak and cupping something in the palm of her hand. Instinctively she reached out grabbing a chair to steady herself.

Her mind was all over the place. Her knees knocked as her eyes steadily followed Hyacinth's disappearing back. She didn't know what to think, but one thing she did know for sure was she couldn't wait for their day out.

Hyacinth continued to play Beth like a fiddle throughout the rest of the day, deliberately coming close to her then pretending she needed to be somewhere else.

Seeking solitude Beth headed into the tranquillity of the deserted poolroom. Spectacular in both engineering and design, the outside tinted glass wall was manufactured to open up giving the indoor pool an outdoor feel. Walking between the tall palm trees, a particular favourite of Hyacinth's, Beth sank down into a deep comfortable recliner, partially hidden from view beside a fountain where a large statue of Venus stood in the centre. With a bit of luck Stuart wouldn't find her in here.

She stilled her mind, rejecting what she considered to be unnatural thoughts.

Laughter from the swimming pool disturbed her solitude. Two of the women she had been introduced to earlier must have followed her in and were splashing each other in the pool. Beth sat up, straining her eyes to see.

Voyeurism had never been on her agenda until today, but she couldn't tear her eyes away as she watched them kissing each other. The redhead, Alison, was all over Serena, the young blonde. And Serena wasn't stopping her. Beth gasped. She watched Serena drop the top of her swimsuit and push her tits into Alison's face.

Beth squeezed her eyes tight shut so she couldn't see what was happening. It was exciting her too much. Of course, curiosity won. First she opened one eye to peep, then the other. Disappointed that the pool was now empty, she was curious to know where they had gone. She needed to get out of there. Standing up to leave she was embarrassed to feel moistness between her legs.

Unobserved, Hyacinth watched Beth's reactions with mounting carnal lust. In her book this beauty was certainly rompworthy. She was going to enjoy this chase and conquest more than any before.

The remainder of the party passed Beth by in a daze, as did the drive home. Although glad to be alone in her bed she was unable to sleep. Every time she closed her eyes all she could see was Hyacinth moving among her guests shining like a star in her kingfisher blue outfit, and the two women in the pool turned into herself and Hyacinth. Why couldn't she block these feelings? They were driving her crazy. And the vision of Hyacinth wearing a purple cloak, what was that all about?

Chapter 6

The following morning, exhausted by lack of sleep, Beth met Ann, the anaesthetist, ready to start their list in the operating theatre. Beth needed to push all thoughts of Hyacinth out of her mind for the sake of her sanity. Ann had other ideas. She wanted to know all about the charity bash, her questions never stopped.

'You lucky thing!' Ann was green with envy. 'I hope I get an invite to the next one.'

'You probably will. It was nothing really. Nice food though. Val said the catering would be good and it was.' Beth played it down.

Why couldn't Ann just shut up? Beth had to concentrate on work. Ann wanted a blow by blow account.

'What was their house like?'

'Nice.' Beth busied about pretending to look for something.

'Is that it? Nice? What was the garden like then?' Ann followed her into the store cupboard.

'Big.'

'Big? Well then, who was there?'

'Lots of people.' Beth dropped a packet of dressings.

'For God's sake Beth! Don't give too much away will you.'

'Sorry. I'm tired today.' She bent to retrieve the packet.

'Oh, I see. I suppose Stuart stayed over last night.'

'No. No, he didn't actually.' Her tone was cool as she regained her composure.

'Oh. Well then! What's Hyacinth Dickinson like? They say she's gorgeous.'

Beth's stomach lurched. Searching for words to reply as Hyacinth's face swam into vision before her eyes, she was saved as the theatre doors swung wide and the first patient was wheeled in. Beth thanked her lucky stars.

It was a busy day so Ann had no chance to continue her questions before she had to hurry off to keep an appointment leaving Beth to finish writing up patients' notes.

As Ann left the Operating Theatre, Hyacinth parked her Mercedes in the reserved parking bays. She always looked good, but today she had taken particular care with her appearance and looked ravishing in a red Valentino trouser suit. Swinging her car keys, another of her habits, she stubbed her cigarette out under her expensive boot before entering the hospital by a side fire exit. She knew exactly what she was going to do.

Beth was glad to be alone. It had been a relief to concentrate on work. She'd finished writing up her notes and was checking the theatre to ensure everything was in order before leaving when she thought she heard the outer doors open. Hurrying to investigate, she found no-one so doubled back to check the staff room.

As she walked in she sensed someone behind her then warm hands covered her eyes. She panicked. Was it a ghost?

Every hospital has convincing ghost stories and St. Gregory's had more than most.

Hyacinth dropped her hands onto Beth's shoulders, turning her so they were face to face. Before Beth could speak she kissed her full on the lips. Beth's body responded, instantly shooting into overdrive. She was on fire as realization dawned that this lady meant business. She hadn't called in just to be sociable. Hyacinth's persuasive tongue seduced hers and Beth didn't want the kissing to stop. She was experiencing a type of arousal she'd never felt before, and loving it.

Hyacinth, an expert in the art of seduction and confidant of her effect on Beth, touched her nipples, squeezing and coaxing them as they responded, protruding through the thin material of Beth's theatre greens.

'You **are** pleased to see me, darling.' she whispered.

Beth only managed a nod.

Hyacinth's hands slipped under Beth's loose top, gliding up her back, unhooking her bra. Beth's legs turned to jelly as nerves took over. She held her breath. Please God, help me. This is embarrassing, but pure bliss. What should I do?

Her hands were glued to the wall behind her. While at the back of her mind she was praying she'd put on a decent bra that morning because you dressed for comfort not for style when on duty.

Hyacinth gave a husky laugh. 'Don't be nervous, darling. You know this is fun,' she whispered, 'just relax.'

Easier said than done thought Beth, who suddenly like a soul adrift, was lost in the depths of Hyacinth's Mediterranean blue eyes, hypnotized yet shaken to the core, wanting more, needing more. Her hips started to move with a life of their own, pushing into Hyacinth.

Perfect, just the reaction I anticipated thought Hyacinth congratulating herself.

Beth couldn't believe what she was doing. What was Hyacinth playing at? And why was she here, disrupting her emotions, opening the door into territory she had never dared venture into before? What signals had she given off to make Hyacinth think she could seduce her?

'Ooohhhhh Hyacinth!' she moaned, 'What are you doing to me?' Again she felt the wetness between her shaking legs. This had to stop. This woman was making her lose her sanity. She wanted to push her away, unable to cope with her surging emotions. She couldn't.

Hyacinth's hands were all over Beth and when she discovered she was wearing stockings and suspenders under her loose fitting trousers she was more than titillated. 'What have we here?' she cooed pulling the suspenders through the green material.

Beth was still rooted to the spot. Then they heard a noise. She panicked; Hyacinth didn't turn a hair just moved her hands away and took a step back as Ann's head appeared round the door.

'I wondered where you had got to Beth. Sister's asking if you can come and check on a patient.' Ann, oblivious to the tension, was unaware she was looking at the women she'd wanted to know all about earlier in the day.

Flustered Beth was finding it difficult to pull herself together and act naturally.

'Yes! Yes, of course, I can Ann. I'll be right there!'

Ann left as quickly as she'd arrived.

Although furious at being interrupted, Hyacinth was much too clever to show it. Cupping Beth's face in her hands, she kissed her. 'See you at the weekend, darling,' she murmured, then calmly turned on her heel and walked away.

Unexpectedly Beth felt a rush of excitement at almost being caught in such a wonderfully compromising situation.

Chapter 7

After another sleepless night, thanks to visions of the encounter with Hyacinth tormenting her, Beth struggled to concentrate on the ward round, grateful no surgery was scheduled.

She noticed a patient's blood transfusion running low and asked a new auxiliary nurse to fetch more blood from the fridge, only half explaining it needed to be warm so that when it was used the patient wouldn't go into shock. It was a simple enough request, or so Beth thought. Didn't everybody know to warm a bag of blood you wrapped it in a pillowcase and held it under your arm for a while so your body heat takes the chill off. Easy.

Because she was missing for what seemed like an eternity Beth went to look for her and found her in the kitchen. The woman was warming a pan on the cooker. Standing in the doorway Beth watched horrified at her attempts to pour the blood back into its bag. Then hysteria kicked in and Beth became helpless with laughter. Later she explained to the bemused newcomer what 'warm it up' actually meant and they laughed together.

The harmless incident served to remind Beth that she should have made herself clear. She must not allow other things to cloud her mind. It was all Hyacinth's fault. Relieved when her shift finished, she escaped back to the safety of her flat where she sat drinking endless cups of coffee, hopelessly trying to clear her mind when all she could feel were Hyacinth's hands on her body.

That night she dreamt Hyacinth was making love to her. When she woke she felt on the brink of orgasm. She had never had this happen to her before. She needed to block all thoughts of this woman from her mind and throw herself into her work.

Perhaps she should make an excuse and cancel that trip to the Lakes. Yes, that's what she would do. Cancel the day out then she needn't see her again. That way she could put her feelings safely to the back of her mind and ignore them.

Working in theatre with David, she couldn't look him in the eye without seeing Hyacinth, making it impossible for her to dismiss the fact of just how much she wanted to see her again. Stuart was working in theatre too. He irritated her even more today.

Despite her decision to block Hyacinth out, it was impossible. Every time Beth thought about her she felt excited, butterflies in her stomach, the whole thing. She just had to be with her, like a teenager with a crush. She was so smitten she couldn't eat. Dangerous thinking. Her decision to cancel did not materialize. Every time she picked up the phone, full of good intention she faltered, should she ring her or should she not? The gremlins in her subconscious battled it out between them until the weekend arrived and Beth hadn't made the phone call.

She was up at the crack of dawn. She wanted to look perfect and went through her entire wardrobe carelessly flinging clothes on the floor in her search for something that she considered suitable. Why didn't she have some glamorous walking gear? she fumed while putting in her favourite diamond stud earrings.

Hyacinth wouldn't have cared if she'd worn a black bin bag, she had plans for Beth. Soon she would have to introduce her to her friends, but she didn't want to share this one, not yet. She was still kicking herself for getting carried away with the situation in the staff room. She could have blown it, yet her gut instinct had been right. Today, she told herself firmly as she drove into town, she would be on her best behaviour. Absolutely no touching. She smiled to herself as the memory of Beth's body caused her to place her hand between her legs.

Beth heard the sound of a car horn, looked out of the window and saw Hyacinth, waving her down. Better not go in, thought Hyacinth, or we'll never get to the Lakes.

Conversation was lively during the journey. They talked about all sorts of things. Hyacinth looked about twenty today, her hair fastened up in a ponytail, wearing the trendiest clothes. Today was her fortieth birthday, but she wanted to forget about it. It was good to laugh about silly things that happened at work and Beth turned out to be a good storyteller. They were hysterical about the student who was sent to another theatre for a set of fallopian tubes returning with two lengths of plastic drainpipes which the porter had obligingly given her, and Beth's auxiliary trying to refill the bag of blood.

Hyacinth mesmerized Beth. The more they talked the more Beth fell under her spell. Davinia and Julie became a topic of conversation. Beth learned Davinia's daughter, Felicity, ran an outrageously expensive livery yard on the family estate and was a successful event rider. When she wasn't with the horses, Felicity, a single twenty-five year old, enjoyed night clubbing and partying with her gay friend, Dan.

Hyacinth smirked when she said the Macfarlines had staff to attend to their *every* need, especially Petra, the Swedish Housekeeper. She described Petra in detail, wild, wavy dark blonde hair, sexy pale blue eyes, and a svelte figure. Glancing sideways to check the effect she was having on Beth, smug at the angry sparkle in Beth's eyes, she continued her description emphasizing Petra's amazingly long legs.

Suddenly Beth felt jealous, an unknown emotion for her. Did Hyacinth and this Petra person have something going between them she wondered, and was this Hyacinth's way of telling her she had competition? Or had she got it all completely wrong? She felt confused, which is exactly what Hyacinth intended.

Feeling smug at Beth's reaction to the information about Petra, Hyacinth almost allowed herself to reach out and touch her, so impatient was she to move things forward. But experience and her strong will held her in check. One wrong move and her game plan might go wrong, though she was pretty certain it wouldn't. She forced herself to keep both hands on the steering wheel, licking her lips at the thought of what could come later. Better have another cigarette to keep both her hands busy.

They arrived in Langdale, a beautiful part of the Lake District. Hyacinth drove slowly along the twisting roads enabling them to enjoy the scenery. Passing the entrance to The Country Club, the road climbed slightly running alongside a fast flowing beck. Hyacinth parked behind Wainwrights Pub.

'We'll eat here later, darling, shall we?' Hyacinth smiled across at Beth as she opened the boot. 'They do an excellent full English breakfast.' Her eyes sparkled at the thought of an overnight stay. She planned to engineer that later in the day.

Beth didn't answer. Quickly changing into walking shoes, carrying their small backpacks, they wasted no time in heading off towards Langdale Pike to enjoy a day in the glorious sunshine.

As they walked Hyacinth turned and hugged Beth, 'Darling! You look absolutely gorgeous…I just love those shorts.' She ran her hands down Beth's back cupping her buttocks, drawing her into her groin. The expression in her eyes made Beth blush as she stammered her thanks for the compliment. 'We're going to be such close friends, darling. We'll share our secrets.' Hyacinth whispered.

Releasing her grip, Hyacinth grabbed Beth's hand. 'Come on, darling. I've got lots to show you.' And you don't know the half she thought wickedly.

Beth followed her like a lamb to the slaughter. Hyacinth knew the area well so was able to point out various landmarks, but soon she was back on the subject of her friends and their party games. Beth was spellbound, sure she was dangling a carrot to see if she was interested. Who could fail to be? Hyacinth described beautiful women enjoying themselves, and each other, in beautiful surroundings. Petra's name kept cropping up making Beth wonder if she was doing it on purpose to get a reaction. If so, she certainly succeeded.

'Is Petra involved in the parties?' Beth asked sharply while walking up yet another hill.

'Oh, she is, my darling, she most definitely is!' Hyacinth replied smiling, 'but don't you get any ideas.' She reached out and took hold of Beth's hand.

'As if!' Beth exclaimed, laughing and glancing round to make sure that no one could see them. She had no need to worry, other walkers were well away in the distance.

Beth couldn't believe she was having this conversation, becoming overwhelmed by erotic thoughts about these women.

This was a whole new ball game. She remembered having a crush on her female P.E. teacher when she was school, but didn't everybody? Now here she was seriously fancying this woman and enjoying it. She loved the way Hyacinth's clothes clung to her body, even though her shapely tanned legs were just a touch too slim for the thick socks and hiking boots. Her lilac checked shirt, casually tied under her bust, showed off her tanned waist and had been deliberately left unbuttoned to give Beth a clear and inviting view of her bare breasts.

Beth hadn't mentioned her feelings for Hyacinth to anyone, not even her best friend. She felt too embarrassed. After all it could be just a passing phase. Plus Hyacinth was married to her boss and how complicated was that. Beth didn't know how far she would want to take this - this thing that was happening between them.

Hyacinth was still teasing her about Petra when they came across a large flat rock, the perfect place to stop for their picnic lunch. The view was unbelievable.

'I have a friend who lives over there.' Hyacinth pointed in the vague direction of Ambleside, 'You'll like her. She's crazy, dances around naked when there's a full moon!' Hyacinth laughed out loud.

Beth grinned, 'Yeah, right! I believe you, thousands wouldn't!' and concentrated on unwrapping her lunch.

'Oh, it's true enough darling…and she makes the most exquisite jewellery. Tell you what, I'll take you to meet her one day. She'll love you.'

'Jewellery? How interesting. What sort? Costume?'

'Oh no, darling. Meg's designs are beautiful, truly original and she only ever works with the real thing.'

'The real thing? What do you mean?'

'Darling, you are slow! Gold, silver, sapphires, that kind of stuff, but especially diamonds. Oh yes…Meg's a whiz with her diamond creations.'

'Really?'

'Do you like diamonds, Beth?'

'Doesn't every girl? You could say they are one of my weaknesses.' Beth lifted her hair and angled her head to show off her prized diamond studs.

Hyacinth nearly choked on her sandwich. 'And what are your others, darling?'

'I think I'm just finding out.' As if challenging her, Beth looked directly into Hyacinth's eyes.

'You know darling, we have such a lot in common…my friends are going to love you.'

Hyacinth deliberately stopped the conversation there. She wanted Beth to concentrate on what she'd said about her beautiful friends. She knew she was rushing things, but couldn't help it and discovering Beth's love of diamonds was a wonderful unexpected bonus. She hadn't planned to tell her anything like she had today, but had been unable to stop herself as she described some of their antics, picturing Beth in the leading role. Another bonus would be to get her into bed with Petra. That would be some threesome. She was currently enjoying pitting her wits against the feisty Swede confident she would get her way in the end. She never failed too.

Ready to continue their walk, they stood up and collected their belongings. Hyacinth lead the way along the rocky path. As Beth turned for a last look at a shimmering Elterwater she stumbled and fell, banging her head on the rock they had used as their dining table.

In an instant Hyacinth was kneeling down beside her. 'Are you okay? What happened?'

'Sorry, I don't think I can get up I feel a bit dizzy.'

After checking her eyes, Hyacinth cradled Beth's head in her lap. 'You silly girl. Can you remember what you did...did you faint?'

'No...I just turned round... I wanted a last look at the lake. I shouldn't have bothered. I must have slipped.'

Hyacinth bent forward and kissed Beth's forehead, 'Poor baby.'

Chapter 8

Beth slept most of the way home, only waking when the car engine was switched off.

Hyacinth leaned across and spoke softly, 'I thought you would prefer to come home with me for a while. We need to make sure you're okay…you could have a slight concussion after hitting your head.' She placed a hand on Beth's forehead, ostensibly checking to see if she had a temperature, using any excuse to touch her.

Half asleep, Beth nodded in agreement. She wanted to spend as much time as possible with Hyacinth. This was a good excuse.

Knowing the house would be empty, Hyacinth had battled with herself throughout the entire drive back. She wanted to take Beth to bed, to explore her voluptuous body, and this was the perfect opportunity, but she didn't want to blow it especially if the girl wasn't feeling well.

Switching on the lowest voltage lamps in the hall and living room, to keep the mood, Hyacinth settled Beth on the sofa and went to make coffee.

Beth couldn't wake up, she was sleeping when Hyacinth returned. Sitting on the floor Hyacinth stroked Beth's face, tracing every detail, lingering over her lips. Beth's eyes flickered open.

'Are you awake, darling? I've made coffee. Why don't you take a shower? You'll feel more refreshed.'

'Thanks Hyacinth. I'd appreciate a shower, but it's not really worth it. I don't have a change of clothes.'

'Oh, that's not a problem, darling. I'll find you something.'

Twenty minutes later sitting on a chair in the dramatic black and gold bathroom, Beth glanced around appreciating the luxurious design. This was some guest suit. She undressed, eager to feel the warm water ease her aching muscles, all the while conscious of where Hyacinth could be and what she might be doing. Working up a rich lather with some beautifully scented soap, she almost slipped when the shower door opened and Hyacinth stepped in behind her, naked.

'You're full of surprises, aren't you? Do you make a habit of sneaking up behind people?' she snapped, terrified, but wildly excited, standing rigid not knowing what to do or expect.

Hyacinth didn't answer, kissing the nape of Beth's neck she started sliding her fingers up Beth's thighs as the warm water cascaded down over them both. Putting her arm round Beth's waist she turned Beth to face her; so close their nipples touched.

Beth felt ready to explode. Dizzy with fearful ecstasy, yet despite the hot water she was covered in goose pimples.

'Are you cold, darling?' Hyacinth whispered as she nuzzled her ear.

'N…n…n…no!' Beth shivered, her teeth chattered, she couldn't stop herself from barking, 'Just because you're a gynaecologist Hyacinth doesn't mean that you have automatic access you know!'

Hyacinth's shoulders shook with laughter, 'At last I've found a woman with a sense of humour.' Then bending her head, she kissed her. Long, sweet and lingering.

Beth had been waiting for this, but now it was happening she didn't know what to do. Should she touch Hyacinth? She wanted to, but didn't want to make a fool of herself by fainting on the spot. It must have been the knock on the head that was making her feel so dizzy, so out of control. She didn't know if she was brave enough to follow her heart. Her mixed up thoughts were spinning around in her head like a merry-go-round, as her arms nervously crept around Hyacinth responding to her kisses.

Hyacinth was just about to make her next move when the doorbell rang. Cursing, she wrapped herself in a robe. Instructing Beth to 'just stay in the bathroom darling until the coasts clear' she disappeared to deal with the unwelcome caller.

Beth waited for what seemed liked hours, although it was only minutes. With the passion completely knocked on the head she dressed in her borrowed clothes, deciding the minute Hyacinth re-appeared she would make her excuses and leave. What if it's David? She couldn't do this. And she had the most splitting headache.

Hyacinth opened the front door.

'You're ready for bed early!' the visitor looked her up and down, 'Have you got someone in there?'

'No. No. I'm tired, that's all. I've had a long day, darling. Is this the parcel?' Hyacinth reached out. 'Thanks for bringing it, darling. I'll make sure everything's ready for the big night.' She leaned forward, kissed her visitor on both cheeks, dismissing her.

Pushing the parcel in the corner of the hallway, she took the stairs two at a time, anxious to get back to Beth, only pausing to check her reflection in the mirror outside the bathroom.

'Darling, what a nuisance! Just a friend dropping something off for me.' Her face dropped when she saw Beth was dressed. Keeping her composure, determined to continue, she tried to pull Beth into her, disappointed when Beth resisted. Oh fuck, fuck! I almost had you.

Beth started mumbling her thanks, 'I really must be going now. Would you please order me a taxi?' She needed to escape.

'Of course, darling. But first you must promise to come to London with me. We can go shopping, see a show, go dancing, my treat of course.'

That stopped Beth in her tracks. Looking into those hypnotic blue eyes she couldn't refuse, and a weekend shopping in London would be nice, she might even pick up a new diamond bracelet from Asprays. So after pretending to think about it, she agreed. 'Thanks Hyacinth. I'll look forward to it.'

'Leave it all to me, darling. I'll arrange something really special.' Hyacinth moved closer allowing her robe to slip open showing off her perfect naked body.

Beth gasped. She couldn't take in much more today. Hyacinth sensed that. Taking Beth by the hand she led the way downstairs sitting her on the cream leather sofa while she rang for a taxi.

Ten minutes later going out through the flower filled front porch, Beth spotted a roll of purple material standing in a corner.

Hyacinth noticed. She smiled convincingly, 'Our disturbance darling, material for some new drapes.'

Beth had a fleeting thought that this gorgeous shade of purple wouldn't match anything she had seen in Hyacinth's house. Her head still aching, she forgot about the material as the taxi drove her home through the darkness, but she couldn't stop herself reliving the shower scene.

As the taxi pulled out of her driveway, Hyacinth returned to her bedroom. She spoke into her mobile phone without any preamble. 'Darling, I've found our missing link!' She bounced on her king-sized bed. 'Yes, she's perfect…leave it all to me.'

Chapter 9

Beth imagined everyone in the hospital was looking at her. They weren't of course. She was bursting to tell someone what had happened. She couldn't. It was their secret, hers and Hyacinth's.

She kept thinking what it would be like to have sex with a woman. Not just any woman, Hyacinth.

She didn't feel any guilt, just excitement, and carried on working with a secret smile on her face all the while visualizing their weekend in London. After the interrupted shower experience she knew the trip was going to be some learning curve.

She continued to see Stuart. Her mind was in a turmoil, not knowing who she wanted to be with. When she was with him there was something missing. Although he was tender, sensitive and kind, he didn't excite her as Hyacinth did. There was no comparison. He was the wrong gender.

Thoughts of Hyacinth continuously danced through her mind, which was exactly what Hyacinth had planned. Checking patient's records, actually in a 'Hyacinth' daydream,

Beth almost missed the apology from Countess Dracula, the Night Nursing Officer.

A voice interrupted her thoughts causing her to look up. Standing by the side of her desk, Daphne was smiling, but looked agitated.

'Beth...like I said I'm sorry I caused such a commotion the night you were attending Mr. Green.' She hesitated briefly wanting to be sure she had Beth's full attention. 'He should be settled back home now, shouldn't he?'

Beth nodded.

Daphne continued, 'I wondered if I could buy you a drink, by way of an apology?'

The invitation seemed genuine and friendly.

'Why thanks Daphne, that is kind, but there's really no need. I think the student could have used a shot of brandy at the time though. Don't you?' Beth laughed.

In daylight Daphne had a look of Amanda Burton. As she persisted with her invitation Beth felt it would be churlish to refuse and arrangements were made for the following Tuesday night when Daphne was off duty.

Then Beth remembered Hyacinth. Would she mind? How could she? It's only a drink with a work colleague and more to the point was it any of her business?

Beth purposely dressed down for her night out with Daphne. Comfortable cowboy boots, denim jeans and a matching denim shirt were all she felt able to aspire to. Her luxurious long dark hair was pulled back, caught up in a beautiful diamond butterfly comb. Of course she wore her diamond studs too. She didn't feel dressed without them.

She pulled up outside Daphne's neat little semi, situated in a residential area popular with a lot of hospital staff because of its close proximity to St. Gregory's. When the old Audi Coupe rattled into the cul-de-sac, she noticed with amusement how several sets of curtains twitched. She really must do something about buying a new car, and soon.

Before she could turn off the engine Daphne hurried out and jumped into the passenger seat.

Always polite and attempting to break the ice, Beth said, 'Oh that's a nice skirt, Daphne.'

Daphne beamed, 'Thank you. I'm glad you like it.' She really had made an effort tonight, pleased her long flowered skirt had turned out to be a good choice. She suggested they go to a country pub she knew near Morpeth. Good food if you were hungry and not too busy on Tuesdays.

Despite it being June, the evening was cool and they were grateful for the roaring log fire in the lounge at the Drovers Arms. Settling into easy chairs with a bottle of red wine on the table between them, Daphne started drinking fast while she talked non-stop about the hospital.

What have I let myself in for? Beth thought fighting to keep her tired eyes open.

Half an hour later Davinia and Julie walked in. Thankful to learn they were friends of Daphne's, Beth invited them to share a bottle of wine. She saw it as being rescued.

Davinia was in a 'sit down and pay attention' mood whereas Julie was in a silly mood, telling naughty tales between fits of laughter. She recalled the time she had taken Davinia sailing and how they'd drank too much rum. Davinia had tried to climb up the mast, the boat tilted over so far she had fallen overboard. Luckily she was wearing a life jacket, although Beth reckoned her under-wear would have given her good buoyancy.

Beth was delighted when Julie invited her to come along with Daphne to Davinia's birthday party at the Manor.

'All women, of course,' she winked lewdly in Beth's direction.

Beth accepted prettily, she'd never been to an all women party before. She wondered who else would be on the guest list. Would this be the kind of party Hyacinth talked about? At the end of an unexpectedly enjoyable evening they wished Davinia and Julie goodnight and set off home. During the drive Daphne described the Manor to Beth, it seemed as though she was a regular visitor. Beth was impressed. It sounded baronial and grand. She loved old property and couldn't wait to see it.

While they were driving along an unlit road in the middle of nowhere Daphne asked Beth to pull over. Thinking she must be feeling ill, Beth immediately stopped the car. She could feel Daphne looking at her.

'What's wrong? Are you ill?'

'No. I've been waiting to do this since the day I met you.' Daphne leaned over and kissed her.

Beth was shocked. She didn't respond. Alarm bells began ringing in her head. She didn't want to do this with Daphne, not at all. Not in any way, shape or form.

It wasn't the same as being kissed by Hyacinth. Fleetingly Beth thought how confusing life was. Suddenly women were making advances towards her. Why now? Why not when she'd been sixteen and hormones were raging and sex was sex without questions or analysis. Or better still at University where they had a Lesbian Group. Beth's sexuality needed looking at and here were two women wanting to do just that! Joking aside Beth had always felt there was something different about her, but didn't know what. Perhaps this was it. After all she had always been more comfortable and in tune with women than men. Maybe she should stop denying it.

Disengaging herself from Daphne's arms, Beth managed to tell her that she didn't know how she felt, saying with total honesty she was confused. Daphne told her not to worry, they could take things slowly. Beth tried again. She told her about Stuart, but Daphne just smiled as they drove home in silence.

Chapter 10

Beth hadn't seen Hyacinth since their day in the Lakes, which was just as well as she needed time to get her head into gear after the shower experience. Hyacinth deliberately stayed away, but knowing the effect it would have on Beth, she telephoned periodically always late at night ostensibly to ensure Beth was suffering no ill effects from the fall, ensuring she would be the last thing on Beth's mind before she went to sleep. Hyacinth moved her plan forward.

Knowing Beth was scheduled for a long weekend off she planned to take her to Scotland before they went to London. They could celebrate the Summer Solstice together, along with three of her other close friends.

'Hello darling…how are you?' Hyacinth purred into the telephone when Beth answered.

'Hyacinth, hello…I'm fine…and you?'

'Oh you know, darling…tired…in need of a break, which is why I'm ringing actually. How do you fancy a few days in Scotland with me? I have a little place in the Highlands I'm dying to show to you.'

'That sounds good, but when did you have in mind? Duty rota's and all of that.' Beth tried to sound cool, but her pulse was already racing.

'I know it's short notice, but how are you fixed for this weekend, darling? I thought we could leave Thursday evening. What do you say?'

'Why that's perfect timing and it sounds too good to resist. Would you believe this is my long weekend off?'

'Is it darling?' Hyacinth was so convincing. 'How bizarre. It's obviously meant to be. Pick you up at six then. Bye darling, see you then.'

It was almost midnight when they arrived at Hyacinth's highland retreat, yet daylight still lingered across the Cairngorm Mountains. Well, Saturday is midsummer's day, thought Beth loving the ethereal light.

When Hyacinth had mentioned her little place, Beth had envisaged a small cottage, not the lovely big house set in over twenty acres they were parked outside of.

'So! This is your *little place*?' Beth said standing in the drive looking at The Old Manse.

'Do you like it, darling? It's one of my favourite places in the world…and it *is* mine, not David's. He doesn't come here.' Her matter of fact tone held no malice.

'Hyacinth, it's beautiful. What a wonderful place to live.'

'Come on in…Angela should be here waiting.'

The door opened as she spoke and a stunning brunette came out, 'Hyacinth, darling, you're here at last.'

The women embraced each other warmly then Hyacinth took Beth's hand.

'Angela, darling, I want you to meet someone very special. This is Beth.'

'Beth! It is so good to meet you. Hyacinth has told me all about you.'

Has she, thought Beth, reaching out to shake Angela's outstretched hand. What is it with Hyacinth's friends? They are all beautiful and Angela was no exception, slim, elegant, with shiny shoulder length hair. Simply, yet stylishly dressed in loden green moleskin jeans, cream shirt and a plaid needlecord jacket, she wore no jewellery except a shimmering diamond solitaire that caught the light as she moved her hands. Beth liked her instantly. It was going to be a good weekend.

The house was traditionally furnished, warm and welcoming. Angela had food ready for them and after eating they relaxed for a while in a comfortable snug, chatting and drinking the local malt whisky before going up to bed.

Since receiving the invitation Beth had been excited. She had anticipated sleeping with Hyacinth and struggled to hide her disappointment when Hyacinth showed her into a guest-room. Noting the expression on her face, Hyacinth was delighted, but kissed her on both cheeks then left her alone.

Waking late on Friday morning, Beth rejoiced in the peacefulness. No traffic noises, only birdsong and the occasional sheep bleating could be heard. She stretched out under the duvet curling and uncurling her toes. Despite her disappointment at sleeping alone, she had slept soundly. This was the most comfortable bed, and the whisky had probably helped.

Wrapping herself in a thick robe, she headed down to the kitchen where Angela and Hyacinth were already eating breakfast.

Angela made a great fuss of scrambling eggs for her. 'It's lovely to be able to do this, you know. Our housekeeper hates me being in the kitchen and I love to cook.'

'Thanks, Angela, this look delicious.' Beth tucked into her breakfast while Hyacinth and Angela discussed plans for some get together on Saturday night.

'It's the Summer Solstice darling. I know you'll want to be part of our celebration.' Hyacinth smiled encouragingly at Beth.

'Yes, yes of course.' She managed to reply without spitting out a mouthful of food, imagining a small gathering with canapés and champagne.

'Right then, Angela, I can leave all of the arrangements to you so Beth and I can just enjoy our day.' She lit a cigarette and leaned forward to kiss Angela on the cheek, 'Thank you, darling.'

They spent a fun day exploring Hyacinth's twenty acres on quad bikes then a lazy evening eating out at an intimate Bistro in Aviemore. At ten pm they returned to sit outside in the warm night air and drink brandy. It must be tonight, thought Beth, she must sleep with me tonight.

An hour later both women were in separate bedrooms. Beth sat in the window seat watching the almost full moon beset by doubts about Hyacinth. Perhaps she had totally misread the entire situation. Despite her inexperience she was sure she hadn't.

If Beth could have seen Hyacinth pacing the floor her doubts would have vanished. She was in a terrible state almost overcome with desire and wanting. The effort of forcing herself to hold back was proving too much. She pulled on some old clothes, slipped downstairs and out of the kitchen door heading for the Loch.

Twenty minutes later she was sitting by the water watching the moonlight reflecting on its surface. She had to be one hundred and ten per cent sure, there was so much at stake. Not just the sex, but with Beth it wouldn't stop at sex, she already had feelings for her that she was reluctant to acknowledge. It was the business side of things that really held the sway. If only she had a crystal ball. Don't be so bloody soft, she told herself, she's only a passing fancy; business *always* comes first.

Midsummer's day dawned and Beth stirred in her bed, disturbed, the dream vivid in her mind. It wasn't a bad dream, it was the clarity of it that disturbed her.

After a shower she headed to the kitchen to find Hyacinth already waiting for her.

'I didn't want to disturb you darling, you were so peaceful when I looked in.'

Beth's stomach plummeted. So you hadn't wanted to come and climb in beside me she thought, disappointed.

Accepting a cup of tea, looking at Hyacinth's long fingers, Beth imagined them touching her again, invading her intimate places. God, she must stop this.

'I thought we could have an easy day, darling. Perhaps go for a walk? There's a beautiful Loch nearby I'd love to show you.'

'Yes. Okay.' Beth answered casually, consciously suppressing images of her dream.

They spent an idyllic day together, walking round the Loch, and then picnicking until Hyacinth suggested it was time to return to The Old Manse and prepare for the midnight celebrations.

Beth was surprised at the mention of midnight, then chided herself for not knowing better. What other time would you celebrate the Summer Solstice?

After enjoying a luxurious soak in the bath she still couldn't decide what to wear. She had no idea what would be considered appropriate.

She needn't to have worried for laid out on her bed was a white silk Grecian style gown with a note from Hyacinth:

Darling Beth,
For you to wear tonight.
H

Beth was enchanted. Trust Hyacinth to think of everything. She pulled on the gown. It hugged under her bust, emphasizing her shape and was split down both sides almost from top to bottom revealing everything if she turned too quickly.

Five pairs of eyes turned to assess her as she walked down the stairs into the hall.

'Darling! I just knew you would look sensational.' Hyacinth paused while the other women all murmured and nodded in agreement. 'Come, meet my friends.' She moved to the bottom step to take Beth's hand before making the introductions.

Fiona, Sheena and Morag stepped forward, kissing Beth on both cheeks. She thought it odd that all three women had the same long, straight black hair. Perhaps she should have thought it odder that they all wore the same Grecian gowns.

Then it was everyone to the kitchen to collect the trays of food Angela had spent the day preparing. Leading the way Hyacinth carried the first tray followed by Beth and the others. They walked in single file through the warm night air along a narrow pathway to a sheltered spot where a large circle of candles burned. In the centre of the circle a huge fire crackled spitting embers high into the night air, casting dancing shadows over the piles of cushions set around the circle. Glasses, bottles of wine and mead were already placed beside the cushions.

Angela has been busy, Beth thought. I wonder what we do next.

The trays of food were carefully placed on the ground around the fire. Hyacinth opened a bottle of wine, filled six glasses and handed one to each woman, leaving Beth till last before making a ceremonial toast to the Moon Goddess.

Forming a circle around the fire they all stood and raised their glasses echoing Hyacinth's words, then settled into the cushions to enjoy the fabulous banquet.

Beth was touched by the energy of the ceremony. It was beautiful. She had never been involved in anything like this before; had not known what to expect and laughed at her expectation of drinks and canapés in Hyacinth's drawing room. It was much nicer to sit outside under the stars like this.

After they had eaten Angela and Morag started to dance, slow movements set to raise the energy of the group. Fiona and Sheena joined in and finally Hyacinth and Beth. It was approaching midnight when they all joined hands around the fire.

Hyacinth spoke. 'Ladies…it is time to write down your dreams and desires to be delivered to The Goddess.'

'Hyacinth! What am I supposed to do?' Beth whispered.

'Write down your heart's desire, your deepest wishes…but be careful what you ask for as wishes have a way of coming true.'

'Why do we do this…what do we do with our letters?'

'We burn them, darling. It's part of our celebration. Now hurry, it's almost midnight.'

Beth wrote quickly, the first thing that came into her head, then turned to Hyacinth. 'Okay, I've done it.'

At midnight with the moon riding high in the sky above them they stood in silence around the fire ready to throw their letters into the flames. Hyacinth passed a wooden bowl filled with vervain herbs and dill for each one to take a handful. On her command they threw the herbs and their letters into the fire.

'Now, my darlings, you have sent your deepest desires to the Universe…forget about them and leave it in the hand of destiny.' She handed out glasses of mead poured in readiness, raised her glass to the full moon and spoke, 'We stand before you Moon Goddess in our nakedness, ready to do your bidding.'

On her words the women released the shoulder clasps that held their gowns in place and they slipped to the floor. Beth stood still, uncertain until Hyacinth reached across and unhooked her gown.

Naked they all held hands and circled the fire, feeling the rise in energy, the fire warming their naked bodies. Eventually they turned to wish each other peace and happiness. While holding Hyacinth's hand a vision of a much younger Hyacinth handing a gorgeous cherub of a baby to a nurse shot through Beth's mind so fast she was unable to anchor it. The vision instantly faded when Hyacinth released her grip.

Beth was enchanted by the celebration, the gentleness and camaraderie reached into her soul.

Alone in her bed in the early hours of the morning she tried to analyse what she had been part of; how her previous night's visions had been of the clearing with the bright fire and magic circle. As usual she had no answers, only questions. She had no doubt she had taken part in a coven's ritual, in itself that didn't disturb her, what did was the brief vision of Hyacinth and the baby.

Chapter 11

Beth had been trying to contact Hyacinth since their trip to Scotland. She was smitten, her feelings alternating between incredible lust, desperate to get into bed with her and total self-doubt seeing herself as a stupid fool who had got the situation entirely wrong. Despite leaving several messages Hyacinth hadn't returned her calls. What was she playing at? Beth was anxious to make contact, needing some sort of re-assurance.

Beth presumed her silence meant she wasn't going to Davinia's birthday party. She convinced herself Hyacinth was playing with her mind, she didn't appear to want to play with her body. The party might help to lift her spirits. Despite going with dreary Daphne she was looking forward to her first glimpse of Melton Manor. From Daphne's description the MacFarline residence sounded impressive.

On the night of the party they rattled along in Beth's old car. The Manor was well off the beaten track, the endless private drive twisted through acres of open parkland. Finally they arrived. Built more like a castle, Melton Manor was imposing, and much bigger than Beth's home. She couldn't wait to see inside.

To create an atmosphere, not that they needed to because the place had enough of its own, strategically placed torches were positioned to cast long shadows. Beth loved it.

The minute they stepped out of the car Beth's keys were taken by a handsome young man who drove it away to be parked out of sight. Apparently Daddy didn't like the place to look untidy and her old boneshaker of a car would certainly lower the tone. Liveried staff ushered them towards a red carpet leading into an arched doorway that spilled out warm welcoming light.

This is some way to live Beth thought walking into the grand reception hall, where a string quartet played in an alcove large enough to house a family. Davinia and Julie were waiting inside to receive their guests. Beth was amused that they were immaculately and identically dressed in purple silk shirts under flowing black kaftans.

'Come in, darling girls. Have some champagne.' greeted Julie, kissing Beth on both cheeks. Then thrusting a glass in one hand, she grasped the other continuing, 'come with me Beth. Daphne knows lots of people here, but let me introduce **you** to someone so you don't feel left out. Daphne's sure to get sidelined, she always does!' Julie chuckled.

Barely giving Beth time to wish Davinia a happy birthday, Julie led her into the garden room. A lovely mellow yellow room with tall windows reaching down to the floor opened in such a way you could step out into the walled garden. Numerous fruit trees jostled with each other from behind shrubs in various stages of bloom, providing a riot of colour. A summerhouse, almost hidden by rhododendron bushes, was just visible in a far corner - perfect for secret liaisons.

Holding tightly on to Beth's hand, afraid of losing her in the throng of chattering women, Julie headed towards a woman sitting alone on one of the comfortable sofas. As they approached the woman turned her head, glossy dark hair swung across her shoulders and brown eyes smiled up at them. Constance held out her hand in greeting. Julie, confident that Beth was in good company, hurried back to Davinia. Like a lost puppy Daphne had trailed across the room behind them, spotted someone she knew and promptly scuttled away.

Beth didn't mind, she discovered she liked Constance, who was chatty, not at all stuck up, as she'd initially expected her to be. Constance spoke briefly about her job saying matter of factly how she worked long hours as a corporate lawyer with a large firm in Newcastle. Beth thought it must be lucrative as she spent weekdays in her upmarket city penthouse, travelling to her country hide-a-way for quiet weekends. Sometimes work took her to London, she said. Not her favourite place, she was always glad to get back up north to the more sensible pace of life.

Beth mentioned her forthcoming trip to London to spend a weekend shopping and clubbing with a friend. Dipping into a small shoulder bag, Constance passed her what looked like a business card.

'This is an exclusive night club. Strictly 'Ladies Only' with a *very* discerning membership. Go. I know you'll enjoy it.'

'Thanks.' Beth took the card and sank back into the sofa to read it.

Constance excused herself to fetch them more drinks, giving Beth a chance to survey the room. Although the furniture had been pushed back against the walls to allow more floor space for all of the inevitable food and drink, it was evident this room was well used by the family. She could understand why. Beth was idly looking at the other guests, a diverse selection of women in all shapes and sizes, when she noticed one or two of them wore the same diamond pendants as the three glamorous girls she'd met at Hyacinth's charity bash. How weird they all chose the same design. Others wore long silk scarves in the same shade of purple as Hyacinth's new curtain material. Stranger still, purple isn't one of this season's colours, she mused, it's all yellows and creams. She was still pondering on the pendants when Hyacinth stalked into the room.

Dam! What's she doing here! Flustered, Beth looked for Daphne who was on the far side of the room deep in conversation.

Muttering an excuse about needing fresh air to Constance, who had just returned, she ran out into the garden hoping to become invisible amongst the cherry trees. Knowing there was something wrong Constance followed and found her lurking in the shadows.

'Are you running away from Hyacinth?'

'Sort of.'

'Why? Has she done something to you?'

'Yes. I suppose she has, but I can't talk about it. I didn't expect her to be here.'

'I had a brief *affaire* with Hyacinth years ago. And let me tell you, she's extremely jealous, and volatile.' Constance was matter of fact.

'Really?'

'Trust me when I tell you that you want nothing to do with her. She's trouble with a capital 'T'. She's involved in......
well, I don't know what really or actually how to describe it. It's some kind of rituals they do. Oh I know it sounds crazy, I would even go as far as saying she dabbles in...magic! Anyway there are some weird goings on with her and her little group of special friends. Have you noticed the stunning women wearing the identical pendants? Take my advice Beth. Stay well away from her. From all of them.' Constance, holding

both of Beth's hands, looked at her, genuinely concerned. 'Are you going to London with Hyacinth?'

'Yes!'

'Oh my God! How did that happen?'

It was a relief for Beth to talk. She stood nervously squeezing her hands, saying how she was besotted with her, deliberately not mentioning Scotland or the ceremony on midsummer's night. She must be crazy opening up to a stranger like this.

'Please, please take my advice, Beth. Let her go. She can be an evil bitch! How that poor husband of hers puts up with her, I really don't know. Are you listening to me? I don't think you appreciate the seriousness of what you're getting into! Look, if nothing else, think about your career.' Constance was trying her best. Beth wasn't listening and she knew it.

She decided to find Hyacinth. Sooner or later Hyacinth would find her. Her gut instinct told her it would be wiser to approach her first. Of course she ignored Constance's advice, all that silly hocus-pocus cloak and dagger stuff, was just that....silly! Magic! As if! Although, she supposed, their celebration could be classed as white magic. She thought of it as working with mother earth's energy and there was nothing wrong with that.

Constance wasn't the only person to notice Beth's reaction to Hyacinth. Julie's sharp eyes missed nothing. Not wanting any upsets, and knowing Hyacinth of old, she organized Davinia to show Beth round the Manor. That would take them both safely out of the way while she had a few words with Hyacinth.

When Beth stepped back into the garden room Davinia appeared like a vision at her elbow. Knowing Beth had a keen interest in old property from their first meeting, it didn't seem unusual for her to offer a personal tour of the Manor. Perfect timing and what a saving grace. Beth accepted gratefully.

Davinia led the way into a vast mirrored ballroom where a female disc jockey was busy setting up her equipment ready for the dancing. Beth wondered what sort of scenes these mirrored walls had witnessed over the years. Before she had time to register some naughty thoughts Davinia swept her into the drawing room with its regal display of family portraits. Generations of Macfarline Lords and Ladies gazed down from the gold silk lined walls onto antique regency furniture. An exquisite Venetian chandelier graced the ceiling. Nothing ostentatious here then, Beth thought sarcastically.

They moved into the formal dining room dominated by an impressive mahogany table capable of seating twenty-four people comfortably. At the far end of the room a fireplace filled the entire width of the wall. Davinia explained how a tunnel ran behind it coming out somewhere in the gardens. It had been built to allow a safe route for escaping priest's centuries ago. Curious to know more, Beth asked if she had ever explored the tunnel. Davinia went into peels of laughter, spluttering that she would probably get stuck if she tried. The priests had been on the small side.

They crossed the hall, moving between the guests, to the foot of the wide staircase with an incredibly high ceiling. Beth commented how she wouldn't like to have to decorate it, which set Davinia off laughing again as she led the way up the stairs. At the turn in the stairs a high window looked out over the garden and across the parkland. Beth paused and glanced down. Hyacinth and Constance were talking. She drew back and hurried after her hostess.

Davinia ushered her along the first floor landing one by one flinging open the doors to the bedrooms. Every room was decorated in a different colour and Beth lost count after the fifth or sixth. They were all comfortably furnished with heavy, dark furniture and solid four poster beds. In sharp contrast the ultra modern bathrooms had wonderful old Victorian style bathtubs. Beth lingered imagining herself soaking in deep scented water surrounded by rose petals.

Hardly pausing for breath Davinia bombarded Beth with so much history she almost missed her invitation to be a house-guest. When the words registered she accepted graciously. Davinia prattled on, saying they should arrange the visit soon. She wanted to know all about Beth's work, did she got much time off, what were her career plans, what did her family do and how did she find David Dickinson? Beth was surprised at Davinia's interest in her and her family, she bordered on being downright bloody nosy.

Continuing along the endless landing Beth thought there just had to be a ghost or two lurking about somewhere. No self-respecting house of this size would be complete without one. They were crossing to another landing as Daphne climbed up the back stairs with a positive spring in her step.

'There you are!' she greeted them, 'I've been looking for you. I'll come with you. I love mooching around this place.'

Davinia looked at Daphne, nodded and winked, 'Tell you what Daph…why don't you show Beth around…after all you know the place well enough and I really should be getting back to the other guests.'

As Davinia hurried towards the main staircase, Daphne took Beth's hand leading her into the nearest bedroom. Two steps into the room, she pulled Beth down onto a sofa. Beth realized she'd been drinking.

She had difficulty keeping Daphne's wandering hands at bay, and was fast loosing her patience. They didn't hear Petra come in until she was standing right in front of them. Running her hands over her body, taking time to unfasten the top button of her blouse, Petra lifted her leg to rest her foot on the corner of the sofa next to Beth.

Daphne's wandering hands finally stopped, she glared up at Petra giving her a warning look.

Beth breathed a sigh of relief. Because Hyacinth had described Petra in such detail she knew immediately who she was.

'Can I mik it wiz you?' Petra spoke.

'Make it? Make what?' Beth asked.

'Lurve. Is zat what you English zay?'

'Lurve?' Beth could feel the laughter bubbling. Was this woman serious? Did she want a threesome? It was all too much, still she couldn't tear her eyes away from the top of Petra's stockings where those long shapely legs disappeared under her short skirt.

Daphne forced a thin smile and patted the seat, inviting Petra to sit beside her.

Is it the drink or do these women act like this all of the time? Beth wondered. As for being the housekeeper, Petra was dressed more like a French maid, her peculiar accent more French than Swedish. High heels, black stockings, the shortest black skirt that moved invitingly higher when she'd lifted her leg, and a dainty white apron. Her slinky white blouse gave a tempting glimpse of her deep cleavage. Bizarrely Beth remembered Davinia telling her that she designed all of the staff uniforms herself. What a surprise!

Petra didn't sit down. Instead she remained standing, beckoning Beth to her. When Beth didn't respond she reached forward and took her hands, pulling her slowly to her feet. Placing Beth's hands on her breasts she held them there. Beth felt Petra's nipples harden under her palms as she closed her eyes, starting to murmur in Swedish. Beth hadn't a clue what she was saying, but had a tremendous urge to kiss her pouting red lips. Playing hard to get, Petra tipped her head back out of Beth's reach, making Beth think twice. She paused momentarily and made to step away, and then Petra came to life. Hands on either side of Beth's head, she pulled her back, their lips met and her tongue searched out Beth's, causing her heart to hammer wildly as the blood surged through her veins.

Daphne was furious. Glaring at them, she slammed out of the room almost taking the door off its hinges.

Chapter 12

Petra led Beth to the bed, not that she took much leading. Undoing her apron and loosening her tight skirt, she wriggled, trying to pull her skirt up with one hand. She held Beth firmly by the waist with the other reluctant to let her go in case she evaporated into thin air. She was going to enjoy this.

Without warning the door burst open and Hyacinth stormed in. She was absolutely blazing. Alarm bells rang in Beth's head. God knows she'd just been warned about that temper and jealous streak, and now she was about to witness it first hand.

Daphne, unaware of the situation between Beth and Hyacinth, had gone down stairs moaning bitterly about what was happening in the bedroom with the girl she had brought to the party.

With surprising strength Hyacinth wrenched the two girls apart pushing Petra away towards the door. Failing to gain control of herself she drew back her hand and delivered a resounding slap across Beth's face.

Momentarily stunned, Beth raised her hand and slapped her back, delivering an equally stinging blow. Then she rounded on Hyacinth with a fury to match hers.

'What the hell do you think you're doing? How bloody dare you!'

It was Hyacinth's turn to be shocked. No-one ever dared retaliate against her; although her temper was shooting off the Richter Scale in that instant some respect for Beth was born. Still, it took her a huge effort to steady herself.

Conscience-stricken she reached for Beth, 'Darling! I'm so sorry. I didn't mean to hit you. Truly I didn't. You gave me such a shock, kissing that hussy.' Dramatically she pointed at Petra. 'Can you forgive me, please, my darling?'

'Forgive you? You've never returned one of my bloody calls since we got back from Scotland. What the hell do you want from me Hyacinth?' Beth's angry words struck home.

'Darling, I'm sooo sorry. I over reacted.' Shit, Hyacinth silently cursed, shit, shit, shit. She *must* learn to control her temper, it would be her downfall. Standing as petulant as a small child, one hand on her heart, the other behind her back so she could cross her fingers, she gave Beth her most imploring look.

Petra faded away like morning mist in the sunshine slyly blowing a kiss behind Hyacinth's back as she slunk out of the door.

Beth didn't like this side of Hyacinth. She didn't like it at all. All the apologies in the world would never make her forget that stinging slap.

On a losing streak, Hyacinth moved on to Plan B. 'I have strong feelings for you, Beth. So strong I'm finding them difficult to deal with. I was jealous! And I'm sorry I haven't been in touch, I've had staffing problems at the Unit...I've hardly been home.'

Surprised by her admission, Beth's face softened but she couldn't resist saying, 'What! Not even time for a quick phone call.'

Gotcha, thought Hyacinth. Genuinely relieved she pulled Beth into her arms kissing her passionately, her hands sliding under Beth's silk shirt. She was almost panting in anticipation. Suddenly she stopped, looking towards the door.

'Listen…someone's coming!'

'What?' Then Beth heard the voices too.

'Quick, into the dressing room.'

Davinia, with her friend the ultra-chic Clarice arrived in the room. An avid collector of antique furniture, Davinia appeared to be showing Clarice her latest acquisition, a set of drawers. Opening each drawer carefully, looking in, neither spoke. After a couple of seconds Clarice solemnly tapped the middle drawer. The two women stripped off their clothes. Davinia opened the middle drawer, lifted up a box and turned to Clarice.

'Yes, Davinia. That will do nicely.'

Beth watched Davinia take a dildo out of the box. There was no reaction from Hyacinth.

Beth whispered, 'What on earth are they going to do with that?'

'Sssh. Keep quiet or they'll hear us. We don't want any embarrassment. Watch darling. You're about to find out.'

From their secret vantage point they watched, as Davinia pleasured Clarice with the pink toy, almost smothering her with her over-generously proportioned body. They shook with silent laughter and Beth was convinced she would never be able to look either woman in the eye again. Eventually, after much puffing and panting they stopped both out of breath. Their fun over, they disposed of the toy, dressed and left the room.

Hyacinth and Beth almost fell out of the dressing room. An intriguing thought came into Beth's mind. We're supposed to be going to London soon, will Hyacinth be chasing me around the room like that, or will she leave me alone like she did in Scotland?

They rejoined the other guests separately hoping no one would notice they were missing for so long together. Of course Petra knew. She slipped Beth her telephone number and whispered she wanted to see her again so they could continue their unfinished business, running her hand lasciviously over Beth's firm bottom so as to leave her in no doubt of her intentions.

Collecting a glass of Chardonnay and looking around at the women in the garden room, Beth stood watching Clarice talking to Maria. The two were supposed to be the best of friends with Davinia and Julie, often going out in a foursome, to the theatre, for dinner and even on holiday together. Lighting a cigarette, she wondered if Julie and Maria got up to anything. Perish the thought.

Subdued, Daphne joined Beth while they ate supper. Afterwards it was everyone for themselves on the dance floor as the mirrored walls of the ballroom reflected some of the wildest and most erotic dancing Beth had ever seen. She never sat down, she loved to dance. Some of the women she'd met at the Dickinson's charity bash were there. Each one sought her out to dance, charming her with their offers of friendship. The party ended in the early hours of the morning when everyone was on the brink of exhaustion. Hyacinth, passing Beth in the grand hall, whispered she had some good news and would see her soon.

Beth refused Daphne's sly invitation to come in for coffee knowing full well it wasn't coffee that was on the agenda. All she wanted was to collapse into her own bed and sleep.

Unwanted flashbacks of Davinia chasing Clarice came into her mind as did Hyacinth's angry outburst. She could almost feel that stinging slap again. In retrospect, the party had been a lot of fun. Beth enjoyed the buzz from the attention a lot of the women had paid her, along with invitations to go shopping, have lunch and the offer of membership to the exclusive Hogan's Gym. Alison, the owner, had promised to call her soon. So many women had taken her telephone number, wickedly she wondered who would be the first to ring. In the meantime, she had Davinia's invitation to look forward to.

Chapter 13

Hyacinth pulled away from the ferry terminal. The package delivered safely by the courier was zipped into her handbag. It meant a trip to her London bank sooner rather than later. She didn't like keeping the diamonds in the house. The nagging voice in her head kept urging her to organize a safe deposit box in Newcastle. This was a personal consignment after all; it had nothing to do with the Group.

At six in the morning Daphne was disturbed by the telephone ringing. Anticipating a hospital emergency she paled when she recognized her caller's voice.

'Daphne, I have been thinking about you. I have decided I would like you to be the new Matron of my unmarried mother's unit in Carlisle. You know we call it a unit, but really it's such a beautiful Georgian house and I need someone with your expertise…..and someone I can trust.'

Daphne attempted to speak.

'No Daphne. You must listen to me. This is how it's going to be. You will move into the self-contained ground floor flat within the house; I will double your hospital salary, provide you with a new car, secure your pension and increase your holidays. In return you will hand in your resignation today, when you go on duty, then I want you to go on holiday until you come to me in Carlisle. There is one other thing I want you to do. You must never see or try to contact Beth McConnell again.'

There was silence while Hyacinth allowed Daphne time to digest the implications and seriousness of her words.

'Hyacinth, thank you. What can I say? I don't really want to go to Carlisle, I'm quite happy here.' Daphne floundered, dreading the consequences if she dared to refuse.

'Are you, darling? Do you think the Hospital Board will want you to stay when they learn about how you prey on the female student nurses and the dreadful things you make them do so they score good marks in their ward assessments.' Hyacinth spoke calmly. She knew Daphne would accept her offer. She could afford to be patient.

'Why are you doing this, Hyacinth? I've never done anything to hurt you. I've always been protective.'

'That's exactly why I know I've made a good choice and I can rely on you to make the right decision.'

'You've given me no choice, have you? I'll submit my resignation today.'

'Good. Welcome aboard. We'll speak later, darling. You won't regret it.' Hyacinth replaced the receiver, admired herself in the dressing-table mirror, all the while congratulating herself on her latest plan. That was Daphne neatly moved out of the Beth equation and she had the perfect Matron into the bargain.

Three hours later Daphne handed in her notice, collected her belongings and left the hospital without telling a soul.

Later that day, rushing along the corridor between wards, Beth, half asleep, literally bumped into Hyacinth.

'Hyacinth! What are you doing here?'

'Hello darling. I've come to tell you my good news.'

'News? What news?'

'I've taken a new job, darling,' she lied.

'Oh! Have you. Where?'

'Here, of course. I wanted to be close to you. They've been head hunting me for ages so I thought why not. It's the perfect opportunity for us darling, isn't it? I officially accepted this morning, but I won't be starting for a few months. But we have to keep it to ourselves until the official announcement.' She flicked her hair seductively, expecting Beth to be delighted.

Beth didn't know if she was or not. It was a bit of a bombshell. Through gritted teeth she forced a smile, 'Well, isn't that nice. Congratulations Hyacinth.'

Linking Beth to walk with her she continued, 'I've booked our London weekend. We're going to have a wonderful time darling. So be ready to go two weeks on Friday. We'll take the early train then David can drive us to the station.' She loved rubbing his nose in it. 'Oh and I have some more friends I want you to meet, so I'll arrange a little get together.'

'Now Hyacinth, don't jump the gun. I could be working.'

'No darling you're not, I've checked with David.'

Beth should have known she would have it all worked out. Stroking Beth's arm now, getting too close for comfort, she wished Hyacinth would stop treating her like a pet Poodle.

'Darling, you have forgiven me for last night, haven't you?'

'Yes, of course.' Pulling away, saying she would look forward to the London trip, she escaped before anyone had the chance to see them. God, it'll be like this all the time when she works here. We'll be continually ducking and diving. Uncharacteristically she crashed through the doors into the ward. Hyacinth liked to take risks, she didn't. She decided she had put it off long enough, it was time to talk to Lindsay. She could trust her life long friend. She would ring her tonight.

Chapter 14

Lindsay ran her hand through her short light brown hair, she was tired and it had been a bitch of a day. What she needed was a strong drink. Murders always meant long hours, although this one was all but solved. Closing the door to her minimalistic two bedroomed first floor apartment, she dropped her jacket onto the hall chair then poured herself a large whisky. Carrying it carefully across the cream carpet of her neat and tidy living room she pulled open the patio doors. She intended to relax on the balcony and catch the last of the sunset. She was just settled into her comfortable lounger, long legs stretched out, tired blue-grey eyes about to close when the phone rang. 'Shit!' cursed Lindsay, 'that had better not be work.' She leaned back, reaching behind the curtains and picked up the phone.

'Inspector Powell.' She crossed her fingers, please not more trouble. The desperate voice on the other end brought an immediate change to her features. 'Hi Beth. What's wrong?'

Sensible Lindsay listened without comment to her friends garbled tale. A down to earth, matter of fact woman, she let Beth talk without interruption until she ran out of words.

Lindsay loved her like a sister. She'd always believed Beth had gay tendencies, strengthened when she'd introduced her to a girlfriend once, as Beth hadn't been able to take her eyes off her. They'd been friends since childhood, sharing secrets, looking after each other, and Beth had often been her alibi, getting her out of awkward situations with demanding girlfriends.

They missed each other terribly when Lindsay gained promotion and transferred to Brighton. At the end of their long conversation Beth felt elated and knew exactly what she needed to do.

Chapter 15

Two boring weeks followed. Despite the altercation with Hyacinth, Beth couldn't help looking forward to their London trip. During this time she broke up with Stuart as a direct result of her conversation with Lindsay. The surprise resignation of Daphne left her mystified. Her departure from the hospital, taking all her annual leave and going off on holiday, was the talk of the place.

At last the day for the trip to London arrived. Beth was both excited and apprehensive. David drove them to catch the train, and as he stood smiling waving them off, Beth wondered if he had any idea what Hyacinth got up too. Perhaps he didn't care; she'd heard rumours about his dalliances with his secretary.

The train was half full, mainly with shoppers on cheap day return tickets. But the first class carriages were not so busy. Hyacinth wanted to hold Beth's hand under the table. Beth was reluctant, she looked around while trying to pull her hand away, frightened people would see them. Hyacinth didn't care, but eventually she gave up. She thought Beth's attitude totally boring so instead started reading her newspaper. Relieved,

Beth sat back in her seat and relaxed, looking out at the fields and the overcast sky before glancing around the carriage.

An attractive blonde sitting further along on the opposite side, reading a magazine, was surreptitiously watching them. When Beth looked along the carriage she deliberately caught her eye and smiled.

Beth smiled back thinking, mmmm, nice. Now, where have I seen her before? Staring, unaware she was analysing the other woman's appearance, taking in the cut of the expensive black trouser suit and dark red ribbed silk top, it clicked. I know her. It's the actress, Lou Scott.

Lou didn't want to go to London. She wanted to jump off the train when it pulled into York station and rush home to her rustic Yorkshire farmhouse. She wanted to see Frances, to check on the horses. Instead she had to travel to London and meet with her agent to discuss a possible film offer. Not something she could ignore, no matter how much she wanted to.

Running a hand through her long wavy honey blonde hair, a gesture she used when stressed, she reached into her Louis Vuitton overnight bag for the current editions of Horse and Hound and Eventing. She'd only just had time to buy them before jumping on to the train. Her good nature was quickly restored. She couldn't be grumpy for long especially when her attention was drawn by two attractive women sitting further along the carriage.

The blonde, the older of the two, was pestering her companion to hold hands. It was obvious to Lou she was embarrassed by the way she nervously slapped her friends hands away. Interesting.....Lou opened a magazine pretending to read, covertly watching them. Their antics might give some light relief to her enforced journey.

When the younger woman returned her smile, Lou's world was rocked. Their eyes held, sending Lou's senses spinning in reaction to the brunette's exquisite looks, and for a brief moment time was suspended, they were alone in the Universe.

Hyacinth, who had been engrossed in the newspapers for the past half-hour, subconsciously remembered Beth. Coming back to the present from The Times crossword, she felt the need for strong coffee.

'Be a darling, Beth. Run along to the Buffet Car and bring me some black coffee.' Hyacinth dismissed her with a wave of her hand. That should keep her busy for a while, she thought. Surely Beth wouldn't turn out to be an empty headed beauty who couldn't occupy herself for a short space of time, like the length of a train journey to London. With any luck there would be a queue and she could finish the crossword undisturbed. Wishing she had arranged for them to fly down - she loved flirting with the cabin crew and had pulled on more than one occasion, the inventor of the Mile High Club - she resumed the crossword.

Initially surprised by the demand, Beth obediently stood up and headed towards the Buffet Car. As she walked past Lou Scott fate took a hand. The train swayed almost tipping her onto Lou's lap. Automatically Lou reached to steady Beth to stop her falling.

'Thanks! Sorry! Not a very smooth ride, is it?' Beth was embarrassed.

The blonde smiled, 'No, it's not, is it? Lou Scott. Pleased to meet you.'

'Hello. Yes, I know...that you're Lou Scott that is!' Stop talking like an idiot Beth shouted to herself, 'Beth, Beth McConnell. It's great to meet you. I watch all of your programmes.' Beth extended her hand in greeting expecting to briefly shake hands, instead Lou held on for what seemed like an eternity.

Still holding her hand, Lou indicated to the empty seat opposite her, 'Please, sit down for a while, or is your friend desperate for her coffee?'

Beth glanced over her shoulder to check on Hyacinth. Good, she thought, it looks like she's dozed off. I can take my time. Then she wondered had Lou been watching them and listening to their conversation. Maybe she'd seen them briefly holding hands? Beth didn't care. She sat down before Lou could change her mind.

She had always thought Lou attractive when she'd seen her on television. Now, meeting her in the flesh, she was thunderstruck. Gorgeous, sensuous, beautiful smooth hands, the small screen didn't do her justice. She was a Goddess. Beth felt something spark between them. Did Lou feel it too?

Lou was just so easy to talk to, they got on famously. Flattered by her interest in her, Beth was asked a hundred and one questions. Probably just killing time, Beth decided, nevertheless she was happy to talk about her medical career, explaining how she had recently returned to it. Lou thought her decision was a brave one. Then admitted she couldn't stand the sight of blood, and could never envisage how it must be to be a surgeon. They laughed loudly, causing Hyacinth to stir in her seat.

Through subtle questioning, Lou gleaned all of the information she wanted from Beth, although Beth was totally unaware of it. She knew she had been sitting with Lou for ages, but she couldn't tear herself away, captivated by her soft brown eyes, honey blonde hair and mellow voice. Lou's wicked sense of humour became apparent when she did some of the different accents her acting career had called for, and her attempt at Geordie had them laughing out loud again. Leaning back, looking into Lou's eyes, hardly daring to breathe, Beth had an overwhelming urge to kiss her.

Not trusting herself she leapt out of her seat, startling Lou. 'God! I must get Hyacinth's coffee. She'll kill me!' she blurted.

'Oh, all right then. It **was** nice......chatting. Maybe we'll run into each other again? I hope so. Let me...'

Beth interrupted her, 'Yes, yes. Me too. Bye.' She hurried away certain they would never meet again, but she would *never* forget her brief encounter with Lou Scott.

Her feelings for Hyacinth paled into insignificance in comparison to the torrent of emotions taking control of her now. In a blur Beth got the coffee and returned to her seat, crestfallen when she saw Lou's was empty.

'I only sent you for coffee. Where the hell have you been... Brazil?'

Bitch thought Beth. 'No! There was a queue. Anyway, I thought you were asleep.'

'Just dozing, darling, just dozing.' Hyacinth snapped back.

'Oh Hyacinth, you're so sharp sometimes, you could cut yourself! You know you had your head stuck in the crossword.'

'What's happened while you've been getting that coffee?' Hyacinth peered intently over her designer reading glasses. 'Have you been buying some attitude as well?'

'Don't be silly. You're talking rubbish, Hyacinth!' Beth's tone was harsh. She picked up a magazine. She couldn't be bothered with Hyacinth's cutting remarks right now. Bad tempered cow. If Hyacinth continued like this, theirs would be a very short friendship.

Every female face staring up from the pages looked like Lou. Unable to control her thoughts she visualized Lou's naked body standing in front of her. Could Lou read her thoughts? She glanced along the carriage to where Lou had returned to her seat. They smiled at each other, a slow sensual knowing smile. As the excitement welled up in Beth, the train slowed, pulling into Kings Cross.

Impulsively leaving a disgruntled Hyacinth to collect their things, Beth dashed along the carriage to catch Lou before she left the train. Too late, she'd disappeared. Beth felt gutted, empty. She couldn't believe the impact Lou Scott had had on her. Returning to a fuming Hyacinth, Beth was hit with the devastating thought, what if I never set eyes on her again?

Chapter 16

A short taxi ride took them to the Grosvener Hotel, where the Concierge ushered them through to the reception desk. While they were booking in music from the lounge drifted across. The resident pianist was in good form.

Their room was on the third floor. Beth didn't like lifts, but held her composure, she didn't want any more sniping off Hyacinth. Walking into the plush room Hyacinth went straight to the mini bar. In the short time it took the porter to unload the bags, Hyacinth downed a brandy. Then simultaneously tipping him she pushed him out, hanging the 'Do Not Disturb' notice as she closed the door.

Pausing to gather her thoughts, she decided to ignore Beth's strange behaviour. Turning on the charm she gave Beth a devastating smile. Seduction the name of her game. 'At last darling...I've got you all to myself! Now, what will I do with you?' slipping off her jacket, she sat on the king sized bed and beckoned Beth to her.

Beth shuddered, suddenly she wasn't ready. Playing for time she said, 'I'm really tired after the journey. Aren't you? Let's just have a couple of drinks and relax shall we?'

She sounded so sweet and sincere. Hyacinth couldn't refuse her. Hoping Hyacinth would consume enough brandy to fall asleep and not bother her, Beth reached into the mini-bar. She wasn't a drinker, but managed half a bottle of white wine on an empty stomach. Not a good idea. She felt queasy, put it down to hunger then promptly fell asleep in Hyacinth's arms.

She woke to find Hyacinth, unaffected by the brandy, showered, dressed and ready to go down for a meal.

'Come on Beth, darling. Stir yourself, or we'll never get out to the club.' Hyacinth lit a cigarette.

'Oh God. I don't feel well Hyacinth. It must be the wine. I'm not a drinker, as you know.' Beth crossed over to the bathroom and closed the door, not sure if she wanted to be sick.

'You'll feel better when you've eaten, darling. Now get a move on!' Hyacinth shouted through to her.

Beth looked in the mirror. Her ashen reflection stared back making her feel worse. Wishing she hadn't drunk the wine she took her time in the shower. Deliberately dressing down, she emerged from the bathroom into a cloud of smoke as Hyacinth lit another cigarette.

'Hyacinth! Do you *have* to smoke so much? It's a wonder the smoke alarms haven't gone off.'

With a look of scathing disdain, Hyacinth silently collected her things and walked out of the room.

Feeling slightly better for having eaten, Beth was surprised when Hyacinth bothered to ask if she was feeling well enough to go to a nightclub. Not wanting to spend time alone in the room with her, Beth was quick to say yes. Hyacinth had heard of a trendy basement club in Oxford Street. So off they went.

It wasn't easy to find. The doorway was hidden between two boutiques. Going down the dim stairway was like descending into the bowels of the earth. A dark, hot, thick smoky atmosphere pervaded. Groups of women, although at first glance Beth wasn't sure if they were all women, stood around a dimly lit room, the only real light illuminated the bar. The dance floor was a mass of moving bodies. Beth watched the dancers move as one to the sensuous beat of the music. The beat grew louder, relentlessly thumping in her ears, taking her into a stomach lurching light-headedness.

'Hyacinth...I've got to get outside, into the fresh air.' Beth turned towards the stairs. Hyacinth followed, concerned. She managed to reach the first step before she fainted. Hyacinth helped her up. She went down again. Willing hands came to help.

Once into the fresh air she gradually began to feel better, upset that she had caused their first night in London to be knocked completely sideways. Back at the hotel Beth went straight to bed, to sleep.

The next day she was feeling much better so they decided on a trip to Windsor Castle. They took photographs of each other standing beside the Guards. They had fun, unfairly pulling faces at them, knowing they couldn't laugh. Poor things, not allowed to move at all. Such composure. Their attempts at the ministry of silly walks imitating John Cleese from Monty Python, didn't even result in a smile. Although a group of Japanese tourists enjoyed their performance, frantically clicking away with their cameras.

The afternoon was taken up shopping in Harrods. Hyacinth, determined Beth would not suffer another day from lack of food and be well enough to enjoy the night out she had planned, insisted they go to the Dorchester for afternoon tea.

Shown to a table with a perfect view of the room, Beth sat back, teacup in hand surveying the scene. Naturally her mind wandered to Lou, she couldn't stop herself. She had a vision of Lou walking into the room, the only welcome vision she'd ever had.

She froze as Lou materialized through the door. Oh my god, this is no vision, she's actually here.

Lou wasn't alone, a small attractive woman carrying a bulky briefcase was by her side. They were shown to a nearby table. As she was about to sit down Lou spotted Beth and flashed her a radiant smile.

Elated, Beth couldn't help grinning like a Cheshire Cat. She had convinced herself that she would never see Lou again, yet here she was. She might as well be a hundred miles away came a sobering thought. In her wildest dreams Beth couldn't imagine them getting together. She'd only met her once, for God's sake. Still, she supposed there's no harm in dreaming.

Hyacinth oblivious to Beth's distraction tapped her feet to the piano. Beth wanted to linger. She wanted to sit and savour watching Lou and started to pour more tea into Hyacinth's cup.

Placing her hand over her cup Hyacinth said, 'No, darling. I think we've had enough tea, don't you? We should go and have a rest. We've got to allow ourselves enough time to get ready for tonight.' Her other hand squeezed Beth's knee under the table.

Anxious to escape Hyacinth's touch, Beth excused herself, pretending she needed the Ladies Room. Perhaps Lou would follow her. She felt terribly deflated when Lou didn't appear.

Beth was in the bathroom when she heard the phone ringing. It was impossible to hear the conversation over the noise of the power shower although she could hear the tone of Hyacinth's voice, loud and annoyed. Stepping out of the bathroom wrapped in a white fluffy towel to ask who was on the phone, she was surprised when Hyacinth, eyes blazing slammed the receiver down.

'Bloody silly room service. I told them that I hadn't ordered anything, but the bloody fools kept insisting I had.' Viciously stubbing out her cigarette, she stormed over to the bathroom. Mentally kicking herself, she stopped. Pulling Beth into her arms she kissed her wet hair. 'You are finished in there, aren't you darling?'

'Almost, just a couple more minutes. Are you sure you're alright?' Beth's concern was genuine. She knew it wasn't Room Service that had got Hyacinth so rattled.

She could have sworn she'd heard her shouting at someone called Lady Corday, yelling she was not in a position to dictate terms.

Hyacinth was too angry to make a move on Beth. As a result they were ready to go out much too early so sat in one of the hotel bars for a while. Beth briefly pondered on the Room Service telephone call and Hyacinth's reaction after it, and then surprised herself by feeling disappointed Hyacinth hadn't made a play for her.

Chapter 17

Beth was haunted by thoughts of Lou, angry for allowing her mind to be taken over by a woman she'd only met briefly. She had had a massive effect on her, the like of nothing before and she couldn't stop Lou's beautiful face dancing through her mind no matter how hard she tried. Lady Luck couldn't make their paths cross again - could she? Beth certainly hoped so.

The sound of the piano interrupted her thoughts. She was ready to dance then perhaps she could push all thoughts of Lou out of her head. I wonder where she is now?

Wrapped up in herself she was unaware of the white rage Hyacinth was fighting to control and the several large gins she had downed in quick succession.

It was better they sat in silence because Hyacinth couldn't trust herself to speak for fear of her anger bursting out. She needed to calm down. If Penny fucked up the delivery of the diamond consignment they could all be in real danger. Hyacinth would kill her if she did; hopefully Alison would be able to save the deal. She needed to be in Tynemouth, not in London seducing a woman she suddenly had doubts about. Shit! Just wait till she got her hands on Penny.

They had arranged to meet Constance at nine-thirty so had another hour to kill. Beth happily preoccupied with thoughts of Lou, looked over at the piano and gasped, 'Wow!' Lou was playing the Baby Grand.

'What? Did you say something, darling?' Hyacinth asked vaguely.

Leaning forward in her seat, Beth rubbed her eyes hard. Lou disappeared, while the piano played on.

'It's nothing, Hyacinth. I thought I saw someone I knew. Another g and t darling?' Beth mimicked.

Hyacinth nodded absently, not paying attention, missing the sarcastic darling euphemism. Fury still surged through her over the phone call from her number one. How dare she try to dictate the terms of sharing? How bloody dare she remind her about the basic rules of the group when she should have been out meeting the Contact.

Hyacinth controlled the group. She made the rules. Every one of her women had been only too keen to become part of it and enjoy the benefits.

Time dragged until they were able to get into a taxi and head for this supposedly exciting, wonderful club, both hoping it wasn't like last nights. When they arrived it was so exclusive Beth thought they were going to ask for their dental records as proof of identity. Fortunately Constance was already waiting for them and whisked them into the VIP lounge. Beth's eyes became like two huge saucers. She stopped in disbelief looking around at the women, she couldn't believe what she had been missing all these years. Fragments of her conversation with Lindsay came to mind as she allowed herself the liberation to appreciate her feelings without censoring them.

Constance led them to a table and introduced them to some lovely women. She was immediately monopolized by

Hyacinth leaving Beth rather at sea until one leaned over and spoke.

'Hello Beth, how are you?'

'Angela! I didn't realize it was you, how lovely to see you again. You're a long way from home.'

'Yes, I'm staying in my Kensington apartment. You'll like this club, Beth it's safe. You can be yourself in here.'

'What about your husband, is he in London with you? Does he know you come here?' Beth asked intrigued.

'Oh yes...my husband.' Angela laughed, tossing her long dark hair back from her aristocratic forehead, crinkling her brown eyes. 'Well, we have our little arrangement. Ours is a marriage of convenience and it works. We each have our own circle of friends, including our special friends, then we have the friends we need for keeping up appearances. You'll find a lot of that here. Works like a charm.' Angela downed her drink in one, reaching for Beth's hands. 'Come and dance with me, Beth. You'll do me a power of good. I think we can be friends, you and I. No strings. No ulterior motives. What do you say?'

'Yes thanks...that would be lovely.'

They stood ready to move to the dance floor. Beth turned to speak to Hyacinth first. She was *still* talking to Constance and stubbing out another cigarette, muttering someone could bloody well please themselves.

'Come on, let's dance.' Angela took Beth's hand, 'No point trying to butt in on that conversation.'

A couple of dances later and back in their seats Beth looked across the dance floor towards the bar. She rubbed her eyes, my mind is playing tricks on me again. Lou was standing in the middle of a group of women at the bar. She didn't disappear, this time she was real. Beth's heart flipped as she watched her scan the room. If only you were looking for me she craved.

Savouring the way Lou's blonde hair shone, loving how her cream satin shirt clung to her breasts, with all her might she willed her to turn, and see her, to come over and ask her to dance.

What's love got to do with it? Tina Turner sang. Suddenly Hyacinth grabbed Beth's hand, 'Come on darling, one of my favourites. Let's dance!'

In the midst of the crowded floor Hyacinth was over zealous spinning Beth too fast. God, what a hopeless dancer, she's pathetic Beth thought. What's wrong with her?

Hyacinth hadn't really wanted to dance. She was only doing it to keep Beth sweet. Wishing the dance over, anxious to return to her conversation with Constance, she spun Beth too hard watching helplessly as Beth started to fall.

In a heartbeat Lou caught her, pulling her in as if her life depended on it. She had known their bodies would be a perfect fit and surrendered to the moment. It was sheer joy to hold Beth close. With her arms around her waist, she held her even tighter whispering, 'I've got you. I wouldn't throw you into the arms of another woman!'

Fleetingly wondering why she felt as if she had come home, Beth lifted her head to thank her rescuer and made eye contact with Lou. The words died in her throat and she thought she had died and gone to heaven.

Hyacinth spoke first putting her hand on Beth's arm as if to pull them apart. 'Why, thank you, darling. I'm afraid my partner is not used to drinking. You really must stop drinking so much, Beth,' she scolded expecting Beth to remain silent and walk away with her.

Neither Beth nor Lou moved.

'Thanks. Thank you.' Beth whispered back. Brief words, huge impact.

Dragging her eyes away from Lou she rounded angrily on Hyacinth saying in a steely voice, 'I am neither your partner, nor have I drank to much Hyacinth. And I'll thank you not to make false statements!'

Her outburst delighted Lou. In one sentence she ensured Lou knew the score. Hyacinth was startled. This was the second time Beth had unexpectedly retaliated, but it was enough to make her realize she could be mishandling things. Apologizing, she propelled Beth back to the safety of their table making a show of sitting her comfortably, then topping up her champagne.

Ignoring Hyacinth, Beth silently sipped her drink, her thoughts on Lou and their sweet all too brief moment of heavenly contact. Hyacinth, sure Beth was sulking, renewed her conversation with Constance and ignored her.

She wasn't sulking, far from it. She had just been hit with the terrific realization Lou was gay and anything was possible. They could be together. Surely Lou felt the chemistry when they held each other. It was electric.

A hand touched her shoulder and Lou's face came close to hers, 'Dance?'

'Love to.'

She was on the dance floor before Hyacinth, mouth agape, had time to speak. Both Constance and Angela laughed, neither had seen Hyacinth lost for words before. Nice one Beth, thought Constance, maybe the Queen Bitch has finally met her match.

'Did you mean that?' Lou asked.

'Mean what?'

'Hyacinth's not your partner?'

'Hyacinth has a husband. I'm just a new toy.'

'Come to me tomorrow morning, eleven o'clock at The Dorchester. The Concierge will bring you to my Suite.'

Before Beth could answer they were interrupted by one of Lou's friends pulling her away; they were moving on to another club.

'Eleven o'clock. Remember…I'll be waiting!' she disappeared into the throng of women and out through the door.

What about Hyacinth? Beth puzzled, looking innocently into her stormy eyes when she returned to her seat. She would have to think of something good enough to get rid of her for the day. Looking across the table she had an idea.

'Constance. How do you feel about going with Hyacinth to Madam Tussards tomorrow instead of me?'

Constance held Beth's unflinching gaze. 'Why? Where are you going?' Her request was not sharp, but almost joking.

Beth couldn't read the expression on Hyacinth's face as she swung round to look at her, blonde hair flying, blue eyes piercing. About to demand an explanation she thought better of it. She'd upset Beth once tonight, she'd better tread carefully.

Following an instinct that Hyacinth wouldn't make a scene, she casually said Lou had invited her to have lunch at The Dorchester and she hadn't felt able to refuse.

If Hyacinth had needed something to jerk her back to reality this was it. Constance, sensing it wasn't just lunch, was more than happy to agree. In her opinion Beth was far too good to be in Hyacinth's clutches.

Hyacinth, however, had been given a wake up call. She was attentive and charming for the rest of the evening. Soon they were all giggling like naughty schoolgirls. Beth didn't need the champagne to make her feel happy, her thoughts of Lou did more than that. Not wanting a repeat of the previous night, she drank very little alcohol.

Chapter 18

Hyacinth decided not to make her move on Beth that night. She thought she wasn't ready. She was right. Beth was relieved when Hyacinth wished her goodnight and promptly fell asleep.

Beth couldn't sleep, she was too excited tossing and turning thinking about her liaison with Lou. What would destiny bring for her?

They had an early breakfast served in their room. Hyacinth was back in good form, touching her, paying her compliments, giving her a long lingering kiss before she left to join Constance for the day.

Arriving at the Dorchester Beth was shown to Lou's Suite. Suffering a tremendous attack of nerves and self-doubt she paced the hallway unable to bring herself to knock on the door. What the hell was she doing here? When she finally found the courage to knock, there was no reply.

Fool, she cursed herself. You bloody fool, how could someone like Lou be interested in you? Disappointed she turned towards the lifts, about to walk away, when her inner voice said, Wait. Knock again. Sighing Beth turned, raising her hand just as Lou opened the door, nearly knocking on her nose.

Beth's face dropped as glancing quickly over Lou's shoulder she saw the same woman who had been downstairs with Lou the previous day.

'Beth! At last you're here. I've been waiting…I was scared you wouldn't come.' Lou, elegant, sophisticated with her hair swept up, reached out, drawing Beth to her, she kissed her on both cheeks. 'Come in. This is Sarah, my agent. We've just finished.'

Beth's relief was instant.

'Hi Beth. Nice to meet you.' Sarah said as she crossed the room to shake Beth's hand. She picked up her briefcase saying to Lou, 'Well, I guess that's it. I'll be off now, but the minute I hear anything I'll give you a ring. I'm sure it will be good news.'

Closing the door behind her Lou said casually, 'There may be some film work in the pipeline for me in America. But it's early days yet and nothing's certain in this business.'

Beth nodded, not taking in what she was saying, just enjoying the sound of her voice, and the joy of being able to look at her again. The suite was exquisite, the whole scenario surreal, she felt like pinching herself to make sure she wasn't dreaming. It was uncanny, even though they'd only had the briefest of meetings she felt as if she'd met her soul mate.

Lou switched on some soft music, collected a champagne bucket from behind the bar and set it down beside two glasses already on the coffee table. Beth stood like a statue overwhelmed with desire. She desperately wanted to kiss Lou, to taste her lips, to feel her breath against her face, to smell her skin again, oh that exotic smell. Tension was building up in her body. Lou's voice interrupted her thoughts, the energy crackled between them.

'Close your eyes, I've got a surprise for you.'

'What is it?'

'It won't be a surprise if I tell you.'

'I love surprises.' Beth closed her eyes.

Lou hadn't been sure Beth would turn up. She had taken a huge risk asking her here today. She was always protective of her personal life, keeping herself out of the media spotlight in all matters of the heart. What was she playing at? She didn't know what Beth was feeling. Could she trust her? Too late now. Her desire to be with Beth was so strong, she couldn't stop it, didn't want to.

She loved her aristocratic features, being able to breathe in her presence. Something special was happening here. Surely Beth must feel it too. Unable to control herself any longer, Lou leaned forward.

Sensing she was standing right in front of her, Beth dare not open her eyes. Her pounding heart almost exploded when she felt the softness of Lou's lips touching hers, instantly her arms reached out. Entwined, they experienced the kiss of a lifetime.

Eventually Lou led the way into the bedroom. She pushed Beth onto the four poster bed, smiled into her eyes, whispering, 'Watch and enjoy.'

Swaying in time to the music, slowly raising her hands to pull the comb from her hair, she released a shimmering blonde curtain. Beth was spellbound.

Lou's erotic, rhythmic dancing continued with the beat. Running her hands over her body, sliding one hand up her thigh she raised her skirt showing the lacy pattern around her stocking top. The other found her nipple protruding through the thin shirt material. She licked her lips, enjoying the effect she was having on Beth. Holding her gaze she began to strip. Reaching one hand behind her back she unhooked her skirt and dropped it to the floor revealing shapely legs encased in silk stockings. Teasing, she leaned close to Beth inviting her to undo the buttons on her shirt.

Beth's shaking hands fumbled their way down one, two, three, four, five she counted, holding her breath.

Lou whispered, 'Take it off.'

Beth, churned up with emotion, almost pushed Lou off the bed as she sat bolt upright trying to ease off the shirt.

'God, Lou, I'm sorry.'

Lou laughed, 'Relax lovely. Gently does it. I'm not going to bite you…not yet anyway.'

Beth slipped the shirt over Lou's shoulders, it floated to the floor revealing her perfect barely covered body.

Lou continued to sway slowly, gyrating from bedpost to bedpost, tantalizingly bending in towards Beth, her breasts skimming Beth's face. She moved in front of her again. Leaning back she ran both hands up the inside of her thighs, drawing Beth's eyes to the dampness coming through the thin material of her panties. Her fingers rubbed over her damp patch lingering briefly before moving to caress her nipples as she removed her bra with great panache. Beth watched her in wide eyed wonder.

'You're overdressed Beth. Let me give you a hand to make you more comfortable.'

Lou pulled Beth to her feet, stripping her in seconds then laid her back into the pillows.

'I have a special treat for you.' Lou whispered, 'don't move an inch.' She disappeared, leaving Beth feeling unexpectedly vulnerable.

She returned holding a giant tub of yogurt.

'Yogurt? I'm not hungry!'

'It's not to eat silly…not with a spoon anyway.'

Pulling the lid off Lou carelessly dropped it onto the floor. Balancing the pot in one hand, using the other to remove the thin wisp of material that covered her pubes, she climbed onto the bed. Beth groaned out loud as she settled astride her, blonde pubic hair greeting black.

Dipping her fingers into the pot she smeared yogurt slowly, seductively over Beth's nipples, squeezing, tweaking. As her fingers travelled down to her navel Beth moaned again, her rigid nipples straining to meet Lou's lips as she dropped her head to lick it off. Taking each one in turn into her mouth, she awoke Beth's direct line to her clitoris, exciting her till she was ready to explode.

Lou, still licking, teasing, started stroking Beth's body, exploring, caressing, discovering erogenous zones Beth didn't know she had.

At the back of her mind Beth was praying she wouldn't go near her belly button, something she couldn't stand, a silly phobia. When the inevitable happened, Beth screamed in panic. Trying not to laugh and risk feeling stupid, she realized she should have said something earlier, but what could she have said. Oh Lou, before we start, don't go near the bellybutton!

Luckily it didn't alter the mood. Lou decided to order more yogurt from room service, requesting ice cream as well. She rang for the butler, within minutes he was knocking on the door.

It was one mad scramble as Lou tried to find her robe, not knowing she still had yogurt around her mouth and on her nose.

Carrying a tub of rich chocolate ice cream she returned to the bedroom. Before she had chance to say anything Beth slid off the bed.

'My turn now I think.'

Lou's body was so hot the ice cream melted as soon as Beth smeared it onto her, running in little rivulets off her erect pink nipples staining the sheets. Soon they were in a sticky mess. Lou's body arching as Beth slowly licked the remains of the ice cream from around her nipples and down between her breasts. Savouring the new experience, yet with the art of the practiced lover, her tongue gently caressed one nipple as her fingers tenderly squeezed the other. Simultaneously Lou's hands were working on Beth's erogenous zones, working their way round to her groin to excite some more. Her fingers found Beth's wetness, and because she couldn't wait any longer, she slid them inside. Rolling Beth on to her back, encouraging her to thrust onto her hand Lou moved to lie beside her so that she could bend her head. Her tongue searched out Beth's clitoris, savouring her taste, both girls moaning with pleasure. Working her tongue and hand together Lou brought Beth to a sensational climax.

This is it Beth thought, an orgasm, I'm having an orgasm. Here she was in her late twenties having her first proper orgasm thanks to a woman. She wanted it to last forever. Her body writhed with pleasure as she enjoyed one orgasm after another. She held Lou tightly, her skin flushed and hot. Is this what they call a multiple? Later as she tried to analyse it, the only thing she could liken it too was a sneeze or a series of sneezes. You know it's coming and you don't want anything to stop it.

Beth turned to Lou who almost burst at her tenderness when she tentatively touched her nipples, nearly coming there and then. Determined to hold out, wanting to prolong their lovemaking, she guided Beth's fingers until the spasms of her orgasm took control. Both wanted this time to last forever.

Later they showered together, soaping each other all over. Inevitably one thing led to another and they were making love again. There was no stopping Beth now, she was over any uncertainty. This was the best day of her life.

Passionate promises to keep in touch were made, telephone numbers exchanged and Lou promised to ring as soon as she returned to North Yorkshire. Carefully, Beth tucked Lou's number safely into her purse. Leaving their parting as late as they dared, they reluctantly took the lift to the foyer to where Hyacinth and Constance were already waiting.

Chapter 19

Hyacinth was trying to analyse the situation. Pretending to be full of Madame Tussaud's, telling how Constance bumped into a man, apologized, then realized it was a wax dummy of Bob Geldoff, she took centre stage. Hawk-like she watched every move Beth and Lou made, looking for telltale signs that would confirm her worst fears. She was wasting her time. Lou was on to her, being purposely cool. She wasn't an accomplished actress for nothing.

Constance watched Hyacinth's performance with awe. What a cracking good liar she is. We haven't been there at all yet I actually believe her. As Hyacinth flashed her a smile, Constance quickly squeezed her hand under the table honoured and relieved to have been taken into the inner circle. Easing her sore buttocks into a more comfortable position, sure the insides of her legs were bruised, she ached from the rough sex Hyacinth had insisted on as part of her initiation package. Until this morning she had never thought about bondage and had been amazed how much it turned her on. Now she was looking forward to being a slave. Her hand went to the diamond pendant hidden beneath her top. A gift from

Hyacinth and tangible evidence of her new found importance. And that wasn't all. Despite currently having a little discomfort Constance felt very smug.

Hyacinth sat back, relaxing for the first time that day. She had done the right thing taking Constance into her confidence. No, she corrected herself. She had done the right thing taking Constance. The sex had been great; she now had a perfect slave. That would teach Penny to step out of line. She couldn't wait to see her face when she told her. She would have to teach her a lesson first though.

Beth was adrift in the middle of the situation as the other three made polite conversation. Her heart already starting to pine over her separation from Lou.

Lou had to leave for an important appointment. Shaking hands lastly with Hyacinth, maintaining steady eye contact, she solemnly thanked her for allowing her to enjoy Beth's company, before majestically walking away.

For the second time that weekend Hyacinth was speechless, and Constance's shoulders heaved with silent laughter. Beth felt a twinge of guilt about her liaison with Lou, but it evaporated as an image of David came into her mind.

What a beautiful couple Beth and Lou would make Constance thought as she kissed Hyacinth and Beth goodbye. And it would just serve Hyacinth right.

It was time to change for dinner when they arrived back at their hotel. Hyacinth was still feeling uneasy, yet there was nothing she could pinpoint. Beth seemed to be the same. Maybe she should never have left her, what if she *had* gone to bed with Lou? Given the chance, she would. Mentally shaking herself, she turned the full force of her charm on Beth.

'Darling, I forgot to mention, I've booked tickets for The Vagina Monologues.'

'Oh that's wonderful Hyacinth.'

They had two of the best seats in the house. When the show finished Hyacinth was keen to get back to their hotel. Beth, shattered after her mind-blowing experience with Lou, just knew what Hyacinth had planned.

'Mrs. Dickinson!' a receptionist called as they were about to step into the lift. 'I have an urgent message for you!' she ran across to them and handed Hyacinth an envelope.

'Thank you, darling.' Hyacinth tore open the envelope, scanned the message and pushed it into her handbag.

'Everything alright, Hyacinth?'

'Oh, it's nothing, darling. Just a friend wanting some advice.'

'But the receptionist said it was urgent.'

'Yes. My friend probably wanted to make sure I got her message. Now don't you worry your pretty head about it. We're not going to let anything spoil our special night, are we darling?'

Beth didn't answer. Hyacinth took her silence as agreement.

They stepped out of the lift and Hyacinth opened the door into their suite saying, 'I'll just make a quick phone call, darling. Why don't you go and have a nice soak in the bath. Use some of the new bubble bath I bought for us today. You'll find it on the shelf. I'll join you shortly. This won't take long.'

Relieved, Beth ran the bath. She was dying to know who Hyacinth was talking to, so kept her ear to the door for ages. She could hear snippets of conversation, the rise and fall of Hyacinth's voice. Twice she heard her shout, 'Now you listen to me. She's not ready yet, she won't be for a long time.'

Who is she talking about? Hyacinth's voice droned on, then there was a long silence. Beth thought she must have finished and was just about to jump into the bath when Hyacinth angrily shouted. 'She's not ready. How many fucking times do

I have to tell you? Penny, I hate to admit it, but I may have been wrong about this one.' Another pause. 'Yes, there's a first time for everything, isn't there darling?' Hyacinth faked a laugh then her tone changed. 'Remind Serena patience is a virtue. And you would do well to remember that yourself, darling. I will be paying you a visit soon to remind *you* personally.'

As Hyacinth replaced the receiver Beth turned off the taps. Despite running the water slowly the bath was full. Sloshing the water to create bubbles she undressed and stepped into the tub expecting Hyacinth to walk in any second. She didn't. Is she on the phone again? Who is she talking to now?

Hyacinth searched Beth's handbag, discovered Lou's personal telephone number and destroyed it. She was taking no chances. Satisfied with herself she went into the bathroom.

Her seduction of Beth was slow and purposeful. Sitting on the side of the bath she started to soap Beth's body, hardly believing the surge of excitement the contact generated. Beth closed her eyes pretending it was Lou, making her start to enjoy it.

Beth didn't attempt to touch Hyacinth, it didn't feel right. In a crazy way she felt unfaithful to Lou. Fortunately, Hyacinth put it down to shyness. Their lovemaking wasn't the success Hyacinth envisaged. Afterwards in bed wrapped around Beth she promised next time would be better. Beth pretended to be asleep. As far as she was concerned there may not be a next time.

Chapter 20

Beth couldn't get Lou out of her mind. Like a seed, once planted her feelings started to grow as thoughts of Lou dominated every waking moment. She knew they had made a tremendous connection, not just on a physical level but also a spiritual one too. She needed to know how Lou felt. But was she being silly? Unsophisticated? She didn't think so. As soon as she arrived home she looked in her bag for Lou's number. It had gone. Frantically she tipped everything out scattering the entire contents over the living room floor. She knew exactly where she had put it. She had placed it securely in the inside zipper pocket. Sickened, it dawned on her that Hyacinth must have searched her bag and destroyed it while she was soaking in the bath at the hotel. Beth was furious. How dare Hyacinth go through her things, how dare she? Just who the fuck did she think she was?

Tuesday morning and Beth was working alongside David Dickinson. While they were scrubbing up he enquired pleasantly as to whether she'd enjoyed the weekend away with his wife. Everyone's ears pricked. Beth smiled, nodded and immediately walked into the operating theatre. She had no intention of answering any questions, or giving the staff thought for gossip. That might come soon enough.

It won't be long now before Hyacinth comes to work at the hospital and she still couldn't decide whether it was a good or bad thing. Good for the hospital, maybe not so good for her. She'd have to wait and see. In the meantime she had no intention of getting in touch with her.

Hyacinth showed the last patient out of her Carlisle office. It had been almost three weeks since she had seen Beth. She had struggled with her decision not to make contact, but Constance had proved an obliging diversion and if Penny didn't heed her warning Constance would take over from her as a willing Number One.

She felt bad at the beating she had given Penny, but there wasn't a bruise visible. She had needed to be taught a lesson. No-one, but no-one, questioned Hyacinth's decisions.

And how could Penny know the pressure she was under. It was nothing to do with sharing Beth. If she allowed herself to dwell on the situation she feared she would fold. For the first time in her life she was frightened and it took a lot to frighten Hyacinth. The Syndicate took no prisoners. She had told no-one. After all who could she tell?

Luckily today had been slow. Perhaps the number of unmarried mothers was on the decline. If the staff attended to any casual callers she had time to ring her girls before she left to drive home to Jesmond. After all she had promised Beth a get-together with her special friends and what better time than this with David away for the entire weekend. She would hold a swim party with some interesting games and the girls could stay over. Beth would love it.

She started dialling the members of her inner coven, making arrangements, insisting she wanted everyone present by eight on Friday evening with the usual regalia ready for the full moon at midnight. The choice of partner was theirs. She loved the full moon rituals, the sharing, giving and receiving, the wild, abandoned sex. Finally, her blood racing, she rang Beth to extend her personal invitation. Furious to hear the busy signal she crashed the telephone down into its receiver. There was a timid knock on her office door. She cursed under her breath. She would have to try Beth's number again later. She rapidly composed herself smiling like an angel as her senior nurse entered the room.

Lou had dialled Beth's number only seconds before Hyacinth. It seemed to ring forever before Beth answered.

'Remember me?' a haunting voice asked.

'Of course I remember you! How could I forget?' Beth whimpered embarrassingly, so excited she nearly wet her knickers. Thank you God she thought. Her eyes shone with happiness, as the past three weeks silence faded away. 'Where are you?'

'I'm in Yorkshire. I wondered if you would you like to meet up somewhere for a romantic night or two?'

'When and where?' her hand went up to her mouth as her conscience questioned what she was saying, and the speed of her answer.

'I know a quiet country hotel, discreet with five star service. It's about half way between us.'

Lou gave directions; Beth wrote them in her diary. Two pm Friday. Yes, yes, yes! She dropped her pen on the table then turned Robbie Williams up to full volume on the radio as she danced around the room.

The phone rang again. Lou must have forgotten something. Beth ran across the living room and grabbed the receiver only to be stopped in her tracks.

'Hello darling. Have you been avoiding me?' Hyacinth purred.

She had.

'We need to catch up darling. I'm having a swim party this weekend. Of course you'll know David's going to be away at a conference. I was just saying to the girls, a couple of them are here now, that it seems a perfect opportunity for us all to get together. What do you say? Be here for six on Friday.'

Thinking on her feet she lied, gushing, 'Oh Hyacinth. Thank you so much for the invite. How very kind of you. I'm so sorry, but I can't make it. You know that I'd love too, but I need to go home. There's some family business I have to attend to that simply can't wait.'

Hyacinth was gutted, 'Well never mind, darling. There'll be other times. Call me when you can.'

Anticipating a barrage of questions, Beth was startled by Hyacinth's calm acceptance.

The telephone rang for the third time. It was Isobel with exciting news. Beth was an aunty. Catherine's daughter had been born so quickly she almost caught them out. Beth promised to visit after the weekend, but ordered a huge bouquet complete with teddy bears to be delivered immediately.

Friday morning, Beth awoke excited at the prospect of her impending rendezvous.

She did the usual things. Showered, washed her hair, not forgetting to shave the armpits and legs. She didn't want Lou to think she was growing sheepskins. Wearing her sexiest lace underwear, musk body spray, a dab of Chanel No.5 behind the ears, she was ready to go.

She was first to arrive at the hotel. Lou had booked them in under her name and Beth was enchanted to be shown into a suite that was absolutely fabulous. Apparently, over a century ago, the hotel had been a family home. When the present owners bought it they turned it into a five star hotel, cleverly keeping the homely atmosphere while introducing the perfect tone in ultimate luxury. There was a private cinema, a superb restaurant, and a small gymnasium with an inviting Jacuzzi.

Waiting for Lou, Beth investigated the ground floor settling in the drawing room. She ordered coffee. Generations of family paintings on the walls and the huge fireplace reminded her of Davinia's home. Restless, she wandered over to the long windows overlooking the expansive gardens and curving drive, her churning stomach lurched when she saw Lou's car turning into the drive. Shivering with delight she had a flashback to their time in London.

Chapter 21

After checking in Lou went in search of Beth. As she walked along the inner hallway Beth stepped out from the drawing room to meet her, body quivering. Lou had the sexiest smile, lips so luscious and inviting that Beth had a burning desire to rip her clothes off right there and then. They headed up to the suite to say a proper hello to each other. There was no need to rush today. There was time to talk, to get to know each other. After a while, and because it was a pleasant day, they decided to look around the hotel grounds and explore the extensive gardens.

After walking a couple of miles, both savouring the joy of just being together, they crested a hill and discovered a lake. Down by the water it was quiet and peaceful with the silence broken only by the sound of birds singing, and ducks coming in to land. Wandering along the banks, enjoying the sunshine and their personal solitude while sharing life's secrets, they stopped to sit on a pile of stones and drink from Lou's pocket flask.

Inevitably Lou's conversation turned to Hyacinth. She wanted to know all about her. Beth was honest in her answers.

After all Hyacinth had awakened something in her she had been denying, although Lou was her first real sexual encounter with a woman. Lou was silent. She felt far too much for this vivacious creature. Overpowering chemistry charged between them and wasn't this just the worst time for her to meet the woman of her dreams. The American offer was almost in the bag, too good to refuse. She might have to leave for LA any day now to secure the deal. She didn't want to go, yet she would be mad not to. Offers like this only came along once in a lifetime, if ever. Maybe she would be able to get Beth out of her system after this weekend. It could fizzle out naturally, it had happened before in fact it usually did. Perhaps Beth was just experimenting like lots of women do. On the other hand, if she were feeling the same, would she wait for her? Lou leaned back against the warm rock.

'What about you?' Beth wanted to know, 'Is there someone in your life?'

Throwing caution to the wind she replied, 'Yes and no.'

'What sort of answer's that? What do you mean?'

'Well, there is someone I've been involved with for about a year. It's always been very on and off, more like a friendship really. Nothing heavy and in truth more off than on. Definitely off now I've met you.' She never mentioned LA.

Overjoyed at Lou's statement, Beth's mind raced. She wanted to throw herself into Lou's arms, beg her to never leave her, and then she got a grip. These feelings were alien to her, she didn't know what to do with them, how to react. Her head was like scrambled eggs. She was scared too. What if Lou changed her mind, met someone else on her travels. Distance and lifestyle could come between them. She didn't acknowledge Lou's words, staying silent.

As they walked back to the hotel they stumbled upon an ancient stone formation, many resembled phallic symbols.

Laughing, they reckoned it probably had something to do with fertility rights. Drawn by the magical atmosphere they sat for a while among the stones. Lou held Beth's hands and as she did a vision of Universal Studios passed through Beth's mind, but she forgot about it as Lou covered her palms with kisses. Both lost in their own thoughts they returned to the hotel.

Once inside their mood lightened. The health spa beckoned. It was deserted. They had the Jacuzzi to themselves. Lou, sitting opposite Beth, started to play footsie with her while bobbing about in the water. Beth giggled as she felt toes walking up the inside of her leg. She yearned for Lou's touch, relishing the tangible excitement building between them. She could see little beads of perspiration on Lou's brow when she moved to sit next to her.

Lou got hold of Beth's hands, their fingers locked as the now familiar tingle surged through Beth's body. Lou, overcome with lust, couldn't wait any longer. She moved to stand in front of Beth, watching her close her eyes as she locked her legs around Lou's waist.

Her fingers trailed over Beth's forehead, before moving slowly down her cheeks. As they reached her lips, Beth sighed, the Jacuzzi bubbles bounced off her hot body. She slipped a finger into Beth's mouth. Beth sucked on it lingeringly. Lou's hands slid down to caress Beth's ripe, breasts.

Waiting with baited breath for Lou's lips to touch hers, Beth found the gentleness so erotic she was gasping for air.

'Lou. Let's go back to the suite. Anyone can walk in here.' she managed to gasp.

Lou shook her head, 'No! I can't wait. We'll hear if anyone comes along the hallway. Anyway, it will be worth the risk.' She kissed Beth again, 'Like I said, I can't wait. We'll live dangerously.'

As Lou whispered sweet nothings Beth was transported to a tropical beach with palm trees and turquoise seas. It was the Jacuzzi bubbles, but the palm trees were real enough. Thoroughly exploring each other's bodies, testing reactions, tantalizing each other, until Beth daringly took the initiative and slipped her hand inside Lou's bikini bottoms. She was overjoyed at the slippery wetness that greeted her probing fingers. Lou responded by spreading her legs as Beth's thumb rubbed gently against her protruding clitoris. Suddenly Lou drew her legs together and Beth was overcome with emotion as she realized what was happening. Lou's body went rigid then jolted as her orgasm made her writhe in the water, climax peaking. A vocal lover, the sound of her pleasure echoed around the room.

Subconsciously Beth worried someone would hear them but she was so turned on her own orgasm thundered the second Lou touched her.

Hearts pounding they lay back in the water. Beth had never experienced such ecstasy. Eventually they sauntered back to the suite, collapsing on the bed to sleep in each other's arms.

Two hours later they awoke hungry, so a mountain of food was ordered from room service along with champagne. More bubbles, they both giggled.

By the time they'd eaten their way through to the cheese and biscuits they were well and truly stuffed. Talk turned to Hyacinth again. Lou wanted to know how much time they spent together, just how deep, and committed, was Beth's involvement. Beth told her about the swim party, explaining how she'd been invited to spend the weekend at Hyacinth's to meet her special friends. She reeled off the names of the women she knew would be there explaining how she'd met some of them.

Lou knew she could have a serious rival in Hyacinth, but Beth was with her now. She intended to keep it that way. To hell with LA. Not trusting herself to speak, needing to create a diversion, she flicked the remote control and the television sprang into life with the news. They were feeding each other grapes when Beth picked up on the presenter's story of a missing woman. Police were concerned about the whereabouts of Serena Gardener-Shaw.

'Lou? Did he say Serena Gardener-Shaw?'

'Wasn't paying much attention, my love. Why?'

'Well. I'm sure she was going to Hyacinth's swim party. You know, the one I've just been telling you about.'

'Really! Do you know her?'

'To be honest, I can't remember if I've met her or not. She may have been at their charity thing, I don't know for sure. I met so many people that day. The name is familiar though.'

'Well, let's hope she turns up safe and sound, eh?'

Serena forgotten, they lay back on the bed. Asking each other thousands of questions, wanting to know everything at once, Beth was surprised to learn Lou loved horses and actually kept two Eventers at home cared for by a live-in groom. Beth asked if she knew the MacFarlines and mentioned her invitation to be their guest, to ride out with Felicity. 'Come with me. Davinia said to bring a friend. I would love it, if you could.'

'Felicity MacFarline. Yes. I've heard of her. I might even have met her once or twice. Quite a beauty, if she's the one I'm thinking of.' Lou said in more of a statement than a question. 'You bet I'll come with you. It'll be fun. I can't wait to see you in tight jodhpurs. In fact I'll look forward to it.'

Beth blushed happily. Rolling onto her stomach she replied, 'That's wonderful…. Guess what I saw when I went to Davinia's birthday party.'

Lou looked puzzled. 'What?'

With great clarity Beth recalled the incident between Davinia and Clarice, making Lou laugh so hard Beth thought she'd need hospital treatment. Even during their bath together she kept giggling.

Chapter 22

Much later they went down to the bar. Slightly tipsy from the champagne, all Beth could manage was an orange juice. They were nearly falling asleep when Lou's curiosity was kindled. Sitting to attention she nudged Beth, indicating to the far side of the room.

'You know, I think that's Penelope Corday over there. Lady Penelope to be precise. Look, near to the door. She's sitting with another woman, short blonde hair, red suit.'

Beth's stomach lurched. She'd heard that name before in London when Hyacinth was shouting on the phone. 'I don't know her, Lou, but I think Hyacinth does.'

For once the mention of Hyacinth's name went over Lou's head. Her attention was concentrated on Penny Corday. 'I always thought she was gay you know, but never had it confirmed.'

'Confirmed? How the hell do confirm that?.....She's married to Lord Corday, isn't she? Don't be silly Lou! Plus the fact they're quite a social pair, always in the news for something or other. Fund raising and stuff, you know what I mean.'

'Fund raising? Marriage? Sounds familiar don't you think? It doesn't stop Hyacinth, does it?'

Beth thought for a moment before answering, 'Mmmmm. Yes. I suppose you have a point there.'

Like super sleuths they covertly watched Lady Corday's body language and eye contact with her friend. Both attractive women, almost mirror images of each other; short blonde hair, brown eyes. Penny Corday's burgundy shirt, smart black trousers and black leather belt suited her gamin figure perfectly. Her friend was similarly styled in red.

They were flirting with each other. Were they just friends or lovers?

'We could go over and talk to them.' Lou suggested.

'How? We don't even know them.'

'Do we not?' Lou laughed. 'Watch, listen and go along with me. Okay?'

'What?..Okay. You're crazy!'

Neither woman was aware of them until Lou interrupted their conversation. Full of charm she greeted Lady Corday exuberantly, 'Liz...hello! How lovely to see you again...how are you?'

Startled Lady Corday looked up, speaking sharply, 'I'm sorry. You are mistaken. My name is Penelope, not Liz.'

Lou dazzled her with a thousand-watt smile, graciously apologizing, 'Oh dear, I'm sooo sorry. I do this all the time... I meet so many people. I really thought you were someone else.'

Simultaneously both women recognized Lou.

'Penny Corday, delighted to meet you.' She thrust her well-manicured hand into Lou's, 'You've interviewed my husband Bertie many times.' Not giving Lou time to reply she continued, 'And you must be Beth.'

117

Funny thought Beth, how could she know my name, Lou hasn't mentioned it, or has she?

Beth wasn't given time to answer as Lady Victoria Ashton indicated to the empty chairs, 'Please, join us.'

Lou looked at Beth with a I told you so expression as they sat down. Conversation was lively. Penny's tongue loosened by countless glasses of sherry told them, in confidence, she only married because it was expected of her and she'd been unable to rebel against it. She happily stands by her man in public, while in private she prefers female company.

Later when Beth climbed into bed next to Lou, snuggling up, revelling in the feel of Lou's naked body next to hers, the silkiness of her skin, she began to fully appreciate why Penny preferred female company. This was pure bliss.

Saturday dawned sunny and warm. After a leisurely breakfast in their room Beth challenged Lou to a game of golf. A seasoned player, she wanted to show off a bit.

Lou was game for a laugh. After a short lesson on how to hit the ball, they walked to the first tee. It was a nine-hole course so Beth thought it shouldn't take too long. Wrong. Every time Lou tried to hit the ball, she missed or hit it out of bounds. Occasionally loud grumbles could be heard from other golfers. The girls allowed a group of grumpy men to pass through, nodding and smiling at them, pretending not to speak English then played on regardless, determined to finish the course. Finally, at the 9th tee, Lou shaded her eyes and looked at the flag on the distant green.

'Beth?'

'Yes.'

'Is that the hole over there?' Lou pointed into the distance.

'Yes. If you can, aim straight down the fairway. And remember not to lift your head when you hit the ball.'

'Yes, ma'am!' she saluted.

Lou placed her ball on the tee, took up her stance and swung the club. The ping echoed as the ball sailed through the air way down the fairway. It landed on the green, bounced twice, then rolled into the hole.

'Like that, Beth?' Lou smirked.

'You *can* play!'

'Yes. I'm afraid so.'

'Well…why on earth have you had me showing you what to do? You couldn't hit the ball when we started out!'

'No, I couldn't, could I?' Lou chuckled, 'I was a bit rusty at first. It's been ages since I've played. And you were doing such a good job, as a teacher. Having you wrapped round me showing me how to hold the club……well, I ask you. Would you have stopped it?'

'Honestly Lou. I feel such a pratt!' Beth laughed picking up the clubs ready to head back, 'No, I guess I wouldn't have stopped it either.'

Hungry, they returned to the hotel for a meal. While the waiters were settling them at their table, Lou dropped her napkin, 'Beth, be a love. Pick up my napkin.'

As Beth bent down, Lou opened her legs. 'Take a look.' She was naked under her skirt.

Flustered, Beth bumped her head off the table giggling as Lou promised, 'Yours - for afters.'

After the meal they wandered into the bar. Penny and Victoria were there again doing justice to a bottle of red. Penny waved them over. Talk was mostly about golf and Lou's hole in one, yet Beth sensed all was not well with Lady Corday. She was edgy, knocking back wine like there was no tomorrow, immediately ordering more.

During a lull in the conversation Beth enquired if everything was all right. Penny looked shifty yet assured her she was fine. Beth didn't believe her, whispering that if she wanted to talk they could meet up in the drawing room on Sunday morning. Penny didn't acknowledge the invitation. As the women wished each other goodnight she slipped Beth a note. Eleven am was scrawled out in black eye pencil.

Beth decided not to mention anything to Lou. She didn't want her to get the wrong idea.

Lou, glad they were alone, said slyly, 'I have a surprise upstairs for you.'

'Another one. You know how I love surprises. Not more ice cream and yogurt though.'

'No, something else. How about a soak in our Jacuzzi first?' Lou hugged Beth from behind.

'Mmmmm that would be nice.'

The minute they closed the door Beth stripped and was first in the tub hitting the button to turn on the bubbles. Lying back she watched Lou take off her clothes, like a sex goddess.

About to step into the tub Lou slipped knocking a bottle of bubble bath into the water. Bubbles overtook the bathroom as Beth tried to find the off button. Laughing together they flicked bubbles at each other.

'I can't believe we are here, doing this.' Beth said. 'How long can it last?'

'As long as we want it too, my lovely. As long as we want.' Lou leaned over and kissed her.

Languidly stroking each other until it got too much, Lou lead the way to the bed. Settling Beth on top of the duvet she reached for a bottle of rich massage oil.

Taking charge, she rolled Beth onto her stomach. Drizzling oil down her spine, she started to massage the bottom of her back. Moving slowly, sensuously up to Beth's shoulders then working down her arms using a heavier stroke.

Kissing the back of her neck Lou moved to sit astride Beth's buttocks. Beth loved it experiencing waves of pure ecstasy as Lou maintained her continuous massage, spreading her fingers on each upward stroke and pushing her pelvis into Beth's buttocks.

Just as Beth felt she would sink through the mattress Lou turned her over, massaging from her shoulders down to her breasts. Kneading lovingly, caressing her nipples, all the while sitting astride her grinding into her pubic bone, exerting just the right amount of pressure, moving back and forth, both were eaten up with lust as they exploded with pleasure.

Later while Lou was sleeping, Beth lay gazing into space, dreading the thought of returning to reality the next day. All too aware she was falling in love and feeling out of her depth, sleep evaded her. As day dawned, she dozed, only to be awoken by Lou's kisses.

Chapter 23

Lost in their own thoughts neither had much to say over breakfast, courtesy of room service. Lou left first, she had to meet her agent. After lingering parting kisses and promises to ring, Beth was left alone feeling desolate. At least Lou had mentioned the visit to Davinia's before she left. A good sign.

Her things packed, she was ready to check out. First she had to meet Penny Corday in the drawing room. Why on earth had she offered? she asked herself while making her way downstairs to where Penny was waiting.

Urgently taking Beth by the arm Penny led the way to the farthest corner of the leafy conservatory, to a table almost invisible behind a wall of greenery. Beth was not prepared for what Penny had to say. Apparently she was being blackmailed.

Horrified at her statement, Beth's kind heart immediately started to think of a way she could help. Poor Penelope was in a particularly vulnerable situation. The blackmailer was threatening her husband's career.

Because Beth had mentioned she had a good friend in the Police Force, Penny thought she may be able to help her. Beth stared at the letters Penny dropped onto the table, reluctant to touch them. Sinister words demanded a five hundred thousand pound payment otherwise the press would be sent a photograph of Penny and Victoria in a passionate clinch. Lady Ashton had received an identical demand. Too distraught to openly discuss the situation she had already left the hotel.

A waiter appeared at the table. Penny didn't try to cover up the letters but quickly ordered two large gin and tonics. Agitated, she said to Beth, 'I'm staying a little longer. I need to keep a low profile while Bert is in London for a few days.'

The waiter returned with the drinks. Draining her glass she gazed out of the windows, 'Oh Beth. What a mess. What am I to do? I've always tried to be so careful.' Tearful, she searched in her bag for a handkerchief.

Beth handed her a tissue, and pushed the other drink over to her. 'Have mine, I'm driving anyway.' Penny took a gulp, staring miserably into the glass.

'Have you any idea who could be doing this?'

'No. None. I have a circle of trusted women friends, you know what I mean dear, don't you? Of course you do.' Penny managed a smile and patted Beth's hand. 'We are all loyal to each other. We have to be. I can't go to the Police, we all have a lot to lose.' Still tearful she implored Beth, 'Please, please could you ask your friend to help me?'

Reluctantly Beth agreed, 'Yes, I suppose so. But I expect she'll advise you to contact the local police. Did I mention my friend is based in Brighton?'

Penny shook her head.

'Perhaps I should ask her to contact you direct.'

Penny didn't answer.

'Yes, I'll do that. So Penny, when Inspector Powell rings you'll know who she is. Okay?'

Penny's hand shook, 'Inspector Powell…What if Bertie gets wind of things? No, we should do it through you. It will be safer. Please Beth.'

'Yes, I suppose so. Don't worry, I'll try to speak to her today.'

Leaving Penny weeping into her gin she went to check out and wasn't surprised to find Lou had settled the bill. Typical. She glanced up the stairs, gasping as Hyacinth disappeared out of view from the top step.

She asked the receptionist if Hyacinth Dickinson had booked in.

'Dickinson, did you say Madam?' the receptionist glanced up, 'Sorry. That's not the name of the guest who has just checked in.'

Beth held her gaze. 'No? …. Oh! I must be mistaken.' Like hell I am. She hurried outside to scan the car park for the silver Mercedes. It wasn't there. Perhaps she was mistaken. After all, she hadn't had much sleep.

Beth drove home enjoying the warm weather, reliving her time with Lou. Once home she would ring her first, then Lindsay, provided the car made it back. It was making an awful noise, rattling like a bag of hammers. She would have to make the effort to buy a new one. It wasn't as if she couldn't afford too, the only thing she was short of was time. Plus she hated the waffling of car salesmen who irritated her to death automatically assuming she had no idea what was under the bonnet, when in actual fact she could have shown them a thing or two.

Lou wasn't home so Beth left a message with her answering service asking her to get in touch. Then she rang Lindsay and told her about Penny's problem.

Lindsay listened carefully. She would like to read the letters and as she was due for a few days leave she would drive up on

Wednesday. Could Beth arrange for her to meet with Penny? Beth was keen to keep the call short because she was waiting for Lou to ring, so promised to tell Lindsay every detail of the weekend when she came to visit.

Unable to sleep because the erotic phone conversation with Lou had her wet with desire, she ached to be able to reach out to touch her, so she did the next best thing and pleasured herself.

Chapter 24

Back at work Beth found it difficult to focus on her patients. She arranged for Penny and Lindsay to meet on Thursday morning. Penny seemed grateful.

On Wednesday morning Janet received a phone call saying Beth's new car would be delivered at lunch-time. Knowing Beth was in theatre most of the day she took delivery on her behalf, leaving the keys with her messages.

After a hard day Beth was looking forward to going home and planned to check her messages then leave. Thankful nothing urgent required her immediate attention, except the small matter of a car. Rereading Janet's neat writing she learned her new XJS (nice choice dear-remember to drive safely) had been delivered. It was sitting in her personal parking bay.

Perfect car, thought Beth, big mistake. Someone must be going crazy wondering what had happened to their new motor. She dialled Janet's home number. No mistake, Janet assured her. The car was definitely hers.

The only thing to do was to return it to the garage. Picking up the keys and paperwork Beth went to find the car. She groaned in despair at the beautiful motor, a silver blue dream machine with a navy hood. Opening the door she slid into the driver's seat breathing in the smell of new leather.

On the passenger seat laid a bouquet of red roses with an envelope addressed to her. Lou had written:

Happy Birthday, my love. Enjoy!

See you soon.

L.

xxxxxxxxxxxx

Gob smacked, her mind recalled her conversation with Lou about getting a new car, when she'd moaned about how she hated the hassle, but this gesture was too much.

Nevertheless she stroked the leather seats, admired the sexy curve of the bonnet and drank in the luxury. Unable to resist, she turned the ignition, and the engine roared into life. Just wait until Lindsay gets an eye full of this, she thought. Of course she couldn't possibly keep it, even as a gift. Lou knew she appreciated life's luxuries and loved surprises, but this was one serious piece of luxury and one hell of a surprise.

Chapter 25

Lindsay pulled off the motorway into a service area. Time for a break. Washing her hands in the Ladies Room her attention was caught by two striking looking women deep in conversation. They would make an attractive pairing she thought, holding her hands under the automatic dryer longer than necessary. The darker blonde, as if aware of Lindsay's scrutiny, looked up making a knowing eye contact. Their eyes held momentarily, Lindsay caught up in the depths of the Mediterranean blue.

Checking her reflection, she smoothed her short light brown hair. Yes, she'd made the right decision to have the gold highlights, made her look more of a babe. That blonde certainly thought so. Maybe she would follow her into the restaurant. With that thought Lindsay tried to catch her attention again, without success. Hyacinth had more pressing things on her mind.

Half an hour later, after finishing the strong coffee and croissants, Lindsay was ready to leave. She stood up, dropped a generous tip on the table then spotted the blonde in the car park. Alone this time, she looked angry, her deep blue eyes blazing. Always the police officer, Lindsay moved out of sight as the Mercedes cruised past the restaurant windows crossing the car park, then turned to head north.

The image of the two women played on her mind for a while, she enjoyed taking them through sex games until she had to stop, her imagination interfering with her driving. Anyway, she wondered, what sort of sex games was Beth playing? She couldn't wait to find out. This blackmail business was a wonderful excuse to visit, suss out Hyacinth and hopefully meet the lovely Lou who had knocked her best friend for six.

Arriving early evening, she expected Beth to have company when she saw the Jaguar parked outside. Instead she was staggered at the change in her best friend who tried to make coffee, tell her about Lou and her new car all at the same time, talking twenty to the dozen. Lindsay had never seen her so euphoric.

'Slow down! You're making me dizzy. So Lou sent you the car? A present?'

'Yes. Are you not listening? Honestly, you're supposed to be a police officer!'

'Tell you what Beth, you've landed on your feet there. I wish I had someone who would give me a Jag and take me away for luxury weekends.'

'She talked about going on a cruise some time. What do you think I should do?'

'Do? The first thing you should do is get the keys and take me for a spin. That's some car. And honey, if you don't want to go on the cruise, I will!'

'No chance. Come on then, let's go.'

After a fast test drive they spent the rest of the evening catching up on Beth's news. Lindsay wanted to know everything.

At eleven sharp the next morning Penny Corday arrived with the blackmail letters including the one sent to Victoria. Sitting around the dining room table, Beth was concerned for Penny, she looked pale and drawn.

Lindsay studied the letters. Someone had gone to a lot of trouble. Each envelope showed a different postmark.

'Could you get some coffee, Beth? Penny looks like she could use a hot drink.'

As Beth left the room she heard Penny nervously gabble, 'Thank you so much for coming. You've no idea how much your help means to me. I've wracked my brain and come up with two possible suspects, though it's hard to believe either of them would resort to blackmail. They might be from an old flame, Baroness Claire Cavendish. We had a five-year affair.' Penny sobbed into her handkerchief. 'I was the one who ended it about six months ago. The Baroness…do you know I can't bring myself to call her Claire anymore…was very bitter.'

Beth returned carrying a tray of coffee. Penny took hers without pausing for breath.

'We got together just after the Baron died. She was in such a state. I had to support her, she was so fragile, but she became increasingly demanding. I didn't notice at first, you don't do you? You do what you can. She turned into an over-possessive monster and when she said she wanted to move in with me…well that was it. She gave me no choice. I finished it. I hadn't realized that we'd been together for five years. Time just rolls by, doesn't it? She did threaten to hurt me, to get even. Of course I didn't take her seriously. Not until now.'

Lindsay's businesslike manner calmed Penny. 'You said two?'

'Two? Oh, yes. Rose.'

'Rose?'

'Yes, Rose.' She dropped her head. 'I thought she was genuine and trustworthy.'

'Yes? But who is she?'

'Oh silly me. Rose is my housekeeper, Girl Friday, call her what you will. She came very well recommended. You could say she had the seal of royal approval. If you know what I mean.'

Lindsay nodded. 'Yes, I understand. Why would Rose want to blackmail you?'

'I don't know that she would. Except that I don't have any secrets from her.'

Lindsay looked at Beth, 'How do you feel about doing a bit of detective work? Could you go to Penny's house, say tomorrow, for a chat with Rose?'

'Be glad to.'

'Afternoon tea,' Penny suggested, 'I often have friends in for afternoon tea, so she won't think anything of it. I could disappear for a while, then you can talk to her.'

Lindsay took notes about the Baroness. She would investigate her personally.

How could someone be so cruel to such a lovely person, Beth thought while Lindsay tried to persuade Penny to have full police involvement. She refused point blank. One thing was for sure though. Lindsay would catch whoever was doing this.

'Penny, if you won't allow official police involvement then you need to keep your nerve. An assigned police officer can give support, you know.'

Penny still shook her head.

'Okay then. If you're absolutely sure?........I'll check out police records on both suspects and report back if I have any news.'

She paused to light a cigarette. While rereading the letters, she noticed the smudgy letter 'm' on each one.

'Whatever you do, do *not* hand over any money. And I mean both of you. Understand?'

Penny nodded.

'If either of you receive another letter then I need to have it immediately.' She handed Penny her card across the table. 'You can contact me on that number, but if there are more letters please give them to Beth. She knows how to get things through to me in a hurry.'

'Be careful with the Baroness. She has a nervous disposition. Oh dear, I'm sorry. I don't mean to tell you how to do your job, but she can be giddy, can the Baroness.'

'I can keep the letters, can't I?'

Penny, startled by the request, reluctantly agreed. Then she left.

Back at the table, eating a late lunch, Lindsay's sixth sense was troubled.

'There's something not right there, Beth. I've got this gut feeling.... she's not all she makes out to be. Just how well do you know her?'

'I don't know her at all really. Only what I told you. We met her at the weekend, in the Hotel, like I said. She seems so sweet and genuine though. Honestly Lindsay, you've seen the dark side of life for too long.'

'Really? And you always see the good in everybody, don't you? Too trusting for your own good sometimes. Anyway, see what you make of Rose, then ring me. I should get home around five. Look for a typewriter, an old fashioned one, but don't get caught. Right?'

Beth nodded patiently. 'I'm listening. I'm not stupid, you know.   I do watch Agatha Christie!'

Lindsay laughed, 'How I miss your sense of humour. Seriously though…this typewriter, right…?If you find one, try to type a word with the letter 'm' in it. No, don't ask. Just do it.'

Beth laughed, 'Yeah, okay. I know better than to ask. You will sort this out though, won't you?'

'Course I will. Have you ever known me to let you down?'

The phone rang. It was Lou. 'Hello beautiful…how are you? How's Inspector Lindsay?'

Beth had told Lou about the visit, but not the real reason why.

'I'm home for the weekend. Why don't you both come and stay. I'd love to meet Lindsay. She can tell me all of your dark secrets.'

'Lindsay has to go back first thing tomorrow, but I'd love to come.'

'That's even better, I was hoping for just the two of us. Pack lightly babe, you'll not be needing much.' Her suggestive tone flustered Beth.

Lindsay gave her a knowing look. Lucky Lou. She simply couldn't afford to be jealous, although it was hard not to be. If only she'd been brave enough to make a move on Beth years ago instead of enduring all those sleepless nights. She'd thought she had her feelings in check. Wrong. Oh, well, she'd just have to get over it. Lou may not last anyway, and why spoil a lifelong friendship by letting sex rear its ugly head. Who was she trying to kid?

Leaving Beth to her phone call, she carried the letters into the living room, laying them out on the coffee table to study them again. Her gut feeling hadn't changed. These were not as kosher as Penny Corday would have them believe. Why? What was going on here? Hyacinth's name came into her head.

She would like to meet Hyacinth. She had a bad feeling about her, yet despite trying to dig up some dirt, had drawn a blank. Not even a speeding ticket.

Pouring herself a drink, she rummaged through the magazine rack, seeking something to distract her. Medical journals were her only choice. Idly, she flicked through one, her attention drawn by a photograph. She couldn't be a hundred per cent sure, but the face in the picture was the same blonde female she'd seen in the motorway services.

Scanning the pages she gasped. Looking back at her was Hyacinth. She started to read.

It was an interesting article about the hard work and fundraising the Dickinson's did for an unmarried mothers' unit. The photograph showed the stunning Mrs. Dickinson officially opening the unit in Carlisle, where her practice was based. The magazine was two years old, but the face hadn't changed.

They ate in. Lindsay's idea. Another gut feeling told her that she didn't want to take the chance of running into Hyacinth while she was with Beth. And she had a thousand questions to ask Beth about her, without wearing her police officers hat. Difficult.

Reluctantly passing up the chance to meet Lou, Lindsay left early keen to run checks on Penny and Victoria, and another one on Hyacinth. She had a dreadful feeling that her precious friend was heading for trouble.

Chapter 26

Beth spent a few hours at the hospital before going to Penny's house in North Yorkshire. The Jag purred all the way there, an absolute joy to drive.

Penny's Georgian mansion was similar to Davinia's, but surprisingly on a much bigger scale. Impressive, thought Beth.

Penny was in the garden when Beth arrived and ushered her through French doors into a comfortable sitting room. There was no time for her to have a look around the mansion. It was straight down to business.

She looks ill, Beth thought, as Penny pressed the servant's bell by the fireplace for Rose to bring tea and biscuits.

Rose appeared almost immediately with a heavily laden tray, placing it on the table. Penny excused herself for a moment and left the room.

Beth gave Rose a friendly smile, 'Lady Corday tells me you worked for the Royal Family?'

'Yes. Milk or lemon?' Rose replied quietly.

She's nice, decided Beth, ' Milk, please. Have you been here long?'

'Two years now.'

'You must enjoy your job.' Beth looked straight into her eyes.

'I do. Despite the low salary and long hours,' she said with humour as she set down the tea pot, 'Still there's compensation in other ways' she matched Beth's look, unflinching.

'Sounds interesting. What ways?' Beth asked raising an eyebrow.

'Well, I get to meet interesting people, enjoy good holidays with her Ladyship, and have a roof like this over my head.'

Beth changed track. 'Did you ever go to Balmoral in your last job?'

'Yes. It's a beautiful place.'

'I've been to the Castle quite a few times.' How lucky we have something in common to talk about, Beth thought.

Once they had exhausted the Balmoral topic, Beth cleverly manoeuvred the conversation to talk about the London gay scene deliberately mentioning Jesters, a popular gay nightclub. Rose wasn't fazed by the turn in the conversation.

'I met Sarah, my partner, there. Except we're miles apart now.' Rose pulled a face, 'She's in the police force and was posted to Brighton a while back.'

'Does Penny know?'

'Yes. Although she's my boss, she's always been interested in my personal life. Good about time off too, means I can visit regularly. And she doesn't mind my having visitors here.'

'What? You mean she lets Sarah come here…to stay?'

'Oh, yes. His Lordship's away such a lot and when the house is empty we can have it to ourselves. It's a useful arrangement all round I think. Works for me, anyway.'

Beth knew Rose was not their blackmailer. She had way too much to lose.

Rose showed Beth a photo of Sarah. She kept it tucked in her bra, keeping her close to her heart at all times, she said.

Sweet, Beth thought. Sarah was not the best looking bird on the perch, but she matched Rose's homely looks.

Lady Corday returned just as Beth's mobile rang.

'Can I ring you back?' Beth asked.

'Where are you?'

'In a meeting,' Beth lied to the caller.

'Oh, sorry. I thought you'd be finished by now.'

'Last minute change of plan. I'll call you back. Bye.'

Rose dismissed herself, 'Nice to meet you Miss McConnell.'

'And you Rose. I hope we meet again.'

The second Rose closed the door Penny spoke, 'Well, Beth. What do you think?' she demanded.

'Sorry...I really don't know. I need to have a word with Lindsay.' Her suspicions were aroused. This was turning out to be rather odd. She refused to be drawn.

Penny moved on to discuss the Baroness.

The Royal Ascot Race Meeting was imminent. Claire always attended Ladies Day. Penny intended to go, inviting Beth and a friend to join her party.

'You'll be able to talk to the bitch yourself!'

'Thanks,' Beth completely taken aback by the venom in Penny's voice, tried not to show it. 'You did say that I might bring a friend?'

'Yes, of course, my dear. But please make sure it's someone with a sense of style. Your friend Lou will fit the bill perfectly. We *will* be in the Royal Enclosure.'

Bitch, 'Naturally.' Beth smiled. Lou had more style in her little finger than Penny had in her whole body.

'Actually, it will be better for you to have someone who is so well known with you and Lou will certainly attract Claire's attention. She's a big fan.'

Not given the opportunity to check out the typewriter situation, Beth left shortly afterwards, anxious to speak to Lindsay. There was something odd going on and it wasn't just the blackmail letters. A few miles down the road Beth pulled over. Thank God for mobile phones she thought. After speaking to Lindsay she rang Lou.

'I'm on my way, sweetheart. Be with you in about an hour.'

Lou gave her directions and then rushed round the already tidy house plumping up the cushions again. She wanted Beth to love this place as much as she did. If she was honest she wanted Beth to feel she would never want to leave.

An hour later Beth was pulling up in front of Lou's rustic farmhouse. It's warm stone walls glowed a welcome in the early evening sunlight and Lou was waiting outside to greet her.

Chapter 27

The second Beth stepped out of her car Lou wrapped her in a bear hug. 'I have missed you sooo much.' Lou's defences were down as she kissed Beth passionately.

'Me too. You don't know how glad I am to be here.'

They stood locked in each other's arms.

'You're hungry, I hope? I've cooked for us.'

'You have? Why, that's wonderful. I'm starving.'

'Good. Let's eat first, shall we? And then I'll show you around the place. You're going to love it here.'

All thoughts of Penny's situation evaporated as Lou led the way through the front door along a wide hall and into the comfortable living room. Using her best crystal and china she had spent ages setting up a small dining table for them, arranging and re-arranging the setting, until she felt she had got it right. She had placed the table in front of the French windows hoping Beth would be impressed with the wonderful view across the dale, and then arranged the curtains to create an intimate alcove. Burning candles flickered soft shadows across the table and the velvet petals of the red roses she had cut from the garden. Gentle music played discretely in the background completing the romantic ambiance. Beth was enchanted.

'Please make yourself at home.' Lou said then hurried off to the kitchen to get the food giving Beth a chance to survey the room.

Beth thought it was perfect and had it been hers she would have furnished it in much the same way. She loved the soft yellow on the walls and the two comfortable cream leather sofas arranged to face each other in front of the fireplace, with a heavy reclaimed pine coffee table between them. Around the room several other occasional tables held either vases of fresh flowers or stacks of books and magazines. There were several attractive oil paintings of horses hanging on the walls and Beth correctly presumed they were of Lou's horses. Normally the room would be filled with light, the heavy curtains pulled well back, but tonight because of the way Lou had arranged the curtains, it generated a cocoon of warmth and intimacy, just as Lou had hoped it would.

'I hope you haven't gone to too much trouble Lou.' Beth called when she heard the sound of clattering dishes coming from the direction of the kitchen.

'No,' Lou fibbed. 'I love cooking.' Another fib. She never interfered with cookers if she could help it and couldn't claim to be a domestic goddess.

She nervously dished up the meal, desperate to make a good impression. She began to feel flustered as she carefully set out the dishes on a tray ready to carry through to the living room. She could have really made a splash and set everything out in the formal dining room, but she had wanted something much more intimate and that's why she had spent hours preparing the food, and the setting. She prayed she hadn't undercooked or burnt anything. But right now she wished with all her heart that she had got the caterers in.

She needn't to have worried. The meal was a success and Beth enjoyed every morsel of it.

After dinner Lou was keen to show Beth around. They started outside as she proudly told her the history of the place.

'There were lots of outbuildings. More stables, barns and buildings than I have now. Some were demolished or simply fell to bits. Even this brook,' Lou jumped over the stepping stones, 'is supposed to have been rerouted.'

'What about the wood over there?' Beth pointed, 'Was that chopped down and replanted?' she was trying not to laugh.

'I do go on, don't I? But I just love this place.'

They larked about like a couple of kids, splashing water as they jumped backwards and forwards across the stones. Suddenly Beth froze.

'Lou,' she spoke sharply, 'do people have access to the woods, or to your land?'

'No. This is all private property. Strictly invitation only. Why?'

'I've just had the weirdest feeling…I think someone's watching us.' Beth felt edgy.

'Don't be daft. There's no-one here but us.' Lou chided. But as the sun dropped, she wasn't so sure.

She pulled Beth to her, 'Do you feel safe now? I'd never let anyone hurt you, you know.'

'Yes, I know.'

Lou kissed her. Beth's senses leapt in response. The trees swayed with the breeze and so did she.

The splash from further up stream distracted Beth unsettling her again. She was sure someone was out there, watching.

'Listen! What's that noise?'

'Probably a duck.'

'Well, fuck the duck. Come on, let's go back.'

Tears streaming down her cheeks with uncontrollable laughter, Lou gave in. 'Okay, you win. You are just so sensitive. Your imagination is running away with you.'

Once in the house, Beth insisted Lou lock all the doors. She couldn't explain why she felt so badly shaken.

'Brandy for you.' Lou insisted. Going to the global drinks cabinet in the living room she poured a generous measure and handed the glass to Beth.

'Thanks. This is a lovely room.' Beth waved her arm, anxious to recreate some warmth and intimacy. 'Did you do the interior design yourself?'

'Yes. I did the entire house. Would you like to see the bedroom?'

'Love to.'

'Right then gorgeous. Come with me. Bring the brandy - it's playtime.'

Beth lay back on the king-sized bed while Lou slipped into the bathroom and came out wearing a stunning diaphanous negligee. Beth's eyes were out on stalks as Lou floated across the room to the bottom of the bed, then running her hands up Beth's long legs she loosened her jeans, pulling them off, appreciating the underwear. She kissed Beth's toes, trailing kisses up her legs sensuously massaging as she went. Beth was swimming in desire as Lou eased her briefs off.

She dipped a finger into the brandy before putting it to Beth's lips, then slid it momentarily into her mouth. Turned on, Beth lifted Lou's negligee exposing her firm pink nipples. In a flash Lou was straddling Beth and both gasped with pleasure as they made contact with one another. Lou instinctively started to move, pushing hard as Beth arched in response. Leaning forward so Beth's face was almost lost between her breasts, she reached into a bedside drawer and pulled out a vibrator.

Startled Beth cried, 'What the fuck is that?'

Lou paused.

'More to the point, what are you planning to do with it? God, Lou, I've never used one of these before. Is it safe? Will I get electrocuted?'

'Oh, you silly thing, trust me. Of course you won't get electrocuted. Tell you what though,' Lou giggled, 'these are fun!'

Without loosing her momentum, she switched the vibrator on. Beth was surprised, but also wildly excited as Lou teased her nipples with it, bringing on sensations resembling Jacuzzi water jets. Lou ran it over Beth's body, up and down her arms and legs, generating a myriad of tingling sensations.

'Oh, this is fun, Lou. It would be great for people with arthritis!'

'Beth! Be serious!' Lou's laughter exploded. 'If I push a little harder, will you be more serious?' Her pubic bone ground into action.

Soon Beth was matching her rhythm. Lou lubricated the vibrator easing it between their legs, into their steaming moisture, both enjoying the full pleasure. Almost reaching orgasm Lou eased herself up slightly. Beth grasped the vibrator and thrust it into her. Lou rode it with passion, her juices soaking Beth's hands as she reached her peak.

Their hands clasped, fingers locking, as Lou fell forward to kiss her. Her beautiful skin flushed and deliciously warm.

Exhausted they lay together. Happy, still intimately exploring each other, while enjoying the afterglow.

Holding Beth tight, Lou said, 'Beth, I have something important I need to say to you.'

Beth's heart sank at her seriousness, suddenly scared in case she wanted to end the relationship. She looked directly into Lou's eyes, 'Is something wrong?'

Leaning on one elbow, Lou looked intently back moving to cradle Beth's face in her hands. 'No, Beth. There's nothing wrong. It's never been more right. In fact I want you to move in with me. I have waited all my life for you. I don't want to be apart from you for a second longer than necessary. I love you Beth McConnell.'

Struck dumb, Beth's mind careered into overdrive. She wanted to say yes, but there was such a lot to consider. Was it too soon? This lifestyle, as luscious as it was, was still new territory. She did love Lou. She knew that for sure. *So what's the problem?* her mind reasoned.

'Well, beautiful…what do you say?' Lou asked anxiously.

'Sweetheart, I'm flattered, I really am.'

'But?'

'Well…' Beth was floundering, 'there's such a lot to consider. And, darling, this is really sudden, unexpected.'

'That's not a no then?'

'No, it's definitely not a no. But let's sleep on it, shall we? We'll talk about it in the morning. I'm whacked.'

Satisfied she couldn't push the issue, Lou agreed, reaching over she switched off the bedside light, then held Beth tight.

Beth didn't sleep much. Millions of questions and 'what ifs' whizzed round in her head.

Over breakfast the next morning, Beth gave Lou her answer. She would live with her.

Despite the early hour Lou cracked open a bottle of Krug to celebrate.

Hugging Beth, 'I am sooo happy. Promise you'll move in soon. We'll have a wonderful life together, you'll want for nothing. You don't even have to work if you don't want to. I have more money than I know what to do with.'

'I promise I will move in soon. I love you too and I do want to be here, with you, for us to be together. God, it's going to be hell going back tomorrow.' Beth dreaded the parting. 'I can't not work Lou. I love my job and besides I'm bloody good at it. But I can travel until I find something suitable at a hospital nearer here.'

Overwhelmed with love they spent a euphoric weekend. Beth met Frances, the groom, fell in love with the horses, and they made exciting plans. They would cruise the world, fly to New York for Christmas shopping at Macy's, skate in Vanderbilt Plaza, ski in Aspen, ride in a gondola in Venice. Their list was endless and they were floating on cloud nine.

Chapter 28

On Sunday afternoon, mentally exhausted, dizzy with happiness, Beth was hit by a reality check.

Sitting at the kitchen table, drinking coffee, she allowed some unwanted sanity to seep into her thoughts. Lou was outside talking to Frances oblivious to Beth's doubts. Wearing a white polo shirt, thumbs hooked in the back pockets of her slim fitting blue jeans Lou looked gorgeous.

What am I to do? Beth pondered. Organizing her work schedule would be difficult, to say the least. And it was possible for Lou to be away for days, even weeks at a time, so sometimes she would be returning to an empty house. Not the ideal. Then she thought about the route, up and down the busy A1, and driving in and out of Newcastle could be a nightmare. Already she felt exhausted. And to cap it all a surgeons work isn't nine to five. She was never sure when her day would finish. Often she stayed over at the hospital if she was concerned about a patient because she liked to be on hand. Surgery required a sharp mind and a steady hand. Then she remembered that Lou had mentioned work in America. What was happening with that? A final sobering thought brought her crashing back to earth. What about Hyacinth?

She could only imagine how life would be living with Lou, but the thought of being without her was unbearable. Maybe this was what you would call the honeymoon stage, what if it all turned sour? Then where would she be?

After a tearful parting, during the long drive home Beth's mind ran away with her and she began to panic. *What on earth have I agreed to do?* She didn't want to lose Lou yet she felt terribly pressurized. She concluded, rightly or wrongly, that Lou was rushing things. Her newly discovered lifestyle offered a lot of uncharted territory. Maybe she should give herself time to explore it, instead of nesting. She had certainly suppressed her feelings by refusing to acknowledge her true self for long enough. She blamed Hyacinth for all of this, there again, if she hadn't met Hyacinth she would have continued to go around in ever decreasing circles denying the real Beth.

In any case she decided that she would advertise for someone to share the apartment with her, which was something she'd planned to do anyway. Then, if things worked out with Lou, that was one problem solved. Perhaps it was the fear of losing her independence that spooked her. She had no intention of becoming a kept woman, and when she thought about it, Lou buying her the car put her into that category. Over the weekend she had tried several times to discuss the matter, but Lou refused point blank. She knew exactly how much the car had cost so had left a cheque under the pillow. Lou would find it when she went to bed, no doubt there would be a phone call when she did.

And what would her family think about her living with a woman, having a lesbian couple in the family. She didn't think they would have a problem. Her mother, a liberal thinker, had raised them to be the same. But could she risk it? Oh, decisions, decisions.

Her concentration was wandering and she had developed a thunderous headache. Hardly surprising with everything she had on her mind. Although she was almost home, she needed a break from driving, so pulled into Washington Services. She would have a cup of tea, the eternal comforter, and maybe browse through the magazines. She might even resort to taking a couple of painkillers.

Heading into the café her attention was caught by a familiar face. Not wanting to be seen she ducked behind some advertising boards neatly avoiding Penny Corday. What was she doing here? And who was she with?

For a split second Beth thought it was Hyacinth, but the blonde hair was slightly darker, the body although just as lithe was actually a little slimmer. Then it dawned on her, this must be the same girl she'd caught a glimpse of going upstairs in the hotel. She must have been meeting Penny.

Trying to get a better look, wishing the girl would remove her sunglasses, Beth bumped into some advertising boards. Diners nearby turned to stare at her clumsiness, but luckily the clatter didn't halt the conversation between the two women.

She didn't dare move. Penny would see her if she looked across the cafe. On the wall behind her were some local advertising notices, she side stepped pretending to read them, now she could see the clear reflection of Penny and her companion in the glass window.

They were so relaxed in each other's company it was obvious to Beth that they must know each other well. Beth silently cursed because she couldn't distinguish any part of their conversation. The vibration of a heavy wagon driving past distorted the reflection just as she thought she saw the unknown female furtively push a small parcel across the table towards Penny. Penny dropped it swiftly into her large shoulder bag. Dam that wagon, Beth couldn't be a hundred per cent sure now. Strange going's on. She'd better get in touch with Lindsay about this. God she's going to be sick of me, Beth thought. But Lindsay had insisted she felt all was not as it should be with Penny Corday.

She watched as the women left the cafeteria, walking arm in arm across the car park. Thankful for the huge windows, she could see clearly across to the far side where a couple of old nondescript cars were parked. Without pausing the women parted, each getting into one of the cars then driving out towards the southbound slip road.

Chapter 29

Arriving back in Brighton Lindsay searched the police computer records thoroughly, without success, except for an incident a couple of years earlier when Penny Corday's name appeared in a boating accident report. Exactly what had happened was never discovered. Puzzled Lindsay scratched her head. Why should an ultra-expensive Interpol investigation have been conducted? And despite that investigation still no answers were found for the accident and the deaths. Apparently there was no evidence to go on. Penny, the only survivor, claimed to suffer complete amnesia. How very convenient for her, Lindsay mused, a cynic to the end.

Thankful for their efficient system, she found the relevant files in police archives without difficulty. Carefully sifting through the contents of several dusty boxes her adrenaline raced as she picked up a file marked 'Lady Penelope Corday - Strictly Confidential - Issue on a need to know basis only'. Boy, this woman must have friends in high places she thought, as holding her breath, she flipped the file open. It was empty.

Beth put the key in the lock just as the phone started to ring.

'Hello Beth. How was the weekend?'

'Well…do you want to know about Lou and I first or Penny Corday?'

'Come on then. Tell me about you and Lou.'

'Well,' Beth paused briefly, 'Lou wants us to live together!' she blurted out.

'Wow, Beth. That's a bit sudden, isn't it? Aren't you rushing things? After all, I haven't met her yet.' Flatly attempting to joke, her statement was serious. 'Well, what are you going to do? Did you give her an answer?' Distracted, running her fingers through her hair she reached for the whisky, her initial panic allayed as she listened to Beth explaining her plans. She must meet this Lou, and soon, just in case Beth did something stupid. She'd got herself in with a funny crowd and Lindsay didn't know if Lou was part of it.

Discussing the information both had gleaned on Penny Corday, Lindsay, knowing there could be more to the situation than the supposed blackmail, regretted she could not divulge the Interpol connection. Lindsay was intrigued with the news that Penny was with a Hyacinth look-a-like.

Hanging up the phone from Beth, Lindsay decided to ring an old flame who just might be able to help. It had been a long time, but they had parted on good terms. She dialled the number and waited.

'Hello Nance, this is Lindsay……..yes, ages…..Me, why I'm fine, thanks for asking. And yourself?' Lindsay wanted the small talk over so that she could get to the point. Patience is a virtue, she reminded herself, splashing more single malt into the tumbler, then adding ice from the bucket, while she listened to Nance bringing her up to date.

'You've made yourself an interesting circle of friends from the sound of things.' she said as Nance paused.

'Yes, I have.'

'Have you come across a Beth McConnell?'

'Beth McConnell...the surgeon? Why do you ask? Is she in some sort of trouble?'

Lindsay was surprised Nance knew Beth's name. 'No, no trouble. And I don't want her to get into any. She's an old friend. Listen. What do you think about this?'

Lindsay explained, in detail, everything she could about Penny Corday, Lou and Hyacinth.

It was dark when Lindsay finally hung up, but she was satisfied that Lou, at least, was genuine. Thank God she had no worries on that front.

As Lindsay dialled Nance's number, Beth was dialling Lou's. They ended up having a totally erotic conversation, whispering sweet nothings, reliving the weekend's sexual activity.

Lying back on the bed, Lou stretched out her arms. Ready for sleep she pulled Beth's pillow into her, wanting the smell of her perfume. Surprised, she discovered an envelope tucked underneath and inside was a note from Beth with a cheque for the car. She was touched. After all she had a lifetime to shower her with gifts and she had every intention of pampering her outrageously. She tore the cheque into tiny pieces, and then went into the bathroom and flushed the pieces down the toilet.

Work commitments stopped any chance of Beth and Lou spending time together for the next few weeks. Penny's invitation to Ascot went to the wall. While Lou was working on a series of holiday programmes in Cornwall, Beth almost lived at the hospital; they were exceptionally busy. Deliberately avoiding contact with Hyacinth, she decided to visit her family when she did manage to have some time off duty.

Bruno was overjoyed to see her. While she and Catherine sat gossiping in the garden he repeatedly brought sticks for her to throw. There was a chill in the air, but the sheltered walled garden afforded them the full benefit of the late autumn sunshine.

Isobel fussed over her daughters, bringing them hot drinks. Catherine looked radiant, motherhood suited her and Isobel was amazed at the change in Beth who was positively glowing. Despite her probing questions she couldn't discover the reason why, but was pretty sure Beth was in love.

'So, you're not seeing Stuart now?' Isobel couldn't resist asking her daughter again.

A shadow passed over Beth's animated face, 'No Mother. I've already told you I'm not!' Came the curt reply.

He's not the cause then, thought Isobel undeterred, but she's not going to tell me anything today.

After an early supper Beth and Catherine settled by the fire in the drawing room. Isobel went to play bridge with some friends, and Giles disappeared to help Angus on the estate.

'Who is it then?' Catherine had her back to Beth as she poured two drinks; gin and tonic for Beth, tonic for herself.

'Who is what?' Beth asked airily, fully aware of what Catherine was leading up to. She reached forward to take the drink.

'You know...I've never seen you looking like this before.'
'Like what?'
'You know.' Catherine insisted. 'Glowing, happy, in love perhaps?'

Beth couldn't bring herself to say the words, deliberately evading direct answers.

Catherine persisted. 'Are you hiding something?'

Beth didn't answer. Bruno snored on the rug in front of the fire as a log shifted sending a fountain of sparks up the chimney, briefly illuminating the room. Beth stood up and walked over to the fire to check no sparks had jumped out. Satisfied Bruno was not singed she turned to look at Catherine and tried to analyse how she would take the news.

Her heart was pounding as she contemplated whether to tell her or not. Then she heard herself saying, 'Yes, sis, there is someone, but it's rather delicate.'

'He's not married, is he?'

'Noooo. No, for goodness sake it's nothing like that.' Beth's words were slow.

Catherine sat forward to reach out for her sister's hands. 'We've never had any secrets, you and I. We've always been able to talk. What is so awful that you can't tell me?'

'It's not awful, sis. Just different.'

'Different? How different? What do you mean? Is he a lot older than you or younger even? Is he a medical student?'

'None of those actually.' Beth finished her drink and went to pour herself another. She silently lifted the bottle of gin to Catherine, who nodded and passed her her empty glass.

In that instant Beth made her decision. It's now or never. And she had nothing to be ashamed of, so why should she hide who she was from her family, the people who loved her most. Splashing generous measures of gin and tonic into both of their glasses she passed Catherine's back to her and then returned to stand by the fire.

Leaning on the mantelpiece, she blurted out, 'It's a woman.'

'What's a woman?'

'For God's sake use your imagination Cath!'

'What? Oh my god, Beth.' Catherine catapulted out of the armchair and stood in front of her. Eyes wide she took Beth by the arms as if to shake her.

'A woman? You're in love with a woman? You're going to bed......having sex with a woman?'

'Yes.' Beth's answer was calm, quiet and dignified.

'Well I never!' Catherine flopped back into her chair. 'What made you do that? How did it happen? Who is it?....... Not Lindsay! We all know about Lindsay. But you!.....Here,' she leaned forward and pushed her glass into Beth's hand, 'pour me another gin.'

'I know I've given you a shock.' Beth topped up the drinks.

'Actually sis, would you believe you haven't. I sort of always knew, but now you've said it, well, it makes it real.'

'It's real all right.' Beth handed the full glass to her sister.

'Right...I want to know all about her. *Everything...* how you met, the whole thing. So you'd better get yourself comfortable Elizabeth, fill your glass and start talking.'

They settled either side of the fire. Beth smiled as she said, 'Cath, can you remember that series of holiday programmes that was presented by Lou Scott?'

'This is no time to talk about holidays, Beth.'

'It's Lou Scott.'

Catherine spluttered her gin.

Beth tossed her a box of tissues. 'We met on a train.' Beth chuckled, 'A bit like Brief Encounter,' she paused, remembering, 'I was going down to London......'

They talked well into the night, not hearing Isobel coming home. She didn't disturb them, pausing at the drawing room door for a while before heading upstairs. She went to check on her grand-daughter, Hannah, in the nursery. Gazing at the sleeping baby she was consumed with love. My girls, I love them both, and you little one, which path will be mapped out for you? Bending to kiss Hannah's forehead, she left her and went to bed.

Chapter 30

The run up to Christmas was manic. Beth didn't have time to spit let alone plan moving. Maybe that was a good thing as Lou got a last minute call to do some filming in the Canary Islands, which meant she would be away over Christmas and possibly New Year. Thank God for mobile phones and emails thought Beth when she heard the news.

Her fear of explaining the situation to Hyacinth had not materialized. Not that it was any of her business, but she was such a force to be reckoned with. If Beth had allowed herself time to think about it she would have realized how out of character Hyacinth was behaving. Relieved she hadn't taken up her new position at the hospital, Beth coasted along living for the next time she could speak to Lou and refusing to think about their being separated over Christmas. Because of the separation she volunteered to work, reasoning she may as well be at the hospital than miserable alone at home.

Christmas Eve morning brought the first cover of winter snow, causing mayhem on the roads and resulting in a spate of bad accidents. Beth spent most of the day in theatre patching people up.

At midnight she sat with Val, reluctant to go home although she could have left hours ago. Dragging her outdoor coat on she told Val to ring if she needed her then reluctantly headed out into the freezing cold night.

Wrapped up in her heavy duffle coat, holding the hood tight under her chin, fighting against the biting cold north wind that was doing its utmost to blow her off her feet, she struggled home in the darkness. Head down she was unable to appreciate the myriad of colours generated across the snow from the Christmas lights, all she could think was how blissful it would be to be soaking up the sunshine in the Canaries with Lou, instead of sliding around on the ice like a novice skater trying to stay upright.

Relieved to be home without falling down she turned the key in the lock letting herself into the dark hallway. Wishing with all her heart that Lou would be waiting for her, she had failed to see the upstairs lights were burning.

She headed for the kitchen intending to make a hot drink before going to bed, but froze when she heard footsteps coming along the hall. Certain she had burglars, she nearly fainted when Lindsay burst through the door.

'Hello you, where the hell have you been, do they keep you chained to the hospital?'

'Lindsay! What are you doing here? What's wrong…is it Lou…the family?' Beth paled.

'Oh no lovely, nothing like that.' Lindsay hugged her. 'I got some unexpected leave and decided to come and keep you company.' She couldn't tell Beth the truth. 'Come on, I've got you a present. It's Christmas morning now, let's sit by the tree.'

Lindsay had switched on the tree lights in the sitting room, lit a cinnamon scented candle and turned the heating up a notch. She had also put two glasses and a bottle of her favourite whisky on the coffee table. Beth thanked her lucky stars that she was not going to be alone today after all. She looked at the presents set around the tree and faltered, everything looked cosy and welcoming.

Lindsay walked over and stood beside the tree. 'Come on, get yourself over here and let's see what Santa's brought us.' Lindsay encouraged her. Bending to pick something up she said, 'Here, open Lou's present first.' she handed Beth a slim gold envelope.

Gift vouchers thought Beth tearing the seal then gasped in surprise.

'What is it?' asked Lindsay.

'You'll not believe this.'

'I won't if you don't bloody tell me.'

'It's a ticket.'

'Well I never!'

'An air ticket, I mean it's a plane ticket. First class to Tenerife for the day after Boxing Day, the start of my days off.'

'You lucky thing.'

'Aren't I just?' Beth smiled smugly holding the ticket to her singing heart. 'Darling, do I detect a hint of jealousy here?' She waved the ticket at Lindsay.

'I guess you do, but only because I'm sick of being single.'

Beth took hold of her friend's hand, 'You are so good Lindsay, you will find someone and when the right woman comes along believe me, she'll knock you sideways.'

Lindsay didn't answer.

Beth pushed her playfully, 'Honestly, I've never heard you complaining about too many one night stands!'

Lindsay grinned, 'I didn't say I wasn't getting any sex.'

'Enough, enough, too much information.' Beth laughed and reached under the tree for Lindsay's present and handed it to her. 'Happy Christmas. There are some more gifts here for you from the family, but open mine first.'

Lindsay loved the dual-purpose watch. 'Thanks, Beth. It's perfect. The stopwatch will be ideal for when I go running.'

'Glad you like it. And thanks for the Chanel, I think it's one of the biggest bottles I've ever seen.'

After the family's presents were opened there was one gift remaining. It was from Hyacinth.

'Are you going to open this?' Lindsay asked.

'Suppose so. Pass it over then.'

Beth looked at the beautifully wrapped oblong box. 'I don't know why she's sent me this. I've hardly seen her.' With that she ripped off the paper, opened a purple velvet box and a platinum pentacle studded with diamonds sparkled in her hands. 'Wow! This is beautiful, but what is Lou going to think?'

'Oh no…not diamonds.' Lindsay did a double take.

'What?'

'Nothing. Let's have a look.' Lindsay studied the piece of jewellery, 'Yes, it is very nice and must have cost her a bomb.'

'Well, Hyacinth has a friend who makes stuff like this. I expect she made it.'

'She does? Who's that then, where does she live?'

'Mmmm, I can't remember her name, it'll probably come back to me later. She lives in the Lake District somewhere near Ambleside. Hyacinth was going to take me to meet her, and then Lou happened.'

Beth sighed suddenly shattered. 'Don't know about you Inspector, but I'm whacked. I need my bed. I'll be back on duty before I know it…what are you planning to do with yourself?

You'd better go and see the family while you're here or you'll never hear the end of it.'

'Yes, of course I will. Actually I've arranged to meet up with an old flame.'

Christmas and Boxing Day at St. Gregory's passed quietly allowing Beth time to fit in a quick visit to her family before flying out to Tenerife. Lindsay was obviously rekindling her old flame, Beth thought. She hadn't seen her since she'd left for work on Christmas day morning.

Chapter 31

In Newcastle the sound of Christmas revellers drifted up to the penthouse from the busy quayside below.

During a lull in the conversation, Lindsay studied the décor of the large and modern lounge area. We could have lived here quite happily she thought. Perhaps she should have worked harder to keep them together, instead of being so typically blasé. Looking worried she leant forward in her chair. 'How safe are you?' she was trying hard not to show her concern.

'How safe? I don't really know, but you could say I'm at her beck and call and that's just what she likes. To be honest I wish this job was over.'

'Have you met the jewellery maker?'

'Yes, yes I have. And she's just that, a jewellery maker. She's not involved...she's sweet actually. I might go and see her when all this is finished. Has Beth *any* idea about the smuggling?'

'No, not a clue. Luckily she's off to Tenerife tomorrow so if anything happens at least she's safe with Lou.'

'Hyacinth is running scared. The Syndicate is really putting the pressure on her now. And I'm pretty sure Penny's up to something that Hyacinth knows nothing about. Don't know what though. She's a devious bitch, and jealous as hell of anyone who takes Hyacinth's attention away from her.' Constance was trying not to let her temper get the better of her.

'Yeah and that blackmail fiasco is just that, a bloody fiasco. Why on earth is she doing it?'

'Oh that's easy to answer.' Constance said waving her arms expressively above her head. 'Hyacinth's behind it, of course. They were trying to gain Beth's sympathy, to embroil her in a fictitious plot, but they didn't reckon on her meeting Lou. Do you think it was just a coincidence that Penny happened to be at the hotel where Beth and Lou were staying? No. Penny was sent by Hyacinth. Whatever you do, don't underestimate this woman, Lindsay. She's tough and she has more contacts than Vision Express.'

Suddenly they both burst out laughing relieving the tension that crackled in the air.

'Seriously though, she can call in more favours than some Mafia bosses. Sounds ridiculous, doesn't it? But it's true. She's a professional and runs a hellish slick operation, and has done for years. Individually her little group should be loaded. If she'd been wise she would have stopped the smuggling when she had the chance. Do you know she's never needed the money?' Constance didn't give Lindsay time to answer before she continued. 'She's absolutely bloody loaded, her whole family are. It was the buzz she craved and, apart from seducing young girls, her biggest buzz is cheating the system. Now look where it's got her. She's in really deep shit, but she's putting on a good façade of pretending she doesn't care. Of course I'm the only one who can see through it. The Syndicate thinks she's an attractive proposition. You know that old saying, if you can't beat them, join them.'

'Pass the wine. I need a drink. And a cigarette.'

Constance picked up a bottle and collected two glasses from the cabinet as she went over to where Lindsay was looking out of the window at the flashing Christmas lights along the quayside.

'Here.' She handed her the bottle of Rioja. 'This is nice, isn't it? It's been a long time. Shame you're down in Brighton.'

'We were good together.' Lindsay poured the wine then passed a glass to Constance.

'Yes, weren't we?' she agreed, remembering their time together. 'She needs to be careful, does Beth. I'll keep an eye on her the best I can, of course, but Hyacinth is obsessed by her and it's only the pressure from The Syndicate that's prevented her from reeling Beth in. I know about the Christmas present, I went with her to collect it. She's already got Beth's special pendant ready and waiting. Look…' Constance dipped into a drawer, 'this is mine. Don't ask me how I earned it.'

'Honey, sometimes, this job sucks.'

'It's not just Beth we should be concerned about, you know. It's Lou as well.'

Lindsay pulled Constance to stand in front of her, wrapping her tight in her arms, resting her chin on Constance's shoulder. 'And what about you Nance? I'm concerned about you too. Do you know you are as beautiful as ever.'

'Flatterer.' Constance laughed.

'Can you make sure Beth gets on the plane? I have to be in London tomorrow.'

'Yes, I know you do. Don't worry, I'll take a ride out to the airport.'

'Thanks. Come to bed.' Lindsay nuzzled Constance's neck.

'I thought you'd never ask.'

Chapter 32

Hyacinth was bored rigid with playing happy families. Although in her own way she loved her children to bits, but right now wished they were miles away in South Africa with their grandparents. Still, come tomorrow, she would be rid of them all. The kids were going skiing with a crowd of their university friends and David was off somewhere romantic with his secretary. It would be bliss to be alone, to think. She needed some peace and quiet to plan her next move.

After seeing both of the children safely onto the plane the following morning she sighed a huge sigh of relief. Leaving the terminal building, Hyacinth was surprised to bump into Beth.

'Darling. How wonderful to see you…where are you jetting off to? Somewhere warm, I hope.'

'Hello Hyacinth. Yes, I'm off to Tenerife for a few days. Thank you so much for the beautiful Christmas gift, you really shouldn't have gone to so much expense.' Beth hugged Hyacinth as she thanked her, and was overwhelmed with sadness. During the brief time she held Hyacinth, Beth experienced a disconcerting vision of them both being enveloped in a dark cloud. It generated a host of negative energy. She quickly let go as her head started to spin.

Catching hold of Beth's hand, Hyacinth held it tightly, 'You're welcome darling. Think nothing of it. How is Lou?'

'Errr, she's fine…thank you for asking.' She pulled her hand away; the last thing she wanted was for the vision to recur.

Beth's flight was announced before Hyacinth could speak again. 'Sorry, must dash. That's me they're calling for.' She picked up her bag and fumbled for her passport, looking back at Hyacinth to say goodbye she thought her usually impeccably made-up face looked drawn and tired. Despite wanting to keep things short and sweet, her compassionate nature prompted her to ask, 'Are you okay Hyacinth?'

'Me? Why yes darling, couldn't be better. I just worry about the children even though they insist they're all grown up.' Hyacinth laughed artificially. 'They're off skiing with their friends.'

Beth's flight was called again. Hyacinth hugged her briefly, 'Ring me when you get back, we'll catch up. I miss you.'

Beth was touched, 'Yes, I will. Take care. Happy New Year.'

Driving home, Hyacinth was furious with herself. How could she have let things get so far between Beth and that blasted Lou woman. It was The Syndicate's fault. Compared to their operation hers was less than small fry. Why couldn't they back off and leave her and her girls alone. Anyway, she had decided on her plan of action now. Pulling over she picked up her mobile.

When Beth and Hyacinth went off in opposite directions Constance breathed a sigh of relief. She waited in the airport until Beth went into the departure lounge and then left to meet Hyacinth. She had been summoned.

'Lindsay? Nance here. Beth is safely on her way so don't worry, but you'll never guess what's happened.'

'Thanks. What?' Lindsay braced herself.

'Well, we were all called to H's a couple of hours ago and she announced, calm as you like, that there will be no more diamonds brought in for the foreseeable future.'

'No! Has she got wind that we're on to her?'

'It's not us. It's The Syndicate breathing down her neck that's done it. She reckons if they see that she's stopped shipments then they'll leave her alone and move on to someone else. I told you she was worried.'

'She could be right you know, they might decide to move on to another set-up. Well, we'll just have to wait and see. What have you got to do now?'

'Oh, I've been instructed by the guv to stick with her, just in case she changes her plans.' Constance said dejectedly.

'Oh Nance, that's a bitch. Why don't you come and spend a couple of days in Brighton...I'll cheer you up.'

'It's too risky. I would love too, but can't chance her finding me out. You know that.'

'Keep in touch. I need to know you're alright...and Beth.'

'Okay. You too. Bye.' Constance put the phone down.

Initially rattled by Hyacinth asking after Lou, Beth wondered just how much she knew about them, but she was determined not to let thoughts of Hyacinth spoil the holiday.

Lou had time off from filming so they swam, sunbathed and made love.

After enjoying a glorious week in Tenerife, Beth returned home tanned and happy.

Back at the hospital, she had a spring in her step. She was in love, and it showed. Despite the expensive gift and meeting Hyacinth in the airport, Beth had no intention of making contact, her intuition told her there was something very wrong going on there.

At the end of January Lou returned from Tenerife, arriving back to the worst snow for years. The dangerous driving conditions caused the usual spate of winter road accidents so the hospital was full to bursting. Beth was convinced everyone on Tyneside must have been through its doors with some kind of emergency.

February was no better. Lou's farm was isolated. They kept in touch by phone, e-mail and text messages, but Beth spent so much time at the hospital she almost forgot what her flat looked like, let alone Lou's homely farmhouse.

Like everyone else Hyacinth was hibernating. She had hated refusing a tempting diamond consignment from Enzo, her Italian contact. Only Penny knew about it and she was furious at Hyacinth's decision throwing a hysterical temper tantrum that Hyacinth regarded as completely out of character. She still would not answer Hyacinth's calls and had even returned the huge bouquet of red roses she'd sent to her. Hyacinth was devastated. She missed Penny like hell, but the willing Constance was becoming her constant companion, yet another thing for Penny to be upset about. There was something serious bugging Penny and Hyacinth intended to get to the bottom of it.

Chapter 33

The first days of spring brought welcome sunshine and early daffodils. Everyone's mood lightened. At last Beth and Lou were able to enjoy a long weekend together in North Yorkshire.

Hyacinth and Penny were friends again despite Hyacinth insisting on keeping Constance close. She called her inner coven together to celebrate the Spring Equinox at her home, deliberately including Constance this time. It was the first time in months she had felt safe and secure.

The shutters were drawn around the poolroom, the only light coming from the banks of candles. A huge candle secured in a metal dish was used to represent an open fire. Hyacinth's spell, cast at midnight, was to bring Beth to her. As she held the paper to the flame she almost burned her fingers so great was her desire.

After the ritualistic spell casting, Penny attempted to raise the subject of the diamonds. Hyacinth flatly refused to discuss her decision. Silently seething, Penny was incensed when Alison and Constance went to stand on either side of

Hyacinth lending her their unspoken support. Later, going over the night in her mind, still furious at Hyacinth's adamant refusal to discuss the diamond situation she realized Montanna and Felicity had remained silent and not moved from their seats.

Early the following evening, on returning home from Yorkshire, Beth rushed into her flat to the sound of the telephone ringing expecting it to be Lou.

'Beth. Hi, it's Alison Hogan here. How are you?'

'Oh hello Alison. I'm fine thanks and you?'

'Well I could use some company and I haven't seen you for ages. You promised to come to the gym and I know how busy hospital life is, but I was wondering if you're free tonight. It's exceptionally quiet here.'

Beth pondered for a while before answering, 'Thanks. Yes, I could do with some exercise. Give me half an hour and I'll be with you.'

'Great. We can have something to eat afterwards.'

Alison hung up then dialled Hyacinth's number. 'She'll be here soon so get your skates on.'

Beth was on the treadmill when Hyacinth walked in, but continued with her workout pretending she hadn't seen her. Out of the corner of her eye she watched Alison go over to meet her before they walked casually across to the exercise bikes. Hyacinth gave Beth a friendly wave as she walked past.

A couple of minutes later Alison left Hyacinth and joined Beth. After a strenuous workout, then a refreshing shower, Beth and Alison went to eat in the Salad Bar. Hyacinth joined them briefly before heading home, congratulating herself on convincing Beth to help out at her Charity Auction. She flatly refused to have a garden party this year, but had to be seen to be doing something and a Celebrity Auction was the perfect alternative. Beth was expertly manipulated into helping.

The Auction, held two days later at the beautifully refurbished Quayside Plaza Hotel, was a resounding success, and raised a fortune for Hyacinth's charity. The event was total glitz and glamour, attended by the great and good the likes of which had never been seen on the quayside before.

The area outside of the Plaza was cordoned off to contain the excited crowd as limo after limo drove up to the red carpet. Photographers swarmed everywhere. Beth, arriving in the pink Cadillac Hyacinth had insisted on sending for her expected to just walk in, but she caused a sensation. The photographers would not let her go begging for more as she laughingly posed this way and that, looking like a million dollars in her clinging silver dress. She loved the attention.

Later when she walked on stage holding the painting she was promoting the crowded room erupted and bidding was fast and furious. David, the perfect auctioneer, worked the room until two bidders were left fighting it out. The final bid raised £250,000.

As the hammer fell to thunderous applause, Hyacinth appeared from nowhere to stand beside Beth putting a possessive arm round her shoulders and gazing intimately into her eyes.

'Well done, darling. I knew I could rely on you.' she murmured, 'You see how they all love you.' She indicated to the crowd who were still applauding, some shouting and stamping their feet. The event photographers were frantically clicking their cameras.

'I don't know why, Hyacinth.' Beth laughed.

'Why…it's because you are beautiful, my darling.'

Waving to the audience they left the stage arm in arm.

Beth left the event as soon as she could anxious to telephone Lou who was filming somewhere in France. She couldn't reach her, as stormy weather was interfering with the telephone lines.

It was four full days before they finally spoke. Lou was full of her travel documentary and when Beth started to talk about the auction Lou was called back on set. Frustrated, Beth cursed, and then decided the auction event would be better explained face to face. The last thing she wanted was Lou getting the wrong idea. As with the best laid plans, the opportunity for Beth to tell Lou never really came up and because it did not hold much importance for her, she conveniently forgot about it.

Lou kept the magazine with the stunning photograph of Beth and Hyacinth on the front cover. She felt sure there was a simple explanation. Even so, she didn't trust that bitch Hyacinth. And Beth was so sweet and gullible.

Chapter 34

It was May, and Lou's thoroughbreds, Charley and Saffy, were due to compete soon. Although more than competent in the saddle, lack of time stopped Lou from reaching the dizzy heights of a competition rider. It was Anna, her old school friend and a professional horsewoman who rode them. At first Beth didn't appreciate that the horses were top class eventers. Lou's conversations about them were always low key. It was only when she discovered they were competing at the famous Badminton Horse Trials that it struck home.

No wonder Lou had pushed her to arrange time away from work. This was the biggest event in the country with top national and international riders competing.

They travelled down in Lou's top of the range Oakley horsebox, which was more like a luxury mobile home with five star equestrian facilities to boot. Nothing but the best was good enough for Lou's horses.

Both horses were seasoned travellers arriving at their destination calm and relaxed. As soon as Lou parked up Fran went to check out the stabling arrangements while Anna inspected the horses to ensure they were well and happy after the journey. Later in the day they would be presented for vetting, which Beth discovered, was extremely strict. She couldn't foresee any problems, but kept her fingers crossed. The horses looked absolutely stunning, shining as if Frances had been at them with Pledge polish and were a credit to her hours of hard work.

Eventually they were settled into their temporary stables, next door to each other. Fran would be sleeping in Saffy's box; she brooked no argument on this.

After a successful vetting-in, the Dressage tests due to start tomorrow morning were paramount in everyone's mind. Because she could ride the dressage test in her sleep Anna went with Lou to walk the cross-country course both checking out the shortest, but safest routes.

Beth felt surplus to requirements until she discovered the shopping area where she bought everything for Lou's birthday, tomorrow, that took her fancy. Hurrying back to the horsebox she set all of her gifts out on the bed carefully pushing her special surprise into a pair of leather riding gloves. Then she made sure the champagne was chilling in the fridge and sat down to wait for Lou.

Arriving back at the horsebox Lou was overjoyed with her pile of presents. She went through the bags with squeals of delight, holding the polo shirts and jackets in front of her and posing for Beth to comment. 'You're spoiling me and I love it.' she said, and then bent forward to kiss Beth who was sitting watching from the corner of the bed, feeling very pleased with herself.

'Lou would you be a love and try these gloves on please. I'm not sure I've got the right size and if not I'll need to pop back and change them.' Beth handed her a pair of gloves.

Lou took the soft brown leather riding gloves, 'These are lovely,' she sniffed the leather. 'Oh I do love the smell of leather, but they feel a bit lumpy. Beth, there's something inside,' she paused, 'what's this?' she asked finding a small black velvet box inside the left hand glove. Lou flipped the lid on the little box and gasped, 'What's this...why, it's beautiful.'

'Happy birthday darling, I hope you like it.'

'Like it, I love it, I absolutely love it.' Lou gazed down at the sparkling gold and diamond studded horseshoe necklace that Beth had commissioned especially for her. 'I'll never take it off,' she said with tears in her eyes.

'Oh I hope you will or I'll not be able to give you another one! I am so pleased you like it.'

'This will be my lucky charm. I just know we are going to do well this weekend. Have I told you lately how much I love you?'

'Mmm...well let me think...not for half an hour at least,' Beth laughed, delighted at Lou's reaction to her gift. 'Now come on, let's eat, I think I've excelled myself with some special birthday food and I even managed to smuggle in a bottle of your favourite champagne.'

'You treasure, you've thought of everything, haven't you?'

Eventually the whole place settled down for a quiet night. After a visit to check her horses and have a final word with Anna and Fran, who were both spending the night in the stables, Beth and Lou walked arm in arm back to the horsebox.

In bed Lou pulled Beth closer breathing her in. 'Thank God. Alone at last. Thank you again for my lovely birthday presents, especially the necklace.' She kissed her lovingly, 'I can't stand this being apart all of the time,' she said gazing into Beth's eyes.

'Yes, it is hard, very hard. I can't stand it either. In fact I hate it.'

'We really must try to get things organized so that we can live together, but my working schedule is so crazy.' Lou moaned.

'I know, darling, I know. And I couldn't have travelled to the hospital over the winter. You do understand how important my work is, don't you?' Beth asked, suddenly asking herself the same question. Her need to be with Lou, to be in her space was fast outpacing it.

'Yes, of course I do. Don't worry. I know one way or another we'll sort something out.' Lou hugged Beth tight. 'I know full well just how your elegant fingers can work miracles in the operating theatre.'

'Not just in the operating theatre…' Beth said running her hands over Lou's warm and welcoming body.

Bright and early the next morning owners, grooms and teams of helpers were busy tending to their precious equines. It was a dry day, with no rain forecast and the going was good. Beth was surplus to requirements. The girls and Lou had their routine finely tuned and soon it was just a matter of waiting until Charley was due to do his dressage test.

Standing, leaning on the top of the tailgate people watching, Beth spotted Penny Corday in a crowd of people. She was dying to go over, but was suddenly apprehensive. Penny turned as if looking for someone, spotted Beth and waved for her to join them.

'Lou, I'm going to say hello to Penny Corday. She's with some people over there.' Beth pointed to the left. 'I'll not be long. Okay? Shout if Charley's going before I get back.'

'Okay, sweetheart.'

Beth made her way through the noisy throng of people, dogs and horses towards Penny.

'Beth, how good to see you.' Penny air kissed Beth on both cheeks, 'I've just been informed that *both* of Lou's horses stand a good chance today. How exciting. Fingers crossed the weather holds up.' She looked up at the clear blue sky. Not expecting a response she quickly introduced Beth, 'People, this is my personal friend, Dr. Beth McConnell. She's here with Lou Scott.'

Introductions were made and the talk continued about horses and riders. During a discussion about riding the perfect dressage test, Beth asked discreetly if Penny had ever received any more letters.

Penny said not, but she'd had a couple of odd telephone calls recently where no-one spoke; no heavy breathing, just complete silence. She was considering having a trace put on her calls. Beth's mind flashed back to the incident at Washington Services as she answered.

'Good idea.' Beth said, 'I will mention the phone calls to Lindsay if you wish.'

'Thank you Beth, you are so kind. You haven't mentioned anything to Lou, have you?'

'No, of course not. You asked me not to.'

'Hi.' Lou's voice cut into the conversation. 'How are you Penny?'

'Lou, my dear.' Penny greeted her like a long lost friend, 'Good luck with the horses. Word has it they're in fine form.'

'Why, thank you Penny, nice of you to say so.' Turning to Beth she said, 'it's almost time for Charley to do his bit.'

'Before you go my lovelies,' Penny reached out to hold Lou's arm, 'I would love for you both to join me at Ascot this year, it's a shame you missed it last year. You know what they say…all work and no play.'

'We'd be delighted Penny. Thanks. Just let Beth have the details and we'll be there. Sorry must dash.'

Penny shot Beth a thousand-watt smile, 'I'll be in touch soon dear, now off you go to watch Charley.'

Good luck's echoed after them as they ran to find Anna and Charley in the warming up area.

Beth clapped and cheered louder than anyone while Charley executed the complicated test with ease. He was such a show-off, he loved the crowd and played to them. After Charley was finished Beth stayed put while Lou ran to see Anna. She arrived back as Anna rode into the arena riding Saffy.

Saffy had such style and presence. She floated effortlessly through the test with the panache of a prima ballerina, going out to thunderous applause. Beth was actually reduced to tears, it was so moving.

Both horses achieved excellent dressage scores, and not surprisingly Saffy was in the lead. That night there was a constant stream of callers wishing Lou well.

The following day the horses had to tackle the Cross Country Course. Beth was worried sick. The enormous jumps, although impressive, didn't look half so scary when viewed on television. The fearsome water jump made her grateful Lou wasn't riding and wishing that both horses were safely stabled back at the farm in one piece. Lou was worried too, but wouldn't show it. She didn't want to make Anna nervous. Anna was working on adrenaline, and she had nerves of steel.

Charley and Anna got off to a great start and made good time until they were almost at the water jump where the previous rider had dismounted without permission; both horse and rider were floundering unhurt in the water. A course official stopped them until it was safe to proceed. When Charley finally got to jump the water, he did it perfectly splashing through with gusto as the adoring crowd cheered him on. He galloped home like a steam train, Anna joyfully punching the air after they crossed the finish line making them the current leaders.

With little time for congratulations because Saffy had to run, Fran took charge of Charley leaving Saffy with Beth.

Anna was describing the ride to Lou, explaining some of the trickier fences and praising Charley while Beth stood quietly with Saffy.

As she stroked the mare's velvety muzzle, Saffy snuffled into her hand, 'Take care beautiful,' she whispered to the mare, 'Take no unnecessary chances. Come home safely.' Saffy pushed her head gently into Beth's chest.

Beth couldn't imagine how Anna had the strength and energy to go round again, but before she knew it, it was time for Saffy to go. Anna appeared from the horsebox, impeccably dressed having showered and changed with the speed of an Olympic athlete, then sprang effortlessly into the saddle.

Saffy danced along to the warm-up area then stood in the box waiting like an angel ready to start. Beth was in awe of the way she tackled the course, never appreciating before how horses could enjoy themselves like this. Saffy performed a faultless round. Not as fast as Charley whose huge galloping stride covered great areas of ground, yet not far behind his time because she put in a tremendous sprint towards the finish line galloping flat out to rapturous applause.

Lou was on cloud nine. Fran, wanting to check the horses thoroughly, chased Lou and Beth away, insisting the horses had some quiet time. Anna was instructed to go and rest-up in the horsebox. The final stage of the Event was the show jumping. Tomorrow the horses had to be paraded before the vets for another strict inspection to make sure they were sound and fit enough to go on. Fran wanted her 'babies' to be well rested. It was a tense time, and she was taking no chances.

As they tried to make their way back to the horsebox, Lou was constantly stopped and congratulated. Anna was crashed out and sound asleep when they finally got back.

Hungry, they polished off a couple of ready meals and no sooner had they finished eating when there was a knock on the door. It was Penny wielding a couple of bottles of Bollinger. She'd come to congratulate Lou personally.

She'd also brought a friend, introducing her to Lou first, making a point of telling Lou in great detail how she was totally into horses. Her friend, an American goddess called Montanna, had long glossy brown hair with golden blonde highlights blending through like shafts of sunshine, brown almond shaped eyes, smiling red lips, the whitest teeth Beth had ever seen, and a perfectly toned and tanned body. Montanna was stunning and she dressed to impress. Her tight fitting black outfit, low cut square necked top, trousers with a red leather belt slung casually round her hips and high heeled strappy sandals, were more suited to a fashion show than a horse event. But it was the diamonds that caught Beth's attention; earrings, pendant and ring, all sparkling with a life of their own.

Penny's introduction of Montanna to Beth was purposely brief, but she railroaded Lou into conversation with her. Then Penny started fussing to Beth about finding glasses, deliberately keeping her busy.

At first Beth was prepared to like Montanna and not to judge her, but her opinion changed as she watched Montanna cling to Lou like a limpet. Hanging on to Lou's every word, pushing in to sit beside her, laughing loudly at Lou's jokes and gushing compliments about the horses. The final straw was her wandering hands. She touched Lou constantly.

Beth was furious. She wanted to shout at Penny to get out and take her awful brash friend with her.

Why didn't Lou kick them out? Was she enjoying the attention? Montanna's accent began to grate on Beth; she talked a non-stop load of rubbish, in her opinion all gong and no dinner. Penny didn't have much to say, in fact no-one could get a word in for Montanna's incessant babbling.

When she finally stopped berating Lou and spoke to Penny, Lou pulled a face at Beth, inclining her head towards the door indicating she'd had enough.

During a heaven sent lull in the conversation Lou grabbed the opportunity.

'Right ladies! Sorry to break up this enchanting evening, but I'm sure you'll appreciate we have such an important day tomorrow, we really must get some rest now. Penny,' she extended her hand, 'thank you so much for your kindness, the champagne...and for bringing Montanna to meet Beth and I.'

With that Lou almost pushed them out of the door. Shutting it firmly she said to Beth. 'Did you see how they were looking at each other?'

'Yes, I did. Did you see those diamonds? They must be worth a fortune. And did you see the pendant Penny was wearing?'

'No, hon, I didn't. Why?'

'Well, I couldn't see it clearly, but it looked the same as Montanna's. Why on earth do they wear the same jewellery? There's something strange going on Lou, and I don't like it.' Beth paused, 'And I don't like that bloody Montanna either! She was all over you like a rash.' she exploded.

'Yes, she was awful, wasn't she?' Lou giggled. 'Hey...you're not jealous, are you?'

'Me? Of course not!' Beth snapped, her eyes blazed. 'What on earth gave you that idea?'

Lou grinned, pleased at her reaction. She picked up their jackets, tossing Beth's across to her. 'Come on, hon, we're going to follow them.' Then suddenly serious, 'Let's see if we can find out what they're up to. While we're out we'll call in on Fran, see if she needs anything.'

As they went to step out of the horsebox Anna popped her head round the bedroom door. 'Hey Lou, wait a sec, you'd better take your keys. I'm going to eat and then spend the night with Fran and the horses. Okay?'

'Thanks, Anna. Take your time. We're calling in on Fran, so no hurry.'

Stealthily they moved between the horseboxes, staying in the shadows so they weren't seen as they followed their departing guests, ending up outside of one of the flashiest wagons.

Penny opened the door without knocking, obviously well known to the occupants. Calling out as she stepped inside, 'Hi Fliss. We're back. Have we missed anything?'

'Yes!' a strident voice replied. 'I have a message for Montanna. What the hell took you so long and where the hell is she?'

'She's coming. You know we had a job to do, Felicity, so don't take that tone. It doesn't become you and it isn't necessary.' Penny's voice rang out clearly into the darkness.

'Sorry Pen. I know. But she was so insistent that things went smoothly.......you know what she's like.'

Montanna had lost a sandal; the heel stuck in the ground and snapped. She could hear what was being said while she bent to pull the shoe free. They'd better cool down, she thought, everyone can hear them.

'Girls! Please! Your voices are carrying.' Montanna stepped into the wagon. 'Now, what's wrong, Fliss?....and what does *she* want?'

'For God's sake, shut the door!' Fliss barked, and then indicated to the table.

They sat in silence while she poured four glasses of brandy.

'Four, Fliss?' Penny raised her eyebrows.

'Yes. We have company. Constance should be here any second.'

The door opened as she spoke and Constance stepped in.

'Hi everyone.' Penny and Montanna nodded in greeting. 'Ready Fliss? I've checked round the wagon, we're okay to talk.'

Felicity started to speak as Constance removed her outdoor jacket before picking up a glass of brandy.

Outside Lou and Beth pressed as close to the window as they dared, trying to hear what was being said.

'Well, what do you think? Will she do?' Penny sounded serious.

'No. I don't think she will.' Constance's voice was firm, 'She's not gullible enough. Oh, I know we all thought she was going to be perfect, especially Hyacinth. But no...she's not for this game.'

'That's a pity.' Penny said. 'She would have been a good contact to have at the hospital. No-one would have suspected a surgeon of handling uncut diamonds. And she would have enjoyed the group benefits.'

They all laughed.

'Well,' Penny continued, 'let's not rule her out yet. She could still enjoy the group benefits. The thought of her in purple really turns me on.'

Listening to the conversation, Beth paled. What the hell was going on here? Diamonds? Purple? Group benefits? Were they talking about her? And Hyacinth, why did her name keep cropping up?

Lou held Beth tightly in the darkness. She was just as worried by this conversation as Beth. They remained still, listening.....

Montanna said she thought Lou would be a nice distraction, and laughed when she said she really should thank Hyacinth for coming up with her little plan. Her companions murmured their approval and raised their glasses in a toast to Lou. Then the conversation turned to sexual escapades.

Someone started a horsebox close by, the droning of its heavy engine making it difficult for the girls to hear what was being said inside, but they both heard The Amethyst Group mentioned. Whatever it was, it was apparent Hyacinth was in charge.

'She won't be happy losing Beth, you know.' Penny stated, slurring her words slightly now. 'Hang on Constance, I've got an idea.' She turned her attention to Montanna.

'Do you know, my dear, you look very much like Beth. Don't you think, girls?'

The others nodded in agreement.

'Well, the group will be meeting again soon, having a little ceremony, if you get my drift.' She licked her lips. 'You could take part, Montanna. You could be our.......'

Just then Beth and Lou were forced to move on as a group of people came towards the wagons so they hurried to the stables to see Fran and the horses, staying until Anna arrived.

Back in the safety of their own wagon, they spoke in whispers as they tried to analyse the overheard conversation.

'Who and what are we involved with?' Lou was deadly calm, yet her mind was racing.

'I wish Lindsay were here. She would know what to do.'

'Don't worry hon. I know just what to do. Nothing. Apart from staying well away from them all. Especially that fucking

Hyacinth…she makes my blood boil. What do you think this Amethyst Group thing is?'

'Don't know. But I did see some purple material at Hyacinth's. It was delivered while I was there; supposed to be for new drapes. But to be honest, I couldn't see where they would go. There was nowhere in her house for purple curtains.' Beth paused, thinking back, 'At the party, I noticed some of the women were wearing the same diamond pendants.' she paused again, 'I thought then it was odd, but they were beautiful pendants Lou….you couldn't help notice them, especially if you like diamonds, which I do.'

Beth recalled her memory of Washington Services and the attractive young woman who looked remarkably like Hyacinth. She hadn't told Lou, nor had she mentioned Penny Corday's blackmail letters. Perhaps she should.

At six the following morning the place was alive. Putting all thoughts of the night before out of her mind, Beth focused on the day, and was surprised to realize that she was thoroughly enjoying herself. In a brief moment of reflection she considered how naturally she had moved into a very different lifestyle.

Trying to be useful she gave Lou and Fran a hand where she could. Both horses successfully passed the vets inspection and Fran took them off to prepare for the show jumping.

Lou and Beth went to sit in the owner's area beside the show jumping arena. Beth spied Felicity, who came straight across to join them. She was full of talk about her horse Trojan, he too was doing well. She appeared so normal and sensible that Beth started to think that last night's overheard conversation must have been all in her mind. They must have totally misheard.

'Did you manage to get an early night?' Beth asked.

'Yes, thankfully. I needed my rest after the cross-country course. I was shattered.' Felicity lied.

'Did you see Penny with her friend Montanna at all? They paid us a visit.'

'No, but I was out for the count.' Felicity lied again convincingly. 'God, look at the time. I'd better go and get ready....Good luck Lou.' Her words were genuine.

'Thanks, Fliss. Good luck yourself.' What a cool customer, Lou thought, and what an actress, she's nearly as good as me.

There was no chance to discuss Felicity as Charley and Anna trotted into the arena. They could tell he was tired and this was confirmed when, despite him jumping so carefully, he had the last fence down. Saffy was the star. She had a clear round and the crowd erupted. Lou, ecstatic, rushed off after Anna while Beth hung around caught up in the excitement of it all.

Suddenly Felicity was patting her on her back, hugging her as if she was Saffy's owner. Then she surprised Beth by inviting her and Lou to visit her stables saying how nice it would be if they could all ride out together. Without any hesitation Beth accepted. Firstly because she knew Lou would enjoy it and secondly because she wanted to find out what was going on and this could be a way of doing it. Calling back over her shoulder that she would give her a ring, Fliss ran off to mount Trojan.

Euphoric at Saffy finishing in the top ten they were all talking non-stop, only pausing when Lou pulled into a service station to join a line of horseboxes all waiting for diesel. As Beth climbed out of the cab to stretch her legs she saw Montanna drive in heading towards the petrol pumps at the other side of the café. Beth wasn't surprised to see she was driving a racing green Aston Martin, but she was surprised to see Penny Corday sitting beside her.

Ducking round the side of the wagon hoping they hadn't seen her, she watched Penny walk across to the Ladies Restroom constantly looking around as she went. Why, she's checking to see if anyone's watching her. What is she up to? Beth thought in her Agatha Christie mode.

Beth followed her. As soon as she had stepped into the Restroom she heard hushed voices coming from one of the cubicles. She was sure it was Felicity. She tiptoed into the cubicle opposite so she could listen unobserved.

'Have you got them?' Penny asked.

'Yes.'

'Good girl. You know what to do with them...and I'll see you at the weekend, we'll have some fun. I promise you won't be disappointed.' Penny purred.

'I can't wait, but I'd better go now. Give me a couple of minutes before you come out. And lay off Montanna!' soft footsteps faded away.

A bolt rattled, securing a door, then silence.

Beth held her breath until she heard the toilet flush and different footsteps fading away as someone left the building.

Rushing outside, she watched the women walking off in different directions, Fliss well ahead of Penny. Beth's mind worked overtime throughout the rest of the journey home. She needed to contact Lindsay, bring her up to date even though Lou wanted her to do nothing and forget the overheard conversation completely, wrongly insisting it was just the drink talking. Beth couldn't do that. Lou only knew half the story and Beth wanted to keep it that way.

Chapter 35

Back at the farm when Lou went out to do the late night check on the horses Beth took the opportunity to ring Lindsay. She kept the call short, careful not to be caught.

Lindsay had been expecting a phone call because she knew things were changing, becoming dangerous. She was worried for Beth and warned her to stay away from them all, especially Hyacinth. When pressed she wouldn't expand on it, saying vaguely that she had matters in hand.

Beth told her not to worry because she was taking a holiday from work and staying with Lou for a couple of weeks.

She failed to register the seriousness in Lindsay's voice. Saying she needed to know what was going on and if there was a chance to get to know Felicity better, she would take it and the visit to her stables could be the perfect opportunity. Lindsay ended up laughing at Beth's tenacity, telling her she'd make a detective out of her yet, but repeated she should leave well alone. Beth couldn't do that, even though it was scary she found it exciting and besides, she wanted answers.

Only when Lindsay insisted she let the professionals handle things, did Beth realize something serious was afoot.

Still, she didn't regret giving her mobile number to Felicity. Perhaps Lindsay was just trying to scare her. Her sense of reason refused to be heard.

Felicity wasted no time and rang the farm early the following morning, 'We're having a fancy dress party at the weekend. We'd love for you both to come. Mum said to stay over then we can all ride out together on Sunday. It'll be fun. Please say you will.'

A vision came into Beth's mind of Davinia on horseback and some poor horse buckling at the knees. Attempting to keep the laughter out of her voice she accepted, 'Thanks Felicity. How kind of you to include Lou and I. We'd love to come. Is there a party theme?'

'No, not really. Anything outrageous will do.'

Lou was apprehensive, but because Beth was so excited about the invite, she kept her thoughts to herself. It was bliss having her here, and she didn't want to spoil things.

They enjoyed an idyllic few days. Unknown to Lou, Beth regularly checked with Lindsay to see if there were any developments.

They drove to Melton Manor in Lou's BMW. Felicity greeted them enthusiastically. 'Hello darlings. Sorry Mum isn't here to meet you, but she has left us lunch. She and Julie have nipped out to a boring catering exhibition or something like that. They won't be too long. Now, just leave your bags here and Petra will see to them. I'm *so* pleased you're here… come on through.' She led the way along the grand hallway towards double doors at the far end, pushing the doors open into the enormous kitchen where the table was laid ready.

Felicity and Lou talked about Badminton throughout the meal. Not knowing enough about the horses and riders Beth was unable to take an active part, but she didn't mind.

Perhaps if she'd realized Felicity was deliberately leading the conversation so Beth was excluded she might have tried to put a stop to it. Instead she idly studied the layout and contents of the kitchen imagining which door lead where into the vast house. Her memory of her previous kitchen visit was vague. It's a lot like home, she thought, except there are no dogs. What a waste to have a big place like this without a couple of labradors.

Davinia and Julie returned just as they finished eating. Lou smirked at Beth, the dildo scenario linking their thoughts.

After more hello darlings, Davinia suggested they go for a ride round the park. 'It's such a lovely day and it will keep you all out from under my feet. We need to put the finishing touches to the food for tonight. Don't we Jules?'

'Good idea Mum. Come on girls, you'll need to get changed.'

Ten minutes later they were standing in one of the smartest stable yards Lou had ever seen.

Felicity introduced her horses to them one by one, telling Lou their history and ability in detail. Perhaps she's hoping to make a sale, Beth thought, scratching the forehead of a pretty dappled grey mare.

'I see you've made friends with Phantom.' Felicity came to stand beside her.

'Yes, she's a real sweetie.'

'Would you like to ride her? She *is* a real sweetie, forward going, but gentle as a lamb.'

'Yes, please…..thanks. What about Lou? Which one is she going to ride?' Beth smiled at Lou who looked fabulous in her toffee coloured breeches and cream polo shirt.

'Well, the choice is hers. Any one she fancies.' Felicity flashed her eyes suggestively saying, 'What about it, Lou? Which one's for you?' she moved to stand beside Beth, as though giving Lou the choice between them, her question positively loaded with innuendo.

Lou completely missed it. 'I think I'd like to ride that lovely chestnut, Bamber, isn't it?' she walked across to Bamber's loose box.

Felicity laughed. 'Come on then, let's get them tacked up.'

Lou sat tall in the saddle, shoulders back, her breasts thrusting forward rhythmically as they trotted through a leafy avenue of trees. Beth enjoyed watching her curvaceous bottom encased in the tight breeches rubbing against the saddle and she wasn't the only one.

Felicity was almost dribbling watching Lou. Montanna eat your heart out she thought, kicking her horse forward to ride alongside Lou so she could savour her gorgeous face and sparkling eyes.

Pangs of jealousy assailed Beth. She urged Phantom forward so they were riding three abreast. Bloody Fliss, how dare she try to monopolize Lou! What's she up to? What the hell's wrong with them all? She fumed under her breath.

Felicity was showing off, she was so desperate to make a good impression on Lou. She pointed out various landmarks to her as they rode through the parkland, purposely trying to keep Lou's attention away from Beth. She was proud of the family estate, and she wanted to ogle Lou, and this was a perfect way of doing it.

Despite Felicity's obvious interest in Lou, Beth saw the funny side of it because she knew fine well that Lou would have nothing to do with her. She settled herself down and actually enjoyed the ride. She fell in love with Phantom who carried her as if she were precious china. Galloping flat out along the track taking them back to the stables, out pacing the other two horses, Phantom made sure she was first back. Beth had the horse untacked and her flysheet on before Lou and Felicity clattered into the stable yard.

Henry, Felicity's friend, had arrived with his partner Dan when they returned to the house. The guys were doing their cabaret act at the party and Beth was looking forward to seeing them in drag.

Felicity ushered Beth and Lou up to their room saying, 'Everything is ready for you. Petra will see you have a snack brought up, she'll give you anything you want.' She paused winking at Beth. 'Just ring the bell, she'll come running.' Then to Lou she said, 'If *you* want anything Lou, I'll be happy to see to it personally.' With that she turned on her heel and flounced away leaving Beth and Lou to collapse on the bed in fits of giggles.

They showered and dressed ready for the party. Lou as Robin Hood, and Beth as Maid Marion. From their room they could hear other guests arriving. Sitting close to the window Beth tried to identify their voices then froze as she thought she heard Hyacinth's voice. Straining her ears, listening intently to be sure, no…perhaps she was wrong she decided.

The ballroom was a mass of colour. Flamboyant costumes were favoured, as were exotic masks. It was impossible to guess who was who.

Davinia greeted them at the bottom of the stairs, pushing masks into their hands. 'Girls, you do look divine. And Lou your legs go on forever.' She ran her hand up Lou's thigh. 'My oh my. You are a lucky girl Beth, fancy having those wrapped around you!'

Beth was not at all amused, her eyes flashed in anger. 'Luck has nothing to do with it.'

'Ha, ha, ha, now don't be such a spoilsport, I'm only joking. Now, put your masks on. You can blame Felicity for these, she decided at the last minute we should have a masked ball. Such fun. Enjoy.' she left them to mingle.

Drink flowed freely and people began to loosen up. Petra was overseeing the team of waitresses circulating through the guests, ensuring glasses were never empty. Beth was careful with the wine, she didn't want to become giddy, and it didn't take much. Despite numerous attempts at telling one waitress she had enough, the girl came to refill her glass again.

'Am I talking Swahili or something?' she asked Lou, 'Or is this girl just not listening?'

'Beth, calm down. Put your hand over the glass. Better still, put the drink down and come and join in this daft dance.'

Odysis's Oops Upside Your Head blasted out as everyone rushed to sit in a line. A mass of bodies, legs spread, arms waving, covered the floor.

At the end of the song most of the elegant costumes were in glorious disarray and guests had to scramble hastily off the floor as the opening bars of Hey Big Spender sounded announcing the imminent arrival of Henry and Dan. They glided in, instantly commanding centre stage, to perform Shirley Bassey and Marlena Dietrich numbers with utter brilliance.

Standing wrapped in Lou's arms, swaying in time to the beat, Beth noticed Julie knocking back copious amounts of alcohol; a drunken Bodacia looking so miserable. Instantly Beth's kind heart was touched. Maybe she should talk to her, try to find out what's wrong. There must be something amiss.

As the final strains of Falling in Love Again faded, the room was plunged into darkness.

'Shit! Don't move, hon, be back in a second.' Lou instructed.

Beth had no intention of moving. Sensing someone in front of her she asked, 'Lou, is that you? What's going on?'

No answer. Someone touched her breast, cupped her chin and kissed her, a sweet, unhurried kiss. Her stomach lurched. This wasn't Lou.

Instinctively Beth lifted her hands reaching up into thin air. In the second the kiss finished light flooded the room. Beth looked round expecting to identify her intruder. She couldn't. Everyone was acting normally. Dan and Henry were still waltzing together and hadn't even noticed the blackout. No one looked the least bit suspicious. Beth needed to find Lou, but first she needed to pee.

Returning from the bathroom nearest to the kitchen, she noticed a door tucked away into a corner. Because of the way the hallway turned, it wasn't visible when approaching the kitchen from the main entrance. She couldn't remember this door from her guided tour so she stopped. Curious to know what was behind it she stepped forward intending to open the door and investigate when she heard voices. Her hand froze in mid-air. One sounded terribly familiar.

Chapter 36

Hyacinth passed a crystal brandy balloon to Penny, affectionately touching her cheek. 'We'll have to organize an outing of the Amethyst Club soon. I've heard the weather forecast and next week sounds promising. We could spend a few days on board. Enjoy some sailing. What do you say?'

'Just name the day.' Penny gazed up adoringly.

'Are you up for it Serena?'

'Yes, please. My first sailing trip with the group, how fabulous.' Serena's excited reply was instant. She lowered her eyes coyly, 'Thank you, Hyacinth.'

Flames flickered in the dying embers of the fire, briefly lighting the room, highlighting the heavy old furniture, and laden bookcases. The location of the snug at Melton Manor was the perfect place for secret trysts because the French widows allowed unseen, unhindered access to the outside world.

Only two lamps glowed dimly, casting further shadows onto the three women as they sat by the fire. Penny continued to gaze at Hyacinth. Why did she love her so much? She could be such an obnoxious, demanding bitch. It was bad enough when Beth came on the scene taking Hyacinth's attention away from her, and now here was another. Penny sensed danger in Serena who had pursued her relentlessly, expertly manipulating her way into her bed *and* the group. Penny couldn't remember agreeing to bring her here tonight, yet here she was. She's no different from the rest of us, she thought watching Serena hanging onto Hyacinth's every word. We're all Hyacinths' slaves or pleasure puppets, depending on how you looked at it.

'How's your little game panning out, darling?' Hyacinth's attention returned to Penny.

Flustered, and jerked back to reality, Penny floundered lost for words, 'Oh yes…well…I mean…you know the blackmail was a good idea…'

Hyacinth stopped lighting her cigarette to scrutinize Penny, 'What the hell are you talking about?'

Penny's face was blank.

'Honestly Pen, I wonder about you at times. You told me you were planning to set Montanna up with Lou. What happened?'

'Oh that,' Penny laughed nervously, but long enough to regain her composure, 'well no wonder I forgot about it…it was a complete non-starter. I'd have had more success fielding Fliss than Montanna, she's smitten.'

'Is she, darling?' She looked intently into Penny's eyes, knowing her ability to instil the fear of god into her. 'I'll have to bear that in mind. Perhaps we should bring the ritual forward and get her initiated. What do you know about her friend, the Inspector? Are they really close?'

Penny shrugged her shoulders, 'Friends since childhood.'

Serena sat silent, idly swilling brandy round the glass, fighting the torrent of emotions racing through her, jealous as hell of Penny getting Hyacinth's attention, of being her confidante. She wanted the attention back on her. Now.

In her own way Hyacinth loved Penny, she was loyal, and could be trusted with her life. She moved to sit on the arm of Penny's high backed leather chair appreciating the curve of her breast. Fully aware of the effect it would have on Serena she bent forward to kiss Penny, while slipping her hand down the inside of her shirt. 'I do love your tits, Pen.' She pushed her tongue into Penny's mouth.

Holding the kiss, Hyacinth moved in front of the chair, lifting Penny to her feet she clasped her buttocks and pulled her close into her groin. Penny moaned, why did she allow her to do this?

Serena couldn't take any more. Her poor attempt at subtlety almost made Hyacinth laugh out loud. Jumping up she went to stand behind Penny, kissing her shoulder as she desperately tried to establish eye contact with Hyacinth and get in on the act.

Hyacinth deliberately made her wait, enjoying her anxiety. Only when she felt Penny responding too much, did she look into Serena's eyes. Stretching to touch Serena's tits she barely managed to glance the pert nipple.

'I think I can hear someone.' Serena quickly stepped backwards taking herself out of reach.

Interesting, mused Hyacinth. So the little minx wants to tease. She needs to be taught a lesson. Hyacinth wasn't happy Serena was here tonight, or about how she'd managed to wangle her way into the group in the first place. No one in the group knew anything about her background and Hyacinth's enquiries hadn't provided any answers. Penny never could resist a pretty face, but there again, neither could she. There wasn't really that much to hide at the moment with the suspension of the diamond run, just a little magic here and there. And it might do Penny good to be sidetracked with a young beauty like Serena, hopefully it would take her mind off diamonds.

Releasing Penny, she fired Serena an angry glance. Blast the girl, she'd better check. Easing the heavy door open Hyacinth stepped out to look up and down the hallway. It was deserted as she had expected. Stupid girl.

Time to go, Hyacinth decided. Closing the door and heading for the French windows, ignoring Serena, she looked back over her left shoulder.

'Ring me later, Pen. I need to know when we can go to Cornwall. We might even stay a couple of extra days, do some walking. Oh, and by the way Serena.' Hyacinth looked directly into her eyes, 'I've changed my mind - you're not coming!'

Serena opened her mouth to protest.

Immediately Hyacinth raised her hand, 'No. I said *not* this time.' She dismissed Serena's tearful expression with a cruel sense of satisfaction. Speaking to Penny in a softer tone, 'Penny, darling, we should arrange to go on Saturday then we can spend at least a week sailing. Can you make your arrangements?'

'Yes, Hyacinth,' Penny answered. 'I can make my arrangements all right.'

'What about Beth's initiation?' Serena blurted out. 'Can I seduce Lou for you?' she was desperate to stay on the right side of Hyacinth.

'Don't talk about things you know nothing about child.' Hyacinth's icy voice stopped Serena in her tracks. She was itching to slap her insolent young face, but instead she stepped outside disappearing into the darkness. Seconds later Penny and a glum Serena followed.

Beth heard enough fragments of the conversation to be disturbed. Hiding in the dusty folds of some ancient dust filled drapes, she disentangled herself then rushed off in search of Lou.

Scanning the ballroom for her while trying to identify which mask hid Hyacinth, she drew a blank on both accounts. Most of the guests were singing and dancing while a few had taken up someone's suggestion of playing leapfrog. Their hilarious, drunken attempts hampered by some voluminous costumes briefly drew Beth's attention, but she was too wound up to laugh.

She had to find Lou. She stepped into the ballroom from the doorway anxiously going from one to another asking if anyone had seen her, dreading coming to the mask that disguised Hyacinth.

Eventually Davinia came across to her. Lou hadn't been feeling well she told her and had gone up to bed. Beth glanced at her watch. Well, it was four in the morning. Relieved to be able to excuse herself, she thanked Davinia and hurried to their room.

'Lou! Lou! Are you awake?…You'll never guess what.' she entered their darkened room with the story of the overheard meeting ready to spill from her lips.

'I'm awake.'

'You're eyes are closed.'

'I know, I'm inspecting the inside of my eyelids.'

'Well open them, now!' Beth took hold of Lou's shoulders through the duvet to shake her. 'Davinia said you came up because you weren't feeling well…what's the matter?'

Lou looked sheepishly at Beth. 'Actually hon, I have a confession…there's nothing wrong. I was just tired and couldn't get rid of Montanna.'

'Montanna? I didn't know she was here.'

'Well she is. She arrived late and made a beeline for me. I couldn't be bothered with her, so made up an excuse to escape.

I knew you would follow me.' She patted the bed for Beth to sit beside her. 'Anyway, you're looking a bit fraught…what's up?'

'In the room. Voices.' Beth started pacing backwards and forwards at the foot of the bed.

'Room? What room?'

'I found a room next to the kitchen. When you come in from the main door you can't see it, it's almost hidden behind the drapes. Hyacinth was in there. God, Lou, they're going to initiate me.'

'Initiate you? Hyacinth? What the hell have you been drinking?'

Frustrated by Lou's calm reaction, Beth bounced on and off the bed. 'She *was* in there I tell you, I am not imagining it! *And* she wasn't alone either…there were at least two other women with her. I didn't recognize their voices properly, but I think Penny Corday was one of them and someone called Serena.'

Lou sat up, pulling the quilt round her, 'Beth, honey. Calm down.'

Beth rushed across the room throwing herself into Lou's arms, 'My God, Lou…do you remember in the hotel? That news item? It was on the television. Someone called Serena had gone missing?'

Lou thought for a few seconds, trying to remember, hoping her silence would have a calming effect on Beth. Quietly she answered her. 'Yes, Beth I do. Now calm yourself down and tomorrow we'll ring either the police, or Lindsay. Whoever you want, how about that?'

'Lindsay. Yes, we'll ring Lindsay. Where's my phone?'

'You can't ring now, it's four in the morning. Sweetheart just get into bed and we'll ring in the morning.'

Just then there was a rustle in the corner of the bedroom. Suddenly Beth dived under the cover into Lou's arms. 'What was that?' she started to shiver.

'I don't know hon. Shush…listen…'

Complete silence surrounded them. Then in the dimmed room a faint glow started to emanate from the far corner. They watched fascinated, holding their breath as it drifted slowly, hovering at the foot of the bed.

Half-joking Beth whispered, 'It must be a ghost.'

The bedroom lights flashed frantically on and off before leaving them in inky darkness. Too scared to move Lou whispered she could see something that looked like an apparition. Frozen with fear, both stifled a scream when they felt the bedclothes being pulled away from them. Trying to hold on to the covers, unable to fight the force pulling at them both girls screamed out loud and long as the bedcovers were whipped off completely, leaving them exposed in the darkness.

Within seconds Davinia burst into the room switching on the lights as she did so. Pale and shaking, Beth and Lou both gabbled incomprehensibly about seeing a ghost.

Davinia chortled, 'Oh that will be my great, great grandmother. She is a rascal. She visits occasionally and must have wondered who you were. She gets very inquisitive about strangers - don't worry girls, she won't hurt you. She just likes to look.'

'What!' Beth exploded, 'You're telling us that we *did* see a ghost? Oh My God!'

Davinia, still laughing, left them to the mercies of her deceased relative. 'By the way girls, she had a penchant for the ladies too.' She said closing the door behind her.

Now sober and wide-awake they decided to give their ghostly visitor a floorshow and made mad passionate love; with the lights on. All thoughts of Beth's overheard conversation were suspended, but definitely not forgotten.

Chapter 37

The following morning Davinia, genuinely concerned, enquired if they managed to get any sleep. Both grinned then muttered they had, eventually.

During breakfast Petra came in to clear away some dishes. Felicity and Lou were discussing horses again. Taking advantage of their distraction Petra moved around the table, finally standing next to Beth.

Quietly she asked, 'You enjoy ze party? Yez?'

Surprised, Beth replied just as quietly, but rather pompously, 'Yes, thank you...*we* did,' purposely emphasizing the we.

Petra made no response. Instead she fussed around the table, kneeling to retrieve a serviette from the floor next to Beth's chair. As she stood up she ran her finger tips lightly up Beth's leg whispering, 'Ze lights cauze leetle problem.'

Beth's breath caught in her throat making her cough as Petra winked so only she could see.

Was Petra the one who had stolen the kiss? Determined not to let her go from the room without an answer Beth spoke, 'Did you enjoy the party?'

'Oh but yez. I like - how you zay - err very much to mix wiz zee gueztz…. Davinia ze joinz me in.'

Beth stifled a laugh at her poor English and bizarre accent, supposedly Swedish she sounded more French. She guessed Petra was not at all what she purported to be. 'What did you wear?'

'Vot did I vear?' Petra was surprised to be asked expecting Beth to know. 'Ze coztume, ov courze - I do not know vot you vould call it…it vaz vhite, virginal vhite…did you not zee me?'

Beth decided it was much safer not to answer. Instead, keeping her voice low and trying to sound casual, she asked, 'Did I hear Hyacinths voice last night, was she at the party?'

'Yez, maybe. Zat bitch dizappeared at midnight like Zinderella.' With that remark Petra disappeared back to the kitchen.

Beth still didn't know who had kissed her. She didn't want to mention it to Lou because whoever it was sure had luscious lips.

After breakfast they decided to go for a walk, ostensibly to clear their heads, but in reality so Beth could ring Lindsay and they could discuss her overheard conversation without fear of their being overheard.

Lindsay was exasperated with Beth. Why couldn't she just stay away from those women when she'd asked her to? 'Listen, there *is* something going on, but I can't tell you anymore than that. Will you please trust me and at least try to do as I ask.'

'Oh alright. Don't blow a fuse. Am I in some sort of danger here?'

'You will be if I get my hands on you.' Lindsay tried to joke, 'But seriously Beth you should go home, out of the way, as soon as it is polite to. Don't make any waves. Understand?'

Beth looked at Lou, 'She wants us to leave.'

Lou took the phone, 'What's going on, Lindsay. This is no joke is it?'

'I'm afraid not Lou, just take my word for it and get little Miss Marples out of there. Right?'

'Right. Will do.' She flipped the phone shut. 'Guess we've gotta go hon.'

As they approached the stables the sound of raised voices drifted towards them. Two women were arguing loudly. Keeping quiet they moved closer, staying out of sight behind the half open tack room door. Inside Felicity was crying, and demanding to know why Montanna had been brought to stay at the Manor.

'I don't like her Pen. She's a troublemaker.'

'I know, I know.' Penny tried to soothe her. 'She is a pain, but Hyacinth insisted......you know how she is.'

'Only too fucking well.' Felicity blew her nose.

Putting an arm around Felicity's shuddering shoulders, Penny tried to comfort her, 'Montanna means nothing to me....but she is useful to the group. That's all it is, I promise you. And you know Hyacinth is trying to establish a new route...Okay?'

Felicity nodded, subdued.

'Now, we shouldn't even be discussing this. Come on let's give the horses a gallop and forget about it...Dry your eyes, darling.'

Beth nudged Lou whispering, 'Told you they were together, didn't I?'

'Yes, you did my little Sherlock Holmes.'

'Well, you have to admit it, there is something odd going on. I think I do want to go home. You know, suddenly I don't feel we're safe here. I think Lindsay's right. Am I going crazy, or what?'

'No, honey, you're not crazy…well, no more than usual.' laughter bubbled in Lou's voice. 'Just to be pleasant, and because we don't want them to become suspicious, we'd better go and say our goodbyes. Then we'll get the hell out of here.'

'That suits me fine.'

After a short stroll round the rose garden allowing Felicity time to pull herself together they went back to the stables. Fliss greeted them warmly. She and Penny were almost ready to ride, and despite Lou's loud protestations saddled Bamber and Phantom, insisting they all rode together.

Leaving the stable yard in single file Fliss lead the way heading along a narrow path towards a giant rockery. The path twisted through the middle giving the impression of riding through the Grand Canyon. The sides were extremely high then gave way to woodland thick with bluebells. Riding in single file had made conversation impossible which was exactly what Fliss intended. Unexpectedly the track led into a wide and well cared for clearing where a waterfall splashed over stones into a deep pond filled with carp.

'Why, this is gorgeous.' Beth exclaimed in surprise.

'Yes, isn't it?' Fliss acknowledged.

'Look, Lou, over there. Can you see that funny little door?' Beth pointed towards a group of large rocks.

'Oh that yes, it's supposed to be a tunnel back into the Manor.' Fliss explained matter of factly. 'I don't think it's ever been used. Not in my lifetime anyway, but this is such an old place, as you know. The Manor is supposed to be riddled with secret passageways, the priests old escape routes, you know. I used to play in the cellars during my childhood. I could ride my bike through some of the tunnels. I wasn't supposed to go into a couple of the cellar rooms though, but I used to sneak in. I loved the smell in there, it was like exotic perfume.' She sniffed her wrist as Penny shot her a dangerous look.

'Yes, I know what you mean. My sister and I used to play in the cellars at home too,' Beth said, 'especially on rainy days.'

The horses were becoming restless so they moved on into open space. Penny set the pace. Determined to keep Fliss quiet she kicked her horse forward ensuring the ride was so fast there was no further opportunity for Fliss to indulge in careless talk. Forty-five minutes later they were back in the stable yard. Dismounting first, Penny shoed Beth and Lou away, insisting they were guests; she and Fliss would attend to the horses.

The second they were alone Penny rounded on Fliss angrily. 'What the fuck are you playing at you stupid little bitch? Why did you attach so much importance to the door and the passageways? There was no need. Hyacinth will go ballistic when she finds out. Have you no common sense?'

Fliss burst into tears again, 'Pen, please, I'm sorry. I was only making conversation that's all. Please don't say anything to Hyacinth, please…I'd be in terrible trouble, wouldn't I?'

'Oh stop whimpering, of course I won't tell her. Just stop opening your mouth and letting your brains fall out, if you can.' Penny felt guilty. Perhaps she was being too hard on Fliss. Oh what the hell, the door was only important to them. Why should Beth or Lou attach any significance to it. She kissed Fliss until her crying stopped.

While they tended the horses a voice in Penny's head constantly nagged her about the precious consignment that was due. The biggest yet. She didn't want any cock-ups.

Chapter 38

Back in the comfort and safety of Lou's warm, honey coloured kitchen, Beth sat at the round pine table gazing into space, mentally going over her conversation with Lindsay. She'd told her they were home and about the old door set in the stones beside the pond. She didn't know why she'd done that, but her intuition told her the door was important.

Lou, back from checking the horses, kicked off her boots, walked over to the Aga and poured herself a coffee. She glanced at Beth, concerned. Poor girl looked troubled and she was just about to add to it.

Picking up the coffee mug she sat down at the table and reached out to hold Beth's hands, 'Hon, I've got something to tell you.'

Beth's stomach lurched at the tone of Lou's voice, 'What's up?'

'You remember Sarah, my agent?'

'Yes.'

'Do you remember talk of an offer of work from America?'

'Yes.'

'I've turned it down.'

'Turned what down....what have you done Lou? What exactly have you turned down?'

Lou spoke without any regret, 'I was offered a lead role in a Hollywood Production,' she sipped her coffee, 'with Universal. I've turned it down because I'd rather be here, with you. After all, we haven't spent a lot of time together and I don't want to leave you.' She paused holding Beth's hands tighter, 'I wasn't going to tell you, but these things have a way of getting out into the press.'

'Lou...No...You should have grabbed it with both hands. My God, some people never get a Hollywood offer...I don't want us to be apart either, but you must get Sarah on the phone, right now. Anyway I thought that had gone by the wayside it was months ago when it was mentioned. We had only just met.'

'Yes, it was over a year ago when they first approached me, but these things can take time to happen. I'm not going.' Lou shook her head vigorously emphasizing her decision.

'No, you must go, you absolutely must. I insist. Honest to God, you can't pass this up.'

'I am *not* going. And that's final!'

Beth was almost speechless. Every emotion imaginable was surging through her. Eventually she managed to glean more information about the offer. Her questions of who, what, where and when were answered with a simple calmness. As Beth sat looking at this amazing woman she knew she must persuade her to accept the offer. She couldn't allow her to throw away the chance of a lifetime - a chance most people would give their right arm for.

So Beth talked...and talked...and talked. Eventually Lou grudgingly agreed to phone Sarah, but only because Beth promised to take a holiday and go with her for the first three weeks. Relieved, Beth leaned back in her chair totally worn out, while Lou made the call from the study.

Within minutes of Lou returning to the kitchen, Sarah rang back. The Director was ecstatic and wanted Lou in America in the next two weeks. Sarah would make the arrangements for them both, now it was up to Beth to keep her end of the bargain and arrange time away from work.

Lou switched the answer phone on. They had a lot to discuss and she didn't want any interruptions. She was both excited and apprehensive at the turn of events. Thank God Beth had persuaded her to go. Thank God she would be going with her.

Both were emotionally exhausted when they finally headed for bed. The phone had rang once while they were talking so they went to check the message.

'I'm watching you. Do you hear me?…I'm watching you both.' a muffled sinister female voice threatened.

'I told you I felt as though we were being watched the first time I came here.' Beth stammered.

'I don't recognize the voice, Beth. Do you?' Lou was much calmer.

'Yes. Yes, I do. Oh hell….Why can't I put a face to it?' It sounded like Hyacinth, yet Beth couldn't be sure so she didn't dare say. 'We need to find out who it is and put a stop to it.' Beth was becoming more upset, 'I'm sick of all of this intrigue.'

Lou tried to calm her, 'It's probably someone playing a joke to wind us up. Come to bed, love. Don't worry about it. You've had enough to think about today without trying to take in anymore. We both have.'

Lou promised to phone the police first thing.

Neither of them got much sleep, both were restless, constantly tossing and turning. At one point Beth thought she heard someone outside, but the stable dogs didn't bark so she convinced herself she was wrong and eventually drifted into a dreamless sleep.

Lou was up before first light. Beth found her in the kitchen, sitting on the floor by the Aga, hugging a mug of cold tea. Beth sat down beside her and started talking about her wonderful not-to-be-missed opportunity with as much enthusiasm as she could muster.

Chapter 39

Trying to keep positive was difficult, and tears kept catching both Beth and Lou out at the thought of the separation. They tried to focus on Ascot. Lou wouldn't be leaving until after that so it became their catalyst.

Along with all the upheaval the answer phone message was still on Beth's mind. Unknown to Lou she rang and told Lindsay about it, along with Lou's departure to LA.

She must contact the local police if it happened again, Lindsay said. They could put a monitor on the phone and all calls would be intercepted. What was Beth going to do about Lou, their relationship?

Good question, thought Beth, knowing how long distance relationships could be absolute killers.

Lou's arrangements forged ahead at an alarming speed. On a practical note she decided to have someone live in the house while she was away. Frances obliged, she was willing to move over from the stable flat. Anna offered to stay whenever she could. Beth planned to spend as much time as possible at the farm in the hope of being able to feel nearer to Lou, even though she would only be there spasmodically.

In the middle of all of this Ascot crept up on them almost unnoticed. In preparation they spent a fun day in Harrogate shopping for outrageous outfits. The first visit was to the milliner. Start with the hat and work down was Lou's motto.

The milliner, a poe faced women, looked like she was permanently sucking a lemon. Despite Beth putting hats on the wrong way round causing Lou to have hysterics, she never cracked a smile. A thousand hats later, they made their perfect and totally outrageous choices. Their infectious good humour found a chink in the milliners armour and she couldn't remember when she had enjoyed serving clients so much. She wiped tears of laughter from her eyes as she opened the door for the girls to leave and even stood outside waving them off.

Stunning outfits, elegant shoes and smart handbags were relentlessly hunted out. Laden with bags they finally headed home.

They travelled down to Ascot the day before Ladies Day, to stay overnight with a friend of Lou's, someone who Beth had never met before. For some inexplicable reason Beth was feeling rather nervous and uncomfortable about staying there.

Helen worked in the same profession as Lou and lived in a smart farmhouse on the edge of Windsor Great Park. She was annoyed that work commitments would prevent her from attending Ascot with Lou and her fancy piece.

She had instructed her housekeeper to have a meal prepared ready for when they arrived in the hope that Lou would realize she should be living here with her. She was wasting her time, but Helen's tunnel vision would not allow her to see that.

Helen returned from her day's filming like a ship in full sail. Introductions were made, a bottle of Chianti opened, then she and Lou caught up on some gossip. Helen was ecstatic to learn about Lou's work in LA and expertly excluded Beth from their conversation.

Watching them, there were times, when Beth could have believed they had some romantic history. Helen was overly familiar, shooting dark glances at her when Lou wasn't watching. It amused Beth in a wicked way, it was almost like watching a re-run of the Montanna and Felicity episodes. Of course, it went completely over Lou's head.

The following morning after enjoying a full English breakfast cooked to perfection by the housekeeper, the girls prepared for their day at the races. Helen, out to impress Lou, had arranged for a chauffeur driven limo to collect them.

They stepped into the Bentley, both an understatement of stylish sophistication. The new outfits were perfect, as was the weather, and the hats were as good as a complete disguise. The chauffeur, an absolute charmer, was totally professional and as camp as they come.

Once inside the racecourse, Lou took Beth's elbow and guided her through the crowd, waving and calling hello to almost everyone.

They scanned the boxes looking for Penny. Lou spotted her first, with Felicity. That brought Beth back down to earth with a bump, and then her natural curiosity came to her rescue.

Beth air kissed Penny, not particularly wanting to touch her, before politely enquiring why Felicity was with her. Penny replied rather too loudly that some last minute emergency had prevented Montanna coming, then launched into a rapid and complicated explanation of how she had asked Davinia, who was much too busy with some major catering event. Still gabbling fifty to the dozen, she stressed it was Davinia who suggested Felicity would enjoy the day out.

I'll bet Felicity was more than happy to oblige, Beth thought sceptically. With her face a picture of sincerity she replied, 'How convenient for you.' She popped a canapé into her mouth, almost choking when she noticed they were wearing their identical diamond pendants. She wondered if Lou had spotted them. She figured these pendants had to be some sort of sign or an indication of some connection.

Muttering something about race cards, she pulled Lou away to tell her to check out the pendants.

The mood was good as they perused the days racing pages before heading to the parade ring to savour the top class thoroughbreds at close quarters.

The atmosphere was unique, as was the pageantry. Lou talked knowingly to racehorse owners and trainers, gaining a few tips along the way. Selecting a couple of hopeful winners while sipping champagne, they placed their bets before going in for coffee and pastries.

Beth was having such a good time at first she didn't register the importance of the introduction to Baroness Cavendish. When she did it was glaringly obvious to her this woman could never have been Penny's blackmailer. She was the scattiest person Beth had ever met. The type you can dress up, but didn't want to take out. Talking to her was like driving with the brakes on and Beth nicknamed her Baroness Fidget because she could not keep still…..but she could talk for England and did so, incessantly and in a booming voice, but oh so boring. Obviously a domineering character, thought Beth, but in no way could she ever be a 'secret keeper'. The Baroness appeared to know everything about everybody and loudly announced it to the world. It would be impossible to have a quiet conversation with her never mind anything else.

When the Baroness spotted a trainer she knew she rushed off after him. Then someone told a really funny story about her belated husband. There was a standing joke how for years the Baron had pretended to be deaf so she ignored him saying there was no point in talking to a deaf man. His plan was foolproof and he was left in peace right up to the day he died.

What was Penny thinking about? Beth wondered. There was no way this woman could have blackmailed anyone. She couldn't hold her own water never mind keep a secret.

Leaving Lou alone for a few minutes she sought out Penny, 'I've met your friend the Baroness.'

'Oh Beth. I was wrong to think she could have blackmailed me, wasn't I? Anyway, forget about it. I have,' she placed a hand on Beth's arm, 'I expect it was just one of my silly friends playing an even sillier game.'

'Do you think so?'

'Yes, I do and I over-reacted. Now don't you worry your pretty head about it any more...go and enjoy the racing.' Penny left her to hurry back to Felicity's side.

Beth had enough on her mind and was glad to forget about it, although in retrospect thought the whole scenario was highly peculiar. Whatever did Lindsay make of it?

Turning away from Penny, she thought she'd have a bit of fun with Lou who was chatting to some race horse owners. Collecting a glass of champagne, she caught Lou's attention while lifting the glass to her lips as if to take a sip, instead she ran her tongue around the rim before dipping a finger into the liquid then seductively slipped it into her mouth. She had difficulty suppressing a grin as Lou stared at her in amazement. Fluttering her eyelashes she eyed Lou up and down, her gaze lingering on Lou's crotch. Any minute now, thought Beth, she'll have to come over to me.

Sure enough within seconds Lou made polite excuses before rushing over. 'What are you doing to me?'

'Why? What's wrong?' Beth innocently asked.

Bending into her Lou whispered, 'You know fine well. You're turning me on you little minx. I'm so wet we'll have to find somewhere to go. I can't wait until we get back to Helen's.'

'Oh, I can't! I have to meet someone in five minutes.' Beth feigned shock, playing with her.

'Come with me…now.' Lou took Beth firmly by the elbow. So dominant, Beth shuddered in anticipation.

Unexpectedly Constance blocked their path. 'Hello, how lovely to see you both.'

Lou groaned inwardly. 'Constance! What a nice surprise. We didn't know you would be here today. Have you had a winner?'

'Yes, and I have a hot tip for the big race.'

'Oh. Come on then, spit it out.' Lou invited.

'Never mind that, come with me and we'll put the bet on now.' Spotting Penny and Felicity, she called out to them, 'Girls. Girls…over here….We're going to place a bet now, but come and share some champagne.'

Constance then caught a passing waitress beside a conveniently vacant table. Pushing a generous tip into her hand she asked her to keep their table well supplied with Clicquot Veuve. Indicating to Penny they would be back shortly, she hurried off with Beth and Lou to place their bets.

Constance's strange behaviour was irritating Beth. She seemed to want to keep them all together. Rounding them up like a sheep dog. Or am I just being paranoid? Beth wondered.

As a result of Constance's herding, they spent the rest of the day in the company of Penny, Felicity and Constance, almost confined to Penny's box. Felicity was surprisingly subdued.

Beth's paranoia returned when Constance mentioned she had spotted her much earlier in the day talking to Penny. So why hadn't she come over to say hello then? And why did she keep repeatedly looking at the man with bushy black eyebrows who appeared every time Beth glanced around the nearby faces?

The runners for the Gold Cup came out on to the course, distracting her thoughts. Well, let's see if her bloody tip was right she thought venomously.

'Why, Lou. You do look flushed. Are you sickening for something?' Penny turned to Lou and Beth who were standing close together at the back of their little crowd.

'Must be the champagne.' Lou replied languidly.

'Really? What did you think of that last race? Clever Constance was absolutely spot-on with her tip, wasn't she? And wasn't it just the most exciting climax?' Penny bubbled.

Lou stammered, 'Y…Y…Yes…I must say…I was in a highly excitable state while that race was being run…and as for the climax…well, it's the most excited I've been all day!'

Beth giggled, her hand hidden by the soft folds of her shawl, rested in the wetness between Lou's legs.

Chapter 40

They were all packed and ready to leave for America. Lou had booked them into the Dorchester for the night before the flight. The train journey to Kings Cross was tinged with excitement and sadness, lurching them between tears and laughter. Every time the conversation lulled Beth was rocked by heart-wrenching despair. Once the holiday was over they could be separated for months.

Gazing lovingly into each other's eyes across the table they reminisced about their first fateful train meeting. In no time at all the train pulled into Kings Cross station.

The suite at The Dorchester was exactly how Beth remembered it. Sentimentally Lou had arranged for them to stay in the same one. Closing the door after tipping the porter she said, 'I couldn't resist booking us into this room. Happy memories honey.' She held Beth close kissing her and stroking her hair.

Leaning back in Lou's arms, Beth joked, 'Absolutely no yogurt this time, you hussy, and *definitely* no ice cream. Tooo messy...you'll have to eat it with a spoon like everyone else if you want some.' Giggling, she paused, 'Oh yes, there is something else…we'd better keep any bubble bath well away from the Jacuzzi.'

After a snack from Room Service Lou asked if Beth fancied going clubbing.

'Of course,' she replied, 'but only if we go to the Ladies Only one.'

'Where else, lovely, where else?' Lou said.

The Club was pretty crowded when they arrived. Beth was shocked when Lou pointed out her ex partner, Vanessa, standing with a group of fashionably dressed women at the far end of the bar.

Beth had a thousand questions on her lips, none of which Lou was prepared to answer.

'She's history, lovely. Let it rest.'

'But she's gorgeous…why on earth haven't you told me about her before?'

'Yes, she is gorgeous on the outside, but she's a selfish bitch at heart. There's simply nothing to tell.'

'I told you all about Hyacinth.'

'Yes, I know you did, but I felt Hyacinth was a threat… and I was right, wasn't I?' she kissed Beth hoping to stop her questioning. She didn't want to talk about Vanessa. 'I told you it was more off than on…Vanessa is not a threat to us. Like I said, she's history. She won't bother us.'

Vanessa did stay out of their way, but Beth glanced across a couple of times and caught her watching them. It began to wind her up.

After enjoying a sexy smooch they were distracted from one another and were forced to drift apart to talk to other people. This was the opportunity Vanessa had been waiting for.

Beth needed the ladies room. She headed off unable to tell Lou who was nowhere in sight. Hating herself for doing so, she hesitated, and searched the crowd trying to identify Vanessa's red hair. She couldn't see her. Where had she gone?

Beth could have gone to the loo nearby, but guessing it would be crowded, made for the one upstairs. She would be there and back before Lou missed her. She was right, it was empty.

Heading back she saw two women in a passionate embrace in the shadows of the corridor. No surprise there, until she realized one was Vanessa…and with a sickening gut wrenching lurch realized the other woman was Lou.

Time stood still as she watched Lou returning Vanessa's kiss.

After what felt like an eternity Vanessa noticed Beth and made to dash for the stairs, but Lou grabbed her arm, pulling her back, and they kissed again.

'God, Lou, I've missed you too. Don't worry, of course I'll keep in touch. You'd better look out, you're girlfriend's watching.' Vanessa's eyes never left Beth's face as she looked coldly over Lou's shoulder.

Beth was devastated. For her the expression on Lou's face said it all. Unable to speak she watched Vanessa disappear from view leaving behind an eerie silence.

'Beth…sweetheart…' Lou, trying to hold her composure, held out her arms, 'let me explain.'

'Don't touch me!' Beth's icy tone broke the silence, 'What's to explain? I would say actions speak louder than words, wouldn't you?'

Seething Beth left the club stepping straight into someone else's waiting taxi. Wisely the driver didn't argue.

After frantically managing to wave down a cab Lou followed, expecting the mother of all rows when she got back to the hotel.

'Beth. Honey, please...you've got it all wrong...honest to God it's not what you think.' The words spilled from her lips as she pushed the door to their suite open. There wasn't the angry response she expected and she was shell shocked to find the suite empty. Crazily running from room to room pointlessly searching she realized with sickening certainty that Beth had already left.

Trying to suppress the panic flooding through her she snatched up the telephone summoning Reception. Yes, a faceless female voice confirmed, her companion had left. Lou dropped the receiver into its cradle, cursing herself. What had she allowed to happen? Better get after her quick, put things right. Buzzing reception again, she ordered a taxi.

Sensing Lou's urgency the driver put his foot down and within minutes she was standing in Kings Cross station, watching the northbound train disappear into the distance. She knew Beth was on the train, she'd spotted her down at the far end of the platform about to board. Shouting first, and then screaming Beth's name desperately trying to attract her attention, she didn't care when people turned to stare at the weeping madwoman.

Chapter 41

Two weeks later a despondent Lou, still in her dressing gown, sat in her kitchen gazing aimlessly out of the window, when she should have been in California having the time of her life with Beth. Her search to find Beth had been relentless yet she was no further forward. How could someone just disappear off the face of the earth?

After she had watched Beth step onto the train she rushed back to the hotel, swiftly packed and went straight back to Kings Cross to catch the next train home. Feeling the cold hand of fate closing round her she arrived home expecting to find a fuming Beth ready to do battle. Instead Fran confirmed her fears that Beth had already been and gone, refusing to talk to her.

Driving her BMW like a maniac up to Newcastle, she arrived at Beth's flat to find nothing. It was cold and empty. She left a message on the kitchen pinboard pleading with her to make contact.

She had bombarded Lindsay with phone calls. Truthfully Lindsay insisted she knew nothing, and although she didn't say so, Lou could tell she was furious with her.

She rang the hospital every day seeking information. This morning Janet had promised to contact her should they hear from Beth, patiently explaining again they didn't expect to as Miss McConnell was on annual leave.

Today she had to decide about America. Should she go or should she stay. She didn't care either way. The telephone rang interrupting her reverie. Listlessly she trailed across the kitchen to answer it. It was Sarah.

'Sit down and listen to me Lou.' Sarah spoke firmly.

Lou sat. What the hell, she had nothing better to do.

'It was Beth who made you see what you were turning down. Right?'

'Right.'

'Then you *have* to go, for *her*…if you don't, you'll be letting her down.' Sarah talked. Lou listened, finally heeding her words and her sound advice. Eventually she agreed to go. Sarah would sort out everything for her, like always.

'Sarah…thanks. You're right, I can't stay here. I'll go tomorrow.' And I won't have to act the part: I can play heartbroken by acting naturally Lou thought, full of self pity as she closed the kitchen door behind her, heading for the stables to tell Fran of her plans. She would never ever forgive Vanessa for doing what she did.

At least there wouldn't be any awkward questions in America; nothing had changed with the work situation there.

Chapter 42

Beth stretched across from the sun lounger to reach for her glass of orange juice. She was beautifully tanned from two weeks in the sun, but worry lines were noticeably etched into her normally smooth forehead.

Cannes had welcomed her with open arms. She hadn't planned to come here in her dash to the airport to escape. She hadn't planned to go anywhere in particular, just to get a seat on the first plane out regardless of its destination.

The concierge at The Grand Hotel had felt an immediate empathy with her. Consequently she was ushered into one of their most exquisite suites, her every whim instantly attended to. It all only served to deepen her sadness; she had never felt so utterly alone.

Placing her book face down on the small table beside her, she adjusted her gold rimmed sunglasses and idly glanced around at the other guests in The Grand's plush beach cabana. Some had unsuccessfully tried to befriend her, but gave up when she continually rebuffed their pleasantries. How could they be expected to know her heart was broken and she was incapable of talking to anyone?

Gazing out across the shimmering Mediterranean Ocean, Beth watched a cruise liner drop anchor. Soon its little tenders would start to ferry passengers ashore busily going backwards and forwards for the remainder of the day.

Suddenly restless, feeling the need to be active, she stood up deciding to walk along the Promenade, maybe even as far as the Marina today. I must be feeling better, she thought ironically, I've actually made a decision.

Waving to the waiters who had become her slaves, she collected her belongings, pushed them into her beach bag, wrapped herself in a stylish black and white silk sarong and set off.

It was much hotter up on the Promenade. The warm breeze caressing her face as she walked was refreshing. In another world, a world with Lou, she mused, this would be bliss.

The Marina was about a forty-minute stroll from her beach cabana. Beth observed the beach activity as she walked, people laughing, happy, having fun, together. If only…if only they had never gone to that blasted nightclub. If only Lou was here now. To her mind all the *if onlys* in the world sure as hell would not change things.

Yesterday, she'd got half way to the Marina then couldn't be bothered to walk any further because it was too hot. Instead she spent the afternoon in a secluded corner of a little café listlessly people watching.

Now, deep in thought and walking with her head down, she bumped into someone. Trying to gabble her apologies, she was startled when a young woman grabbed her wrist, speaking her name.

'Beth. I must talk to you.'

Brought back to reality, Beth stared at the woman. A gypsy, with dark skin and long jet black hair, wearing a red and gold flowing dress and flat brown leather sandals, blocked her way.

'What the? Who are you? And how do you know my name?' Beth tried to step back, to pull her hand away.

'Ask no questions. Just come with me. There are things you need to know.' The gypsy pulled Beth to a nearby seat.

At least she's not trying to rob me, thought Beth as her mind started to function.

'Sit.' The gypsy commanded.

'I have no money for you.' Beth said, matter of factly, as she sat down.

'You know I don't want your money, just give me your hand.'

Obediently Beth held out her right hand.

Studying her hand intently, the gypsy began, 'You've been terribly hurt recently, but things will come right. She is a good person. She loves you. It was all a terrible mistake. It will be sorted, in time. Think about it and you will see.'

Beth gasped in surprise, wanting to snatch her hand away, but at the same time wanting to hear more. How could this woman know? Why hadn't she known herself?

The gypsy continued, 'You must avoid the diamond people. They are dangerous and will hurt and use you. You must not let them.' She released her hold on Beth's hand. 'Heed my words, Beth. I've been sent to help you.'

Beth dropped her head fighting back tears, swallowing hard. Searching in her bag for her purse, she wanted to give the gypsy some money, she pulled out a handful of notes then looked up to say her thanks. She was alone.

Standing up, shading her eyes from the sun she couldn't see the gypsy woman anywhere. Where had she gone?

The only people around were a couple walking a black standard poodle through the nearby gardens. Beth approached them. Describing the gypsy, she asked if they'd noticed which way she went. The couple shook their heads, they had seen no-one.

Beth returned to the seat and sat down again, pushing the money back into her purse. Confused and convinced she was finally losing the plot, she sat for a few seconds with her eyes closed until a shadow in front of her blocked out the sun. Ha, she's come back for her money, Beth thought.

'Beth, darling, it *is* you. How wonderful. This is my lucky day.'

Beth stared vacantly into Hyacinth's face.

Taking her arm, Hyacinth cooed, 'Come with me, darling. I have The Amethyst docked in the Marina. We can spend some time together, catching up. We'll drink some champagne, I have your favourite on board.'

Like a zombie, Beth allowed Hyacinth to walk with her arm-in-arm to the berth where The Amethyst was moored.

Hyacinth was concerned about the state Beth was in. Instead of cracking open the champagne she ordered the chef to prepare smoked salmon and scrambled eggs on toast. Treating Beth with a care and tenderness she normally kept well hidden, she fussed over her, ensuring she ate every bit of the food.

The girl looks dreadful, she thought, heartbreak definitely doesn't suit her. A thousand questions were bursting to be asked, but she kept them in check, talking quietly, casually.

Full and relaxed for the first time since seeing Lou kissing Vanessa, Beth fell asleep.

Hyacinth sat with her like a guardian angel.

Eventually Beth stirred opening her eyes, 'Hyacinth I thought I was dreaming.'

'No, you're not dreaming, darling.' She signalled the cabin boy to bring some cold drinks. 'I've been thinking.' She paused. She had to play this sympathetically, strike the right note. 'Why don't you stay on board with me? No, don't decide now. Let me tell you what I'm planning first, see if it appeals to you.'

The cold drinks arrived. Beth took the chilled glass of lime and lemon without speaking.

'You've probably already realized I have a professional crew to look after everything,' Hyacinth waved her hand in indication, 'so much easier this way.'

Beth nodded.

'They are a good crew, they've been with me for some time. Now, darling, I don't plan to stay here in Cannes much longer, a couple of days perhaps, no more.' Hyacinth sipped her drink allowing the words to register in Beth's mind. 'I plan to sail across to Majorca and drop anchor for a while, and call in at Corsica. I haven't decided which way round to do it yet. What do you think? Perhaps Corsica first might be a good option?' she took another sip of her drink trying to gauge Beth's reaction, 'No strings, darling. I know you're unhappy, and I know why. I'm offering you some real time out. Absolutely no strings…one friend looking out for another.' She smiled her most devastating smile, so genuine it was almost tangible.

Beth was surprised at Hyacinth's invitation. They hadn't seen or spoken to each other for ages, yet here she was offering the hand of friendship. It sounded very tempting.

'Let me think about it, Hyacinth. I am grateful, really I am…but I'll not be good company and could spoil your holiday.'

'Of course you should think about it darling. Trust me, I'm a doctor and pampering in the sunshine, enjoying the sea air and getting some good food into you are just what the doctor ordered.'

Beth couldn't help but smile at the pun. Perhaps it wouldn't be such a bad idea after all.

'Sleep on it, darling. I'll still be here tomorrow. I have to meet an old friend tonight. Where did you say you're staying?'

'At The Grand.'

'Well, what a co-incidence. That's where I'm meeting my friend.'

The conversation lulled, Hyacinth didn't want to push it. She lay back on the lounger, pretending to read, yet still watching Beth. Had she pitched it right, would Beth accept her offer? Time would tell.

While Beth dozed, Hyacinth showered and changed ready for her meeting. Wearing a stunning black evening dress she gently shook Beth awake.

'You could sleep for England. I guess that's because you feel safe with me darling.'

'You know, Hyacinth, you could be right there.' Beth answered. In that moment she decided to accept Hyacinth's offer. It was good to feel safe and secure, but she would wait and tell her tomorrow.

They took a taxi to The Grand. Sitting together in the back Hyacinth took Beth's hand. Putting her original plans on hold she said, 'Why don't we explore the coastline tomorrow?'

Beth wavered, uncertain how to answer.

'Well darling, will I come to collect you in the morning?'

Beth nodded in agreement.

'About ten? We'll take The Amethyst and go and explore some beautiful coves. What do you say?'

'Thanks. It sounds wonderful.' Beth glanced out of the window, wondering if she would see the gypsy again. Turning her attention back to Hyacinth she asked, 'Why are you doing this?'

Hyacinth smiled, patted Beth on her knee, but didn't reply.

'Surely you must have better things to do. This is your holiday time after all.'

'It's a sort of working holiday, darling…and you are my friend.' She took a compact out of her handbag, flipped it open, checked her lipstick then finished answering, 'We may have had our differences, Beth, but you know how fond I am of you. And a friend in need and all that.' Her sympathetic tone almost reduced Beth to tears. 'I heard about Lou, and I am so sorry.'

This was the first time Lou's name had been mentioned all day and it nearly cracked Beth up. She swallowed hard, fighting to stem the flood of tears that threatened.

As they walked across The Grand Hotel's majestic reception hall she accepted Hyacinth's offer to join her on the boat, putting Hyacinth in an exceptionally good mood.

Before she could escape to her suite Hyacinth insisted on introducing her dinner companion. Expecting some glamorous woman Beth was gob smacked to meet Enzo Gonzales. A pleasant, rather nondescript man despite his expensive dinner suit, shook her hand. His only distinguishing feature apart from his mop of jet-black hair and edgy manner were his thick bushy eyebrows. He reminded her of a man she had seen at Ascot. Still, it was nothing to do with her who Hyacinth was meeting, she decided as she walked to the lift. As the lift doors opened at Beth's floor she thought it was time to let Lindsay know she was still on the planet.

Chapter 43

Hyacinth and Enzo were shown to their table in a secluded corner of the restaurant. As she walked Hyacinth's eyes swept the room for familiar faces. As usual it was full of the rich and famous. A group of twenty something's had taken over all of the window tables and were noisily enjoying themselves. Expensive gems flashed under the chandeliers, but nothing sparkled as vividly as the diamond necklace nestling around Hyacinth's throat.

She didn't care for Enzo, didn't like the way his sweaty hands carelessly wandered, but she had to be pleasant and put up with his schoolboy groping. He was essential to her plan. It was hard for her to concentrate on business when all the time her soul was singing out with the joy of finding Beth. Selfishly relishing how Lou's loss was now her gain. Penny would be furious.

At last the coffee and brandy arrived and as was the way of business between them, Enzo dipped into his pocket and pushed a small parcel, no bigger than a pack of cigarettes, across the table.

Hyacinth examined the contents, smiled, withdrew a fat envelope containing a wad of money from her handbag and pushed it across the table towards Enzo. The swap was done casually, mimicking an exchange of gifts between lovers, culminating with kisses.

Hyacinth wanted to be sick at the sloppy contact of Enzo's lips, cringing as his hands brushed her nipples. It took all of her willpower not to whack him across his smug Italian face. Steady girl, she warned herself, this is not the time to spoil the façade. She had not been able to resist a little personal trading while enjoying her solitary sunshine break.

They left the restaurant a short while later, standing close together in the warm night air maintaining the charade before climbing into different taxi's to go their separate ways. Hyacinth desperately wanted to storm Beth's room as incredible lust assailed her. Knowing she couldn't possibly do that, she returned to the boat to pleasure herself.

Constance held her breath as Hyacinth's eyes skimmed over her without any sign of recognition. The plain middle aged woman disguise worked perfectly. She was able to sit with her new friends and observe the exchange of parcels; diamonds and cash, no doubt. Excusing herself from the table, she telephoned her contacts alerting them to the situation, then went back to finish her meal. No need to draw attention to herself by leaving, and besides the food was delicious.

Chapter 44

Showered and wrapped in a fluffy bathrobe after another harrowing day, Lindsay hurried to answer the telephone.

'Hi'

'Beth! Where the fuck are you?'

'So nice to speak to you too.'

'I thought, hell…I don't know what I thought. Are you okay? Have you been in touch with Lou? She's frantic with worry. She's been pestering me every day. She doesn't believe I don't know where you are.' Pausing, expecting a response, she continued when none came, 'Where the hell are you?' her angry tone changed to concern, 'Do you need anything?'

'First off I'm staying at The Grand in Cannes and no thanks I don't need anything.' Beth deliberately didn't acknowledge the mention of Lou's name.

'Cannes, eh? Trust you to go somewhere plush.'

'Actually, it wasn't planned. I just got on the first plane I could. It didn't matter where it was going, Timbuktu or Toronto, I didn't care.' She paused to sip the chilled champagne she was holding. 'Cannes is a bonus though.'

'I'll bet it is. Beth, we have to talk about Lou.'

'No Lindsay we don't.'

'She's desperate to know where you are.'

'Tough.'

'Let me tell her you're okay at least.'

'Yes, you can tell her that, but no more. Make sure you let her know I don't need *her* to be able to get on with my life.'

'Beth…I thought you were in love with her.'

'I am, but that's not the point.'

'What is the point?'

'Vanessa.'

'Who?'

'Exactly!' Beth sipped the champagne again as her emotions started to run riot. 'Ask her, and then see what she's got to say for herself.' Another sip, 'She didn't tell you about Vanessa, did she?'

Lindsay knew Beth would say no more so changed track. 'Okay I will. So…what are you doing with yourself? What are your plans?'

'I have the best tan ever.' Beth managed a chuckle knowing how Lindsay would be jealous, as her pale skin only ever burned red.

'Bitch.' Lindsay laughed.

'Tomorrow I'm joining a friend on her boat. We're going to explore the coastline.'

'Oh, sounds wonderful.'

'Yes, and you'll never guess who it is.'

'No, you're right, I won't.'

'It's Hyacinth.'

Lindsay wanted to scream in frustration. Here was her dearest friend with no idea she was being drawn into the midst of a diamond smuggling ring. And what was worse she couldn't tell her or yell at her to get on the next plane home. Drawing on all of her years of calm persuasion she knew she had to come across as normal.

'Well, fancy that. Hyacinth in Cannes. At least you've got a friendly face there now. What's her boat like?'

Beth described The Amethyst as best she could. She hadn't taken much notice of her surroundings whilst on board, but she did remember to mention the professional crew. Then she explained how Hyacinth turned up right after the encounter with the gypsy.

Lindsay wasn't surprised about the gypsy, and said so. Beth had always refused to acknowledge her unusual psychic gift, to learn and explore its possibilities.

'Give me your telephone number so I can keep tabs on you or at least switch your mobile on.' Lindsay joked.

'Okay, I'll give you the hotel number and I'll switch my mobile on in the morning.'

'I'll ring you tomorrow night. You can tell me about your day with the lovely Hyacinth.'

As soon as Lindsay replaced the receiver her telephone rang again.

'Hello.'

She listened briefly before interrupting, 'Constance, we have a problem. I've just spoken to Beth. She's in Cannes with Hyacinth.'

Beth was enjoying a blissful day on board The Amethyst. Hyacinth, the perfect hostess ensured everything was relaxed, without pressure or effort.

They anchored at a jetty in a beautiful secluded cove over lunchtime swimming in the clear blue water while the crew set up everything for the chef to prepare a beach barbecue.

After lunch, while Beth and Hyacinth were stretched out under purple and pink beach umbrellas, three attractive women appeared from a narrow pathway hidden between the rocks.

Dumping their stuff a good distance away from Hyacinth's party they ran for the coolness of the water, noisily splashing each other and generally larking about.

Disturbed by their frivolity Hyacinth raised herself up on her elbows watching them with the intensity of a predator. Beth gave them no more than a cursory glance before closing her eyes again. They didn't raise a flicker of interest in her.

When the women came out of the sea they shook out their colourful beach towels ready to stretch out in the sunshine. Hyacinth got up from her lounger and walked over to them. Her gracious offer of cool drinks was immediately accepted and soon all four were enjoying Bucks Fizz, chatting like long lost friends.

Beth could hear snippets of the conversation, but had no inclination to join in. Wishing they would shut up and go away so she could sleep, one sentence hit her with crystal clarity. They said they were on holiday from California. That did it. Suddenly she was wracked with a gut wrenching longing for Lou. Drowning in waves of emotion she gripped the sides of the sun lounger to steady herself in a vain effort to suppress the sobs threatening to overcome her; the mention of California had finally cracked her emotional paralysis.

She needed to be with Lou. Her sense of reasoning managed to scream at her, successfully breaking through the solid wall she had built in her mind, launching her onto an emotional roller coaster.

Sitting bolt upright she looked over at Hyacinth who was still entertaining the strangers. Overcome with urgency she scrambled to her feet then started to gather her things together.

Hyacinth was quick to notice Beth's distress and, leaving her new found friends, hurried back.

'I'm sorry, Hyacinth, but I have to go. I need to find Lou. Really, I do.' Beth's voice although quiet was determined.

'Yes, of course you do, darling.'

Two hours later Beth was back in her hotel suite preparing to leave for LA. Her flight arrangements were already in place, organized by the experienced hotel reception staff.

Hyacinth helped her to pack, adding a little surprise package of her own, and then accompanied her to the airport in a taxi holding her hand all the way. She was gutted Beth was leaving her, but in true ice maiden style she wished Beth well while successfully hiding her real emotions. She imagined her heart would break as she watched Beth walk away from her again.

Chapter 45

With butterflies in her tummy, and an aching body and soul from lack of sleep, Beth's plane touched down in LA.

Had she done the right thing? Was Lou still here? She'd find out soon enough.

Her chauffeur driven limo glided through the traffic taking her to The Ambassador Hotel. The hotel she should have been staying in with Lou. It seemed as good a place as any to start looking. In her rush she never thought to contact Sarah, Lou's agent, who would have been more than pleased to tell her exactly where Lou was staying.

Lou's director thought she was marvellous. He was in awe of someone so young and beautiful who could portray a grieving widow with such depth and intensity. She is an enigma though, Al decided. All work and no play. She wouldn't even go for a meal or a drink with some of the crew after the days shooting finished, preferring to head straight back to the house they had rented for her in Bel Air.

Today he had been able to call a wrap in record time despite the fact they had reached a particularly intense part of the film and he'd envisaged doing take after take. He had even boosted the budget to cover it. Clever Lou had got it in one and saved him a fortune. To show his thanks he was determined to take her to dinner tonight. He wasn't going to take no for an answer, and was surprised when she accepted his invitation to dine with him and his wife Zandra. Perhaps it was because Dee was going to be there too. He had noticed how Dee was the only person who Lou really talked to. He was wise to the fact that actors liked to keep makeup artists sweet knowing they could make or break them, but his intuition told him this was something more.

Lou had been feeling peculiar all day, uneasy, sort of expectant yet still in the depths of despair. She dialled Lindsay's number and was devastated to learn Beth was in Cannes. She should be crying she told herself as she replaced the receiver, but she was way past tears.

Dry-eyed and without thought, she showered and dressed for dinner. At least Dee would be there with Al and Zandra so the night should not be too tedious. Dee had instinctively sensed Lou's anguish, and became a friend and confidant, giving strong unconditional support just when Lou needed it most.

Checking her reflection in the full-length dressing room mirrors before leaving Lou was appalled at the sad, frail reflection staring back. The expensive black dress did nothing for her except to emphasize her over thin body and the haunting sadness in her eyes.

Right Lou, this cannot go on, she sternly told herself. Get changed, you're supposed to look glamorous for God's sake not like a skeleton in mourning.

Going back to the closet she pulled out the slinky, scarlet Versace gown she had bought especially to wear for Beth.

What is the point of saving this she thought, sensuously fingering the liquid material, it's not going to happen. Beth's on the other side of the world thanks to Vanessa. She would never understand in a million years why Nessa had done what she did. Even when she'd demanded an explanation Vanessa had refused point blank to give one, and was shifty and evasive, insisting she had her reasons, but unwilling to look Lou in the eye.

Lou changed, leaving the discarded black dress on the floor. The red dress was perfect. The silk skimmed her figure, rising high at her neckline, dipping low on her back. Its sumptuous folds disguised her protruding bones and put some much needed colour into her pale face. After applying scarlet lip-gloss she rummaged through her shoeboxes searching for suitable shoes, but was disturbed when the gate buzzer sounded. She had to rush, her driver was impatient to take her on her way.

In The Ambassador Hotel restaurant Al, Zandra and Dee were already seated at their table waiting for Lou. Ultimately, they enjoyed a pleasant evening with Dee fussing over Lou like a Jewish mother and Lou actually managed to eat a little of the fillet steak the head chef cooked especially for her.

While Lou was in the restaurant, Beth was upstairs contemplating her next move. She sat out on the balcony in the warm night air gazing at the bright lights along Wilshire Boulevard asking herself why she had been so foolish to come here. Feeling silly at her impulsive flight to LA, lost because she was here alone and couldn't reach Lindsay on the telephone, she had an impulse to get out of her room, to explore the shopping mall in the hotel. The need for retail therapy, she decided, should not be ignored. Picking up her shoulder bag she headed for the lifts.

Sifting through the stylish clothes on offer, Beth's attention was naturally drawn to the jewellery section. Here items were cleverly displayed in glass cabinets enabling browsers to view the goods and see into the restaurant. Obviously done this way so romantic purchasers can look into the restaurant and imagine the exotic gems adorning their lovers thought Beth. Perfect for impulsive gestures.

While she studied a tray of diamond rings a flash of scarlet in the restaurant distracted her. Peering through the glass into the crowded room she saw Lou wearing her beautiful scarlet gown. Laughing and at ease in the company of three other people; she didn't give the impression of a woman suffering any kind of heartbreak.

Transfixed Beth stood watching her, torn between the desire to rush in and take Lou in her arms or turn tail and run. They looked like a happy foursome enjoying an intimate get together. The dark skinned beauty was paying Lou a lot of attention. When she lifted Lou's hand to her lips and kissed it Beth cried out in anguish as her tears started to flow. Devastated at what she had seen she ran to the lifts and the safety of her room.

Lou's happy, she looks great, she has someone else, and she doesn't need me. I was stupid to think she might. Beth's harsh thoughts punished her relentlessly. Home, I must get home, get the hell out of here she sobbed.

Lou was not enjoying the evening, although no-one would ever have known. Pulling on every resource learned from her acting career, she portrayed the successful, happy, carefree young woman with convincing panache. Even when Dee paid her the huge compliment of being the easiest actress in the world to make up, kissing her hand in appreciation, her heart cried out for Beth. Would she ever see her again?

Finally the meal was over and Lou was able to excuse herself because of an early morning call. Thanking Al and Zandra for a delightful evening, she insisted they stay with Dee and finish their brandy, then left the noisy restaurant desperate for the solitude of her temporary home in Bel Air.

Two taxis left The Ambassador hotel from different exits, sitting alongside each other, engines idling, waiting to join the line of traffic. Both girls sat back, eyes closed, experiencing different kinds of relief. Simultaneously both cars moved forward gliding effortlessly into the traffic, heading off in opposite directions. One to Bel Air and the other to the airport. If only Lou or Beth had looked up, both of their prayers would have been answered.

Chapter 46

Three weeks later Beth returned to work. She did her job with the utmost professionalism as always, returning late every night to her empty flat, deliberately exhausting herself so she was too tired to think before falling asleep. After three solitary weekends she felt the need to go and spend time with her family.

Calling at Fenwick's Department Store in central Newcastle, she bought everything for her little niece that took her fancy including a huge teddy bear she would need to strap into the passenger seat.

The weekend was successful. It was exactly what Beth needed, but she was ready to return to Newcastle early on Sunday evening. Catherine tried several times to talk about the situation with Lou. Stubborn as ever, Beth refused to be drawn into a discussion, closing her ears and her heart to Catherine's attempts to help.

Waving goodbye she headed back to Newcastle, to meet up with Hyacinth who was proving to be a real friend. Despite still being in Cannes she had arranged extra time away from the hospital for Beth when she'd returned from LA, and kept in constant touch with her. Tonight Hyacinth was home from the Med. and they were meeting for supper. Unsurprisingly, David was not at home.

Hyacinth had prepared a table for them beside the indoor swimming pool. She planned to keep things easy and relaxed, plus this gave her the chance to see Beth wearing very little.

Beth was flattered at the trouble Hyacinth had taken for her and after supper said so.

'It's time we had you back in circulation, darling.' Hyacinth poured Beth another glass of champagne.

'I'm not ready, Hyacinth. It's hard enough going to work at the moment.'

'Nonsense! I know just the thing…a party.'

'God, not a party. I can't be bothered to socialize. It's hard enough being with people at work without having to have to talk to people I probably don't even know.'

'But you do know them, darling. It's Julie's birthday party I'm talking about…and you and I are going together.'

Beth frowned.

'Don't scowl darling, it doesn't suit you. Just trust me…you know I won't let anything awful happen to you, don't you?' Hyacinth stepped behind Beth's chair and started to massage her shoulders.

'I guess so, Hyacinth.'

Beth felt the knots in her tired, weary body relaxing under Hyacinth's expert fingers. The poolroom was a haven of tranquillity. Candles burned between the plants casting flickering shadows, the temperature was just right and the reflection from the pool danced on the ceiling.

Beth started to unwind for the first time in weeks. She liked the feel of Hyacinth's hands on her shoulders. She tried to find the words to thank her for her help.

Graciously brushing her thanks aside, Hyacinth sensed Beth was becoming sexually aroused. Keeping up her constant stroking and massaging she brushed her hands over the rise of Beth's breasts, savouring every second of doing so.

Beth's body was responding to Hyacinth's touch. She really should stop her, but couldn't, and she gasped with pleasure when Hyacinth's hands slipped down the top of her swimsuit to caress her bare breasts.

'Are you ready, darling?'

'Yes.'

Hyacinth took Beth's hand and led the way to the guest bedroom. At last Beth was going to be hers.

The telephone rang only once before Hyacinth snatched it up. 'I told you I didn't want to be disturbed tonight.' she growled.

Her caller was brief and to the point.

'Give me half an hour and I'll be there.'

The caller hung up.

Checking Beth was still sleeping, Hyacinth slipped out of bed, pulled on some black jeans and a black zipped jacket then headed for the Quayside.

Her contact was waiting and the small package passed between them without comment. This was an unexpected delivery. Selecting Enzo's number in her mobile phone, she drove home slowly, puzzled by his answers. It was obvious he was hiding something, but what? He seemed scared and her blood ran cold at the thought of The Syndicate putting pressure on him.

Beth was still sleeping when she returned. Had anyone needed to ask her she would have sworn Hyacinth had been with her all night.

Chapter 47

The following night Hyacinth and Beth called at Penny's, something to do with Julie's birthday party arrangements, Hyacinth told her. They hadn't been there long when Penny asked Beth if she would mind fetching her diary from her office. Beth found it difficult to be rude, so she went along to the office to get it. While she was searching around the surprisingly untidy room she noticed an old typewriter half hidden behind a pile of books. For some unknown reason the blackmail letters clicked into her mind. Grabbing a piece of paper, she rolled it into the typewriter then hit every key as fast as she could hoping no-one would hear the clatter. Stuffing the paper into her jeans pocket, she grabbed the diary and hurried back to the drawing room.

Back home she checked the typed sheet against the blackmail letter she still had. On both sheets the 'm' key was misaligned. The witch, she's done them herself. But why?

Come on Lindsay pick the phone up.

'Lindsay thank goodness I've caught you.'

'Beth, what's wrong, has something happened? It's not Lou again is it?'

'No. It's the typewriter, I've found it at Penny's.'

'Typewriter, what typewriter?'

'The one used for the blackmail letters to Penny and Lady Ashton.'

'Oh that typewriter.'

'Penny must have typed them herself, I checked the keys and the wonky *m* key matches the letters.'

'Yes, I know, it was a rouse. I should have done her for wasting police time but she was clever and never made it official.'

'Oh well thanks very much for telling me!' Beth was annoyed.

'Sorry love, but I completely forgot about it. How are you doing? Are you feeling stronger?'

'Yes I'm okay thanks.' Beth purposely didn't mention her dalliance with Hyacinth.

'I'm glad you're feeling stronger because I'm going to be out of circulation for a while. I have to go undercover. I can't expand, as usual, but there is something big going down and I shouldn't be out of reach too long.' Lindsay loved the buzz undercover work brought with it even though it was terribly risky. So she had a long-standing arrangement with Beth in case things went pear shaped and something terminal happened to her.

Chapter 48

Julie's party night arrived. The dress code on the invitation had been specific; evening dress and diamonds. Beth had found the perfect dress, a slender pale lilac creation in shimmering silk, with a deep plunging halter neck. She had decided to wear her hair down and was the perfect match for Hyacinth, who wore a rich purple Valentino dress and her hair, like Beth's, was flowing free around her shoulders. Entering the ballroom Hyacinth bore Beth on her arm like a trophy and Beth's choice of dress unintentionally made them look very much together. The knowing glances exchanged between some of the women were lost on Beth as the crowd parted allowing them clear access across the ballroom floor to where Julie and Davinia were seated.

Beth's birthday gift to Julie paled into insignificance against the exotic dragonfly diamond pin Hyacinth presented to her.

'Hyacinth, what a beautiful piece of jewellery.' Beth exclaimed in delight.

'Yes, it is exquisite, isn't it darling. My friend at Ambleside made it, do you remember I mentioned her to you ages ago... the day we went walking in Langdale.'

Beth looked puzzled, concentrating, then her memory clicked, 'Why, yes Hyacinth. I do remember. Her work is divine. I would like to meet her, perhaps she would make something for me.'

Savouring the prospect of a weekend at The Country Club Hotel with Beth, Hyacinth answered, 'My darling, I'll take you. Soon.'

Hyacinth never left Beth's side, sticking to her like glue, subtly ensuring her champagne glass was never empty. A number of guests recognized Beth and waved to her in acknowledgment. Beth was enchanted at the attention. This was briefly dampened somewhat when Daphne, whom Beth had not seen since she left St. Gregory's, totally ignored her. Petra was kept busy supervising the hired in staff and didn't have any time to mix with the guests. Beth thought this was probably a good thing, being kept fully occupied she wouldn't have the opportunity to cause mischief and get Beth into trouble.

When Beth managed to slip away alone to the bathroom she saw Penny and Felicity disappear into a bedroom.

Should she be a spoilsport and go in? No, she couldn't spoil their fun. Or could she? Feeling wicked she went to open the door. As she reached for the handle the floorboards creaked. Shit, I'm going to blow this, she thought. Turning the handle she pushed the door open laughing at the scene she expected to see, already apologizing, 'Whoops, sorry! Thought this was the bathroom.'

The room was empty. But how could that be? She had just watched them come in. How had they got out? There was only one door. Where the hell were they?

Mystified she rejoined the party. Penny and Felicity were nowhere to be seen; they seemed to have disappeared into thin air. And where was Hyacinth?

Beth walked the full length of the ballroom looking carefully at the women dancing. As she passed one or two tried to pull her into the throng. Tactfully she refused.

Standing by the far window gave Beth the perfect vantage point for surveying the entire room. Suddenly her attention was drawn to the mirrored walls. Light reflected in response to the movement of a concealed door opening behind one of the large sound speakers. Funny, she hadn't noticed it before.

Felicity emerged seeming to float across to the drinks table. Collecting two bottles of wine she floated back out the same way.

Intrigued Beth followed her. Making her way towards the doorway, she stopped to chat briefly so that her intention was not obvious. Ducking behind the speaker she pushed at the mirrors until one moved revealing a passageway.

Aha, so this is how they do their disappearing act. This old place must be riddled with secret passages she thought, pausing to allow her eyes time to adjust to the darkness. Even so she could barely see and could just about distinguish a dim light in the distance. She crept forward carefully, lifting her long skirt with one hand, stumbling a little on the uneven flags as she felt her way along the wall with the other.

The unpleasant atmosphere, cold, damp and musty, repelled her. She shuddered at the thought of huge spiders dropping onto her bare shoulders when cobwebs brushed across her face, but carried on regardless, overcome by curiosity. She stopped dead in her tracks when she heard voices. Straining her ears, she listened, not daring to move. She couldn't tell what they were saying. It sounded like gibberish, some kind of chant. Then it stopped and an eerie silence hung in the air.

Beth held her breath, audibly gasping when Hyacinth spoke, her voice carrying clearly.

'Ladies…the diamonds!'

Why, it's as if she's giving a toast, Beth thought. How bizarre. Why would anybody want to toast diamonds? God. I must have drunk too much, my head's swimming. Time to go back to the party.

As she turned, her foot slipped and she fell heavily, dropping the glass she had been clutching. The crystal shattered loudly as it hit the flagstones. Shit, she cursed oh shit, now I've blown it, they'll have heard that.

Hopelessly she tried to scramble back onto her feet without cutting herself. She couldn't get up. The drink was really taking effect now and there were shards of glass everywhere threatening to cut her fingers. Sitting still in an attempt to get her head back into gear, she tried to focus on an approaching figure.

Felicity hurried towards the noise, her purple silk cloak billowing around her. 'Beth. What the hell are you doing here?' she demanded while carefully helping Beth to her feet.

Beth tried to answer, unable to take her eyes off the diamond pendant hanging around Felicity's neck. 'Shorry, Flissh! Made a mishtake, opened the wrong door.' she slurred, 'Nish pendant!'

'Oh Beth you opened the wrong door all right. And you're drunk. What has Hyacinth given you to drink? You had better come with me. Be careful of that broken glass.'

Felicity led the way into a circular room that Beth, even in her confused state, recognized as some kind of grotto. The room glowed in candlelight yet Beth was not able to see everything clearly. She was conscious of other people standing in the shadows all wearing the same sort of cloak as Fliss.

Lavish purple and gilt regency style sofas were arranged in a circle. Fliss led her into the middle and Beth was surprised to be standing on a rug. Funny place to store such lovely furniture she thought ironically.

The grotto was silent. Beth looked towards an altar draped in purple and silver silk holding exotically scented candles arranged to represent the eight compass points. The candle's heady fragrance filled the air wafting on unseen thermals. Beside them glasses of red wine were placed in a figure of eight representing eternal infinity. Beth wobbled, she was having difficulty standing up and her eyes blurred into double vision.

Even so she thought the alter looked beautiful especially when the centre of the candles began to sparkle. Before she could make out what it was that was sparkling, Penny spoke.

'Sit down, Beth.'

'Err, I fink I'd better get back to the party Penny…if you don't mind.' Beth said nervously.

'No, Beth. That is not possible. You have seen too much… sit down.' It was a command, not a request.

Beth sat. Scared now and feeling claustrophobic she wondered who else knew about this weird place.

Penny spoke again, gentler this time, 'Well, Beth dear. Now that you are here, we can play a little game together, can't we?' She was in front of Beth now bending forward to touch her cheek, her silk cloak brushed Beth's shoulders.

'Game? A game Penny? How nish. What sh…short of game do you want to play?' Beth giggled.

The other hooded figures, standing motionless until then, turned in unison to face Penny.

'A game of truth.' Penny said triumphantly.

Well, this should be easy, Beth thought, they're just messing about. All she need do was humour them then they would leave her alone. She was rapidly sobering up.

Felicity stepped forward with a blindfold as Penny pulled Beth's hands behind her back, tying them with a silk scarf just tight enough to make Beth wince, and panic. Good grief, maybe this is not a silly game after all.

'Hyacinth!' she shouted. 'Hyacinth! Where are you…? I *know* you are here. What are they doing to me? What's going on?' Beth's voice echoed along the myriad of passageways.

Hands on her shoulders pushed her forward off the seat until she was kneeling on a cushion. Someone smeared a sticky substance onto her lips, it was tangy, and tasted like bitter orange. She tried to keep her lips together, failing as a segment of orange was forced into her mouth. It was too bitter a taste to be just fruit.

They've dipped it in alcohol or maybe poison, Beth thought. She was forced to eat it, unable to refuse otherwise she would have choked.

She was woozy when Penny spoke again, 'Beth you must tell me what you know about the diamonds.'

'Diamonds? What diamonds? Do you mean the one's Hyacinth was toasting just now? That's a funny thing to do, isn't it? I've never heard anyone do that before.' Beth's voice was vague.

'Tell me what you know about the diamonds, Beth. Who have you told about them?' Penny insisted.

'What do you mean?' Beth paused. 'The diamond pendants some of the girls wear? What a funny question Penny. I haven't told anyone about them. What's to tell? The girls have excellent taste.'

'Yes, Beth, they do. Well done! Now, can you tell me anything else?'

Beth paused briefly before answering, 'Well, no I can't. Except that I would like to have one of those pendants…they are very beautiful and I adore diamonds and the way they sparkle…like stars in the sky. Do you think you can you get me one Penny?'

The energy in the room lightened and standing beside the altar Hyacinth breathed a massive sigh of relief.

Beth began to feel clammy and shaky. Where was Hyacinth?

Then Felicity spoke, 'We should initiate Beth into our little group Penny. She's such a beauty.'

Nice of you to think so, Beth thought. She didn't reply, just listened, still curious and still woozy.

'Once you are part of us, Beth you can't leave. We will always look after you, in all respects, but I must warn you however, if you got any silly ideas and tried to hurt *any* of us then you would face serious consequences. Or your family would. Have I made myself clear?' Penny said firmly.

Beth's heart started racing. What is this *us*? It must be a gang of sorts, but who was in it? What had she got herself into? She wanted the blindfold off, her hands untied and the hoods removed from the women so she could see their faces. Anger stirred in her veins as she tried to stand up, only to be pushed back down again.

In her befuddled state Beth heard the footsteps and voices echoing along the passageway. As they came closer she heard the group greet Julie and Davinia.

Then the chanting started again. Beth could sense people moving nearer to her, circling. Someone sprinkled her with water.

Her knees had started to cramp and her back ached. Her bones felt as if she had been in this position forever. She'd had enough of this silly game. She wanted out, now.

Warm breath fanned her face, someone was too close invading her aura, lips touched hers. Was the truth game turning into a sex game? What was coming next? Matching her thoughts she felt a series of soft lips sensuously brushing across hers.

Next several pairs of hands started to touch her, stroking, seeking, invading, moving all over her body. She felt herself surrendering to the erotic sexual sensations. Not resisting as her clothes were removed with the minimum of effort. She was aware of standing naked, except for the blindfold.

Someone wrapped a robe around her before she was lowered on to a bed of cushions on the floor. Laying either side of her, the women took it in turn to languidly lick her nipples and then their tongues seemed to be everywhere at once.

She reached out to touch her seducers, but someone took hold of her hands whispering, 'No, darling, just go with the flow. I promise you'll enjoy this.'

Will I Hyacinth? Beth wanted to ask, but she was unable to speak. The blindfold remained. She wasn't capable of thinking clearly. She wasn't capable of thinking much at all. What had they put on the orange and what was in the delicious wine they kept feeding her?

Her legs were parted, her body invaded by hands and tongues working to bring her to a state of tremendous arousal. Every woman wanted a piece of her. Tongues and fingers worked in and out of her wetness, teasing, making magic. Beth was moaning with pleasure when the dildo slid inside of her. Successfully wrenching her hands free she pulled off the blindfold. She had to see who was on top of her, riding her.

'Lou!'

'Sssshhhh, relax baby, it's me.'

Her body responded of its own accord as her hips rose up eager to greet the sensations Lou was creating. Tossing her head to the side as she went over the edge into orgasm she opened her eyes momentarily. Petra was lying beside her. 'Going down!' she slavered, licking her lips in greedy anticipation.

Beth was being devoured and loving it, relishing the caresses of the women, her body soared. She was the kingpin in this glorious orgy of feminine abandonment, and loving it.

She felt Lou roll off her, watching in amazement as she started to fuck a total stranger.

Then Beth cried out as Petra's tongue expertly teased her clitoris. She was just about to crest her second orgasm when a deafening bang exploded in her head.

Chapter 49

Beth's head ached. Aware she was lying in a bed, she raised her arm to shield her eyes and found herself next to Petra. Struggling to lean on her elbow, she tried to focus on her surroundings.

Where was Lou and the other women? Beth tried to remember. Then she saw the dildo at the bottom of the bed. She rubbed her eyes hoping she was dreaming.

Closing her eyes she willed herself to wake up again. But she was awake. Vague images began to filter through her mind. Exactly what had gone on the night before? For the life of her she couldn't remember.

Struggling, she sat up. Petra was sleeping. Had she slept with her? A picture flashed through her mind, she could almost feel Petra's tongue caressing her clitoris. Other images crowded in, Lou sitting astride her. Hyacinth stroking her breasts while cradling her head, Fliss and Penny exploring her naked body, women she didn't know having uninhibited sex together, taking turns with her.

Dazed, Beth swung her legs over the side of the bed, examining herself for evidence of sex. She was sore and sticky and the inside of her legs was starting to bruise.

Petra opened her eyes.

'Please, tell me what happened.'

'Did you not enjoy, my Beth?'

'I can't remember anything - who else was here? Was I drugged?'

'Vot do you mean? Drugged? Are you crazzzy? Who elze vould be here exzept uz?' Petra was indignant.

'I had this dream. It was so vivid. Lou was in it, she was making love to me.'

Petra smiled impishly, but gave nothing away, just snuggled back into the bed, holding the duvet up around her neck making it impossible for Beth to see if she was naked.

Beth tried to convince herself Petra was just being a bitch. But deep down in the pit of her stomach she had a terrible feeling her visions were real.

Sitting on the side of the bed shivering, Beth tried to piece together the events of the previous night, from when she and Hyacinth arrived at the party. She couldn't. Her memory was like a jig saw puzzle with the main pieces missing.

Warning Petra not to tell anyone what had happened between them she left her looking smug and went to find Felicity.

She was alone drinking tea in the conservatory.

'Good morning, Beth. Is Petra looking after you? Hyacinth told her she mustn't leave you until she got back. You do know she's been called to the hospital, don't you?'

Beth didn't acknowledge Felicity's words, but immediately bombarded her with questions about the coven.

Treating Beth as if she had completely lost the plot, Felicity pressed her to sit down and drink a cup of hot, sweet tea. She went on to explain in detail how she and Penny had put her to bed after finding her worse for wear on the bathroom floor.

Of course, Beth didn't believe her. She got the distinct impression Felicity was being deliberately blasé, covering something up.

In her dream, if that's what it was, she had been given something that tasted bitter. She was sure they had drugged her, but why? It couldn't have been just for the group sex. What the fuck was going on?

In an attempt to stop Beth's barrage of unwanted questions Felicity invited her to go riding with her and Penny.

How can she act so normal? Beth wondered as Felicity put down the morning paper.

'Go on then. Get ready. The fresh air will help to clear your head. By the time we have a canter through the park Hyacinth should be back. Okay?'

Reluctantly Beth agreed, 'Yes, alright. Give me time to shower and change.'

Beth returned to her room expecting to find Petra waiting for her. She had left and in her place was a breakfast tray laden with hot coffee and warm croissants. The room was in perfect order, curtains fastened back and the bed made. Housekeeping must have swept through like a tornado, Beth thought, picking at the croissants.

Felicity had the horses ready and waiting when Beth arrived in the stable yard. When Beth pulled on her riding hat, it felt like a vice, but was pleased gentle Phantom was her ride. Mounting gingerly, wishing she was somewhere else, she said, 'I'm sorry. I can't do this. I feel terribly sick. I'll have to get off. I need to lie down.'

Penny would not hear of it. 'Oh come on...you'll feel heaps better once you get some fresh air into your lungs. Too much champagne, Beth. You really must learn when to stop.'

'That's if it was the champagne,' her eyes challenged Penny who did not respond.

Phantom, aware there was something wrong with her rider, took responsibility. Beth was able to sit easily and let the horse carry her, allowing her to observe the interaction between Felicity and Penny. She needed to know if they had anything to do with last night's events, actual or imagined. But they weren't giving anything away.

If I can get a good look around the house on my own, she thought, I might find that grotto.

If there is one - her sense of reason chipped in. When they arrived back at the stables Penny insisted Beth go and rest. Shaking her head in such a way an aunt would do to her favourite niece, she turned Beth by the shoulders, pointed her towards the house, patted her bottom just a little too hard and said she would see to Phantom.

'A nice warm bath is what you need now. Get Petra to run it for you - she can wash your back.' Penny leered at her. Felicity giggled.

Stuff the bath, thought Beth. She was off to do some searching.

Hurrying across the courtyard into the kitchen she noticed Davinia and Julie were busy in the rose-garden. Knowing she was safe for a while because Davinia would keep Julie there for ages, she smiled politely at the cook before heading to the ballroom.

She found Lord Macfarline in there. She couldn't breeze in and start tapping on the wood panels nor check the wall mirrors or he would think she was bonkers.

Backing out of the doorway before he noticed her, she ran upstairs into the bedroom where Penny and Felicity had disappeared. Closing the door quietly behind her she started to methodically feel along the walls. She discovered a button, like a doorbell, at the side of a long wall mirror. Tentatively she pressed it and the mirror slid silently to one side revealing a steep, stone spiral staircase.

Bingo! She flicked a light switch on just inside the doorway and a dim light shone onto the stairs lighting up the gloom below. Just then she heard floorboards creaking along the hallway. Someone was coming. Grabbing the handle on the back of the mirror Beth stepped over the threshold and pulled the mirror across, sealing the doorway. Crossing her fingers that she would be able to get back out, she decided that she may as well investigate further.

The dim glow lit her way as she crept carefully down the steps, feeling dizzy by the time she reached the bottom. A familiar smell of damp greeted her as she crept along the passageway. Beth was surprised, and grateful, when the sensor lights in the wall lit up. At the end of the passageway she found the grotto.

Not knowing whether she was relieved or not, fear gripped her. God, it hadn't been a dream after all. Standing in the middle of the room she closed her eyes, concentrating hard, trying to relive what had happened.

But, how could she? She was unable to separate fact from fiction. Opening her eyes she walked the circle of the grotto. There was no furniture stored in here, no evidence of candles or regalia, but there was a strong smell of incense; she did recognize that.

The place was empty. As she looked closer at the area where the altar had been set out she spied a mound of candle wax that had dripped onto the floor.

Deep in thought she walked back and climbed gingerly up the steps to the bedroom, but couldn't find the fiddly catch to let herself out. She wasn't fazed by that, just tired and unhappy. She retraced her steps. She would find the other door and get out that way. At a fork in the passageway she hesitated unsure of which way to go.

The second tunnel led to where she had entered the previous evening from the ballroom. Easing the door slightly open she could see Lord Macfarline still messing about in there. Cursing him under her breath, she turned back again to try the other route. This one led into a small opening, just big enough for her to crawl through. After she managed to squeeze through she was faced with a solid wooden door. Grabbing the handle she pulled hard. It refused to budge.

Panic raced through her. I'll never get out of here. I'm trapped and nobody knows I'm in here. I want Lou, the love of my life. I need to see her to sort things out. Doubting Lou would be prepared to give her the time of day, she looked up in despair and saw a flicker of daylight high above her head.

Convinced the only way out was to climb up to the light she decided to take the chance. As she started to climb her hand encountered something warm and furry. Sure the rats from hell had descended on her, she screamed and dropped back to the ground.

She fought for air as palpitations rushed up into her throat threatening to choke her. Unable to breathe as panic took hold she tried desperately to get a grip and put her sensible doctors head on. She talked to herself, telling herself to take some deep breaths and control this horrible panic attack. She eventually succeeded, and was relieved to be able to breathe normally again.

Her best option was to go back and wait by the door leading into the ballroom. Lord Macfarline would not be in there forever, would he? Why didn't you think of that before? her inner voice chided.

After slowly counting to one hundred to steady her breathing and stem the panic still simmering within her, she started to make her way back to the ballroom. Pausing in the grotto, she experienced several realistic flashbacks. Visualizing the altar wall, she stared in disbelief as the images lingered enabling her to identify its exact position. It was like recalling memories from the twilight zone.

For goodness sake Beth, it's only a stone wall, her subconscious shouted. Regardless, she needed to examine it again. In her mind she could see lighted candles set in a circle. She reeled when a faint whiff of exotic fragrance stirred her senses.

Digging into her jacket pocket for the torch she suddenly remembered she'd brought, she flashed it across the floor. She had no idea what she was looking for, but there had to be something to confirm the activities in here.

Kneeling down, holding the torch in one hand, she brushed the other carefully over the cold stone floor, disappointed nothing was to be found except a piece of glass. She picked it up, shone the torch on it and gasped. Nestled in the palm of her hand a diamond the size of an old fashioned sixpence sparkled.

With sickening certainty she knew for definite that last night had been real. Something had sparkled in the candlelight, it must have been diamonds, and then there was Hyacinth saying *to the diamonds* or something like that. And Penny's peculiar interrogation about diamonds. What a weird going on. Lindsay will just love this one. There's something much more than sex games happening here.

She knew she had to get as far away from here as possible without raising any suspicion. Racing back to her room through the now empty ballroom she packed her bag and left Melton Manor without a backward glance. Driving the Jaguar like someone possessed she arrived back at her flat in record time.

Double locking and bolting her flat door behind her, she rang Lindsay immediately and without pausing for breath told her everything. Lindsay was astonished at Beth's story about the sex orgy in the grotto, but not surprised to hear about the diamonds.

'Beth, I know this will sound heartless after what you've told me, but I need to know…where is the diamond you found?'

'Why, I have it with me, of course. It's in my jeans pocket.'

'I need you to put it somewhere safe. You must not tell anyone about it. Do you understand?'

'Yes. I'm not stupid you know.'

'Well the jury's still out on that one. I don't know, the things you manage to get yourself into. Anyway, listen. I've been trying to get in touch with you because Lou's…'

'Lindsay, I….'

'No. Now Beth, shut up and listen to me. Lou's provisionally booked a ticket for you to fly out to LA in a couple of day's time. And you lady, are going.'

Briefly Beth's heart sang. Obviously Lou still loved her, but what about the grotto?

'Lindsay, please don't…you know how much I love her, but how can I go now?'

'You *are* going, because I'm putting you on the plane myself. No arguments. I'll be with you tomorrow and after we've dealt with the other stuff we'll go out and buy you some new gear so you'll look even more drop dead gorgeous, than usual. She'll not be able to resist you.'

'Thanks Lindsay. What would I do without you?'

'God knows, girl. God knows. Just one more thing and this *is* important, best not let anyone know you are home. Especially Hyacinth.'

'Why? What's going on? Why especially Hyacinth? She's been good to me lately - it's something to do with this diamond, isn't it?'

'Can't say...just promise me?'

'Okay, I promise.' Beth knew it was pointless to argue.

Chapter 50

Lindsay arrived mid-afternoon the following day. True to her word Beth had not left the flat despite being driven crazy by the constant ringing of the telephone.

Sitting at the dining room table, which was now covered in pages of Lindsay's notes, Beth knew how it must feel to be under interrogation. Lindsay wanted to know every single detail about the party. Who was there, what they wore, even what they ate, going over it again and again until Beth was certain she'd told her everything she could. When she was confident Beth couldn't tell her anymore, Lindsay dropped her bombshell.

'You do realize we'll have to go back there, don't you? I need to suss out this place for myself.'

Beth had already handed the diamond over and as far as she was concerned, that was it, she was never going back. 'I can't Lindsay. I'm sorry, I just can't go back there. And you shouldn't ask me to, you don't know what I went through in that grotto, I don't exactly know myself. No, sorry. Not going. I'm a surgeon for God's sake, not a police officer.'

Lindsay hugged Beth, knowing she was traumatized and hated herself for insisting. 'Don't worry. We'll not be going alone and we won't be announcing our arrival. We'll sneak in from the grounds, through that door you told me about...'

Panicking Beth cut her short shouting, 'Don't worry! Are you mad? And who else will be coming on this expedition?'

'Constance.'

'Constance? Why her? What has she got to do with this?'

'Beth, listen to me - there is something you need to know.'

'Oh God...now what?'

Five am and they were up with the larks. Looking like an advert for Charlie's Angels the three girls swooped on Melton Manor.

Beth dropped Lindsay and Constance off at the back of the stables where there was a little used drive that couldn't be seen from the main house. Then she parked nearby, waiting, worried to death about what they were doing and hoping she hadn't messed up the plan she had drawn them. Providing she had got it right, Lindsay would know exactly where to go. It should take them under an hour to do their search.

Lindsay and Constance synchronized watches then set off. Running, keeping low, Lindsay led the way skirting through the grounds successfully finding the door near to the carp filled pond.

The heavy door looked as though it would be difficult to open, but with one good tug it swung back on well-oiled hinges. Interesting, thought Lindsay.

Nodding to Constance they stepped inside switching on powerful torches to light their way.

Lindsay spoke, 'For God's sake be careful.'

Constance nodded closing the door behind them.

Waiting in the car Beth tried to pass the time by concentrating on Lou; they would be together again soon. If it wasn't for this bloody carry on, she could have been on a plane today. She was aching to see her.

And Beth still didn't fully believe the story Lindsay told her. It was only because Constance had so convincingly backed her up that she'd agreed to help today. Who is Constance exactly, just what is she all about? Beth's thoughts raced on. She's a friend of Hyacinth's, and Penny's. And Constance had warned her off Hyacinth, said she'd had an affair with her and that she was a vicious bitch who dabbled in magic. The magic turned out to be true enough though, but then Constance had been with them all at Badminton and Ascot.

Whose team is she really playing for, the police or Hyacinth's? Beth didn't know. Giving up on the puzzle she checked her watch for what seemed like the millionth time.

Her thoughts switched to Hyacinth. Beth was furious at the way Hyacinth had used her, watching and encouraging the women in their sex games with her in the grotto scenario. How could anyone be so callously perverted? Beth shook her head in despair. In her heart she would ensure that one day Hyacinth paid for what she had done, yet Beth still could not believe it had really happened.

The minutes ticked by, it was over an hour now. Where the hell were they? Checking her watch again, Beth was starting to worry, she decided to wait another ten minutes. If they had not come back by then she would go and look for them.

Ten minutes later she climbed out of the car and ran swiftly through the grounds. At one point she nearly bumped into the gardener. Careful, Beth, she warned herself as she crept round the back of the house dodging between the trees and shrubs.

She remembered from her first visit here how Davinia mentioned a tunnel hidden behind the dining room fireplace that came out somewhere in the garden. She wondered if Lindsay and Constance might turn up at that exit. Frantically she searched for something that resembled a doorway of sorts. Sighing with relief she thought she had found it. She was wrong.

She decided to call upon her angels for help. Standing still, she raised both arms high above her head, closed her eyes and concentrated hard on Lindsay and Constance.

Val had always insisted she had a gift, but what a time to put it to the test.

Minutes later instinct directed her towards some unused buildings. As she went in she heard tapping. Looking up she saw a small door a good way up a high wall.

She needed something to stand on to reach it. Pulling an old chair from under some bits of wood she dragged it across the floor and positioned it underneath. The chair wobbled, it was riddled with woodworm. Crossing her fingers she climbed up praying she could reach. The tapping started again.

'Lindsay. It's Beth. Is that you? Are you both all right?' she called.

'Beth, how did you find us? No, never mind just get us out.' Lindsay's voice sounded hoarse. 'We're fine, but we're stuck in here. This sodding place is a maze of tunnels, we took a wrong turn.'

'Beth, is the door locked? We can't budge it.' Constance asked.

'Yes. It's got a whacking great padlock on it.'

'Shit!' Constance cursed.

'Don't worry guys. I'll get you out.' Beth said with more confidence than she felt.

What she needed was a wrench. Jumping off the chair she searched around for something suitable and found an old metal bar. Perfect. Balancing on the chair again, with the grace of a ballerina, but the strength of a builder, she eventually managed to lever the door open.

'Did you find what you were looking for?' Beth asked when they were safely back in her kitchen sitting round the table drinking hot coffee.

Constance answered, 'No, not a bloody thing.'

Lindsay remained silent, turning her head to gaze out of the window deliberately avoiding Beth's eyes. She had never been any good at lying to her.

'We'll have to leave it now. Let the powers that be take it on from here.' Lindsay eventually spoke.

'What about Hyacinth?' Beth asked.

Lindsay shrugged her shoulders, thankful when Beth went to answer the phone.

It was Lou ringing from LA. At first the conversation was shaky, neither girl knowing exactly what to say, both worried they would get it wrong. Beth desperately wanted to pour out how much she loved her, what a fool she had been, how she ached for her, needed to see her, but foolish pride and a terrific sense of guilt held the words back.

'Did Lindsay tell you about the flight?' Lou asked cautiously.

'Yes. Thank you.'

'Will you come?'

'I don't know. There's a lot going on here.' Understatement, she thought.

'Beth, I love you.'

'I love you too, but you still have a lot of crawling to do.' And so will I if everything that happened in the cellar's true.

That did it. The conversation turned the corner and Lindsay, listening from the hallway knowing Beth would soon be safely on other side of the world, went to tell Constance.

Chapter 51

As promised Lindsay personally put Beth onto the plane, suitably impressed that Lou had booked her a first class ticket. Only the best was good enough for her friend, and Lou had better do right by her. She'd had several long, strong telephone conversations with her on that score, but in her heart knew she had no need to worry. Hyacinth had a lot to answer for though.

Beth hugged Lindsay tight before they parted, thanking her for being the best friend in the whole world. And the best liar, Lindsay thought, as she hugged Beth back.

On board the plane, Jerry the campest air steward ever, rushed to fuss around Beth, he always laid claim to the most beautiful girls. He would die to have this one's cheekbones and made a great show of taking Beth to her seat and settling her in.

After searching for travel bands in her handbag, she glanced around at her fellow travellers. Not many people in first class she thought, idly noticing the empty seats opposite her. A member of the cabin crew was about to close the door when a young blonde girl jettisoned unceremoniously into the cabin. Jerry was not pleased about this late arrival and scowled at her, allowing his disdain to show.

Serena had only just made the flight by the skin of her teeth and did not want to cause any waves. She was under strict instructions to be inconspicuous, so with a smile that would charm the hardest of hearts she summoned Jerry to apologize.

In response to her buzzer, he minced along the cabin to her seat. Serena hit him with dazzling blue eyes, softly spoken apologies, made it obvious they were on the same wavelength, and minutes later he was her slave.

Beth was impressed. She had just witnessed a performance worthy of Hyacinth. Come to think of it, the girl bore an uncanny resemblance to Hyacinth, and she was sure they had met before.

Once airborne she tried to strike up a conversation with the younger girl who was seated opposite, but Serena feigned sleep. If she messed up Penny would kill her.

Beth didn't care. Her real thoughts were completely taken up with seeing Lou again, generating butterflies in her tummy. Restlessly she switched between trying to read her book, watching the in-flight film and dozing.

Coming in to land Beth sensed a change in the cabin's energy. Jerry, in particular, seemed uneasy. Beth half expected an announcement from the Captain informing them something was wrong. None came. The plane landed without incident and taxied to a halt.

Looking out of the window Beth was surprised to see armed police standing on the tarmac. She glanced across the aisle at Serena. Why, thought Beth, she looks terrified.

Serena was terrified and certain the police were waiting for her. Her blue eyes became dark pools of fear when two officers, one plain clothed, the other uniformed and carrying a gun, entered the cabin.

With a faint attempt at normality, Serena picked up her handbag, opened it and was about to reach inside when her wrist was grabbed by the uniformed officer and held rigid.

'Looking for something Miss?'

'My lip gloss, Officer.'

'Serena Gardner-Shaw I am arresting you on suspicion of diamond smuggling. You do not have to say anything, but anything you do say will be taken down and may be used in evidence against you.'

Beth and the rest of the passengers watched in horror as the plain clothed officer handcuffed Serena and escorted her off the plane into a waiting police car.

'Of course, I knew all along.' Jerry could be heard saying to his fellow crew members. 'She had that look about her. You know what I mean.'

Beth doubted his colleagues had any idea what he meant, but she knew. Oh yes, she knew - just wait until she got on the phone to Lindsay.

Chapter 52

Beth passed through customs and into the waiting car Lou had arranged to collect her. As she climbed elegantly into the back of his limousine chauffeur Kevin approved of Lou's choice. No wonder she has been so miserable leaving this beauty behind. And Miss McConnell has a nice personality too, he thought as they chatted about the weather while he expertly negotiated his way out of the airport onto the Freeway. He knew all to well from past experience that sometimes these lookers were as hard as nails, but not this one, she was the genuine article. Lucky Lou.

Beth was impressed with Lou's temporary home in Bel Air. She was aware that Lou would still be filming on set, and was not prepared for the genuine warm reception the housekeeper gave her. Typical, Beth thought, everyone loves Lou.

She gratefully accepted the housekeeper's offer to run her a bath, she could certainly do with a long soak after eleven hours sitting on a plane. Waiting until the woman disappeared out of sight at the top of the curved marble staircase Beth checked her watch and then picked up the telephone.

'I am sorry madam, I'm afraid it is not possible for you to speak to Inspector Powell,' a reedy female voice told her.

No it wouldn't be, thought Beth, she's probably off somewhere secret by now, doing God knows what. She spoke firmly to the reedy voice, 'It is imperative that I speak with Inspector Powell. Please ask her to ring me on this number, regardless of the time.' She repeated the telephone number twice and then made her repeat it back.

Pushing all thoughts of Lindsay, Hyacinth and diamonds out of her mind, she went to soak in the bath to prepare herself for Lou.

Scented and ready, Beth lay on the bed. Jet lag struck and she was sleeping soundly when Lou returned from her days filming. Becoming conscious of cramp in her arm, Beth opened her eyes to see Lou's lovely face close to hers.

'Hello sleeping beauty. Welcome to LA.'

Gathering Beth into her arms as if she were the most precious thing in the world, Lou kissed her passionately. Words were unnecessary, actions saying it all.

They had a lot of catching up to do. Between making love, eating and sleeping, they lost the next forty-eight hours in a haven of bliss.

'How about we hit Rodeo Drive today?' Lou asked while they enjoyed an early morning swim.

'Great. We can do some serious shopping. I've always wanted to do the Pretty Woman thing,' Beth laughed as she floated on her back gazing up into the clear blue sky.

Over a poolside breakfast of fresh Californian orange juice and croissants Lou attempted to explain about Vanessa.

Beth didn't want to go there; she had her own dark secret to resolve. Bending forward across the glass topped table she put her finger to Lou's lips, 'Shush now, I want to hear no more about it. We are here, together and that is all I care about.'

'But, Beth sweetheart, I need for you to know I wasn't doing anything wrong. I would never...'

Beth silenced her with croissant kisses, 'I know baby, I know.'

They spent the entire day shopping on Rodeo Drive. Taking a break for a late lunch they went into a restaurant. As they stepped onto the escalator Beth spotted an attractive blonde. Indicating her to Lou, she turned to get a better look when the escalator reached the top unceremoniously throwing her off. Embarrassed, tightly clutching her shopping bags, Beth looked up to see if anyone had noticed.

Of course everyone stopped what they were doing to stare at her. For a second no-one moved, then Beth started to laugh. Several people came to her aid, checking she was unhurt, and asked could they get her anything?

After Beth assured everyone it was just her pride that was hurt she turned shamefully to Lou who laughingly poked her on the arm, 'That will teach you not to ogle other women!' she said.

'Point taken.' Beth giggled while checking to make sure nothing had spilled out of her designer shopping bags.

Later, when Kevin came to collect them, Beth noticed a copy of the LA Times on the front passenger seat. The headline stood out.

Exposed
International Diamond Smugglers

Alongside the text was a photograph of Serena with the caption 'Arrested at LAX'.

'Kevin, do you think I could have your newspaper, please? When you're finished with it, that is.'

'Sure ma'am, with pleasure. Take it with you.'

Beth reached for the paper. This would make interesting reading.

'Lou, are you sure Lindsay hasn't tried to get in touch with me?'

'No, honey, she hasn't. I've checked with the answer service myself.'

Bloody hell, thought Beth, if it's this that's stopping Lindsay from making contact, it must be big.

Back at the house she rang Lindsay's home number, the answer machine kicked in. 'You'd better ring me, you bastard. I want to know what's going on. Serena Gardner-Shaw was arrested on *my* flight.'

Lindsay picked up the phone, 'Hello Beth, how are you?' she enquired sweetly.

'What the fuck is going on?' Beth demanded, struggling not to raise her voice, not wanting Lou to hear the conversation.

'There is nothing for you to worry about. It's all been sorted out. Just enjoy yourself…How is Lou by the way?'

Lindsay's attempt at general conversation was infuriating Beth. 'LINDSAY!'

'Okay, Okay, keep you're hair on. I'll tell you.'

Half an hour later Beth walked into the state of the art kitchen where Lou had started cooking the food left out for them by the housekeeper.

'Everything all right, honey? You're looking a bit off.' Lou asked.

'Yes, fine. Thanks. I'm just a bit tired sweetheart, lack of sleep and too much sex. Probably all your fault.' Beth chuckled. She was turning into an expert liar.

The newspaper was lying on the kitchen bench. Lou pointed to it with a knife. 'That girl…Serena Gardner-Shaw,' she stabbed at the photograph, 'is the girl who had gone missing when we first met up in Yorkshire. What a coincidence.'

They smiled at each other, both recalling the erotic memory.

'Seems the police eventually found her. No wonder she went missing. Have you read this? Diamond smuggling of all things.'

'Really? No…I haven't read it yet.' Beth lied.

'Oh you should. Here…read it now.' Lou pushed the newspaper along the bench towards Beth. 'Would you believe it…it was organized by a group of women.'

Obediently Beth took the newspaper making a pretence of reading the article. Thankfully the food was ready and Lou dished up a delicious looking pasta concoction saving her from continuing the conversation. She would not be raising the subject again and quickly pushed the newspaper into a cupboard in the hope the out of sight out of mind saying would be effective on Lou.

Suddenly Beth lost her appetite. Pushing the food around her plate unable to eat she had an urgent need for fresh air.

'There is something wrong…what's up hon?' Lou asked, concerned.

'Delayed jet lag, I think. I'm sorry, you've gone to so much trouble…cooking, but I just can't eat. I think I need some fresh air. Can we go out?'

Lou was surprised at the request to go out again because they had been out all day. But as far as she was concerned whatever Beth wanted was fine by her. 'I know just the place for some sex al fresco if you're game for it.'

'Mmmm…now you're talking.'

Sitting in Lou's car in the deepening twilight they looked out over the Hollywood Hills watching the twinkling lights in the distance.

'Beth, there is something I want to ask you.'

'Oh, what?'

'Well…oh hell, here goes…the thing is..,' Lou paused to swallow, her throat unexpectedly dry, 'Well, it's like this…I love you and I hate being parted from you. Please come and live with me. I want us to be together.'

It wasn't the question Beth expected. Flinging her arms around Lou's neck she cried, 'Oh Lou. Yes. Yes, I will. I hate being without you too.'

Her lips sought Lou's, and passion exploded the second their lips met. With tongues entwined and hearts racing, Lou's hand stroked Beth's thigh. She was in the mood to tease.

Recognizing Lou's game Beth played along. She kissed her neck, nibbled her ear, played with her nipples. Then she ran her fingers up and down Lou's arms, sensually stroking before she took hold of her hands. Lou was rising out of her seat, wanting more.

Slipping off Lou's jacket and the top that barely covered her breasts, Beth removed Lou's wisp of a bra with one hand. She tickled and licked Lou's nipples with her tongue, curbing the temptation to put her hand between Lou's legs, she wanted her to savour every moment.

'In my bag…a little vibrator.' Lou gasped.

'Lou! Talk about being prepared for emergencies!' Beth giggled as she reached across for it.

She set the vibrator on a slow speed and began to caress Lou's breasts, rolling it in circular movements around her extremely aroused nipples.

Restricted in the front seats they climbed into the back. Beth's fingers pushed between Lou's legs touching her soaked panties, turning Lou on even more. Beth was going to make her wait despite the fact she was bursting herself as Lou's fingers expertly worked her nipples.

She ran the vibrator across the inside of Lou's thighs, before pulling her panties to one side and letting it hover above her bulging clitoris creating tremendous sensations.

'Beth. Please.' Lou moaned. She raised her buttocks urging Beth to slip it inside of her.

'Soon, baby, soon.' Beth whispered, tantalizing her some more before sliding it slowly in ensuring Lou would enjoy the full penetration.

As the vibrator slid into Lou, her fingers took control of Beth's clitoris. Together their orgasms started to flow, waves of ecstasy carrying them into a crashing climax. Holding each other tightly they savoured the joy of riding them out together.

Beth couldn't sleep. Despite the great sex earlier in the evening, the sweetness of reconciliation and making plans to live together, she should be in seventh heaven. Instead her conscience was far from clear. Visions of Hyacinth holding a baby drifted in and out of her mind, mixed up with scenes from the grotto. And then she saw Fliss, Montanna and Lou all floating in a star studded night sky wearing nothing but purple satin robes.

Chapter 53

All too soon Beth would be back in the UK, in a few short hours Kevin would be taking her to the airport. She would have preferred to slip away quietly without another tearful parting, but Lou was determined to get some time off from filming and be there for when she boarded her flight. Pushing off from the side of the pool Beth swam another four laps before flipping over to float on her back contemplating her return to normality. In truth she would have been happy to stay here with Lou. But in reality she had responsibilities her conscientious nature would not let her neglect. However, she had decided to submit her resignation to St. Gregory's as soon as she returned and then hot foot it back to Lou. She was determined they were not going to be separated for a second longer than necessary.

The sound of her mobile ringing disturbed her reverie. Guessing it would be Lou she climbed out of the pool grabbing a towel as she ran across the tiles to answer it.

Without taking note of the caller's number she automatically spoke, 'Hello darling.'

'Why, hello my darling…I knew you would be pleased to hear from me.'

Beth stared at the phone in disbelief. 'Hyacinth!'

'Yes, of course it's me darling. Who did you expect? Oh I know, you thought it was Lou, didn't you?'

There was something eerie in the tone of Hyacinth's voice that Beth couldn't quite make out. Trying to banish the vision of suitcases that Hyacinth's voice conjured up in her mind she had to ask her to repeat what she'd just said.

'You're really not listening darling, are you? I said when you come home I will meet you at Edinburgh airport.'

'What on earth are you talking about Hyacinth? I'm flying into Manchester.'

'No, you're not. You and I are going to live happily ever after in Scotland. You liked my house there didn't you?'

'Hyacinth! Have you lost the plot?'

'Ah yes, the plot Beth. Do you know you have played an essential part in it? I really should thank you for doing it so efficiently.'

'What?' Despite the heat of the day Beth shivered, pulling the towel around her shoulders.

'Well, you're a professional Beth. On behalf of the Amethyst Group I would like to thank you for transporting our cargo around the world….The plot darling Beth as you so simply put it, is that you are carrying our uncut diamonds in your suitcases.'

'What!' Beth flopped down into a chair, the brilliance of the Californian day fading into nightmare alley.

'Yes, I knew you'd be pleased to hear how well you've done.' Hyacinth paused to light a cigarette. 'Now, where were we…oh yes, as I was saying, well, a girl needs some insurance, doesn't she? And you have been terribly obliging darling transporting them with you since Cannes…I helped you pack. Remember?'

'Hyacinth, are you having some kind of breakdown? You're talking in riddles.'

'No riddles, darling, actual fact…and your precious Lindsay won't be able to get you out of this one.'

'I don't believe you. Why are you doing this, why are you lying? More to the point…just what the hell do you want from me?'

'What do I want darling? Hyacinth said in a silky smooth voice. 'I want **you** of course. Now, listen carefully Beth. Go and look in every one of your suitcases…and I mean every one. See what you can find. Better check you're favourite handbag too. Be thorough, imagine you're a policewoman or, better still, airport customs. Now where would they look…? The linings perhaps - always a good place to start.'

Beth didn't answer. Galvanized into action she raced through to the spare room where her partly packed bags were set out. Dropping the phone onto the floor she launched herself at the biggest case examining the lining - nothing. Guided by instinct she started to feel the corners. Carefully squeezing the pleating around the seam she encountered something hard and gritty. Flabbergasted she looked closer at the stitching. It had been tampered with, but so cleverly as to go unnoticed. Frantically she ripped the seam open, pushed her hand inside and pulled out a small purple velvet bag. She didn't need to open it to confirm its contents. She knew this material only too well.

Sitting on the bed, her mind racing, she picked up the phone. 'Why, Hyacinth?'

'Because you belong to me and if this is the only way I can have you then so be it.'

'I don't belong to anyone Hyacinth.'

'Darling, we're going to have such a wonderful life, you and I.'

'No we are *not*. I am going to the police Hyacinth. You'll go to jail for this.'

'You're upset, darling, but don't worry. Of course I won't be going to jail…and neither will you if you play your cards right and do as I say. Now before we continue with our arrangements there is just one more little thing you need to do. Find Lou's cream Prada handbag and check it out.'

'No! I won't!'

'Do it now, Beth, my patience is wearing thin.'

'Don't threaten me you fucking bitch. I'm not frightened of you.'

'Darling, I don't want you to be frightened of me. And threaten you, why I would never do that. Have you got the bag yet?'

Flinging the closet door wide open Beth grabbed hold of Lou's bag. She examined it with shaking hands and found nothing. She had to go over it several times before she discovered the little velvet pouch. Knowing she was beaten she started to retch. What now?

'Now, the fact darling, is that Lou is your accomplice. Clever, eh?' Hyacinth paused allowing the enormity of her words time to register. Callously laughing she continued, 'You can't refute facts, Beth. And now that we understand each other, this is how it's going to be.'

As Hyacinth talked, the cold hand of fear gripped Beth's heart. The devious bitch had it all sewn up. No matter what she tried to do, which way she might try to go, Hyacinth had already been there and blocked her.

'Now don't disappoint me, darling. I'll be waiting.' Hyacinth took a long draw from her cigarette then continued,

'I can see it now darling, just you and I sailing off into the sunset aboard The Amethyst.'

'You flatter yourself Hyacinth. You and I are not sailing anywhere.' Beth's voice was firm.

'We shall see darling. Test me if you must, if you are prepared for your precious Lou to come crashing down off her pedestal that is. I expect you've been completely honest with her, haven't you?' she paused to extinguish her cigarette allowing Beth time to consider her predicament. 'You were such a willing participant at our little gathering in the grotto, do you know darling, the camera's absolutely loved you.'

Beth looked at the stack of velvet bags on the bed; seven in all containing an absolute fortune in diamonds. Oh, she could contact the police, tell them her story, but it would be totally wiped out by Hyacinth's cunning plans and willing accomplices. They would confirm Beth was the kingpin in their operation. Or, she could take the diamonds and put them in a safe deposit box at the nearest bank, but that bastard Hyacinth even had that avenue covered, she had spun her web so cleverly that Beth could see no way out. Beth couldn't risk bringing Lou into this mess; it would ruin her career. But how the hell the diamonds had got into her bag was a mystery that only went to prove how wide Hyacinth cast her net. If only she could contact Lindsay.

Knowing it was fruitless she tried her number anyway. As she'd expected Lindsay's mobile was switched off. Shit, why the hell did she have to be working undercover right now?

Shaking with fear and frustration Beth started pacing the room. What the hell was she going to do?

Chapter 54

Flight 326 from LAX touched down on time. To match the dismay seeping into her soul, they had flown in almost constant darkness. Beth stayed in her seat not wanting to leave the plane until she was the last passenger to disembark knowing when she did her life would never be the same again.

Beth wanted to leave Lou a letter explaining why she could never see her again, but what could she say, not the truth, that was a certainty. Lou had been unable to get to the airport, so Beth was able to board the plane without a backward glance.

Going through customs slowly, trying to draw attention to herself, Beth prayed she would be stopped and searched. The diamonds were deliberately and carelessly pushed into her shoulder bag. Purposely, she'd left it open so that the pouches could be clearly seen. No such luck, she was waved straight through.

With immaculately styled hair, wearing cowboy boots and a long camel cashmere coat over tight fitting denims and a pale lilac sweater, Hyacinth greeted Beth effusively. Linking arms with her she led them straight to the baggage carousel waiting while a porter loaded Beth's bags onto a trolley.

'I want a coffee Hyacinth.' Beth demanded.

'Of course, darling. We'll pop into the restaurant before we go.' Hyacinth spoke to her as she would to a child.

Beth's bags were loaded into a four track and the porter was generously tipped before Hyacinth spoke again.

'I'm so glad you decided to join me, Beth darling. It would have been dreadful if you had made the wrong choice, all that terrible publicity for Lou. She would probably never have worked again, you know, and no doubt you would have been struck off the medical register by the time the press was finished with you. It's so much better this way. I can promise you a wonderful life darling, a Scottish winter and then Paris in the spring.'

Beth didn't answer.

'Coffee was it, darling? Right, let's head over there.' Taking Beth's arm again she had to almost drag her towards the restaurant.

Lindsay watched in disbelief as Hyacinth almost frog marched her best friend through the length of Edinburgh Airport unable to do anything because she would blow her cover. Frustrated she had to watch Beth pass her so closely she could have touched her; it was obvious she was in severe distress.

Hyacinth walked past the restaurant into the deserted bar. Still holding Beth firmly by the elbow she charmed one of the bar staff into bringing their drinks to the table.

'Now darling, how are you?' Hyacinth had the nerve to act concerned.

'Are you stupid?' Beth's tone was icy.

'Don't take that attitude with me Beth. Remember I can make your life unbearable if you don't do as...'she stopped mid-sentence as the waiter brought their drinks undergoing a personality change. 'Thank you for being so kind. Sudden bereavement is terribly difficult to come to terms with.' She patted Beth's hand indicating concern.

The young waiter left them to it. The brunette looked ready to be put into a box herself.

'Drink this.' Hyacinth ordered as she pushed the large brandy across the table. She had requested orange juice for herself.

Beth took several gulps of the amber liquid. She was chilled to the bone. Maybe the brandy would help to warm her up. After ten minutes of total silence she spoke calmly.

'I want to know everything. You owe me that at least.'

'You know everything you need to know darling. Now don't push it.'

Hyacinth held her breath unsure what to expect. In truth she didn't know Beth that well, although she was aware Beth had another side to her, a fiery side, and that all added to the attraction.

Beth was seething. At the very least she wanted to scratch Hyacinth's eyes out and was drawing on every ounce of her reserve to remain calm and collected. She needed a plan, but right now how that was going to be formed, she hadn't the faintest idea.

Finishing the brandy she spoke again. 'As I said Hyacinth, I want to know everything…now.'

'Oh how dreary of you to insist, darling. Actually there is someone who can explain things much better than me, but we need to be home for you to hear it.'

'What are you talking about?'

'Why, darling, the whole world will know about how Penny ran her diamond smuggling ring when they tune in to the late News tonight.'

Beth stood up. Hyacinth was one cool customer, at the moment unchallengeable, but somehow Beth would make her pay for this if it took her the rest of her life.

Purring with satisfaction as they left the bar, Hyacinth was feeling smug. As far as she was concerned she'd cracked it and Beth was hers for good. Eventually they would live happily ever after. She was sublimely convinced of her ability to make Beth fall totally in love with her.

A flight had just landed from Majorca. Its passengers shattered the early morning stillness of the airport as they surged through like a wave towards the taxi ranks engulfing the two women.

Loud and happy after their holidays, one group in particular zig zagged drunkenly in front of them. If Beth hadn't been so withdrawn she might have recognized Lindsay. Right on cue the group crashed into Hyacinth and Beth. Hyacinth was almost knocked off her feet and was forced to let go of Beth. Pre-occupied with staying upright, she didn't see Lindsay push a note into Beth's hand. It was perfectly choreographed.

Chapter 55

Beth read and re-read Lindsay's note:

H struck deal, turned Queen's evidence. P & others arrested. Will send help soon.

Sure this whole nightmare scenario would be resolved soon she tossed the note into the fire that Hyacinth had so obliging lit in the large bedroom. Then she climbed into bed her thoughts briefly bordering on the hysterical as she wondered if she should have eaten the note in true James Bond style, before falling into an exhausted sleep.

Hyacinth was downstairs on the phone listening to her solicitor who was confirming how most of the Amethyst Group, with the exception of Serena, had been arrested. The police were insisting she help flush her out. Hyacinth was furious; this had not been part of the deal and she wanted to scream that they could fucking well find her themselves. It was hardly surprising Serena had gone to ground after they'd cocked-up her arrest in America and had to let her go. She could still be there, or anywhere in the world for that matter.

Basically Hyacinth didn't give a shit about Serena. She knew she had plenty of time to play with before the police would summon her when the kid finally surfaced somewhere or other. Hyacinth intended to devote that time to conquering Beth. It was a pity Beth hadn't come to her willingly, but Hyacinth was so confident in her powers of persuasion she could not foresee a problem. Anyway a little reluctance usually added to the fun.

Beth slept for over twelve hours. When she awoke it was early evening and she could hear voices. Probably the television she thought.

Hyacinth and Angela were sitting outside enjoying the early September evening. It was their voices that drifted up to Beth's open bedroom window.

'Do you really know what you're doing Hyacinth?'

'Of course, I do darling.'

'Don't take this the wrong way, but I am concerned. Remember the rule of three?'

Stony silence as Hyacinth tossed her head impatiently not prepared to acknowledge Angela's words.

'Hyacinth…what you give out will come back three fold… you reap what you sow…need I go on?'

'I know, but I can't help myself. You don't really expect me to go to prison darling, do you?'

'How can I answer that? It's not diamonds I'm talking about Hyacinth…it's Beth. You are taking away her free will. We can't do that. You know that it's against everything we believe in.'

'I have to have her Angela.'

'No, you don't. *If* you are meant to be together, Beth will come to you willingly…not like this. I really don't agree with it. In fact, I'm appalled at what you've done. It's disgraceful, Hyacinth, how could you?'

This was the closest anyone had come to criticizing Hyacinth for years and she didn't like it, yet the element of truth struck its mark. She snatched her glass off the table and stormed into the house. Angela followed, not prepared to give up. The conversation continued inside, so Beth was unable to hear anymore.

Sitting on the edge of the bed, Beth realized she could have an ally in Angela. Better tread carefully though. Could she manage to play along until Lindsay's help arrived? She had no choice, she had to tread carefully until she got proof positive Lou was safely out of danger.

Showered, and dressed in denims and a white cotton shirt, Beth went downstairs into the drawing room. Hyacinth and Angela were discussing the weather and the forthcoming autumn solstice.

Hyacinth jumped up when she saw her, 'Darling, are you rested? You must be starving, come with me,' she spun Beth around and pushed her towards the kitchen, 'we have lots of food ready.' Looking over her shoulder at Angela, 'Come along, darling. We'll all eat together.' For once she did not want to be alone with Beth; she couldn't say why she felt unsettled, but blamed police harassment and Angela's criticism for it. Whatever it was she didn't like this feeling, it was alien to her.

To Beth's surprise the meal and next couple of hours passed without incident mainly because of how well she got on with Angela. The television was switched on in time for the late news. Beth watched the newscaster reporting how the members of an all-female diamond smuggling gang, known as The Amethyst Group, had been arrested. The gang had been under police surveillance for some time, they had operated worldwide and the successful arrests had been made due to the co-operation of an unnamed insider.

'British aristocracy will be stunned to learn Lady Penelope Corday, wife of Lord Albert Corday whose shipping empire is on the brink of bankruptcy, headed the operation assisted by Lady Davinia Macfarline better known to many as 'Davinia's Catering'. Her illegitimate daughter Felicity a successful event rider was also arrested along with Alison Hogan owner of the growing chain of Hogan's Health and Leisure Centre's and Montanna Gilby from San Diego. Several other women ranging in age from eighteen to fifty-nine are being held for further questioning at various police stations throughout the UK, including a jewellery designer from Cumbria, a corporate lawyer from the north-east of England and a Swedish Au Pair.'

Beth hung on to the newscasters every word, horrified at the mention of the corporate lawyer. How could Constance possibly be under arrest? Unable to trust herself to speak she left Hyacinth and Angela and went to her room. She needed to think.

A little while later Hyacinth breezed in. 'You see, darling, we'll be fine. The police can't touch us and we can live happily ever after.'

'I doubt that very much Hyacinth. There are practicalities even you can't sort out.'

'Believe me, Beth, there is *nothing* I can't sort out,' She replied darkly. 'Now, are you going to promise to stay in your room or do I have to lock you in?'

In reply Beth turned her back and walked over to the window.

Frustrated that she hadn't fallen gratefully into her arms, Hyacinth left her, locking the door between their adjoining rooms. Beth might have her own bathroom, but there was no way out except through this door or making a treacherously dangerous jump from the bedroom window. Tomorrow would be a better day. Beth would start to see sense tomorrow, Hyacinth was sublimely sure of it.

Following a night of careful deliberation Beth started to formulate her plan. Not knowing how long it might be before she could have contact with Lindsay, she decided her only alternative was to lull Hyacinth into a false sense of security. Angela could be constructive in that. Knowing how Hyacinth relished a challenge she would delight in taking that pleasure away from her by becoming the demure, subservient type – a mouse. Angela's job would be made easy and she just might relax her guard duties enough to give Beth the opportunity to contact Lindsay. Although how she would do that was another problem.

Over breakfast Beth put her plan into action. Finishing up the plateful of scrambled eggs on toast, although they had nearly choked her, she spoke as if she didn't have a care in the world. 'I was thinking we could have a run into Inverness today.'

Hyacinth was so surprised she almost spat her coffee across the table, 'What…? Inverness did you say?'

'Yes, if you don't mind. There are one or two things I need. We could go shopping together.' Playing it cool Beth sat back in her chair.

'We can certainly go into Inverness tomorrow, darling.' Hyacinth paused attempting to weigh up the situation before she continued, 'We can't go today, I have some business to attend to.'

'Tomorrow's fine.' Beth picked up her cup and went to look out of the window. After a few seconds of surveying the sun shinning on the Cairngorms, she looked over her shoulder, almost smiling at Hyacinth and said, 'It's going to be a warm day.'

Beth's calm attitude was confusing the hell out of Hyacinth.

'Angela will be here soon to keep you company until I get back.'

'Oh will she? How nice.' Beth's expression was tranquil. 'I hope she doesn't have far to travel. She should have stayed over.'

'No need, she's just along the road.' Hyacinth said brusquely.

'I think she's arrived.'

Frowning, Hyacinth picked up her shoulder bag and hurried outside to meet Angela. She didn't come back into the house. After speaking to Angela she climbed into her old Landrover scattering gravel as she sped down the drive.

Chapter 56

The next few days were an emotional roller coaster for Beth. The trip to Inverness never happened and she was unable to make any contact with anyone, despite the fact that Hyacinth was hardly ever home and her only companion was Angela. She fretted herself silly until her inner strength took over.

Angela did her job well. There were no telephones in the house and Beth had no interest in going out so their days were spent in comparative silence, reading and watching daytime television. Beth couldn't even write a letter, all the paper and pens were locked away. Her mobile phone had disappeared, as had her personal supply of pens and notelets. Hyacinth, leaving nothing to chance, had searched Beth's luggage on the first night confiscating anything she thought fit.

Frustrated, unhappy and bored, Beth went within herself searching for an answer, seeking a way out of this god awful mess. She had taken to standing gazing moodily out of the windows watching the ever-changing light on the Cairngorms. Angela felt desperately sorry for her, but was powerless to help.

The word meditation kept flashing into Beth's mind until she consciously acknowledged it. Okay, okay, I'll meditate, she said to herself. I've got sod all else to do and at least I can pretend to be somewhere else.

'Angela, I'm going to my room. I'm so bored I'm going to sleep for a while so please don't disturb me.'

'All right, Beth.' Angela acknowledged her request and settled back with her book.

Up in her room Beth lit a candle, placing it on the floor in front of her as she took up the Lotus position at the bottom of the bed. Resting her hands palms upwards she closed her eyes and cleared her mind with surprising ease. It wasn't as if she'd ever done this before, but it seemed the natural thing to do.

Focusing on the flame of the candle her mind went off on its own and a vision of Lou in LA took shape drifting into her subconscious. First Lou stood silently before her looking happy and radiant in her red silk dress. As that image faded it was replaced by another showing Lou working on set acting out one of the final scenes of her film. Finally she was home in her comfortable kitchen, dressed for riding, leaning against the Aga holding a mug of hot coffee as she often did. Beth could see it all so clearly she was able to identify the steam rising into the air from the hot drink. The aroma of strong coffee filled her nostrils and the hairs on the back of her neck stood on end as she heard Lou's voice and felt her warm breath caress her cheek. A gentle whisper, more like a sigh, 'Beth, my brave Beth, don't worry. You are not alone. We're all here. Waiting. Help is coming and we'll be together soon. I love you.'

Her meditation over, the tears cascaded down her cheeks as she gave in to the despair she'd been holding at bay since Hyacinth met her at the airport. Sobs racked her body as she climbed into bed and cried herself to sleep.

When Angela eventually came up to check on her, she was still sleeping. Reluctant to wake her and feeling guilty about her role as watchdog, she determined to make Beth's stay as pleasant as she could. After all, not even Hyacinth could keep the girl here indefinitely.

Chapter 57

Hyacinth slammed the gears of the Landrover as she skidded to a halt at the end of the drive. Bloody Angela, she mentally cursed, always lets her estate vehicles go to rot. The brakes took hold just in time to stop her from ploughing into a line of traffic speeding north along the A9. Rackety old thing, it just about bounced my tits off coming down that drive, Hyacinth cursed again. Suddenly laughing at herself she pulled out, crossing the now clear road turning right heading towards Perth. Already wishing she'd brought the Mercedes because it would take her at least two hours to reach Dorothy's in this old banger, but knowing it would kill the car's suspension going up the long rutted track, she put her foot down and got on with it.

An hour later her mobile beeped. She had a text message. Pulling over into the next lay-by she stared at the words: *You think you are clever, don't you? I'm watching you.*

Hyacinth had no idea who had sent it. She didn't recognize the number and wasn't sure if she should ignore it or reply demanding an explanation. She stared at the cars parked nearby trying to identify her caller. There was no passing traffic and the assorted vehicles in the scenic viewing parking bay opposite were all empty. Their lucky owners off hill walking, no doubt. She decided to ignore it, someone had obviously keyed in the wrong number. Crashing the gears again she shuddered down the road. If she ever reached her destination in this rust bucket it would be a miracle. Well, she decided she didn't have to put up with it. On the outskirts of Perth she pulled into the Mercedes garage and thirty minutes later drove out behind the wheel of a top of the range four wheel drive.

That's better, Hyacinth thought, and within a short time had bounced comfortably along the rough track to Dorothy's isolated home.

As she skidded to a halt outside of the front door her mobile beeped again. *Changing your car won't stop me* the message told her. Hyacinth looked around, there was absolutely no-one in sight, if there had been she would have been able to see them from up here, you could see for miles.

Who the fuck was messing with her and what the hell did they want? It'll be something to do with Penny Corday she was certain of it. She would make that bitch pay, revenge is sweet and not even Penny could imagine the terrible repercussions her betrayal of Hyacinth would generate.

Rattled, Hyacinth locked the four-track and went inside to be mobbed by Dorothy's dogs. She had always found them a nuisance, but today was glad of their large solid Rottweiller bodies, sharp hearing and deep menacing barks. Barks like theirs should be enough to warn anyone off.

Dorothy greeted her like a long lost daughter wrapping her in a great bear hug before pulling her into her over furnished living room. In front of the blazing fire Dorothy had set a tea tray in readiness. She had baked especially knowing that Hyacinth probably hadn't been eating properly. The dogs were going crazy all clamouring for attention and were in danger of upsetting the tray.

Laughing Hyacinth fussed them, 'Well Dot, it may have been a while but they haven't forgotten me, have they?'

'No, they haven't, but then again, who could?' Dorothy smiled fondly at the younger woman. She could still see her as the lost little soul who had stood before her on her first day at boarding school. Lost, but brimming with rebellion. As Matron, she took all of the girls under her wing, but Hyacinth was special and Dorothy had channelled the rebellion into productive energy. As far as Dorothy could see all Hyacinth needed was someone to love her, to care for her and she did just that in her role as surrogate mother. And Hyacinth had done her proud becoming a model student and Head Girl.

Oh Dorothy knew about the affairs with the other girls, and probably one or two members of staff. Naturally, she had turned a blind eye. Love is love and it doesn't matter where it comes from had always been her motto. Yet it had never come her way. Instead she had her dogs and she loved all three of them passionately.

And in her way Hyacinth loved Dorothy. She was the mother she'd never had and the one person she genuinely respected. No matter where her travels had taken her she had always kept in touch, sending letters and cards right up until Dorothy had been due to retire five years ago. Then Hyacinth had bought her this house and sent the deeds and keys together by special delivery. Dorothy had been wise enough not to look a gift horse in the mouth and her home had become Hyacinth's safe haven.

Bored now the dogs went to lie in the kitchen. Dorothy fussed over Hyacinth settling her into one of the two comfortable fireside chairs, plumping the cushions before allowing her to sit down. Then she poured a large cup of strong tea and handed it to Hyacinth. 'You must eat some of this food dear. I've made it especially for you. I think you are looking a tad too thin, I know it's hardly surprising with what you have gone through but you must keep your strength up.'

'Oh don't worry about me Dorothy, I'll be fine. I will have some cake though it looks delicious.'

'How can I not worry about you, you're like my own.'

They sat in companionable silence until Hyacinth spoke. 'It's not going to work with Beth.'

'I know dear, it is a shame for you. She looked beautiful in the photographs you sent me. The tarot cards told me that she wasn't the one for you,' Dorothy patted Hyacinth's hand in a comforting gesture, 'but I knew you wouldn't listen if I'd tried to tell you. You had to find out for yourself. You can't force love, you should know that.'

Hyacinth nodded her head in acknowledgment. She couldn't argue with Dorothy's statement because it was true, and if she had seen it in the cards it only served to confirm it. Dorothy was a much wiser witch than she would ever be and had taught her all she knew about the subject starting when Hyacinth was fourteen years old. Her white medicine was the most powerful stuff Hyacinth had ever come across.

'Someone is sending me strange text messages. Look...' she recalled the messages on her phone and handed it to Dorothy.

'Any idea who it could be?'

Hyacinth shook her head, 'No, but whoever it is, is close enough to know I'd changed vehicles on the way here.'

'Why did you do that? Did you know someone was following you?'

Hyacinth laughed harshly, 'I started to drive down in one of Angela's dreadful old Landrovers.'

'Oh honey, say no more. Wouldn't you think she would look after them better? At least upgrade occasionally!'

'She has, or at least I've done it for her. There was no way I was taking that bloody old boneshaker back.' Hyacinth needed to discuss the text messages. 'Do you think it might just be coincidence and someone's hit the wrong number?'

Dorothy re-read the messages before she answered, 'Mmmm, could be. Guess you'll just have to wait and see. Just be extra careful, don't take any chances.' She handed the phone back to Hyacinth. 'Now, my dear girl, to business. Do you want to leave the diamonds here with me or take them to a bank? I presume that's what you've come for?'

'No, it's a social visit Dorothy. Anyway, I think it would be too dangerous to move them, especially now someone seems to be watching me. And the police will be as well, watching me that is, you know, hoping I'll make a mistake and drop myself in it. They probably think I'm up to something.' She laughed mercilessly. 'Are they still in the well, the diamonds?'

'Yes, safe as houses.'

'Good, we'll leave them there. Thank God I took your advice and didn't put everything into deposit boxes.'

'No, I'm the best deposit box you could have.'

'Do you need any cash or anything?'

'No thanks dear, I'm fine.' Dorothy reached over and patted Hyacinth's hand touched by her concern.

'Can I stay the night?'

'Of course, you don't need to ask. Your room is always ready for you.'

'Tomorrow I'll give them all the run around, the police and whoever else is playing silly beggars, that'll sicken them off.'

Chapter 58

Lindsay's patience was running out. What the hell was taking Constance so long to answer the phone? Drumming her fingers on the dressing table she looked out of the hotel window across the main road that ran through Aviemore. Where the hell was the woman?

'Lindsay, hi how's tricks?'

'How's tricks? Why aren't you with Beth? Getting her away from that moron?'

'Hey, slow down. You know why. I haven't been authorized to go in yet. The second I get the word you know I'll be right in there…are you here…in Aviemore?'

'Yes. I'm at The Seasons Hotel. I booked in an hour ago.'

'Good. We'd better get together tonight then. I'll come for dinner, book us a table.'

At eight that evening, over a delicious meal in the hotel restaurant Constance brought Lindsay up to date with details of the surveillance of The Old Manse. It was under twenty-four hour observation, split into eight hour shifts and officers from the local constabulary were involved. Unfortunately, there wasn't a great deal to report. Beth had not left The Manse and was never alone. Angela stayed with her. Today Hyacinth had gone down to Perthshire and Constance was awaiting information on her destination.

Back in her room Lindsay tried to contact Lou to bring her up to speed.

Lou had not known a moment's peace since she had been unable to get to the airport to see Beth board the plane back to the UK.

The Director had wanted the scene wrapped in one, but uncharacteristically her co-star kept fluffing his lines. His apologies didn't stop the clock ticking and Lou watched in agony as precious minutes slipped away. Finally the scene was completed but only by the time that Beth would have been well on her way home.

Tired, Lou fumbled with the key trying to turn the lock and let herself into the house. She could hear the loud ringing of the telephone echoing from the hallway. Gutted at not being able to say goodbye to Beth and exhausted from the strain of the days filming she crossed the hall.

Who the hell was pestering her at this hour, she thought. Dropping her bag onto a chair, wearily she picked up the receiver.

'Lou this is Lindsay. I know you've just got in I've been trying to contact you for hours and your mobile was switched off. I know it must be half way through the night over there, but there's something I have to tell you. We have a problem...'

Lou sank into the chair as she listened, then, white faced, she replaced the receiver, walked into the living room and poured herself a very large brandy. Her beautiful Beth was in danger and here she was hundreds of miles away stuck in Los Angeles unable to do anything about it. Keep calm, Lindsay had said. How the hell could she keep calm?

Several hours later Lindsay rang again. Lou was sitting outside beside the pool wrapped in the bathrobe Beth had worn during her stay, wide-awake as she had been since Lindsay's first call.

Apparently Beth was in Scotland with Hyacinth, but it was obvious she had not gone with her out of choice. Try not to worry, Lindsay insisted. There was a full police operation in progress. She promised she would keep her informed.

Was Lindsay crazy telling her not to worry? Later that day Lou learned about the Amethyst Group from the CNN newscaster. Horrified she rang Lindsay yelling across the Atlantic demanding an explanation. Why hadn't she told her the full story, just how much danger was Beth in, what the fuck was going on?

Lindsay had to tell her everything, realizing that if she didn't Lou would be on the next plane out of LA and the shit would really hit the fan. When she eventually managed to calm her down she asked about Vanessa again. Lou told her for what seemed the hundredth time about that fateful episode in London.

'Lou, listen carefully,' wrong choice of words thought Lindsay.

'Haven't I just been doing that for the past half hour?' came her icy reply.

Ouch, though Lindsay. 'Sorry. I'm not supposed to say, but we've arrested Vanessa.'

'Oh terrific…how is she involved in this mess?'

'Well, we're not too sure yet…anyway from what you've said I think you should check out your luggage.'

'What! Check out my luggage! Now why would I want to do that?'

'Go over everything you had in London with you. Examine all the corners, the lining, the pleats, everything…imagine you're looking for something.'

'Are you taking the piss because you are failing to be funny?' Lou was not amused.

'No, neither. Sorry love, I am actually very serious here. I want you to search every bit of your luggage, handbags the lot.'

'And just what am I supposed to be looking for?' Lou demanded, scathingly.

'Diamonds.' Lindsay heard Lou's gasp before she answered, soberly now.

'Yes, okay Lindsay. I'll go and do it now.'

'Ring me straight back. Right?'

'Right.'

Lou searched, prodded and poked every square inch of her bags. Up to now only her Prada bag revealed anything and the tiny bag of diamonds that Beth had missed sat on the bedside table in a glass ashtray. Lou felt sick. There was only her Gladstone bag to check now. Her fingers felt around the squashy corners, revealing nothing.

'Lindsay. I've found some diamonds in my Prada bag. It was the handbag I had with me that night in London.'

'Vanessa planted them. We know that for a fact now, she's confessed to doing it.'

'The bitch! Why?'

'Hyacinth of course, but Vanessa daren't say as much.'

'Hyacinth wants Beth to herself, doesn't she?' Lou could never remember feeling so angry.

'Yes, however, we do have a plan and Vanessa has admitted she was paid to set you up. We think that's the reason Beth went to Scotland with Hyacinth, to save you and protect your reputation.' As the enormity of Lindsay's words hit home, frustration at being on the other side of the world took hold of Lou.

'Right, that's it Lindsay, I'm on the next plane out.'

'Thought you'd say that. Now I want you to listen to what I have to say first. No love, don't tell me to shut up. A lot's been happening here, please hear me out.'

Chapter 59

'Does Angela have a burgundy four-wheel drive?' Beth said as she stood in her usual place idly gazing out the kitchen window.

'No she doesn't!' In her haste to get to the window Hyacinth knocked her chair flying. 'Good God!' Pulling open the kitchen door she ran outside as the vehicle stopped.

Beth watched as Hyacinth wrenched the driver's door open and her jaw dropped as Constance fell out of the vehicle into Hyacinth's arms. Now what the hell's going on?

Seconds later Angela arrived and the women came into the kitchen together.

Well it looks like our little party's complete, thought Beth. Bursting to know the latest news, while feigning disinterest, she walked over to the kettle, 'I suppose you'll be wanting a cup of tea.'

It was as though all three had just remembered Beth was in the room. Gathering her wits, Hyacinth replied, 'Why thank you darling, thoughtful as always. Constance and I have a little catching up to do so why don't you bring a tray through to the drawing room for us. You will excuse us Angela.'

Beth loaded the tray with a huge pot of tea, warm buttered toast and Scottish marmalade then carried it carefully through, setting it down on a low table beside Constance.

Ashen and looking in need of sustenance, Constance's voice was shaky as she spoke. 'They couldn't get me for anything, Hyacinth, but what a grilling I got. They're such conniving bastards…honestly I almost admitted to something just to get some peace.'

'Poor darling.' Hyacinth cooed.

'I heard a rumour they've got someone working undercover.'

Hyacinth jumped up, nearly knocking the tray off the table as she started to pace the floor. That would explain the text messages - some smart arse copper thinking they would put the wind up her. No chance.

In the seconds Hyacinth's back was turned Constance managed to give a thumbs up sign to Beth. That was all the reassurance Beth needed. She slipped out of the room and returned to the kitchen where Angela was waiting. 'Shall we go for a walk? I could use some fresh air and they'll be in there forever,' Beth said.

'Why not? Come on, we'll walk round the Loch.'

Constance was alone in the house when they returned and because Angela trusted Beth with her, she was happy to leave them together. After all, she had a thousand and one things to do. 'Tell Hyacinth I'll catch up with her later.'

'Okay. Don't worry…you know she'll be safe with me,' Constance nodded towards Beth, 'Bye for now.' she just about shunted Angela out of the door.

They watched Angela's vehicle disappear down the drive before Constance spoke, 'I was willing you to get back before Hyacinth did. We've got to get you out of here.'

'I can't go.'

'Don't be stupid, go and get your things together. Better still, bloody well leave them. I told you not to get mixed up with her, remember that night at the party.'

'Constance, you don't understand. Hyacinth framed me, she put diamonds in all of my cases and I've been carrying them around the bloody world for her. But that's nothing compared to what she's done to Lou…'

'Go on,' Constance encouraged when Beth's voice faltered, 'tell me.'

'Somehow, and I have no idea how she did it, she planted diamonds in the lining of Lou's handbag. That's why I'm here. She's threatening to say Lou's involved.'

'Where are the diamonds? Still in Lou's handbag?'

'No I got them out and brought them with me. Hyacinth has them along with the ones she planted in my cases. I can't trust her, she's a devious cow, and she could have planted *anything* in Lou's bags.' Tears of frustration ran down Beth's cheeks. 'I don't know how the hell she does it.'

Constance knew. She had poured over the suspects' information long enough, from the so-called ring leader to the numerous minions willingly doing whatever Hyacinth wanted them to. 'Probably a stupid statement Beth, so forgive me for saying what might seem obvious, but you do realize I'm still under cover.'

Beth managed a smile, 'Yes, I haven't completely lost the plot, although I want Hyacinth to think I have.'

'Good girl. Now listen to what I'm going to tell you.'

They sat side by side at the kitchen table so they could watch the drive for Hyacinth returning while Constance talked.

'Does the name Vanessa mean anything to you?'

'Vanessa…you're joking, right?'

'She's one of the minions we arrested and she's confessed to planting diamonds in Lou's bag. Lou is in the clear lovely girl. You have absolutely nothing to worry about.'

Beth breathed a massive sigh of relief as Constance continued, 'Serena's arrest was the result of a tip off, but she wasn't carrying anything. Someone just wanted her out of the way. Now she's disappeared and we haven't managed to locate her yet.'

Perplexed Beth listened, but her heart was singing knowing her beautiful Lou was no longer in danger.

'The lovely Hyacinth has turned in all of her precious girlfriends and Penny is to blame. It seems Penny is in financial dire straits, thanks to Bertie's gambling, she tried to arrange a huge diamond run herself. She was also planning to set Hyacinth up, but Hyacinth found out by accident and tried to stop the handover. The whole thing back fired because Penny wasn't as clever as she thought she was. The police had an anonymous tip off and picked Hyacinth up. We know now that it was Penny who tipped them off.' Constance paused to take a drink of her now cold tea. 'Penny hates Hyacinth with a passion, but at the same time loves her so desperately she can't think straight. Penny had all of the girls convinced they were doing the run on Hyacinth's instructions, but they weren't. Of course Hyacinth's solicitor struck a deal, it's surprising what money can buy, and in return Hyacinth sang like a bird. We've even got Enzo.'

'Enzo...why he's the man she introduced me to in Cannes.'

'Yes I know. I was in Cannes at the time.' Beth's mouth dropped open as Constance continued, 'It doesn't stop there, Beth. Hyacinth needed to keep a low profile because she'd drawn attention to herself and her operation, seems it was getting too big. She was scared and under pressure. Penny

Corday could have got her killed, organizing a scam behind her back. The Syndicate had approached Hyacinth. They wanted the Amethyst Group to start working for them and they don't take kindly to being snubbed. They thought Hyacinth arranged the diamond run after she had promised to stop invading their turf. They had no idea it was Penny. To them Hyacinth was rubbing their noses in it.'

'I can't believe it…this is so dangerous. Does Hyacinth need money?'

'No, not at all. She has more money than Tetley have tea-leaves. She does it for the thrill, for the excitement. She needs the buzz.'

Despite everything Beth couldn't help but smile at the tea leaf reference.

'Why did Penny do what she did and go behind Hyacinth's back? Surely *she* doesn't need the money. I've been to her mansion, it's huge, and the lifestyle of the entire group is luxurious to say the least.'

'Actually she does, or rather did. Penny's husband is strapped for cash, or more to the point, he's in financial ruin. Apparently he's an addicted gambler. Horses, dogs, flies climbing up a wall, you name it and he'll bet on it, but it was the roulette table that finally finished him. Penny tried to sort things out in the only way she knew. And do you know, in a way I feel sorry for her. She's lost everything. Somehow, and we still don't know how, Hyacinth found out what she was up to. I think Penny is lucky to be alive. A few years in prison and she'll be out, able to start again as good as new. But Hyacinth won't forget, or forgive, what Penny's done. She'll be waiting and planning some terrible pay back.' Constance paused to refill her cup, 'The sad thing is, if Penny had only told Hyacinth about the predicament she and Bertie were in, then Hyacinth would have bailed them out and none of this would have happened.' Constance stood up and walked round the table to stretch her legs. 'She still can't let things lie though. The silly bitch has got her immunity, right, and she's in danger of blowing it. We have reason to believe she's out there now trying to move diamonds.'

'But why?'

'Who knows? She's going to end up in serious trouble.'

'I don't know where she goes or what she does.'

'We've been tailing her. She's been to Perth. Do you know who the woman is that she went to visit?'

Beth shook her head.

'Her old school Matron. Has she ever mentioned her?

'No, she doesn't say much to me now. I'm too boring.'

'Has she heard anything from Serena?'

'No, not as far as I know.'

'We're still trying to locate her and my boss figures sooner or later she'll make contact with Hyacinth.'

'Well she hasn't yet, at least I know she hasn't been here. Do you know something Constance, I'm not a vindictive person but I would like to see Hyacinth pay for what she's done to me and Lou.' The strength and determination in Beth's voice surprised Constance.

'Perhaps you can,' she said cautiously.

'How?'

'You need to understand the background on this. Stop me and ask about anything you're not sure about. It's important you understand it all. Okay?'

Over the next hour Constance gave Beth the full history of Hyacinth's life. Bringing a diamond into the country had started out as a game thought up by her grandfather whenever she returned to school from South Africa. As she grew up she re-invented the game to suit herself.

Beth's head was aching by the time Constance finished and now she was faced with a dilemma. It seemed the police could use her help.

She never realized her life had so many loose ends as Constance outlined their plan. Beth wanted to help them, by God she did, but didn't know if she was a good enough actress to pull it off. Then again, was she brave enough? Contemplating that thought fired her inner strength. Of course she was brave enough. She could do anything she put her mind to, Hyacinth must not be allowed to manipulate people any longer, and revenge is sweet.

Constance watched the wave of emotions racing across Beth's face. She had one final card to play, well two actually if the first one missed the mark.

'Lindsay will be close by. She's already in Aviemore.'

'Good...great...hell I don't what to do.'

'No pressure Beth, it's up to you at the end of the day. One way or another we'll sew things up.' Her first card fell flat. 'Why don't I make us some coffee? Like I said lovely, no pressure, but I do need an answer before our hostess returns.'

Beth shuffled uncomfortably in her seat, elbows on the table, head resting in her hands as she tried to clear her mind. For once she would welcome a vision coming through.

The kettle started to whistle in tune with the train whistle that was sounding in her head. Why should she see Hyacinth standing on a railway platform holding a baby in her arms?

Constance was about to ask if she took sugar, but stopped. Beth looked really out of it.

Concentrating on the vision, trying to understand its meaning, the image changed to Hyacinth and was it Serena standing on the same platform, facing each other? It was one of the briefest visions Beth had experienced, flashing in and out so quickly it was impossible to anchor it. Frustrated at her inability to hold on to it she banged both fists of the table. This was the second time a picture of Hyacinth holding a baby had come to her. She must be missing something important.

'Here's your coffee...what is it, Beth? I know you're psychic and can see stuff, Lindsay told me.'

'Did she? It's nothing. I see rubbish, things I can't make out.'

Constance took a small brown bottle from her pocket, the same type that you would get eardrops in. She handed it to Beth, 'Do you recognize this? Take a sniff.' It was time to play her ace.

Absently Beth took the bottle. What the hell was Constance giving her a medicine bottle for? She unscrewed the cap and sniffed. Her mouth fell open. She sniffed again, to be sure. 'What is this? Where did you get it? More to the point were you there? Are you fucking me about or what?'

'Well, yes I'm afraid I was there, but no way am I fucking you about. Tell me what you think happened.'

'What I think happened? What do you mean? Hyacinth told me there was an orgy.'

'That's just it Beth, there was no orgy. You slept like a baby. It was the drug. It's hallucinogenic. Penny fed you some before Hyacinth performed one her magic ceremonies prior to paying the girls in diamonds for what was supposed to be the final time. Afterwards they dumped you into bed and left you there.'

'Yes, but Petra...I woke up with Petra.'

'Ah yes, well that might be another story. Petra isn't part of this, but she is a rampant lesbian. She hates Hyacinth and fancies the hell out of you.'

'Constance, thank you so much for telling me about the cellar. But I *did* wake up in bed with Petra. I think we'd had sex...I can't remember.'

'Sorry Beth, I don't know about that. But I do know about Penny. She is, or rather was, besotted with Hyacinth. As we already know she's a conniving bitch. She hated anyone who took Hyacinth's attention away from her. I don't know much about Petra, best not dwell on it, eh.'

'I need to speak to Lou. She'll be frantic with worry.'

'It's done. Lindsay has kept her in the picture as far as she needs to be. Don't worry, we're keeping her up to speed.'

'Then you can count me in, but I want to speak to Lou first.'

'Marvellous!'

Constance handed Beth her mobile and left her to it. The girls spoke for ages, both declaring their undying love for each other.

Back at the kitchen table Constance studied Beth. She'd been right in her gut feeling; she was some tough cookie. 'Ready? Now this is what we need to do.'

Chapter 60

Early winter snow beckoned skiers to the slopes. Beth could see the first arrivals already teaming over the Cairngorms like ants. It was Wednesday, which meant she would spend the whole day with Angela, free of Hyacinth's constant harping. She was supposed to be working with the police yet it wasn't turning out how she imagined it would.

Beth hardly ever saw Hyacinth and was becoming frustrated with the idle lifestyle. It was ironic how her time here was turning out to be something of a holiday. Hyacinth might be her jailer, but she had kept her distance not making any physical demands and leaving her mostly in the company of Angela and now Constance. It was a relief, but Beth knew there must be a day of reckoning. What then? Refusing to think about it she called to Angela who was somewhere in the house, 'Shall we go up the mountain?'

'Yes, great idea. First, we'll go to that nice designer boutique and kit ourselves out courtesy of Hyacinth, shall we?' Angela grinned sticking her head round the drawing room door. 'Be ready in ten minutes?'

Beth enjoyed Angela's company. They had become good friends over the past few weeks and it had been Angela who had taken her shopping, spent days in the health spar with her, and introduced her to the great golf clubs in the area. Wednesdays were turning out to be their salvation; it was the day they were free of Hyacinth and they both dreaded her return, foul temper and all.

For the sixth Wednesday in succession Hyacinth headed for the airy shopping mall in Inverness, sure her trip today would be another waste of time. Every week for the past six weeks she had received a text message asking her to come to The Coffee House. The sender failed to show every time. She felt stupid for even bothering to turn up today, but she had nothing better to do. And she had a feeling it had something to do with Penny and anything that helped her move towards instigating her revenge was worthy of her time. Ultimately she would ensure Penny paid dearly for her attempted assassination, because one day she would be released from prison and Hyacinth would be waiting. That's when Penny's real sentence would begin.

The police surveillance team was in place, but if nothing transpired today then their Governor was planning to pull them back and leave a skeleton crew to keep an eye on things. Lindsay would leave. Constance would stay with Beth, but they couldn't expect Beth to remain indefinitely and in reality she could walk away now. Up to date she had not been able to find out anything more about Hyacinth's suspected continuation of diamond smuggling than they had.

Hyacinth had not received any more threatening text messages. Instead sexy suggestive messages started coming through. She had no idea who was playing this game with her, except that it was a woman. Eleven am and she was sitting in the open plan café, waiting. Just like the message had requested.

She was glad of the excuse to be out alone, not that she needed one. She could do what she wanted, she answered to no-one.

When the waitress came to take her order, Hyacinth requested a large cappuccino before drifting back into her daydream. What was she going to do? Beth was driving her mad, although she would never admit it, not even to Angela who obligingly kept her entertained. And Constance had been a godsend in that department too. She couldn't stand Beth being in the house and under her feet all the time. How could she have so totally misjudged this girl? The seemingly strong personality had disappeared, in fact she began to doubt if it had ever been there at all. The girl was proving to have absolutely no character whatsoever, and she had no real feelings for her. Dorothy had confirmed that. How could she have got it so wrong? There was no spark, no energy; Beth was completely languid, insipid. Hyacinth needed a woman with some fire in her belly, which was one of the reasons she was here today. Whoever had the gall to continually set her up like this must have some guts.

If Beth had been able to read Hyacinth's thoughts she would have been thrilled that her plan was working so well, but at that precise moment she and Angela were hurtling down the nursery slopes. Hyacinth was reacting exactly how Beth wanted. Realizing her need to be challenged, to be able to exert her control and dominate, Beth had deliberately withdrawn into a shell. She was pleasant, compliant and utterly boring, displaying every characteristic in gentle abundance that irritated and frustrated the hell out of Hyacinth. Also, in her quiet way, Beth was being ultra observant, but despite that she had absolutely nothing to report.

Hyacinth checked her watch. It was almost noon. Someone was playing her for a fool, standing her up again.

The shopping mall had four entrances. Imagination had not been employed in their naming. North Avenue, South Avenue, East and West Avenue all converged on Central Avenue. And it didn't take a genius to work out that The Coffee House was located here.

The place was alive, all geared up for Christmas, the sound of singing Santa's vying with traditional carols bombarded the bustling Christmas shoppers. It looked like they'd come in by the busload today. The place was heaving even though it was snowing heavily. Lindsay was browsing through goods displayed outside the stores along East Avenue; all offering fantastic never to be repeated one off deals. If she wasn't under cover she could have done her Christmas shopping. Other members of her team were dotted throughout the complex thinking the same thing.

Constance was opposite her somewhere along West Avenue. They were all waiting for Hyacinth to meet her fence, but Constance didn't believe she was here for that. Over the last few weeks she had come to appreciate just how precious freedom was to Hyacinth. The woman didn't value much, but her freedom was paramount and Constance did not believe she would put herself at risk of losing it. But the powers that be did. They were convinced Hyacinth was on the make, which is why they were all here, again.

Hyacinth checked her watch again. Twelve forty-five. Another no show. She may as well go shopping. Bending down to retrieve a glove that had fallen to the floor she was surprised when the waitress came across to her table and handed her an envelope. She took it, thanked her and sat back down.

This is it, thought Lindsay, they've made contact at last. She watched Hyacinth read the note, push it back into the envelope then get up to leave, tipping the waitress generously on her way out.

Hyacinth pushed her way forcefully through the shoppers jamming West Avenue, once outside she skipped through the traffic and headed straight for the revolving doors of The Grant Hotel opposite. Taking the stairs to the third floor because she couldn't bear to wait for the lift, she almost ran along the corridor. She reached into her coat pocket and pulled out the envelope containing the door key.

Suit 105 was in darkness when, heart racing with anticipation, she turned the lock and let herself in. Hesitating briefly, allowing her eyes time to adjust to the gloom, she saw the outline of a naked girl dimly reflected in the floor to ceiling mirrors covering the opposite wall.

'Welcome to my world Hyacinth.' Hot breath hit her ear as her hands were pulled behind her back and tied together. Hyacinth's heart started racing with excitement, matching the wetness that erupted between her legs. At last she was going to have some fun.

Chapter 61

Hyacinth rolled onto her back in the king sized bed, sore but totally satisfied. She had never in her life enjoyed herself as much as she had in the past twenty-four hours. Stretching her aching body she reached out expecting to touch her seducer. She was disappointed, but not surprised, to find she was alone.

Two hours later she was still alone. Of course she checked in with Angela casually asking if she had any messages. She hadn't. For once, uncertain of what to do next, she decided she may as well go home, convinced the little minx wanted to continue playing cat and mouse. Well, that was fine with her. It would be fun and something to relieve the mind numbing tedium of her present situation.

It was almost midnight when she arrived back at The Old Manse. Beth was in bed and Angela left almost immediately. During her drive home she had contemplated the situation with Beth. Last night had made one thing crystal clear for sure; Beth was not the one for her.

Last night's lover had been one step ahead of her all the way, pushing the boundaries between them into new realms. Something new to Hyacinth and she'd relished it. The girl would get in touch. Hyacinth had no doubt about that. She probably wanted some kind of payment and Hyacinth didn't have a problem with that either. If the sex continued in the same theme she could have whatever she wanted.

But what about Beth? Switching off the bedside light she fell back into the softness of the pillows, her decision made. She would tell her in a day or so, not just yet.

Hyacinth didn't surface the following day having Angela running after her like a ladies maid, scurrying up and down stairs with trays of food, tending her bedroom fire and finally running her a bath. Poor Angela left, exhausted, when Constance arrived in the early evening.

Of course Hyacinth summoned Constance upstairs immediately. Beth was amazed to be left on her own.

A couple of hours later Constance came down boot faced. It seemed their costly surveillance of Hyacinth could turn out to be a total waste of time and money she moaned, tucking into the Shepherd's Pie Beth had prepared for supper. When pressed she refused to say more, except to ask Beth if she would hang in for a little while longer. Beth felt so sorry for her that she agreed despite her desperate longing to be back with Lou. She was almost certain Lou would be home by now, yet she had been unable to contact her for a couple of days.

Midnight, and a full moon illuminated the snow covering the mountains, giving them a magical, unearthly look. Beth lit her candle, took up her meditation position and focused on the flame. Soon Lou's lovely face was in front of her, smiling, whispering 'home soon baby...together again...forever'. As the vision of Lou faded, Hyacinth and an unknown blonde girl took her place. They were both here, in the drawing room, standing facing each other, silent and motionless. Someone else was standing in the shadows.

Beth's third vision, she was doing well tonight, successfully managing to anchor them, showed a place she didn't recognize, but that was not unusual. A pretty wishing well sparkled in the frosty snow, the ground around it was covered with frozen paw prints. Somebody has a very big dog Beth thought as she let the vision go.

Climbing into bed she snuggled deep into the duvet. She felt she had done all she could for the police here. Hyacinth was not moving diamonds, but she was up to something. Tomorrow she would tell Constance that it was time to call it quits; she wanted to go home, she'd had enough. Her revenge would have to be left in the hands of the police.

At ten the following morning all three women were in the drawing room. Beth standing in her usual position gazing out of the window was watching the activity on the mountain. It was another bright sunny day although bitterly cold. Constance was sprawled in an armchair beside the roaring fire engrossed in the latest Stephen King novel to hit the local bookshop, and Hyacinth was making a pretence of reading a fashion magazine. She was waiting; her seducer had yet to make contact.

They all heard the beep of Hyacinth's mobile announcing an incoming message. Almost moving in slow motion she flipped the phone open. 'I have to go out. Constance you will stay with Beth, won't you?'

'Yes, 'course…where are you off too?' Constance asked casually, as if it were an effort to drag herself out of her book.

'Nowhere…mind your own business.' Hyacinth snapped as she hurried out of the room.

Beth watched her skidding down the drive, 'Must be important to get a reaction like that.'

Constance agreed. She had already alerted the surveillance officer positioned near the end of the drive. It should have been Lindsay, but last night she had been unexpectedly despatched down to Brighton. Information Constance had deliberately withheld from Beth.

Chapter 62

The hotel was bustling with skiers, obviously a favourite haunt of the wealthy. Perhaps I should have come here before, Hyacinth thought, sitting back in her chair, swilling the large gin and tonic round the glass she held in her hand.

She had chosen to sit in the corner furthest away from the door so that she could observe the guests coming and going. Because she was not familiar with the hotel she wasn't aware there was another entrance, and almost fainted when the girl spoke to her from behind.

'Hello Mother. I'm so pleased you waited.'

Silence.

'Shall I sit down?'

Still silence.

In an acid tongue the girl continued. 'What's wrong *Mother*, cat got your tongue?'

Hyacinth tried to stand up, but her legs had turned to jelly. Her mind was reeling. 'Serena! I should have known…why didn't I…? I should have bloody known.'

'But you didn't know, *Mother*, did you? You failed to recognize your first born daughter. Oh no, all you wanted to do was have a shag...now that *is* something for us to talk about, isn't it *Mother*.' Serena hissed, her eyes blazing.

'Serena, darling, I can explain, but not here.' Flustered, Hyacinth waved her arm in the air and looked around, 'it's so public.'

'Why did you tell the police I was carrying diamonds to America?' Serena demanded, sitting down opposite.

'I didn't...it was Penny. She must have set you up. If it's any consolation to you she set me up too...big time.' Hyacinth answered by way of explanation.

'And Penny's not the only one to set Hyacinth up, is she?' a sharp voice interrupted.

Surprised, both women turned to stare at the well - dressed girl now standing beside their table.

'Well?' the girl demanded looking down at Serena.

Hyacinth, still reeling, did a double take as she stared into the face of her mirror image.

The intruder spoke again, calmly and with dignity. 'I'm waiting for your explanation.' She paused to look from Serena to Hyacinth, 'And I'm not the only one.'

'I *can* explain.' Serena insisted passionately.

'Really...?'Then I suggest you try.' The girl sat in the empty seat, removed her fur hat and shook a cascade of honey blonde hair loose. Mesmerized, Hyacinth watched it falling into soft waves around her shoulders.

Confused and numb with shock, Hyacinth stared at the girls. Speechless, she studied them, looking from one to the other. It was scary; their likeness was uncanny. A wave of nausea hit Hyacinth, had she slept with her own daughter?

Attempting to gain control of the situation, she thumped the table, rocking the glasses. 'I want to know what the fuck is going on, and I want to know NOW!'

'I am Serena. I am your daughter. This is Stephanie, my half-sister, the one you had sex with,' the newcomer spoke calmly, 'and she has a lot to explain. She knew I was looking for you and stole the information I had gathered, and borrowed my identity.' pausing briefly to allow her words to register, she continued, 'I was planning to make contact with you, but she beat me to it. Her masquerade was excellent, don't you think? She certainly had Penny fooled.'

Waves of relief washed over Hyacinth. Thank God she hadn't slept with her daughter. That was taking things too far, even for her. Then every maternal emotion she'd denied and kept locked inside exploded. She flung her arms around her daughter and suddenly she was back on the cold, windswept, railway platform alone with her baby. She could feel her baby warm in her arms, hear the whistle of the train, and then cold emptiness and despair replaced the baby's body heat as she walked out of the station alone.

She had never expected to see her first born ever again. She kissed her cheeks, they were both crying now, tears of joy and happiness. Hyacinth never wanted to let her go again.

When Stephanie got up to leave the table without saying a word, Hyacinth didn't attempt to stop her. For now she needed time with her daughter and she was wise enough to know that both girls were going to be a big part of her life from now on.

Most of the police surveillance team had drifted in, surreptitiously surrounding their table, fully expecting to make an arrest. Constance was nearest although Hyacinth would never have recognized her. Pretending to be doing a crossword, she was able to take notes when Hyacinth and the real Serena eventually started talking.

When it became apparent what was going on the team gradually drifted out. They had no need to be here.

Constance's faith in her own judgment was totally restored and she made her way inconspicuously out past their table, kindly acknowledging the waitress who smiled at the pleasant grey haired old lady.

Serena excused herself, apologizing. She had to make a phone call. Grateful of the break Hyacinth looked round to attract a waitress. She needed another drink, a large one. Grabbing a piece of hotel writing paper from the display behind her, she wrote quickly:

Darling Steph,

Please don't run away from me when we have such a lot in common. Stay here in the hotel. Charge whatever you need to your room and I will take care of the account. I will be in touch soon.

H.

Pushing the letter into a matching envelope she handed it, along with a twenty-pound note, to the obliging waitress when she returned with her drink. Five minutes later the note was delivered into Stephanie's eager hands.

Angela was amazed when Hyacinth telephoned just before midnight to say she wouldn't be home that night, but she would be returning some time the following day. Would she mind staying with Beth and could she please arrange to have the guest suite prepared. It wasn't the request that amazed Angela, but the polite way it was asked. Very un-Hyacinth.

A particularly heavy snowfall overnight made the scenery even more majestic, but turned the roads into an absolute nightmare, blocking long stretches of the A9 and bringing the minor roads to a complete standstill. It was mid-afternoon before Hyacinth and Serena arrived at The Old Manse.

Hugging her daughter close as they stood beside the car, Hyacinth, overcome with emotion, could barely manage to speak.

With her arm around her daughter's shoulders she whispered, 'This is where you were born, Serena.'

'I know.'

'You do…how?'

'Penny. She told Steph.' She reached out to take Hyacinth's hand. 'She's obsessed, but it goes way beyond jealousy, she's not just jealous of you, she wants to *be* you.'

In the course of time Hyacinth would ensure Penny paid dearly for the things she'd done to her, and she would pay an even higher price for what she'd tried to do to Serena, but she didn't want to think about it right now, not today. Today was the start of a new life with Serena in it and she wasn't going to allow that bitch Penny Corday to spoil one second of it.

Steph was a sensational bonus. Hyacinth could see them now, sailing the Mediterranean on board The Amethyst, sharing every female they pulled, enjoying sensational threesomes, not forgetting how they would be fucking each other silly. Hyacinth's idea of heaven made her smile, but again, all that was for later. Right now she tightened her grip on Serena's hand ready to take her into the house.

Beth and Angela, waiting inside, observed the brief conversation before Hyacinth breezed into the kitchen.

'Angela, this is my daughter Serena. She's going to be staying here with me. Would you please settle her in while I have a word in private with Beth.' Hyacinth didn't wait for Angela to answer. 'Beth, come into the drawing room please.'

Obediently Beth followed Hyacinth across the hall.

'Sit down.' Not an order, more of an indication as Hyacinth waved towards an easy chair. Appearing somewhat agitated she stood with her back to the roaring fire, clasping and unclasping her hands before she spoke, 'Constance will be calling to collect you shortly. Please pack your things and be ready to leave here when she does.' She waited for her words to sink in.

'Why? I thought you wanted me with you. Do I not turn you on anymore or have you lost your touch? After all, you haven't had the nerve to come anywhere near me,' Beth challenged Hyacinth, wanting answers. She'd learned not to trust this bitch.

The old Hyacinth answered, 'Remember, we have unfinished business, darling. Now fuck off out of here before I change my mind. Keep looking over your shoulder Beth, because one day I'll be back for you.'

Beth leapt from the chair and ran.

Chapter 63

It was Christmas morning. Penny lay on her top bunk staring up at the ceiling. The sounds of the prison dorm invading her mind, already some of the girls were awake and shouting, wishing one another a Merry Christmas. Somebody started singing Oh Come All Ye Faithful and one by one several others joined in. Penny sneered in disgust. Bloody fools, she thought, satisfied with next to nothing and a few paltry gifts. She was rigid with anger. This was not the Christmas she'd planned. Right now she should be enjoying the Caribbean high life with Felicity. Instead she was banged up in this hellhole. While all of the other girls had been placed in open prisons to serve their time, as leader of The Amethyst Group she had been considered too high a risk, too dangerous. Her ten-year prison sentence would be served in a secure unit and it was that back stabbing bastard Hyacinths fault.

But hell, she would still be a young woman when she got out and then she would find Hyacinth and take her revenge. She had years to work on her perfect plan; a plan fuelled by flames of pure hatred. Not for one second did she consider that she'd been instrumental in her own downfall, and she would allow nothing and no-one to distract her from her plan.

Swinging her legs over the side of the bunk, she dropped down and peered in at the sleeping girl who had arrived late last night to share her cell. Well now, she thought, tracing the outline of the girl's lips with her forefinger, maybe there is a Santa Claus after all.

In Brighton, Lindsay stirred in bed. She couldn't remember when she'd felt so good. Wrapping herself round Constance she snuggled into her. There was no need to get up yet, this was heaven.

In Scotland Hyacinth sat in her festive drawing room carefully wrapping presents for Serena. She'd been sitting beside the fire all night adding to the pile of gifts, while her first born slept soundly upstairs.

She should be chastising herself for not feeling guilty. And to all intents and purposes she should be. David had finally left her to move in with his secretary, no surprise there. Although as far as family and friends were concerned their split was by mutual agreement. Their two children had completely blanked her preferring to go and live in South Africa, and her beautiful Jesmond home was going on the market at the turn of the year.

Penny, who she had truly believed to be her loyal and absolute best friend, had betrayed her. She would never forgive her for that. As a result the Amethyst Group was destroyed and her lovely girls...she would always think of them as hers, were separated, scattered around several prisons throughout the UK. She did experience a twinge of guilt here, but knowing the girls would probably get early release for good behaviour and every one of them was loaded, she shrugged her shoulders, and sighed deeply allowing her thoughts to wander on.

Putting down the scissors and red ribbon she reached across the hearth to throw more logs onto the fire. Then there was Beth, supposedly her trophy catch, gone. Not even now, with the unpredictable, demanding and exciting Stephanie on the scene, would Beth ever be forgotten. She should be feeling guilty about her too, but she wasn't. She had seen Beth as a challenge, but had got it so wrong. She still couldn't believe she had such crap judgment. In her book no challenge equalled no interest. But upstairs in the second guest room, unknown to Serena of course, was the challenge she had always been seeking.

For once in her life Hyacinth felt liberated. At last she had no restrictions. Daphne was taking good care of the Carlisle unit leaving her free to spend time with Serena. This was the start of a new chapter in both their lives and she was actually excited about it. She knew one way or another Penny would exact her revenge, but that was years away and she didn't need to devote much time or thought to it just yet.

Today was the start of great times for her and her lovely Serena. It transpired they had a great deal in common, oh yes, Serena was her mother's daughter all right. A carbon copy of Hyacinth's sexual preferences with just the right amount of depravity added. Hyacinth's spine tingled at the prospect of the sexual adventures they would enjoy together. They had already discovered some very accommodating girls spending an extended holiday here in Aviemore, and Hyacinth had been delighted at Serena's seduction techniques. She couldn't have done better herself.

Today was to be their first personal orgy, and it had been Serena's suggestion to include Steph who was joining them for a special dinner party tonight to mark the occasion. Serena had personally designed the after dinner games, and Hyacinth could hardly wait. But first the oriental lovely who was waiting patiently at the other side of the fireplace was to be Serena's first gift of the day.

Hyacinth stood up and held out her hand to the girl. 'Come…I'll take you up now.'

Daybreak was just dawning when Hyacinth kissed her daughter's brow, 'Darling, wake up…time to enjoy your first Christmas gift.'

She left them to it convinced Serena wouldn't notice the tiny infrared cameras recording everything, and even if she did, she wouldn't care.

The large two-way mirror on the wall opposite Serena's bed allowed secret and uninterrupted observation from the adjacent dressing room. Not only could she watch her daughter in action first hand, the cameras were recording from all angles, just in case she missed anything. Wasn't technology wonderful? Leaning back against the wall she laughed out loud as Steph, eyes sparkling in anticipation, and wearing only a short diaphanous Miss Santa costume, slipped into the room beside her - let the games begin…

North Yorkshire was in the grip of one of the coldest winters ever. Inside the farmhouse it was warm. All of the curtains were pulled tight against the cold; the central heating boiler buzzed and logs burned in both grates.

Beth and Lou sat on the floor by the hearth in the firelight. Neither girl wanted to be parted from the other, not even by sleep.

It's perfect here, thought Beth, safe and peaceful. Apart from the fire, the multi-coloured tree lights were the only other lights in the room. The candles on the hearth had burned down ages ago. She sighed deeply, relaxing back against Lou's soft body, comfortably sitting between her legs.

Lou leaned against the sofa, her chin on Beth's shoulder breathing her in, her legs and arms wrapped round Beth's body.

'I love you,' she whispered softly thinking Beth had finally dozed off.

'I love you too,' Beth answered just as softly.

'I have a confession about the filming,' she nibbled Beth's ear, 'it's something you have a right to know.'

'Don't tell me. You have to go back the day after tomorrow.' Beth's heart sank.

'No, that's when I'm going to meet Isobel!'

Instantly wide awake, Beth twisted round to face her, 'Isobel...my mother?'

Lou giggled, 'Yes, we're really good friends now. We have someone very special in common.'

'Oh Lou, that's wonderful. But how?'

'You can thank your sister Catherine for it. When Hyacinth was holding you hostage we had several long conversations. It seems Isobel had overheard the two of you talking about us, shortly after we first met. She was hoping you would say something to her, but Catherine did it for you. I think you have a wonderful family Beth. They love you.' She reached out to stroke Beth's cheek before continuing, 'By the way I still think you should press charges, hon, that woman shouldn't be allowed to get away with it.'

'Honestly I would rather it was forgotten. She's probably already paying in ways she could never have imagined.'

'Yes, I guess.' Lou agreed.

'Let's not talk about her.'

'Ok.'

'So… I've been saved from explaining our situation to my family. They are going to love you too just like I do.'

'Thanks babe, I hope so.'

'Of course they will…but never mind that for now…the filming…come on you'd better tell me the worst. But it doesn't matter what you say, nothing is going to spoil today.'

'Well, the worst is Lindsay and Constance are coming to visit tomorrow. Did you know they'd got together? Apparently there's some history between them.'

Beth pretended not to hear, there was probably history between Lindsay and most of the females on the planet. Instead she shook Lou's shoulders in mock desperation, 'Tell me when you have to go.'

'Mmmm, well yes, I suppose I should be honest about it.' She paused, pulling a face, 'The fact is…well…I *don't* have to go. Not unless it's for a holiday. It's finished, all done, finito!'

Beth promptly burst into tears. She needed to cry. The relief that Lou was not going back broke the dam. She burst into great sobs that wracked her body. Lou held her tenderly, rocking her like a baby, all the while wiping away her tears and constantly repeating how much she loved her until she was crying too. Eventually exhausted, but dry eyed and happy they both fell asleep.

After a while Lou stirred. She stretched over and rummaged for a package she had hidden under the Christmas tree. Kissing Beth awake she pressed it into her hands, 'Merry Christmas baby.'

Still drowsy Beth stared at the gift then carefully removed the gold wrapping paper. A velvet Asprey presentation box nestled in the palm of her hand.

'Go on then, open it.'

She gazed at Lou, dizzy with happiness. 'I have something for you, it's….'

'No, no please...open this first.'

Beth flipped the lid, inside sparkled the most beautiful diamond ring she'd ever seen.

Lou grinned, 'Well, Beth McConnell, diamonds have played such a big part in our lives up to now that it seems only fitting....you know what they say...diamonds are forever sweetheart...and so are we.'

Beth laughed at the irony. Trust Lou. Her laughter stopped when Lou slipped the ring on the third finger of Beth's left hand, saying, 'Together...forever.'

Beth started to speak, 'Lou, darling...I don't have anything like this for you.'

Lou laughed, 'Well I don't expect you have. Shopping isn't high on the list of to do's when you're being held hostage, is it?'

'Not exactly, but I did manage this.' She pulled a folder out from under the cushions on the sofa and handed it to Lou. 'Happy Christmas, my love.'

Lou screeched while she read the tickets and itinerary for an extended cruise round the Mediterranean.

'I know it's not until May so I got you this to be going on with.' Beth reached into her jeans pocket and pulled out a small green and gold box.

Now it was Lou's turn to be stunned as she gazed at the beautiful square cut emerald ring.

'Beth...thank you...this is so beautiful.'

Following her lead, Beth removed the ring from its box saying, 'Together forever Lou... that's us...forever and ever.'

Outside it started to snow again. In the stables Phantom and Bamber stirred, whinnying softly to Saffy and Charley.

Epilogue

Six months later, the cruise liner Oriana, dropped anchor in Cannes Bay. Beth and Lou, tanned and happy, stepped down into the tender, anxious to be the first ashore. Beth was searching in her beach bag for some sunscreen when a vision of Hyacinth flashed into her mind.

'Beth...Beth, what's wrong? You've gone as white as a sheet? Are you feeling seasick?' Lou asked, taking hold of Beth's hand.

'No. Would you believe it, I've just had a vision. Maybe it's something to do with the past, and being back in Cannes again.' Beth shook her head as if shaking the vision of Hyacinth out of her mind. 'Don't worry, it's probably nothing.'

'I do worry.' Lou reached up and smoothed Beth's hair. 'I worry because I nearly lost you.'

Alone, in the seclusion of the little boat, they sat as close to each other as they possibly could. Beth spoke quietly, 'I had a vision during the night too.'

Knowing by the tone of her voice it must be important, Lou waited.

'Yes,' Beth hesitated before whispering, 'you and I...there was a baby asleep in a cot...we were standing watching over it.'

'Wow, Beth! That's some vision.' Lou looked intently at Beth as she asked, 'Do you want a baby?'

'Do you?' Beth turned the question on Lou. Beth remembered her wish list, hastily scribbled out and tossed into the fire during the magic ceremony in Scotland. The first part had already come true.

'Pass me the champagne, darling.'

Serena lifted the bottle out of the cooler and passed it across the table.

'Looks like another cruise liner anchored in the bay.' Steph spoke lazily.

'Well, darlings, if you wish, we can always go and check out the talent as they disembark from the tenders. We all know how some of these good looking girls like to experiment when they're away from home, don't we?' Hyacinth laughed wickedly. 'I love Cannes. Don't you, darlings?'

THE END

About the Author

After fifteen years working in the National Health Service, Ellen left it all behind and established an award winning business.

She lives in the north of England with her partner and various animals, is an avid photographer, keen golfer and is active in amateur dramatics. She has a huge interest in vibrational energy, complementary therapies and all things mystical.

Ellen has written articles for national magazines and regional newspapers.

Beautiful Strangers is her first novel. She is currently working on the sequel.

Printed in the United Kingdom
by Lightning Source UK Ltd.
118338UK00001B/10-18

9 781425 954468